SOUTH WIND

Norman Douglas was born in 1868, edu-
cated at Uppingham and in Germany
and spent some early years in the Diplomatic Service, chiefly in St Petersburg
and Naples. The publication of *Siren
Land* in 1911 first brought him to the
notice of the public as a writer of individuality and unusual distinction. Two
further travel books followed in quick
succession, *Fountains in the Sand* (1912)
and *Old Calabria* (1915), but it was his
novel *South Wind*, published in 1917,
which made his name widely known to
two continents, and this is now accepted
as a fiction classic. Although, or because,
his output was a limited one he holds a
unique position in the literature of our
time. He died in 1952.

SOUTH WIND

NORMAN DOUGLAS

With an Introduction by
Norman Lewis

PENGUIN BOOKS

Penguin Books Ltd, Harmondsworth, Middlesex, England
Viking Penguin Inc., 40 West 23rd Street, New York, New York 10010, U.S.A.
Penguin Books Australia Ltd, Ringwood, Victoria, Australia
Penguin Books Canada Limited, 2801 John Street, Markham, Ontario, Canada L3R 1B4
Penguin Books (N.Z.) Ltd, 182–190 Wairau Road, Auckland 10, New Zealand

First published in 1917
Published in Penguin Books 1935
Reprinted 1953, 1962, 1976
Reprinted with an introduction by Norman Lewis 1987

Printed and bound in Great Britain by
Cox & Wyman Ltd, Reading
Set in Monotype Times

INTRODUCTION

Norman Douglas's life and work are best understood if we remember his conviction that the world has never been the same since the loss of the joyous paganism of Ancient Greece and its replacement by Christianity – offering, in exchange for present joy, the remote bliss of the hereafter. He sets out, therefore, to convert as well as to entertain.

A furious energy, both physical and of the mind, allied to a certain ruthlessness distinguished him from the literary figures of his day. Norman Douglas was without self-criticism. He *knew* that he was right, went his own way and had no regrets. Inherited money saved him at first from the necessity to work for a living, but his energy and insatiable curiosity were taskmasters who saw to it that he was kept well occupied. He started in boyhood as a naturalist and was absorbed like a religious devotee in butterflies, 'stones', then snakes. There was no mountain within reach that he failed to scale in search of fossils. He objected to killing for mere sport but admitted to having carried out hecatombs of small animals and birds in the name of scientific curiosity, and he lived among a mausoleum of specimens pickled in spirits. Six years of schooling in Germany added thoroughness and erudition to these pursuits. By the time he was twenty he was making a name for himself by his published treatises on such subjects as the *Herpetology of the Grand Duchy of Baden* (in German with Latin headings), was an acknowledged expert in the coloration of birds' eggs, and had investigated the fauna of Santorini, in the course of which he discovered an exceptional frog that he asked to be named after him. For ten years he continued to contribute to leading zoological journals, then an increasing fascination with language lured him away from science. The collection and arrangement of data no longer sufficed. He became a creative writer absorbed in the craftsmanship of his trade – and, of course, with the propagation of his ideas.

At first he wrote travel books, the most successful in this category being *Old Calabria*, which was received with huge acclaim. To some extent it suffered as a work of art under the sheer weight of its author's limitless interests and his determination to pack everything in. There are few passages in the literature of travel to excel in freshness and descriptive power his accounts of the Italian far south, of the Sila and Aspromonte as seen with his own eyes. But too often we are deprived of such first-hand experiences as the author goes off in search of history, or drags us after him to investigate the prodigies of St Joseph of Copertino, the flying saint.

The financial reward of his travel writing was meagre, and his friend Joseph Conrad suggested he could earn more money by turning to fiction. *South Wind* was the result: it was the first and best of his novels, and a stunning success – although he claimed to have received only £72 from the four impressions that appeared in the first year alone following publication. Nonetheless, it established his fame not only with the literary world but the reading public. He had been working on the book for four years when it appeared in June 1917. It was not an altogether propitious moment, because he had been due to stand trial the previous January for an offence against a minor – one of several such incidents that cropped up from time to time in his life. The problem was that he had skipped bail and fled to Italy, and was wondering whether it might not be better for the book to be published anonymously. Fortunately the idea was dropped.

In fact, as it turned out, part of *South Wind*'s success was due to the accident of its timing. It was published at a period when England had been at war for three years, an endless winter of the spirit from which Norman Douglas offered his readers an escape to Nepenthe. Here he showed them a corner of Europe where the old amoral, derisive, life-loving spirit of pagan antiquity miraculously survived; where – in his own words – 'life was so intense, palpitating, dramatic'. Nepenthe was Capri, famous since the time of Tiberius for its often extravagant effect upon those who took up residence there. Norman Douglas's central character – although his least convincing one – is a visiting Anglican bishop, shown to be so completely overwhelmed by the notorious atmosphere that in a matter of weeks even a murder has become palatable to him.

The abruptness and the improbability of this conversion is perhaps the book's one weak point and was noted at the time of its appearance by critics who were otherwise enthusiastic. They found it hard to accept that a notable churchman, successful in his struggle against the devil in Africa for so many years, should have succumbed in Nepenthe almost immediately after the first sniff of its perfumed air.

This apart, the critics were unanimous in their praise; some, like the famous Professor Saintsbury, were rapturous. One or two ran into some small difficulty in tracing the thread of the plot through so closely woven a tapestry of learned disquisitions, argument and wit. All were agreed that the secondary characters were not only diverting, but real – as they had every right to be, since they were the natives and expatriates of Capri, drawn by the author with mordant accuracy from the life. They have a tendency to share his vehement likes and dislikes, to be fulsome in praise of Athens of old and to protest against 'the preposterous old Hebrew system of right and wrong'. A typical visitor is knowledgeable about crystals, approves of Mormonism, and finds chastity 'an unclean state of affairs, and dangerous to the community'.

The message of the book is go your own sweet way, and be damned to them. After the long, grey years of self-denial, regimentation and sacrifice in the name of king and country, it was a counsel with a special appeal for the young.

South Wind was a cult book of its period. Many years later one saw people reputed to have undergone minor personality changes after reading it, usually with a tendency to spirited self-indulgence. It is hard now to imagine that such side-effects can have existed, for Norman Douglas is unlikely to have retained the power to induce moral waverers to cross forbidden frontiers these days. It remains the liveliest of period pieces, thought-provoking still, and an incomparable account of expatriates at play.

Norman Lewis
1987

CHAPTER 1

THE bishop was feeling rather sea-sick. Confoundedly sea-sick, in fact.

This annoyed him. For he disapproved of sickness in every shape or form. His own state of body was far from satisfactory at that moment; Africa – he was Bishop of Bampopo in the Equatorial Regions – had played the devil with his lower gastric department and made him almost an invalid; a circumstance of which he was nowise proud, seeing that ill-health led to inefficiency in all walks of life. There was nothing he despised more than inefficiency. Well or ill, he always insisted on getting through his tasks in a business-like fashion. That was the way to live, he used to say. Get through with it. Be perfect of your kind, whatever that kind may be. Hence his sneaking fondness for the natives – they were such fine, healthy animals.

Fine, healthy animals; perfect of their kind! Africa liked them to 'get through with it' according to their own lights. But there was evidently a little touch of spitefulness and malice about Africa; something almost human. For when white people try to get through with it after their particular fashion, she makes hay of their livers or something. That is what had happened to Thomas Heard D.D., Bishop of Bampopo. He had been so perfect of his kind, such an exemplary pastor, that there was small chance of a return to the scenes of his episcopal labours. Anybody could have told him what would happen. He ought to have allowed for a little human weakness, on the part of the Black Continent. It could not be helped. For the rest, he was half inclined to give up the Church and take to some educational work on his return to England. Perhaps that was why he at present preferred to be known as 'Mr Heard'. It put people at their ease, and him too.

Whence now this novel and unpleasant sensation in the upper gastric region? Most annoying! He had dined discreetly at his hotel the evening before; had breakfasted with moderation. And had he not voyaged in many parts of the world, in China Seas and round the Cape? Was he not even then on his return journey from Zanzibar? No doubt. But the big liner which deposited him yesterday at the thronged port was a different concern from this wretched tub, reeking with indescribable odours as it rolled in the oily swell of the past storm through which the *Mozambique* had

5

ridden without a tremor. The benches, too, were frightfully uncomfortable, and sticky with sirocco moisture under the breathless awning. Above all, there was the unavoidable spectacle of the suffering passengers, natives of the country; it infected him with misery. In attitudes worthy of Michelangelo they sprawled about the deck, groaning with anguish; huddled up in corners with a lemon – prophylactic against sea-sickness, apparently – pressed to faces which, by some subtle process of colour-adaptation, had acquired the complexion of the fruit; tottering to the taffrail. ...

There was a peasant woman dressed in black, holding an infant to her breast. Both child and parent suffered to a distressing degree. By some kindly dispensation of Providence they contrived to be ill in turns, and the situation might have verged on the comical but for the fact that blank despair was written on the face of the mother. She evidently thought her last day had come, and still, in the convulsions of her pain, tried to soothe the child. An ungainly creature, with a big scar across one cheek. She suffered dumbly, like some poor animal. The bishop's heart went out to her. ...

He took out his watch. Two more hours of discomfort to be gone through! Then he looked over the water. The goal was far distant.

Viewed from the clammy deck on this bright morning, the island of Nepenthe resembled a cloud. It was a silvery speck upon that limitless expanse of blue sea and sky. A south wind breathed over the Mediterranean waters, drawing up their moisture which lay couched in thick mists about its flanks and uplands. The comely outlines were barely suggested through a veil of fog. An air of unreality hung about the place. Could this be an island? A veritable island of rocks and vineyards and houses – this pallid apparition? It looked like some snowy sea-bird resting upon the waves; a sea-bird or a cloud; one of those lonely clouds that stray from their fellows and drift about in wayward fashion at the bidding of every breeze.

All the better-class natives had disappeared below save an unusually fat young priest with a face like a full moon, who pretended to be immersed in his breviary but was looking out of the corner of his eye all the time at a pretty peasant-girl reclining uncomfortably in a corner. He rose and arranged the cushions to her liking. In doing so he must have made some funny remark in her ear, for she smiled wanly as she said:

'*Grazie*, Don Francesco.'

'Means thank you, I suppose,' thought the bishop. 'But why is he a don?'

Of the other alien travellers, those charming but rather metallic American ladies had retired to the cabin; so had the English family; so had everybody, in fact. On deck there remained of the foreign contingent nobody but himself and Mr Muhlen, a flashy over-dressed personage who seemed to relish the state of affairs. He paced up and down, cool as a cucumber, trying to walk like a sailor, and blandly indifferent to the agonized fellow-creatures whom the movements of the vessel caused him to touch, every now and then, with the point of his patent-leather boots. Patent-leather boots. That alone classes him, thought Mr Heard. Once he paused and remarked, in his horrible pronunciation of English:

'That woman over there with the child! I wonder what I would do in her place? Throw it into the water, I fancy. It's often the only way of getting rid of a nuisance.'

'Rather a violent measure,' replied the bishop politely.

'You're not feeling very well, sir?' he continued, with a fine assumption of affability. 'I am so sorry. As for me, I like a little movement of the boat. You know our proverb? Weeds don't spoil. I'm alluding to myself, of course!'

Weeds don't spoil. ...

Yes, he was a weed. Mr Heard had not taken kindly to him; he hoped they would not see too much of each other on Nepenthe, which he understood to be rather a small place. A few words of civility over the *table d'hote* had led to an exchange of cards – a continental custom Mr Heard always resented. It could not easily be avoided in the present case. They had talked of Nepenthe, or rather Mr Muhlen had talked; the bishop, as usual, preferring to listen and to learn. Like himself, Mr Muhlen had never before set foot in the place. To be sure, he had visited other Mediterranean islands; he knew Sicily fairly well and had once spent a pleasant fortnight on Capri. But Nepenthe was different. The proximity to Africa, you know; the volcanic soil. Oh yes! It was obviously quite another sort of island. Business? No! He was not bound on any errand of business; not on any errand at all. Just a little pleasure trip. One owes something to one's self: *n'est-ce pas?* And this early summer was certainly the best time for travelling. One could count on good weather; one could sleep in the afternoon, if the heat were excessive. He had telegraphed for a couple of rooms in what was described as the best hotel – he hoped the visitors staying there would be to his liking. Unfortunately – so he gathered – the local society was a little mixed, a little – how shall we say? – ultra-cosmopolitan. The geographical situation of the island, lying near the converging point of many trade-routes, might account for this. And then its beauty and historical associations: they attracted strange tourists from every part of the world. Queer types! Types to be avoided, perhaps. But what did it matter, after all? It was one of the advantages of being a man, a civilized man, that you could amuse yourself among any class of society. As for himself, he liked the common people, the peasants and fishermen; he felt at home among them; they were so genuine, so refreshingly different.

To such-like ingratiating and rather obvious remarks the bishop had listened, over the dinner-table, with urbane acquiescence and growing distrust. Peasants and fisher-folk! This fellow did not look as if he cared for such company. He was probably a fraud.

They had met again in the evening, and taken a short stroll along the quay, where a noisy band was discoursing operatic airs. The performance elicited from Mr Muhlen some caustic comments on Latin music as contrasted with that of Russia and other countries. He evidently knew the subject. Mr Heard, to whom music was Greek, soon found himself out of his depth. Later on, in the smoking-room, they had indulged in a game of cards – the bishop being of the broad-minded variety which has not the slightest objection to a gentlemanly gamble. Once more his companion had revealed himself as an accomplished amateur.

No; it was something else that annoyed him about the man – certain almost contemptuous remarks he had dropped in the course of the evening on the subject of the female sex; not any particular member of it, but the sex in general. Mr Heard was sensitive on that point. He was not disheartened by experience. He had never allowed his judgement to be warped by those degrading aspects of womanhood which he had encountered during his work among the London poor, and more recently in Africa, where women are treated as the veriest beasts. He kept his ideals bright. He would tolerate no flippant allusions to the sex. Muhlen's talk had left a bad taste in his mouth.

And here he was, prancing up and down, sublimely pleased with himself. Mr Heard watched his perambulations with mixed feelings – moral disapproval combining with a small grain of envy at the fellow's conspicuous immunity from the prevailing seasickness.

A weed; unquestionably a weed.

Meanwhile, the mainland slowly receded. Morning wore on, and under the fierce attraction of the sun the fogs were drawn upwards. Nepenthe became tangible–an authentic island. It gleamed

8

with golden rocks and emerald patches of culture. A cluster of white houses, some town or village, lay perched on the middle heights where a playful sunbeam had struck a pathway through the vapours. The curtain was lifted. Half lifted; for the volcanic peaks and ravines overhead were still shrouded in pearly mystery.

The fat priest looked up from his breviary and smiled in friendly fashion.

'I heard you speak English to that person,' he began, with hardly a trace of foreign accent. 'You will pardon me. I see you are unwell. May I get you a lemon? Or perhaps a glass of cognac?'

'I am feeling better, thank you. It must have been the sight of those poor people that upset me. They seem to suffer horribly. I suppose I have got used to it.'

'They do suffer. And they get used to it too. I often wonder whether they are as susceptible to pain and discomfort as the rich with their finer nervous structure. Who can say? Animals also have their sufferings, but they are not encouraged to tell us about them. Perhaps that is why God made them dumb. Zola, in one of his novels, speaks of a sea-sick donkey.'

'Dear me!' said Mr Heard. It was an old-fashioned trick he had got from his mother. 'Dear me!'

He wondered what this youthful ecclesiastic was doing with Zola. In fact, he was slightly shocked. But he never allowed such a state of affairs to be noticed.

'You like Zola?' he queried.

'Not much. He is rather a dirty dog, and his technique is so ridiculously transparent. But one can't help respecting the man. If I were to read this class of literature for my own amusement I would prefer, I think, Catulle Mendès. But I don't. I read it, you understand, in order to be able to penetrate into the minds of my penitents, many of whom refuse to deprive themselves of such books. Women are so influenced by what they read! Personally, I am not very fond of improper writers. And yet they sometimes make one laugh in spite of oneself, don't they? I perceive you are feeling better.'

Mr Heard could not help saying:

'You express yourself very well in English.'

'Oh, passably! I have preached to large congregations of Catholics in the United States. In England, too. My mother was English. The Vatican has been pleased to reward the poor labours of my tongue by the title of Monsignor.'

'My congratulations. You are rather young for a Monsignor,

are you not? We are apt to associate that distinction with snuff-boxes and gout and –'

'Thirty-nine. It is a good age. One begins to appreciate things at their true value. Your collar! Might I inquire –?'

'Ah, my collar; the last vestige. ... Yes, I am a bishop. Bishop of Bampopo in Central Africa.'

'You are rather young, surely, for a bishop?'

Mr Heard smiled.

'The youngest on the list, I believe. There were not many applicants for the place; the distance from England, the hard work, and the climate, you know –'

'A bishop. Indeed!'

He waxed thoughtful. Probably he imagined that his companion was telling him some traveller's tale.

'Yes,' continued Mr Heard. 'I am what we call a "Returned Empty". It is a phrase we apply in England to Colonial bishops who come back from their dioceses.'

'Returned Empty! That sounds like beer.'

The priest was looking perplexed, as though uncertain of the other's state of mind. Southern politeness, or curiosity, overcame his fears. Perhaps this foreigner was fond of joking. Well, he would humour him.

'You will see our bishop to-morrow,' he pursued blandly. 'He comes over for the feast of the patron saint; you are lucky in witnessing it. The whole island is decorated. There will be music and fireworks and a grand procession. Our bishop is a dear old man, though not exactly what you would call a liberal,' he added, with a laugh. 'That is as it should be, is it not? We like our elders to be conservative. They counteract the often violent modernism of the youngsters. Is this your first visit to Nepenthe?'

'It is. I have heard much about the beauty of the place.'

'You will like it. The people are intelligent. There is good food and wine. Our lobsters are celebrated. You will find compatriots on the island, some ladies among them: the Duchess of San Martino, for instance, who happens to be an American; some delightful ladies! And the country girls, too, are worthy of a benevolent glance –'

'That procession is sure to interest me. What is the name of your patron?'

'Saint Dodekanus. He has a wonderful history. There is an Englishman on Nepenthe, Mr Ernest Eames, a student, who will tell you all about it. He knows more about the saint than I do; one would think he dined with him every evening. But he is a great hermit – Mr Eames, I mean. And it is so good of our old bishop to come over,' he pursued with a shade of emphasis. 'His work keeps him mostly on the mainland. He has a large see – nearly thirty square miles. How large, by the way, is your diocese?'

'I cannot give you the exact figures,' Mr Heard replied. 'It has often taken me three weeks to travel from one end to the other. It is probably not much smaller than the kingdom of Italy.'

'The kingdom of Italy. Indeed!'

That settled it. The conversation died abruptly; the friendly priest relapsed into silence. He looked hurt and disappointed. This was more than a joke. He had done his best to be civil to a suffering foreigner, and this was his reward – to be fooled with the grossest of fables. Maybe he remembered other occasions when Englishmen had developed a queer sense of humour which he utterly failed to appreciate. A liar. Or possibly a lunatic; one of those harmless enthusiasts who go about the world imagining themselves to be the Pope or the Archangel Gabriel. However that might be, he said not another word, but took to reading his breviary in good earnest, for the first time.

The boat anchored. Natives poured out in a stream. Mr Muhlen drove up alone, presumably to his sumptuous hotel. The bishop, having gathered his luggage together, followed in another carriage. He enjoyed the drive along that winding upward track; he admired the festal decorations of the houses, the gardens and vineyards, the many-tinted rock scenery overhead, the smiling sun-burnt peasantry. There was an air of contentment and well-being about the place; something joyful, opulent, almost dramatic.

'I like it,' he concluded.

And he wondered how long it would be before he met his cousin, Mrs Meadows, on whose account he had undertaken to break the journey to England.

Don Francesco, the smiling priest, soon outstripped both of them, in spite of ten minutes' conversation on the quay with the pretty peasant girl of the steamer. He had engaged the fastest driver on the island, and was now tearing frantically up the road, determined to be the first to apprise the Duchess of the lunatic's arrival.

CHAPTER 2

THE Duchess of San Martino, a kind-hearted and imposing lady of mature age who, under favourable atmospheric conditions (in winter-time, for instance, when the powder was not so likely to run down her face), might have passed, so far as profile was concerned, for a faded French beauty of bygone centuries – the Duchess was no exception to the rule.

It was an old rule. Nobody knew when it first came into vogue. Mr Eames, bibliographer of Nepenthe, had traced it down to the second Phoenician period, but saw no reason why the Phoenicians, more than anybody else, should have established the precedent. On the contrary, he was inclined to think that it dated from yet earlier days; days when the Troglodytes, Manigones, Septocardes, Merdones, Anthropophagoi, and other hairy aboriginals used to paddle across, in crazy canoes, to barter the produce of their savage, African glens – serpent-skins, and gums, and gazelle horns, and ostrich eggs – for those super-excellent lobsters and peasant girls for which Nepenthe had been renowned from time immemorial. He based this scholarly conjecture on the fact that a gazelle horn, identified as belonging to a now extinct Tripolitan species, was actually discovered on the island, while an adolescent female skull of the hypodolichocephalous (Nepenthean) type had come to light in some excavations at Benghazi.

It was a pleasant rule. It ran to the effect that in the course of the forenoon all the inhabitants of Nepenthe, of whatever age, sex, or condition, should endeavour to find themselves in the market-place or piazza – a charming square, surrounded on three sides by the principal buildings of the town, and open on the fourth to a lovely prospect over land and sea. They were to meet on this spot; there to exchange gossip, make appointments for the evening, and watch the arrival of new-comers to their island. An admirable rule! For it effectively prevented everybody from doing any kind of work in the morning; and after luncheon, of course, you went to sleep. It was delightful to be obliged, by iron convention, to stroll about in the bright sunshine, greeting your friends, imbibing iced drinks and letting your eye stray down to the lower level of the island, with its farmhouses embowered in vineyards; or across the glittering water towards the distant coastline and its volcano; or upwards, into those pinnacles of the higher region against whose craggy ramparts, nearly always, a fleet of snowy sirocco clouds was anchored. For Nepenthe was famous not only for its girls and lobsters, but also for its south wind.

As usual at this hour, the market-place was crowded with folks. It was a gay throng. Priests and curly-haired children, farmers, fishermen, citizens, a municipal policeman or two, brightly dressed women of all ages, foreigners in abundance – they moved up and down, talking, laughing, gesticulating. Nobody had anything particular to do; such was the rule.

The Russian sect was well represented. They were religious enthusiasts, ever increasing in numbers and led by their Master, the divinely inspired Bazhakuloff, who was then living in almost complete seclusion on the island. They called themselves the 'Little White Cows', to mark their innocence of worldly affairs, and their scarlet blouses, fair hair, and wondering blue eyes were quite a feature of the place. Overhead, fluttering flags and wreaths of flowers, and bunting, and brightly tinted paper festoons – an orgy of colour, in honour of the saint's festival on the morrow.

The Duchess, attired in black, with a black-and-white sunshade, and a string of preposterous amethysts nestling in the imitation Val on her bosom, was leaning on the arm of an absurdly good-looking youth whom she addressed as Denis. Everyone called him Denis or Mr Denis. People used his surname as little as possible. It was Phipps.

With a smile for everyone, she moved more deliberately than the rest, and used her fan rather more frequently. She knew that the sirocco was making stealthy inroads upon her carefully powdered cheeks; she wanted to look her best on the arrival of Don Francesco, who was to bring some important message from the clerical authorities of the mainland anent her forthcoming reception into the Roman Catholic Church. He was her friend. Soon he would be her confessor.

Worldly-wise, indolent, good-natured, and, like most Southerners, a thorough-going pagan, Don Francesco was deservedly popular as ecclesiastic. Women adored him; he adored women. He passed for an unrivalled preacher; his golden eloquence made converts everywhere, greatly to the annoyance of the *parroco*, the parish priest, who was doubtless sounder on the Trinity, but a shocking bad orator and altogether deficient in humanity, and who nearly had a fit, they said, when the other was created Monsignor. Don Francesco was a fisher of men, and of women. He fished *ad maiorem Dei gloriam*, and for the fun of the thing. It was his way of taking exercise, he once confessed to his friend Keith; he was too fat to run about like other people – he could only talk. He fished among natives, and among foreigners.

Foreigners were hard to catch, on Nepenthe. They came and went in such breathless succession. Of the permanent residents, only the Duchess, always of High Church leanings, had of late yielded to his blandishments. She was fairly hooked. Madame Steynlin, a lady of Dutch extraction whose hats were proverbial,

13

was uncompromisingly Lutheran. The men were past redemption, all save the Commissioner, who, however, was under bad influences and an incurable wobbler, anyhow. Eames, the scholar, cared for nothing but his books. Keith, a rich eccentric who owned one of the finest villas and gardens on the place, came to the island only for a few weeks every year. He knew too much, and had travelled too far, to be anything but a hopeless unbeliever; besides, he was a particular friend of his, with whom he agreed, in his heart of hearts, on every subject. The frequenters of the Club were mostly drunkards, derelicts, crooks, or faddists – not worth catching.

Carriages began to arrive on the scene. That of Don Francesco drove up first of all. He stepped out and sailed across the piazza like a schooner before the wind. But his discourse, usually ample and florid as befitted both his person and his calling, was couched on this occasion in Tacitean brevity.

'We have landed a queer fish, Duchess,' he remarked. 'He calls himself Bishop of Bim-Bam-Bum, and resembles a broken-down matrimonial agent. So lean! So yellow! His face all furrowed! He has lived very viciously, that man. Perhaps he is mad. In every case, look to your purse, Mr Denis. He'll be here in a minute.'

'That's quite right,' said the young man. 'The Bishop of Bampopo. It's in the *New York Herald*. Sailing by the *Mozambique*. But they didn't say he was coming to the island. I wonder what he wants here?'

Don Francesco was aghast.

'Indeed?' he asked. 'A bishop, and so yellow! He must have thought me very rude,' he added.

'You couldn't be rude if you tried,' said the Duchess, giving him a playful slap with her fan.

She was burning with ardour to be the first to introduce such a lion to the local society. But fearful of making a *faux pas*, she said:

'You'll go and speak to him, Denis. Find out if it's the right one – the one you read about in the paper, I mean. Then come and tell me.'

'Good Lord, Duchess, don't ask me to do that! I couldn't tackle a bishop. Not an African. Not unless he has a proper apron on.'

'Be a man, Denis. He won't bite a pretty boy like you.'

'What nice things the lady is saying to you,' observed Don Francesco.

'She always does,' he laughed, 'when she wants me to do some-
14

thing for her. I haven't been on this island long, but I have already found out the Duchess! You do it, Don Francesco. He is sure to be the right one. They get yellow, out there. Sometimes green.'

Mr Heard was intercepted on his way to the hotel by the genial priest, and formally presented to the Duchess. She was more than condescending to this stern and rather tired-looking man; she was gracious. She made all kinds of polite inquiries, and indicated the various sites and persons of interest; while Don Francesco, he observed, had unaccountably recovered from his sudden attack of bad humour on the steamer.

'And that is where I live,' she said, pointing to a large and severe structure whose walls had plainly not been whitewashed for many long years. 'It's an old disused convent, built by the Good Duke Alfred. Wasn't it, Denis?'

'I really couldn't say, Duchess. I never heard of the gentleman.'

'That Good Duke was an unmitigated ruffian,' observed Don Francesco.

'Oh, don't say that! Think of all the good he did for the island. Think of that frieze in the church! I have acres and acres of rooms to walk about in,' she continued, addressing the bishop. 'All by myself! I'm quite a hermit, you know. You will perhaps be able to have a cup of tea with me today?'

'Not exactly a hermit,' Denis interposed.

'To take tea with the Duchess is an experience, a revelation,' said Don Francesco in judicial tones. 'I have enjoyed that meal in various parts of the world, but nobody can manage it as she can. She has the true gift. You will make tea for us in Paradise, dear lady. As to luncheon, let me tell you in confidence, Mr Heard, that my friend Keith, whom you will meet sooner or later, has a most remarkable chef. What that man of Keith's cannot cook is not worth eating.'

'How delightful!' replied the bishop, slightly embarrassed. 'And where,' he added, laughing – 'where does one dine?'

'I do not dine. Madame Steynlin used to give nice evening parties,' he continued reflectively, and with a shade of sadness in his voice. 'Excellent little dinners! But she is so taken up with Russians just now; they quite monopolize her house. Down there; do you see, Mr Heard? That white villa by the sea, at the end of the promontory. She is so romantic. That is why she bought a house which nobody else would have bought at any price. That little place, all by itself – it fascinated her. Bitterly she regrets her choice. She has discovered the drawbacks of a promontory. My dear Duchess, never live on a promontory! It has fearful
15

inconveniences; you are overlooked by everybody. All the island knows what you do, and who visits you, and when, and why. ... Yes, I remember those dinners with regret. Nowadays I must content myself with a miserable supper at home. The doctor has forbidden dinners. He says I am getting too fat.'

Denis remarked:

'Your fat is your fortune, Don Francesco.'

'My fortune, then, is a heavy load to bear. Mr Keith tells me I have seven double chins, three behind and four in front. He says he has counted them carefully. He declares that an eighth is in course of formation. It is too much for a person of my austere temperament.'

'You need never believe a word Keith says,' said the Duchess. 'He upsets me with his long words and his – his awful views. He really does.'

'I tell him he is the Antichrist,' observed Don Francesco, gravely shaking his head. 'But we shall see! We shall catch him yet.'

The Duchess had no idea what the Antichrist was, but she felt sure it was something not quite nice.

'If I thought he was anything like that, I would never ask him to my house again. The Antichrist! Ah, talk of angels –'

The person in question suddenly appeared, superintending half a dozen young gardeners who carried various consignments of plants wrapped up in straw which had arrived, presumably, by the steamer.

Mr Keith was older than he looked – incredibly old, in fact, though nobody could bring himself to believe it; he was well preserved by means of a complicated system of life, the details of which, he used to declare, were not fit for publication. That was only his way of talking. He exaggerated so dreadfully. His face was clean-shaven, rosy, and of cherubic fullness; his eyes beamed owlishly through spectacles which nobody had ever seen him take off. But for those spectacles he might have passed for a well-groomed baby in a soap advertisement. He was supposed to sleep in them.

It looked as though Mr Keith had taken an instantaneous liking to the bishop.

'Bampopo? Why, of course. I've been there. Years and years ago. Long before your time, I'm afraid. How is the place getting on? Better roads, no doubt. And better food, I hope! I was much interested in that little lake – you know? It seemed to have no outlet. We must talk it over. And I liked those Bulanga people – fine

16

fellows! You liked them too? I'm glad to hear it. Such a lot of nonsense was talked about their depravity! If you have nothing better to do, come and lunch tomorrow, can you? Villa Khismet. Anybody will show you the way. You, Denis,' he added, 'you disappoint me. You look like a boy who is fond of flowers. And yet you have never been to see my cannas, which are the finest in the kingdom, to say nothing of myself, who am also something of a flower. A carnivorous orchid, I fancy.'

'A virgin lily,' suggested Don Francesco.

'I wish I could manage to come,' replied Mr Heard. 'But I must look for a cousin of mine to-morrow: Mrs Meadows. Perhaps you know her?'

The priest said:

'We all know Mrs Meadows. And we all like her. Unfortunately she lives far, far away; right up there,' and he pointed vaguely towards the sirocco clouds. 'In the Old Town, I mean. She dwells like a hermit, all alone. You can drive up there in a carriage, of course. It is a pity all these nice people live so far away. There is Count Caloveglia, for instance, whom I would like to see every day of my life. He talks better English than I do, the old humbug! He, too, is a hermit. But he will be down here tomorrow. He never misses the theatricals.'

Everybody seems to be a hermit hereabouts, thought Mr Heard. And yet this place is seething with people!

Aloud he said:

'So my cousin lives up in the fog. And does it always hang about like this?'

'Oh dear, no!' replied the Duchess. 'It goes away, sometimes, in the afternoon. The sirocco, this year, has been most exceptional. Most exceptional! Don't you think so, Denis?'

'Really couldn't say, Duchess. You know I only arrived last week.'

'Most exceptional! Don Francesco will bear me out.'

'It blows,' said the priest, 'when the good God wishes it to blow. He has been wishing pretty frequently of late.'

'I am writing to your cousin,' the Duchess remarked, 'to ask her to my small annual gathering after the festival of Saint Dodekanus. Tomorrow, you know. Quite an informal little affair. I may count on you, Bishop? You'll all come, won't you? You too, Mr Keith? But no long words, remember! Nothing about reflexes and praeternatural and things like that. And not a syllable about the Incarnation, please. It scares me. What's the name of her villa, Denis?'

17

'Mon Repos. Rather a commonplace name I think – Mon Repos.'

'It is,' said Keith. 'But there is nothing commonplace about the lady. She is what I would call a New Woman.'

'Dear me!'

Mr Heard was alarmed at this picture of his cousin. He did not altogether approve of New Women.

'She has long ago passed the stage you have in mind, Bishop. She is newer than that. The real novelty! Looks after the baby, and thinks of her husband in India. I believe I have many points in common with the New Woman. I often think of people in India.'

'Such a dear little child,' said the Duchess.

'Almost as round as myself,' added Don Francesco. 'There goes the Commissioner! He is fussing about with the judge, that red-haired man – do you see, Mr Heard? – who limps like Mephistopheles and spits continually. They say he wants to imprison all the Russians. Poor folks! They ought to be sent home; they don't belong here. He is looking at us now. Ha, the animal! He has the Evil Eye. He is also scrofulous, rachitic. And his name is Malipizzo.'

'What a funny name!' remarked the bishop.

'Yes, and he is a funny animal. They are great friends, those two.'

'A horrible man, that judge,' said the Duchess. 'Only think, Mr Heard, an atheist.'

'A freemason,' corrected Mr Keith.

'It's the same thing. And ugly! Nobody has a right to be quite so ugly. I declare he's worse than the cinematograph villain – you remember, Denis?'

'It is a miracle he has lived so long, with that face,' added Don Francesco. 'I think God created him in order that mankind should have some idea of the meaning of the word "grotesque".'

The proud title 'Commissioner' caused the bishop to pay particular attention to the other of the two individuals in question. He beheld a stumpy and pompous-looking personage, flushed in the face, with a moth-eaten grey beard and shifty grey eyes, clothed in a flannel shirt, tweed knickerbockers, brown stockings, white spats, and shoes. Such was the Commissioner's invariable get-up, save that in winter he wore a cap instead of a panama. He was smoking a briar pipe and looking blatantly British, as if he had just spent an unwashed night in a third-class carriage between King's Cross and Aberdeen. The magistrate, on the other hand – the red-haired man – was jauntily dressed, with a straw hat on one side of his repulsive head, and plenty of starch about him.

'I never knew we had a Commissioner here,' said Mr Heard. Keith replied:

'We haven't. He is Financial Commissioner for Nicaragua. An incomparable ass is Mr Freddy Parker.'

'Oh, he has a sensible idea now and then, when he forgets to be a fool,' observed Don Francesco. 'He is President of the Club, Mr Heard. They will elect you honorary member. Take my advice. Avoid the whisky.'

Denis remarked, after a critical glance in the same direction,

'I notice that the Commissioner looks redder in the face than when I last saw him.'

'That,' said Keith, 'is one of Mr Parker's characteristics.'

CHAPTER 3

CONCERNING the life and martyrdom of Saint Dodekanus, patron of Nepenthe, we possess hardly any information of a trustworthy nature. It is with his career as with that of other saints: they become overlaid – encrusted, as it were – with extraneous legendary material in the course of ages, even as a downward-rolling avalanche gathers snow. The nucleus is hard to find. What is incontestably true may be summed up almost in one paragraph.

He was born in A.D. 450, or thereabouts, in the city of Kallisto in Crete. He was an only child, a beautiful but unruly boy, the despair of his widowed mother. At the age of thirteen he encountered, one evening, an elderly man of thoughtful mien, who addressed him in familiar language. On several later occasions he discoursed with the same personage, in a grove of laurels and pines known as Alephane; but what passed between them, and whether it was some divine apparition, or merely a man of flesh and blood, was never discovered, for he seems to have kept his mother in ignorance of the whole affair. From that time onward his conduct changed. He grew pensive, mild, and charitable. He entered, as youthful acolyte, a neighbouring Convent of Salacian monks and quickly distinguished himself for piety and the gift of miracles. In the short space of three years, or thereabouts, he had healed eight lepers, caused the clouds to rain, walked dryshod over several rivers, and raised twenty-three persons from the dead.

At the age of eighteen he had a second vision. This time it was a young woman of pleasing exterior. He discoursed with her, on several occasions, in the grove of laurels and pines known as Alephane; but what passed between them, and whether it was a woman of flesh and blood, or merely an angel, was never discovered, for he seems to have kept his brother monks in ignorance of the whole affair. From that time onward his conduct changed. He grew restless and desirous of converting the heathen. He set sail for Libya, suffered shipwreck in the Greater Syrtis, and narrowly escaped with his life. Thence he passed onward, preaching to black nations as he moved along, and converting tribes innumerable. For three-and-thirty years he wandered till, one evening, he saw the moon rise on the right side of his face.

He had entered the land of the Crotalophoboi, cannibals and necromancers who dwelt in a region so hot, and with light so dazzling, that their eyes grew on the soles of their feet. Here he laboured for eighty years, redeeming them to Christianity from their magical and bloodthirsty practices. In recompense whereof they captured him at the patriarchal age of 132, or thereabouts, and bound him with ropes between two flat boards of palmwood. Thus they kept the prisoner, feeding him abundantly, until that old equinoctial feast drew near. On the evening of that day they sawed the whole, superstitiously, into twelve separate pieces, one for each month of the year; and devoured of the saint what was to their liking.

During this horrid banquet a femur or thigh-bone was accidentally cast upon a millstone which lay by the shore, having been borrowed by the Crotalophoboi from the neighbouring tribe of Garimanes a good many years previously and never returned to them by reason, they declared, of its excessive weight. There it remained till, one day, during a potent sirocco tempest, the stone was uplifted by the force of the waters, and miraculously wafted over the sea to Nepenthe. Forthwith a chapel was built on the spot, to commemorate the event and preserve the sacred relic, which soon began working wonders for the good of the island, such as warding off Saracenic invasions, procuring plentiful vintages, and causing sterile cattle to produce offspring.

In later years the main church was dedicated to Saint Dodekanus and the relic moved thither and enclosed within that silver statue of the saint which is carried abroad in procession at his annual festival, or on any particular occasion when his help is to be invoked. And all through succeeding ages the cult of the saint waxed in pomp and splendour. Nobody, probably, has done more to foster pious feelings towards their island-patrons than the Good

20

Duke Alfred, who, among other things, caused a stately frieze to be placed in the church, picturing in twelve marble tablets the twelve chief episodes in the life of the Saint – one for each month of the year. This frieze indeed was admired so unreservedly, so recklessly, that the Good Duke felt it his duty to remove the sculptor's eyes and (on second thoughts) his hands as well, in order that no other sovereign should possess works by so consummate a master of stonecraft. There the disciplinary measures ended. He did his best to console the gifted artist, who was fed, henceforward, on lobsters, decorated with the order of the Golden Vine, and would doubtless have been ennobled after death, had the Prince not predeceased the sculptor.

Such, briefly, is the history of Saint Dodekanus, and the origin of his cult on Nepenthe.

Legends galore, often contradictory to this account and to one another, have clustered round his name, as was inevitable. He is supposed to have preached in Asia Minor; to have died as a young man, in his convent; to have become a hermit, a cobbler, a bishop (of Nicomedia), a eunuch, a politician. Two volumes of mediocre sermons in the Byzantine tongue have been ascribed to him. These and other crudities may be dismissed as apocryphal. Even his name has given rise to controversy, although its origin from the Greek word *dodeka*, signifying twelve and alluding to the twelve morsels into which his body was superstitiously divided, is as self-evident as well can be. Thus a worthy young canon of the church of Nepenthe, Giacinto Mellino, who has lately written a life of Saint Eulalia, the local patroness of sailors – her festival occurs twelve days after that of Saint Dodekanus – takes occasion, in this otherwise commendable pamphlet, to scoff at the old-established derivation of the name and to propose an alternative etymology. He lays it down that the then pagan inhabitants of the island, desirous of sharing in the benefits of Christianity which had already reached the mainland but left untouched their lonely rock, sent a missive to the bishop containing the two words *Do dekanus*: give us a deacon! The grammar is at fault, he explains, because of their rudimentary knowledge of the Latin tongue; they had only learnt, hitherto, the first person singular and the nominative case – so he says; and then proceeds to demonstrate, with unanswerable arguments, that Greek was the spoken language of Nepenthe at this period. Several scholars have been swayed by this specious logic to abandon the older and sounder interpretation. There are yet other conjectures anent the word Dodekanus, all more or less fanciful.

If the Crotalophoboi had not devoured the missionary Dodekanus, we should assuredly never have heard of Monsignor Perrelli, the learned and genial historian of Nepenthe. It was that
story, he expressly tells us, which inflamed him, a mere visitor to
the place, with a desire to know more about the island. A people
like the Nepentheans, who could cherish in their hearts a tale of
such beauty, must be worthy, he concluded, 'of the closest and
most sympathetic scrutiny'. Thus, one thing leading to another, as
always happens where local researches are concerned, he soon
found himself collecting other legends, traditions, historical data,
statistics of agriculture and natural productions, and so forth. The
result of these labours was embodied in the renowned *Antiquities
of Nepenthe*.

This book, a model of its kind, is written in Latin. It seems to
have been the author's only work, and has gone through several
editions; the last one – by no means the best as regards typo-
graphy – being that of 1709. The Crotalophoboi therefore, who
procured the sanctification of Dodekanus by methods hardly commendable to decent folks, can be said to have done some good in
the world, if the creation of a literary masterpiece like these *Antiquities*, for which they are indirectly responsible, may be classed
under that head.

It is a pity we know so little of the life of this Monsignor Perrelli. He is disappointingly reticent about himself. We learn that
he was a native of the mainland; that he came here, as a youth,
afflicted with rheumatic troubles; that these troubles were relieved
by an application of those health-giving waters which he lived to
describe in one of the happiest sections of his work, and which
were to become famous to the world at large through certain classical experiments carried out under his contemporary, the Good
Duke Alfred – a potentate who, by the way, does not seem to
have behaved very prettily to our scholar. And that is absolutely
all we know about him. The most painstaking inquiries on the
part of Mr Eames have failed to add a single item of positive
information to our knowledge of the historian of Nepenthe. We
cannot tell when, or where, he died. He seems to have ended in regarding himself as a native of the place. The wealth of material
incorporated in the book leads to the supposition that he must
have spent long years on the island. We may further presume,
from his title, that he belonged to the Church; it was the surest
path of advancement for a young man of quality in those days.

A perfunctory glance into his pages will suffice to prove that
he lacked what is called the ecclesiastical bent of mind. Reading

between the lines, one soon discovers that he is not so much a priest as a statesman and philosopher, a student curious in the lore of mankind and of nature – alert, sagacious, discriminating. He tells us, for example, that this legend of the visions and martyrdom of Saint Dodekanus, which he was the first to disentangle from its heterogeneous accretions, was vastly to his liking. Why? Because of its churchly flavour? Not so; but because he detected therein 'truth and symbol. It is a tale of universal applicability; the type, as it were, of every great man's life, endeavour, and reward.' The introduction to these *Antiquities*, setting forth his maxims for the writing of history, might have been composed not three centuries ago, but yesterday – or even tomorrow; so modern is its note.

Hearken to these weighty words:

Portraiture of characters and events should take the form of one gentleman conversing with another, in the easy tone of good society. The author who sets out to address a crowd defeats his own object; he eliminates the essence of good writing – frankness. You cannot be frank with men of low condition. You must presuppose a refined and congenial listener, a man or woman whom you would not hesitate to take by the hand and lead into the circle of your own personal friends. If this applies to literature of every kind, it applies to history in a peculiar degree.

History deals with situations and figures not imaginary but real. It demands therefore a combination of qualities unnecessary to the poet or writer of romance – glacial judgement coupled with fervent sympathy. The poet may be an inspired illiterate, the romance-writer an uninspired hack. Under no circumstances can either of them be accused of wronging or deceiving the public, however incongruous their efforts. They write well or badly, and there the matter ends. The historian who fails in his duty deceives the reader and wrongs the dead. A man weighted with such responsibilities is deserving of an audience more than usually select – an audience of his equals, men of the world. No vulgarian can be admitted to share those confidences...

The Greeks figured forth a Muse of History; they dared express their opinions. Genesis, that ancient barrier, did not exist for them. It stands in the way of the modern historian; it involves him in a ceaseless conflict with his own honesty. If he values his skin, he must accommodate himself to current dogmas and refrain from truthful comments and conclusions. He has the choice of being a chronologer or a ballad-monger – obsolete and unimportant occupations. Unenviable fate of those who aspire to be teachers of mankind, that they themselves should be studied with a kind of antiquarian interest, stimulating thought not otherwise than as warning examples! Clio has fallen from her pedestal. That

23

radiant creature, in identifying her interests with those of theocracy, has become the hand-maiden of a withered and petulant mistress, a mercenary slut. So things will remain, till mankind has acquired a fresh body of ethics, corresponding to modern needs. It is useless, it is dangerous, to pour new wine into old bottles. ...

He carries out his theory. The work of Monsignor Perrelli is, above all things, a human document – the revelation of a personality cultured and free from prejudice. Indeed, when one considers the religious situation of those days, he seems to be sailing perilously near the wind in some of his theological reflections; so much so, that Mr Eames often wondered whether this might not account for our ignorance of his later life and the manner of his death. He held it possible that the scholar may have fallen into the clutches of the Inquisition, never again to return to the surface of society. It would explain why the first edition of the *Antiquities* is so extremely rare, and why the two subsequent ones were issued, respectively, at Amsterdam and Bâle.

Incidentally, the book contains in its nine hundred pages all that could possibly interest a contemporary student about the history and natural products of Nepenthe. It is still a mine of antiquarian information, though large sections of the work have inevitably become obsolete. To bring the *Antiquities* up to date by means of a revised and enlarged version enriched with footnotes, appendixes, and copious illustrations, was the ambition, the sole ambition, of Mr Ernest Eames, B.A. ...

It was not true to say of this gentleman that he fled from England to Nepenthe because he forged his mother's will, because he was arrested while picking the pockets of a lady at Tottenham Court Road Station, because he refused to pay for the upkeep of his seven illegitimate children, because he was involved in a flamboyant scandal of unmentionable nature and unprecedented dimensions, because he was detected while trying to poison the rhinoceros at the Zoo with an arsenical bun, because he strangled his mistress, because he addressed an almost disrespectful letter to the Primate of England beginning 'My good Owl' – or for suchlike reason; and that he now remained on the island only because nobody was fool enough to lend him the ten pounds requisite for a ticket back again.

He came there originally to save money; and he stayed there originally because, if he had happened to die on his homeward journey, there would not have been enough coppers in his pocket to pay the funeral expenses. Nowadays, having solved the problem of how to live on £85 a year, he stayed for another reason as well;

24

to annotate Perrelli's *Antiquities*. It sweetened his self-imposed exile.

He was a dry creature, almost wizened, with bright eyes and a short moustache; unostentatiously dressed; fastidious, reserved, genteel, precise in manner, and living a retired life in a two-roomed cottage somewhere among the vineyards.

He had taken a high degree in classics, though Greek was never much to his taste. It was 'runaway stuff'; nervous and sensuous; it opened up too many vistas, philological and social, for his positive mind to assimilate with comfort. Those particles alone – there was something ambiguous, something almost disreputable, in their jocund pliability, their readiness to lend themselves to improper uses. But Latin – ah, Latin was different! Even at his preparatory school, where he was known as a swot of the first water, he had displayed an unhealthy infatuation for that tongue; he loved its cold, lapidary construction; and while other boys played football or cricket, this withered little fellow used to lark about with a note-book, all by himself, torturing sensible English into its refractory and colourless periods and elaborating, without the help of a Gradus, those inept word-mosaics which are called Latin verses. 'Good fun,' he used to say, 'and every bit as exciting as algebra,' as though that constituted a recommendation. Often the good form-master shook his head and inquired anxiously whether he was feeling unwell, or had had secret troubles of any kind.

'Oh no, sir,' he would then reply, with a funny little laugh. 'Thank you, sir. But please, sir! Would you mind telling me whether *pecunia* really comes from *pecus*? Because Adams minor (another swot) says it doesn't.'

Later on, at the University, he used the English language for the sake of convenience – in order to make himself understood by Dons and Heads of Colleges. His thoughts, his dreams, were in Latin.

Such a man, arriving almost penniless on Nepenthe, might have passed a torpid month or two, then drifted into the Club-set and gone to the dogs altogether. Latin saved him. He took to studying those earlier local writers who often composed in that tongue. The Jesuitical smoothness, the saccharine felicity of authors like Giannettasio had just begun to pall on his fancy when the *Antiquities* fell into his hands. It was like a draught of some generous wine, after a course of barley-water. Here was Latin worth reading; rich, sinewy, idiomatic, full of flavour, masculine. Flexible, yet terse. Latin after his own heart: a cry across the centuries!

So bewitched was Mr Eames with the grammar and syntax of the *Antiquities* that he had already gone through the book three times ere realizing that this man, who could construct such flowing, glowing sentences, was actually writing about something. Yes, he had something of uncommon interest to impart. And a gentleman, by Jove! So different from what one runs up against nowadays. He had an original way of looking at things – a human way. Very human. Those quaint streaks of credulity, those whimsical blasphemies, those spicy Court anecdotes dropped, as it were, in the smoking-room of a patrician club – a rare old fellow! He would have given anything to have made his acquaintance.

Forthwith a change came over Mr Ernest Eames. His frozen classical mind blossomed under the sunny stimulus of the Renaissance scholar. He entered upon a second boyhood – a real boyhood, this time, full of enthusiasms and adventures into flowery by-paths of learning. Monsignor Perrelli absorbed him. He absorbed Monsignor Perrelli. Marginal observations led to footnotes; footnotes to appendixes. He had found an interest in life. He would annotate the *Antiquities*.

In the section which deals with the life of Saint Dodekanus, the Italian had displayed more than his usual erudition and acumen. He had sifted the records with such incredible diligence that little was left for the pen of an annotator, save words of praise. In two small matters, however, the Englishman, considerably to his regret, was enabled or rather obliged to add a postscript.

Many a time he cursed the day when his researches among the archives of the mainland brought him into contact with the unpublished chronicle of Father Capocchio, a Dominican friar of licorous and even licentious disposition, a hater of Nepenthe, and a personal enemy, it seemed, of his idol Perrelli. His manuscript – the greater part of it, at all events – was not fit to be printed; not fit to be touched by respectable people. Mr Eames felt it his duty to waive considerations of delicacy. In his capacity of annotator he would have plunged headlong into the Augean stables, had there been any likelihood of extracting therefrom the germs of a luminous footnote. He perused the manuscript, making notes as he went along. This wretched monk, he concluded, must have possessed a damnably intimate knowledge of Nepenthean conditions, and a cantankerous and crapulous turn of mind into the bargain. He never lost an opportunity of denigrating the island; he was determined, absolutely determined, to see only the bad side of things, so far as that place was concerned.

Regarding the pious relic, for instance – the thigh-bone of the saint, preserved in the principal church – he wrote:

'A certain Perrelli who calls himself historian, which is as though one should call a mule a horse, or an ass a mule, brays loudly and disconnectedly about the femur of the local god. We have personally examined this priceless femur. It is not a femur, but a tibia. And it is the tibia not of a saint, but of a young cow or calf. We may mention, in passing, that we hold a diploma in anatomy from the Palermitan Faculty of Medicine.'

That was Father Capocchio's way; bald to coarseness, whenever he lacked occasion to be obscene.

To Mr Eames it would have mattered little, *a priori*, whether the relic was a femur or a tibia, of cow or man. In this case, he liked to think it was the thigh-bone of a saint. He possessed an unusually strong dose of that Latin *pietas*, that reverence which consists in leaving things as they are, particularly when they have been described for the benefit of posterity, with the most engaging candour, by a man of Perrelli's calibre. Now, an insinuation like this could not be slurred over. It was a downright challenge! The matter must be thrashed out. For four months he pored over books on surgery and anatomy. Then, having acquired a knowledge of the subject – adequate, though necessarily superficial – he applied to the ecclesiastical authorities for permission to view the relic. It was politely refused. The saintly object, they declared, could only be exhibited to persons professing the Roman Catholic Faith and armed with a special recommendation from the Bishop.

'These,' he used to say, 'are the troubles which lie in wait for a conscientious annotator.'

On another point, that of a derivation of the saint's name, he was pained to discover in the pages of Father Capocchio an alternative suggestion, of which more anon. It caused him many sleepless nights. But on matters pertaining to the climate of Nepenthe, its inhabitants, products, minerals, water-suppply, fisheries, trade, folk-lore, ethnology – on questions such as these he had gathered much fresh information. Sheaves of stimulating footnotes had accumulated on his desk.

When would all this material be published?

Mr Eames had not the faintest idea. Meanwhile he calmly went on collecting and collecting and collecting. Something might turn up, one of these days. Everybody with the slightest pretensions to scholarship was interested in his work; many friends had made him offers of pecuniary assistance towards the printing of a book which could not be expected to be a source of profit to its publisher; the wealthy and good-natured Mr Keith, in particular, used to complain savagely and very sincerely at not being allowed to assist to the extent of a hundred or two. There were days on which he seemed to yield to these arguments; days when he expanded and gave rein to his fancy, smiling in anticipation of that noble volume – the golden Latinity of Monsignor Perrelli enriched with twenty-five years' patient labour on the part of himself; days when he would go so far as to discuss prospective contracts, and bindings, and photogravures, and margins, and paper. Everything, of course, was to be of appropriate quality – not pretentious, but distinguished. Oh, yes! A book of that kind – it must have a cachet of its own. ...

Then, suddenly, he would observe that he was joking; only joking.

The true Mr Eames revealed and reasserted himself. He shrank from the idea. He closed up like a flower in the chill of nightfall. He was not going to put himself under obligations to anybody. He would keep his sense of personal independence, even if it entailed the sacrifice of a life's ambition. Owe no man anything! The words rang in his ears. They were his father's words. Owe no man anything! They were that gentleman's definition of a gentleman – a definition which was cordially approved by every other gentleman who, like Mr Eames junior, happened to hold analogous views.

Gentlemen being rather scarce nowadays, we cannot but feel grateful to the Crotalophoboi for devouring Saint Dodekanus and paving the way, *via* the *Antiquities* of Monsignor Perrelli, for the refined personality of Mr Eames – even if such was not their original intention.

CHAPTER 4

NEXT morning, at precisely 4 a.m., there was an earthquake.

Foreigners unaccustomed to Nepenthean conditions rushed in their pyjamas out of doors to escape the falling wreckage. An American lady, staying at Mr Muhlen's high-class hotel, jumped from her bedroom on the third floor into the courtyard below, and narrowly escaped bruising her ankle.

It was a false alarm. The sudden clanging of every bell on the place, the explosion of twelve hundred mortars, and the simultaneous booming of an enormous cannon – that far-famed gun whose wayward tricks had cost the lives of hundreds of its loaders in the days of the Good Duke – might have passed for an

28

earthquake of the first magnitude, so far as noise and concussion were concerned. The island rocked to its foundations. It was the signal for the festival of the patron saint to begin.

Nobody could have slept through that din. Mr Heard, dog-tired as he was, woke up and opened his eyes.

'Things are happening here,' he said – a remark which he found himself repeating on several later occasions.

He looked round the room. It was not an hotel bedroom. Then he began to remember things, drowsily. He remembered the pleasant surprise of the previous evening – how the Duchess had called to mind a small villa, vacated earlier than she had expected by a lady friend for whom she had taken it. It was furnished, spotlessly clean, with a woman, a capable cook, in attendance. She had insisted on his living there.

'So much nicer than a dreadful room in an hotel! You'll show the bishop all over it, won't you, Denis?'

Walking together, he and Denis, they had been overtaken by another recent visitor to Nepenthe. It was Mr Edgar Marten. Mr Marten was a hirsute and impecunious young Hebrew of low tastes, with a passion for mineralogy. He had profited by some University grant to make certain studies at Nepenthe, which was renowned for its variegated rocks. There was something striking about him, thought Mr Heard. He said little of consequence, but Denis listened enthusiastically to his abstruse remarks about fractures and so forth, and watched with eagerness as he poked his stick into the rough walls to dislodge some stone that seemed to be of interest.

'So you don't know the difference between augite and hornblende?' he once inquired. 'Really? Dash my eyes! How old did you say you were?'

'Nineteen.'

'And what have you been doing, Phipps, these last nineteen years?'

'One can't know everything at my age.'

'Granted. But I think you might have learnt that much. Come to me on Thursday morning. I'll see what I can do for you.'

Mr Heard rather admired this youthful scientist. The fellow knew what he was after; he was after stones. Perfect of his kind – a condition which always appealed to the bishop. Pleasant youngsters, both of them. And so different from each other!

As to Denis – he could not make up his mind about Denis. To begin with, he exhaled that peculiar College aroma which the most heroic efforts of a lifetime often fail to dissipate. Then, he had said something about Florence, and Cinque-Cento, and Jacopo Bellini. The bishop, a practical man, had not much use for Jacopo Bellini or for people who talked about him. None the less, while making himself useful with unpacking and arranging things, Denis dropped a remark which struck Mr Heard.

'The canvas of Nepenthe,' he observed, 'is rather overcharged.'

Rather overcharged. ...

It was true, thought the bishop, as he glanced out of his window that evening, all alone, over the sea into which a young moon was just sinking to rest. Overcharged! A ceaseless ebb and flow of humanity surged before his weary eyes. That sense of unreality which had struck him on his first view of the island was still persisting; the south wind, no doubt, helped the illusion. He remembered the general affluence and kindliness of the people; that, at least, had made a definite mark upon his mind. He liked the place. Already he felt at home here, and in better health. But when he tried to conjure up some definite impression of town and people, the images became blurred; the smiling priest, the Duchess, Mr Keith – they were like figures in a dream; they merged into memories of Africa, of his fellow-passengers from Zanzibar; they mingled with projects relating to his own future in England – projects relating to his cousin on Nepenthe. Mr Heard felt exhausted.

He was too tired to be greatly affected by that cannonade, which was enough to rouse the dead. Something must be happening, he mused; then, his meditations concluded, turned on his other side. He slept well into the morning, and found his breakfast appetizingly laid out in the adjoining room.

And now, he thought, for that procession.

Bells were ringing gaily into the sunshine. From a long way off, he discerned the brazen tones of a band, the chanting of priests and townspeople, shrill voices of women. The pageant came in sight – winding its way through the multitudes under the beflagged arches of greenery, while a rain of flowers descended from windows and balconies overhead. Clusters of children went before, in many-tinted array, according to their various schools or confraternities. Then came the municipal band in uniform, playing the cheeriest of tunes, and escorted by the Nepenthe militia, whose old-fashioned costume of silver and scarlet was most effective. The authorities of the island trod on their heels—grave gentlemen in black clothes, some of them adorned with ribbons and decorations. The Mephistophelean judge, the freethinker, was among them; he limped along, expectorating every ten yards or so, presumably to mark his displeasure at being obliged, as an official, to

30

attend a religious function. The Commissioner, too, was in the ranks. He appeared just the same as yesterday; very informal in his knickerbockers and decidedly pink about the gills.

There followed a long train of priests, clad in lace and silken garments of every hue. They looked like a perambulating flower-garden. Plump, jovial fellows—chanting blithely, and occasionally exchanging a few words with one another. Don Francesco glittered in crimson vestments; he recognized Mr Heard, and gave him a broad smile combined with something which might have been mistaken for a wink. The huge silver statue of the saint came next. It was a grotesque monster, borne aloft on a wooden platform that wobbled on the shoulders of eight lusty, perspiring carriers. As it passed, all the onlookers raised their hats; all save the Russians, the Little White Cows, who, standing aside with wonderment written on their childlike faces, were relieved from this necessity, since the wearing of hats had been forbidden by their leader, their self-styled Messiah, the divinely inspired Bazhakuloff; they were to go bareheaded summer and winter, 'like the Christians of old'. Some ardent believers went so far as to kneel on the stony ground. The Duchess, the Catholic-to-be, had assumed this reverent posture; she was on the other side of the street, surrounded by a number of ladies and gentlemen. Mr Heard, reviewing the crowd, abandoned the idea of piercing that procession and exchanging a few words with her. He would see her in the afternoon.

Then the bishop – the dignitary whom Don Francesco had called 'not exactly a liberal'. He tallied with that description. A wicked old face! He was blear-eyed, brown as a mummy, and so fat that his legs had long ago ceased to be any use save as a precarious support while standing. He rode, in gorgeous apparel, on a milk-white donkey which was led by two pretty choristers in blue. Attached to the end of a long pole, a green umbrella of Gargantuan proportions, adorned with red tassels, protected his wrinkled head from the rays of the sun. One hand clutched some religious object upon which his eyes were glued in a hypnotic trance, the other cruised aimlessly about the horizon, in the act of benediction.

Mumbo-jumbo, thought Mr Heard.

Yet he looked without wincing at this caricature of Christianity. It was like an act in a pantomime. He had seen funnier things in Africa. Among the Bitongos, for instance. They would have enjoyed this procession, the Bitongos. They were Christians; had taken to the Gospel like ducks to the water; wore top-hats at

31

Easter. But liars – such dreadful liars! Just the reverse of the
M'tezo. Ah, those M'tezo! Incurable heathen. He had given them
up long ago. Anyhow, they despised lying. They filed their teeth,
ate their superfluous female relations, swopped wives every new
moon, and never wore a stitch of clothes. A man who appeared
among the M'tezo in a fig-leaf would find himself in the cooking-
pot within five minutes.

How they attached themselves to his heart, those black fellows.
Such healthy animals! This spectacle, he discovered, was rather
like Africa – the same steamy heat, the same blaring noises, dazzling light, and glowing colours; the same spirit of unconquerable
playfulness in grave concerns.

And the Bumbulis, the Kubangos, the Mugwambas! And the
Bulanga – that tribe whom Mr Keith seemed to know so well!
Really, the Bulanga were the worst of the lot. Not fit to be talked
about. And yet, somehow or other, one could not help liking
them. ...

'Good morning, Bishop!' said a voice at his side. It was Mr
Keith. He looked well washed and chubby in his spotless white
clothes. Accompanying him was a friend in grey flannels whom he
presently introduced as Mr Eames. 'Hope you slept well,' he
went on. 'And how do you like the procession? You are doing
quite the right thing in attending. Oh quite. That is why I am here,
though I don't much fancy these ceremonies. One ought to conform to custom. Well, what are you thinking?'

'I was thinking of Africa, and the pain which the natives will endure for what they call their pleasures. I wonder how much those
men are paid for carrying that statue? They perspire pretty freely.'

'They are paid nothing. They pay, themselves, a heavy sum for
the privilege.'

'You surprise me!'

'They have remission of sins; they can be as naughty as ever
they like for a twelvemonth afterwards. That is a consideration.
I will tell you something else about that idol. It is five hundred
years old –'

'Oh, come!' interposed Mr Eames, in a tone of gentle remon-
strance. 'The saint was cast exactly eighty-two years ago; they
used to have a wooden one before that time. Anybody can see
from the workmanship –'

'Have it your way, Eames. Eighty-two years old, I was going to
say, and not yet paid for. They want some rich foreigner to produce the money. They are counting on van Koppen, just now; an
American millionaire, you know, who comes here every year and

32

spends a good deal of money. But I know old Koppen. He is no fool. By the way, Eames, what do you think of this discovery of mine? Of course you have heard of the James–Lange theory of the Emotions, namely, that bodily changes follow directly on the perception of the existing fact and that our feeling of these same changes as they occur is the Emotion. They developed the theory independently, and got great credit for it. Well, I find – what nobody seems to have noticed – that they were anticipated by Professor Maudsley. I've got a note of it in my pocket. Here you are. *Psychology of Mind*, 1876, pages 472–4 *et seq.*; 372, 384, 386–7 *et passim*. What do you say?'

'Nothing. I am not interested in psychology. You know it perfectly well.'

'Why not? Wouldn't you get more fun out of life if you were?'

'I have Perrelli.'

'Always your old Perrelli! That reminds me, Eames. I mean to talk to van Koppen as soon as he arrives about getting that book of yours published. He is good for any amount. Koppen is your man.'

There was a mischievous twinkle in his eye as he said this.

'Please don't,' implored Mr Eames. 'You will annoy me very seriously.'

'Don't be absurd, my dear fellow.'

'You can't think how much you will annoy me! How often have I told you –'

'Then you must lunch with me today, together with the bishop. Don't trouble about driving to the Old Town to see your cousin,' he added to Mr Heard. 'She is sure to be at the reception of the Duchess this afternoon.'

Mr Eames said:

'So sorry. I must go back home. I only came out to speak to a man about a collar – for my dog, I mean. Another day, if you don't mind. And no millionaires, whatever you do!'

He departed, rather awkwardly.

'He is shy,' Keith explained. 'But he can tell you all about this island. And now come home with me, Bishop. I feel as if it were time for luncheon. It must be about half-past twelve.'

Mr Heard took out his watch.

'Half-past twelve to the minute,' he said.

'I thought so. A man's best clock is his stomach. We have only a few hundred yards to go. Hot, isn't it? This infernal south wind. ...'

The Villa Khismet was one of the surprises of Nepenthe. It lay

33

somewhat out of the way, at the end of a narrow, gloomy, and tortuous lane. Who would have dreamt of finding a house of this kind in such a situation? Who would have expected, on passing through that mouldy wooden gateway in the wall, to find himself in a courtyard that recalled the exquisite proportions and traceries of the Alhambra – to be able to wander thence under fretted arches through a maze of marble-paved Moorish chambers, great and small, opening upon each other at irregular angles with a deliciously impromptu effect? The palace had been built regardless of expense. It was originally laid out, Keith explained, by one of the old rulers of Nepenthe, who, to tease his faithful subjects, simulated a frenzied devotion for the poetry and architecture of the Saracens, their bitterest enemies.

Something Oriental still hung about these chambers, though the modern furniture was not at all in keeping with the style. Mr Keith did not profess to be a man of taste. 'I try to be comfortable,' he used to say. He succeeded in being luxurious.

They glanced into the garden – a spacious park-like enclosure terminating in a declivity, so as to afford a view over the sea far below. It was a mock wilderness of trees and bright blossoms, flooded in meridian sunlight. Some gardeners moved about, binding up the riotous vegetation that had sprouted overnight under the moist breath of the sirocco.

'It's too hot to think of lunching out here,' said Keith. 'You should come and see this place in the evening.'

'It must be wonderful at that hour.'

'Still more wonderful in the early morning, or by moonlight. But then I am generally alone. There are twenty-four fountains in this garden,' he added. 'They might help to keep the place cool. But of course not one of them is in use now. You have observed, have you not, that there is no running water on this island? That old Duke built the fountains all the same, and to every one of them he attached a cistern, to hold the winter rains; then a pumping apparatus. Relays of slaves had to work underground, day and night, pumping water for these twenty-four fountains; it fell back into the cisterns, and was forced up again. The Arabs had fountains. He meant to have them too. Particularly at night! If anything went wrong with the machinery at that hour, there was the devil to pay. He swore he could not sleep unless he heard the music of the water. And his sleepless nights were bad for his subjects. They generally hid in caves till the fountains were reported to be in working order again. That is the way to run an island, Mr Heard. One must be a stylist.'

'You might re-activate one of them, at least, with the help of those servants.'

'They have enough to do, I assure you, to re-activate me – keep me young and in good condition. To say nothing of the flowers, which also need a little friendly attention. ...'

Mr Heard enjoyed that luncheon. 'The food, the wine, the service – they were faultless; something altogether out of the way,' he declared with frank conviction.

'Then you must come again,' replied his host. 'How long did you say you were staying here?'

'Ten days or so. It depends upon Mrs Meadows and her movements. I understand she is all alone up there, in the clouds. Her husband's leave has been postponed for the second time. He was going to pick her up on his way to England. She had to leave India before him, on account of the child.'

'A pretty baby. Couldn't stand the climate, I suppose.'

'Exactly. My mother asked me to look in and cheer her up a little, and perhaps take her back with me. And really,' he added, 'it's rather awkward! I have not seen my cousin since she was a little girl. What does she look like?'

'Tailor-made. Looks as if she rode well and knew her own mind. Looks as if she had been through a good deal of trouble.'

'I daresay she has. She was always impetuous, even as a child. That first marriage was not at all a success. Some foreign scoundrel who deserted her and vanished. I was in China at the time, but my mother wrote me about it.'

'A first marriage? She never told me about that.'

'This second one was a love match. They ran away together. They must have had a hard time out there at first, living as they did. No doubt she has learnt to know her own mind; one has to cope with emergencies in a life like that. He has done well, I hear. A charming fellow, from all accounts, though I question whether they are properly married even now.'

'Perhaps they can't be,' replied Mr Keith, 'in view of the earlier affair. But how will they educate that boy in India? It can't be done. India is not better than Bampopo, for such purposes. Did you do much educational work in Africa? I hope you were gentle with my friends the Bulanga?'

'We baptized two or three hundred of them one day. But they behaved shockingly the very next week – quite disgracefully! They are hopeless, those friends of yours, though one cannot help liking them somehow. I got through a good deal of other work of that kind,' he added.

'I see you are a man of action. Sometimes I wish I were. A little money has made me lazy, I'm afraid. But I do some thinking, and a fair lot of reading. I travel, I observe, I compare. Among other things I observe that our English system of education is all wrong. We ought to return to that old Camp-and-Court ideal.'

'All wrong?' queried the bishop.

'Take a case like that young fellow Denis. What is a child of his age doing at a University? No. If I had a son – but I am boring you.'

'I have not been bored since I was twenty.'

'I wish I could say the same of myself. I grow more intolerant of fools as the years roll on. If I had a son, I was saying, I would take him from school at the age of fourteen, not a moment later, and put him for two years in a commercial house. Wake him up; make an English citizen of him. Teach him how to deal with men as men, to write a straightforward business letter, manage his own money, and gain some respect for those industrial movements which control the world. Next, two years in some wilder part of the world, where his own countrymen and equals by birth are settled under primitive conditions, and have formed their rough codes of society. The intercourse with such people would be a capital invested for life. The next two years should be spent in the great towns of Europe, in order to remove awkwardness of manner, prejudices of race and feeling, and to get the outward forms of a European citizen. All this would sharpen his wits, give him more interests in life, more keys to knowledge. It would widen his horizon. Then, and not a minute sooner, to the University, where he would go not as a child but a man capable of enjoying its real advantages, attend lectures with profit, acquire manners instead of mannerisms, and a University tone instead of a University taint. What do you think?'

'It sounds a trifle revolutionary,' commented the bishop, with a smile. 'But it appeals to me. Education is a matter that lies very near my heart. In fact, I had some thoughts of retiring from the Church and devoting myself to it. I feel, I don't know why, as if I could do more in that direction.'

Keith merely observed:

'That is interesting. Perhaps you have reached the end of the Church.'

He liked this young Colonial bishop, and his straightforward, earnest face. Being a complicated nature himself, he was always drawn towards men of single aims and purposes.

The other would have been pleased to know why Keith found

it 'interesting' and what he meant by that other phrase, but for-bore to inquire. He was rather a silent man, though not deficient in mother-wit. He lit a cigarette, and waited.

'Let us discourse of education!' said his host with that elaborate manner which the bishop afterwards discovered to be peculiar to him. 'I think we need not differentiate between the sexes. In proportion as more careers are opened to women, their teaching will tend to converge with that of men. That specifically female education in domestic arts has been rendered superfluous by commercial products. I will tell you what I think. A sound schooling should teach manner of thought rather than matter. It should have a dual aim – to equip a man for hours of work, and for hours of leisure. They interact; if the leisure is misspent, the work will suffer. As regards the first, we cannot expect a school to purvey more than a grip of general principles. Even that is seldom given. The second should enable a man to extract as much happiness as possible out of his spare time. The secret of happiness is curiosity. Now, curiosity is not only not roused, it is repressed. You will say there is not time for everything. But how much time is wasted! Mathematics. ... A medieval halo clings round this subject which, as a training for the mind, has no more value than whist-playing. I wonder how many excellent public servants have been lost to England because, however accomplished, they lacked the mathematical twist required to pass the standard in this one subject! As a training in intelligence it is harmful: it teaches a person to under-estimate the value of evidence based on their other modes of ratiocination. It is the poorest form of mental exercise – sheer verification; conjecture and observation are ruled out. A study of Chinese grammar would be far more valuable from the point of view of general education. All mathematics above the standard of the office-boy should be a special subject, like dynamics or hydro-statics. They are useless to the ordinary man. If you mention the utility of a mathematician like Isaac Newton, don't forget that it was his pre-eminently anti-mathematical gift for drawing conclusions from analogy which made him what he was. And Euclid – that frowsy anachronism! One might as well teach Latin by the system of Donatus. Surely all knowledge is valueless save as a guide to conduct? A guide ought to be up to date and convenient to handle. Euclid is a museum specimen. Half the time wasted over these subjects should be devoted to draughtsmanship and object-lessons. I don't know why we disparage object-lessons; they were recommended by people like Bacon, Amos Comenius, and Pestalozzi. They are far superior to mathematics as a means

37

of developing the reasoning powers; they can be made as complex as you please; they discipline the eye and mind, teach a child to discriminate between the accidental and the essential, and demand lucidity of thought and expression. And the hours spent over history! What on earth does it matter who Henry the Twelfth's wife was? Chemistry! All this, relatively speaking, is unprofitable stuff. How much better to teach the elements of sociology and jurisprudence. The laws that regulate human intercourse: what could be more interesting? And physiology – the laws that regulate our bodies: what more important? Our disrespect for the human frame is another relic of monasticism. In fact our whole education is tainted with the monkish spirit. Divinity! Has any purpose ever been served –'

Mr Keith sighed.

'I wish I had not eaten so many of those prawns,' he added. 'What are you thinking?'

'I think modern education over-emphasizes the intellect. I suppose that comes from the scientific trend of the times. You cannot obtain a useful citizen if you develop only his intellect. We take children from their parents because these cannot give them an intellectual training. So far, good. But we fail to give them that training in character which parents alone can give. Home influence, as Grace Aguilar conceived it – where has it gone? It strikes me that this is a grave danger for the future. We are rearing up a brood of crafty egoists, a generation whose earliest recollections are those of getting something for nothing from the State. I am inclined to trace our present social unrest to this over-valuation of the intellect. It hardens the heart and blights all generous impulses. What is going to replace the home, Mr Keith? And there is another point which has often forced itself upon me. A certain proportion of wealthy children tend to fall back into lower grades of life – manual labour, and so forth. They are born below the level of their parents. No difficulty about relapsing. But a fair percentage of the lowest classes tend to rise; they stand, potentially, above their surroundings. An apparatus has been contrived for catching these children. But it is defective, because devoid of sympathy. I have known hundreds of cases in the East End of London where families have been unable to raise themselves by this means because, at the critical moment, there was not twenty shillings in the house wherewith to buy clothes in which the child could present himself to a good employer with any prospect of success. Worthy of a better fate, he is pushed back. The chance is missed; the family remains in poverty. All kinds of profitable and honourable capacities are being wasted in this fashion every day – peculiar aptitudes for mechanics, talents for art, or music, or acting –'

'Acting!' interrupted Keith. 'I am glad you reminded me. We are just in time to see some theatricals at the municipality. They only come off once a year. It would never do for you to miss them. No, never.'

The bishop, rather regretfully, rose from his seat. He was feeling comfortable just then, and inclined to listen to a few more of Keith's educational heresies. But that gentleman seemed to have exhausted the subject or himself.

'It is only a few minutes' walk,' he observed. 'We'll take a couple of sunshades.'

They stepped into the broiling heat. The morning mists had rolled away from the mountains.

Walking along, Mr Heard began to realize what a rambling and craggy sort of place this was. And how decorative! Almost operatic. The town was full of surprises – of unexpected glimpses upon a group of slender palms, some gleaming precipice, or the distant sea. Gardens appeared to be toppling over the houses; green vines festooned the doorways and gaily coloured porches; streets climbed up and down, noisy with rattling carriages and cries of fruit-vendors who exposed their wares of brightest hues on the pavement. Country women, in picturesque cinnamon-coloured skirts, moved gravely among the citizens. The houses, when not white-washed, showed their building stone of red volcanic tufa; windows were aflame with cacti and carnations; slumberous oranges glowed in courtyards; the roadways underfoot were of lava – pitch-black. It was a brilliant medley, overhung by a deep blue sky. The canvas was indeed overcharged, as Denis had said.

'There are no half-tones in this landscape,' the bishop remarked to Mr Keith. 'No compromise!'

'And yet perfect harmony. They are all true colours. I hate compromise. It is one of the curses of life. That is why I cannot endure England for long. The country is full of half-tones, not only in nature. Because a thing seems good, there must be some bad in it. It seems bad to us – therefore it must be good for us. Bedlamites! I like clean values. They make for clean thinking. This is the only day in the year,' he went on, 'when you will see the population abroad at this hour. The streets are generally quite empty. It is the only day when I would forgo my afternoon nap on Nepenthe.'

'Nearly three o'clock,' said the bishop, consulting his watch. 'What a queer time for theatricals!'

39

'That Duke again. You can ask Eames about him; he must have been a man worth knowing. He always slept in the afternoons. It annoyed him to think that his people slept too. He might suddenly want them for something, he said. He commanded that they should stay awake, and decapitated several hundred who were found napping. When he saw that the habit was ingrained in their natures and that nothing would avail save a total extermination of the populace, he gave way, gracefully. Then he instituted these popular theatricals in honour of the Patron Saint, and fixed them irrevocably for the hour of three o'clock. He meant to keep his faithful subjects awake on one afternoon of the year, at all events. He took it for granted that they could never resist a performance of this kind. He was right. He knew his people! That was ages ago. We shall find the place crammed this afternoon.'

There was barely standing room, in spite of the sirocco heat. Mr Keith, by means of some mysterious formula, soon procured two seats in the front row, the occupants of which smilingly took their places among the crowd at the back.

The bishop found himself sitting between his host and a distinguished-looking elderly gentleman who turned out to be Count Caloveglia. He was dressed in black. There was something alert and military in that upright carriage, those keen eyes, bushy black brows, and snowy moustache. He uttered a few pleasant remarks on making Mr Heard's acquaintance, but soon relapsed into silence. Absorbed in the spectacle, he sat motionless, his chin resting in the hollow of his right hand.

'A fine type,' Keith whispered into the bishop's ear. 'You will like him. I call him the Salt of the South. If you are interested in the old Greek life of these regions – well, he gives you an idea of those people. He is the epitome of the Ionian spirit. I'll take you up to see him one of these days.'

The performance consisted of a series of twelve scenes without words, representing the twelve chief episodes in the life of the Patron Saint, as portrayed in a certain marble frieze in the church. The actors were a handful of the more attractive and intelligent children of the place. They had been trained under the watchful eye of a priest who confessed to some notions of stage-craft and delighted in juvenile theatricals. It was a thrillingly realistic performance; the costumes – designed, long ago, by the Good Duke himself – varied with every tableau. Vociferous expressions of approval accompanied the performance. The Saint's encounter in the grove of Alephane with the golden-haired lady was a masterpiece of histrionic art; so was his solemn preaching among the black natives. Tears flowed freely at his violent death – a scene which was only marred by the erratic movements of his venerable beard; that millstone too, of *papier mâché*, played lovely pranks upon a pea-green ocean. Best of all was the cannibalistic feast of the Crotalophoboi, ending with a tempestuous, demoniacal war-dance. Their blackened limbs emerging from the scantiest of vesture, the actors surpassed themselves. Such an uproar of applause accompanied the orgy that it had to be repeated.

Every year it had to be repeated, this particular tableau. It was by far the most popular, to the intense regret of the *parroco*, the parish priest, a rigid disciplinarian, an alien to Nepenthe, a frost-bitten soul from the Central Provinces of the mainland. He used to complain that times were changed; that what was good in the days of the Duke might not be good for the present generation; that a scene such as this was no incentive to true religion; that the Holy Mother of God could hardly be edified by the performance, seeing that the players were almost nude, and that certain of the gestures verged on indelicacy and even immodesty. Every year he complained in like fashion: Ah, what would the Madonna say, if she saw it?

And every year the entire body of the local clergy, with Don Francesco as their eloquent spokesman, opposed his views.

The play was tradition, they vowed. Tradition must be upheld. And what more? It savoured of heresy to suggest that the Mother of God was blind to anything that happened on earth. Doubtless She saw this particular scene; doubtless She approved; doubtless She smiled, like everyone else. She loved her people in true motherly fashion. She was not born in the Central Provinces. She was fond of children, whether they wore clothes or not. The players enjoyed themselves. So did the audience. The Mother of God liked them to make a cheerful show in honour of that good old man, the Patron Saint. And Saint Dodekanus himself – what would he think, if this ancient act of homage were withheld? He would be very angry! He would send an earthquake, or a visitation of the cholera, or a shower of ashes from the volcano across the water. Piety and prudence alike counselled them to keep in his good graces. And what more? The performance had been established by the Good Duke; and that endless line of godly bishops, succeeding each other since his day, would never have given their sanction to the costumes and the acting had they not known that the Madonna approved of them. Why should She now think differently? The Mother of God was not a fickle earthly creature, to change Her mind from one day to the next.

41

With arguments such as these they endeavoured to controvert the *parroco*, who, being a fighter to the death, a resourceful ascetic of unbending will, never admitted defeat. He bethought him of other shifts. On one celebrated occasion he actually induced the bishop – tired as the old prelate was, after his morning's ride on the white donkey – to attend the performance, hoping to obtain from him some confirmation of his own view, that the objectionable scene should be entirely remodelled or, better still, cut out altogether. The reverend dignitary was supposed to be extremely short-sighted and wandering, moreover, in his mind, from sheer decrepitude. Perhaps he was wily beyond the common measure of man. Be that as it may, he witnessed the spectacle but allowed nothing to escape his lips save a succession of soft purring sounds resembling:

gu-gu-gu-gu-gu-gu-gu-gu-gu

an ambiguous utterance which was constructed by both parties as a verdict in their favour.

Mr Heard, while conceding that the acting was good – first rate, in fact – could not make up his mind whether to be shocked or pleased. He wondered whether such a play had any features in common with religion. His host, who stood for paganism and nudity and laughter, convinced him that it had.

'You would have seen the same thing in pre-Puritan England,' he concluded, at the end of a long exposition. 'And now, if you like, we will have a look at that Club. It may amuse you. There is still time for the Duchess.'

CHAPTER 5

'THIS is the place,' said Mr Keith.

It was one of a row of tawdry modern buildings, the lower floors of which were utilized as shops – an undistinguished sort of place, in an undistinguished street. They climbed upstairs and wandered through two or three rooms, all alike save that one of them had a balcony; square, whitewashed rooms, not very clean, and inadequately furnished with tables, cane-bottomed chairs, and a few prints on the walls. There was a lavish display, however, of bottles and glasses, and several shelves were littered with newspapers in different languages. Acetylene lamps hung from the flat ceiling. An odour of stale tobacco and alcohol pervaded the premises. Flies were buzzing against the window-panes.

Half a dozen nondescript members, looking considerably the worse for wear, loafed about moodily or snored in deck chairs.

Two or three were writing letters. It was the sulkiest hour of the day. Mr Heard noticed a slender young Indian and a blonde-haired fellow – probably a Scandinavian. They were arguing about cigars with a rosy-cheeked old reprobate whom they called Charlie. An adjoining apartment, the cardroom, contained a livelier party, among whom the bishop recognized Mr Muhlen. He had lost no time in making himself popular. He must have found congenial spirits here.

'Well?' asked Keith.

'Cheap and nasty,' suggested the other.

'That's it! They call it the Alpha and Omega Club, to shadow forth its all-embracing international character. It's just a boozing institution, where you run to seed. They come in here, and say the south wind makes them thirsty. Red and Blue Club would be a more appropriate name. That is the whisky they have to drink.'

'Why cannot they drink wine or – ginger-beer?'

'He tries to stop that. He would not be able to make any profits on wine.'

'Who?'

'The President.'

And Mr Keith proceeded to sketch the history of the establishment.

The Alpha and Omega Club had led a precarious existence. Often its life dangled by a thread for lack of members, or because those members who owed subscriptions were unable or unwilling to pay them. Such had been the case before the accession of the new President. It hung its drooping head; had almost withered away. Mr Freddy Parker tended the languid flower, and watered it – with whisky of his own composition.

It revived. Or rather (which amounts to the same thing) Mr Parker revived – sufficiently, at all events, to pay off some of the more pressing of his private debts. Napoleon, or somebody, once remarked: 'L'état, c'est moi.' Mr Parker thought highly of a strong character like Napoleon. He used to say, when talking things over with his lady in her 'boudoir' at the Residency:

'The Club, that's me.'

Declaring that wine was the ruin of the place, he imported – it was the lady's idea, originally – the far-famed 'Red and Blue' brand of whisky, in barrels. The liquid was bottled in the cellars of the Residency. What happened during that process was never revealed. It was affirmed, none the less, that one barrel of the original stuff was more than enough for three barrelfuls of the bottled product. Cultured members, on drinking it, were wont to

43

say things about Locusta and Borgia. The commoner sort swore like hell at Freddy Parker. It made you feel squiffy after the sixth glass – argumentative, magisterial, maudlin, taciturn, erotic, sentimental, sea-sick, ecstatic, paralysed, lachrymose, hilarious, pugilistic – according to your temperament. Whatever your temperament it gave you a thundering head next morning, and a throat like Nebuchadnezzar's fiery furnace. It was known as 'Parker's poison'.

The stuff was served, at an alluring price, out of bottles adorned with a seductive label – a label which had been designed by an impecunious artist who, after running up a rousing bill for drinks, got off payment on the strength of this job. But the prettiest label in the world could not atone for the mixture within. Members often complained of feeling queer. They threatened to resign. Mr Parker did not want them to resign; he wanted their subscriptions. He had a grand way with him on such occasions. Whenever one of them complained too bitterly or too persistently – became damned abusive, in fact – he would patiently wait and see which was the fellow's favourite newspaper. That point settled – it was his lady's idea, originally – he would stop the supply of the journal in question, alleging insufficiency of Club revenues. These Napoleon-like tactics generally brought the offending member to his senses.

Mr Frederick Parker spent a good deal of his time in endeavouring to mask, under a cloak of boisterous good humour, a really remarkable combination of malevolence and imbecility. He was what you call a remittance man. He got so much a quarter – a miserable sum it was – to keep out of England. He travelled about formerly. But no amount of travel, no association with his betters, could pierce his stolid pachydermatous obliquity. He was the worst kind of Englishman; he could not even cheat without being found out. But for the wise counsels of his lady he would have been in the lock-up over and over again. Such being the case, he took a justifiable pride in his Anglo-Saxon origin. Whenever a project seemed too risky – not worth while, he called it – he would say:

'It can't be done. That's a job for a dago. I'm an Englishman, you know.'

He had knocked about the world a good bit, had Mr Parker. His last known domicile was Nicaragua. There he invested in some land affair – a most unfortunate speculation, as it turned out. All his speculations had a way of turning out badly. That was because people, even people in Nicaragua, distrusted him for one reason or another; they said his whole existence was a tangle of

44

shady and ignoble transactions – that he looked like a fraud, and behaved like one. He couldn't help his face; but his face, they soon discovered, was not the only, or even the most, evasive and fugitive part of his personality.

At last Nicaragua, even Nicaragua, got too hot for him.

There was Don Pomponio di Vergara y Puyarola, Nicaraguan Minister of Finance; one might come to terms with a man of that kind. One came to terms. It was arranged between them that His Excellency, who had a large family and many poor dependants, should take over Mr Parker's landed interests; being a native of the place, he might succeed in squeezing a little something out of them. In exchange for this concession an unobtrusive Government job was specially created for Mr Parker. He was appointed Financial Commissioner for South-Eastern Europe, to reside at Nepenthe or wherever else he pleased – unpaid: the exalted social status conferred by such a post being deemed ample compensation. His sole duty consisted in submitting a short annual report, a pure formality, to his Government.

He departed, but not alone. With him went his familiar spirit, his guardian-angel, his lady, his step-sister – a dusky dame of barn-like proportions. Arrived at Nepenthe they rented a small villa, rather out of the way, which they called the Residency. The change of climate did him good. So did the appointment. He was now a person of consequence – the sole representative of a Foreign Power on the island. His official rank procured him not only dignity and a new start in life but what was still more urgent, credit. It brought him into contact with the local authorities – with the red-haired rachitic judge, for instance, between whom and Mr Parker there sprang up an intimacy which was viewed with vague forebodings. The lady, being a Catholic – Mr Parker, too, was suspected of Roman proclivities – was confessed by the parish priest. That was a point gained; the *parroco* being above suspicion, among foreigners at least. She stayed mostly indoors, inventing scandals about people and writing voluminous letters to warn newcomers of the appalling immorality of the place.

To outward appearance the Commissioner and his lady agreed like a brace of turtle-doves. He, too, was a moral and social reformer. But men must live. The refined social status attached to Mr Parker's honorary post producing nothing tangible in the way of ready cash, he began to cast about for some means of livelihood. They were getting into debt once more. Something must be done, he declared.

His portly presence, flushed countenance, briar pipe, knickerbockers, and white spats had already become a familiar object in the streets of the town, when a terrific uproar at the Club – one of those periodical, approximately monthly, rows at which the police, who hated meddling with foreigners, were reluctantly compelled to intervene – suggested to her that something might be done in that direction. She got him elected President for that year, President for the next, the next, and the next; in spite of the fact that, according to the rules, a new President had to be elected every year. Who cared about rules? He was the Commissioner! People were only too glad to have him there. In fact, like Napoleon, he became a sort of Dictator.

He was now in his element. There were emoluments to be picked up here – percentages, perquisites, and profits of all kinds. He made a little arrangement with the Club laundry-woman to take in his own washing as well, gratis. Under the threat of placing the Club custom elsewhere he concluded a number of treaties, each containing a secret clause which referred to fifteen per cent profit for himself, with the grocer who supplied provisions; and with other tradespeople dealing in stationery, soap, crockery (broken crockery was a heavy item in the accounts), and such-like Club necessaries. Next, he took the landlord in hand. He would clear out, by God, and take more respectable premises if the rent were not reduced by twenty per cent! Scandalous! Downright robbery! The landlord being a reasonable sort of man, it was agreed that the old rate should stand in the contract, while the balance of twenty per cent found its way into Mr Parker's pockets, and not, as heretofore, into his own. The same with the servants. From the boy who cleaned the rooms, and whom he changed as often as ever possible, he exacted a monetary deposit as a guarantee of good conduct – a deposit which was never returned, whatever his behaviour had been. Then – the subscriptions. For of course the accounts were never audited; nobody bothered about such things in Nepenthe, with all that south wind hanging about. If they had been, he would have squared the auditor up to any sum – a hundred francs, almost; it was worth while. Pickings, he called them. The place, the system, suited him down to the ground. He had lived all his life on pickings. He was a retail welsher; he lacked the nerve for sweeping enterprises.

On his accession, the Club was in such a state of demoralization, had become such a public scandal that Mr Parker, in his capacity of moralist, would have been the first person to dissolve that assembly of topers and rakes. As financier, he meant to live by it. But how was the place to be purified?

46

Parker's poison solved that problem, besides yielding a fine slice of additional revenue. The hardest drinkers, the inveterate rowdies, refused to believe that it was anything but the ordinary whisky to which they had been accustomed from childhood; or believing, refused out of sheer boastfulness, or force of habit, to reduce their doses. While the moderate realized the truth and acted accordingly, these others insisted upon regarding it as genuine Scotch – with inevitable and dire results. They succumbed. During the first year of Freddy Parker's reign, eight of these stubborn sinners were carried to their graves. And year by year, the same causes being in action, the process of betterment went on. Extremists dropped off, moderates survived. The Club was purged of its grosser elements, the moral tone of the establishment was raised, through the operation of Parker's poison. It was Napoleon's way with the Paris Parliament, he once explained to his lady, who wondered vaguely how long the hero himself would have outlived the effects of that mixture which she brewed, with her own fair hands, in the dim vaults of the Residency.

Even now it was a pretty tough place. New crooks, like the dubious Mr Hopkins, new fire-eaters, new cranks, new sots, were always dropping in from different corners of the globe to spread their infection among the more decent crowd of curio-hunters, gentlemen of commerce, nautical wrecks, decayed missionaries, painters, authors, and other vagrant riff-raff who frequented the premises. There were rows going on all the time – insignificant rows, mostly about newspapers and gambling debts. Mr Samuel got his eye blacked over a harmless game of écarté; Mr White, one of the steadiest members, threatened to withdraw his subscription on account of the black-beetles; a Swedish sea-captain smashed nine panes of glass – just by way of a friendly demonstration, he said – because the great Upsala journal, the *Utan Svafvel*, was missing from its shelf; a muscular Japanese made himself distinctly offensive about the *Nichi-nichi-shin-bum* being out of date, and was going to twist everybody's head off if it occurred again; the excellent Vice-President, Mr Richards, tumbled noisily downstairs, nobody knew how or why – all on a single afternoon. The sirocco happened to be particularly trying that day.

On the whole, there was no denying the fact that the Club flourished under the statesman-like autocracy of Mr Parker. That was partly because, unlike previous presidents, he was generally on the spot. Some great man once made a remark about the need of 'the Master's Eye'. He believed in that remark. If you run a place, run it yourself. He was ever-present, absorbing at other people's expense his own poison, to the effects of which he seemed to be immune; and borrowing money, on the sly, from the richer and more forgetful members. His uproarious joviality, his echoing ha! ha! became a feature of the place; it deceived the simple, and amused the complex. He was ready to talk about anything with anybody who shoved along; he had a fund of naughty tropical stories for the so-called bawdy section, and could be as sympathetic and pious as you please with a contrite youngster suffering from last night's debauch.

'A hair of the dog,' he would suggest with a genial wink, pushing the bottle temptingly nearer.

The regulations had also been improved under his auspices. The entrance fee was imperceptibly raised, while the conditions of entry were relaxed. It was his lady's idea originally. She made it clear that the more numerous the members the greater the quantity of whisky consumed – the greater, therefore, their profits; quite apart from the possibility of additional subscriptions being paid. He agreed. Then, in a sudden glow of commercial enthusiasm, he proceeded to hint that ladies should also be admitted. Regretfully she put her foot down. Anywhere else the proposal would have been welcome. It was out of the question on Nepenthe.

'You're forgetting that Wilberforce woman,' she said. 'She would have to be carried home every night. It couldn't be done, Freddy. We might as well shut up the shop at once. People would get talking about the place – you know how they talk as it is.'

Miss Wilberforce was a pathetic local figure, a lady by birth, with a ready tongue, wiry limbs, and an insatiable craving for alcohol. She would unavoidably have damaged the reputation of the place, to say nothing of its furniture. She had gone from bad to worse lately.

'Perhaps you're right, Lola. It isn't worth while for those few subscriptions. After all, I'm an Englishman. But how about all those Russians?' he added.

'I've often told you to let them in, Freddy.'

'So you have, dear! It was your idea originally. Well, I must think it over again.'

He thought it over and regretfully came to the conclusion that it could not be done. Russians were not people of the right kind. They were not honest.

'Russians are too artistic to be honest,' he declared.

It was a *bon mot* which he had picked up, long ago, from Madame Steynlin, in the days when the lady looked with disfavour on the Muscovite colony. That Lutheran period was over

48

for the present: she was orthodox so far as sentiments were concerned. Nothing could be good enough for the Russians, just then. An acquaintance with Peter, one of the handsomest of the whole batch of religious enthusiasts, had brought about her psychological conversion and altered her outlook upon life. Her heart was in the Urals. But that stupid malicious epigram had impressed itself on the mind of Mr Parker, who was hopelessly insensitive to the flaxen curls of Peter.

'No,' he decided. 'They are not honest. We must draw the line somewhere, Lola. I draw it at Russians. At least I think we ought to. But I'll think it over again.'

That was foolish of him, she opined. For the Muscovites would probably have paid their accounts as regularly as other members; and as to their capacity for raising the Club revenues by the destruction of alcohol – why, many people had said unkind things about them, and yet nobody had gone so far as to accuse them of being unable to stow it away in proper Christian style. No wonder. Because there was nothing whatever in their Bible, the *Golden Book* of the divinely inspired Bazhakuloff, to prohibit or even limit the consumption of strong waters. In the matter of dietary he had only bidden them refrain from the flesh of warm-blooded beasts.

Mr Parker was always thinking things over and coming to the wrong conclusion. It was foolish of him.

She knew him too well to say anything more for the moment. She would have to bide her time because Freddy, of whom she had made an exhaustive study, was a wobbler, and worse than a wobbler. He was stubborn at the wrong season and difficult to manage. He needed careful motherly guidance. All fools, she reflected, were subject to meteoric gleams of common sense. He was no exception to that rule. But whereas they received such flashes with thankfulness, he persisted in regarding them as inspirations of the devil. That was the tragedy of Freddy Parker. It made him into something quintessential – a kind of super-fool. ...

Mr Keith inquired:

'You don't want to become a member of this institution, do you, Bishop?'

The other pondered awhile.

'I am pretty democratic,' he replied. 'We have some warm places in Africa, you know, and I never allowed myself to be beaten by them. Perhaps I might be of use to some of these poor fellows in there. But I like to do things properly. It would entail at first a little friendly drinking, I'm afraid, in order to gain their confidence. It is not in my character to do one thing and preach another. I cannot pose as an abstainer after the way I enjoyed your luncheon. But the smell of the whisky here – it scares me. My liver –'

'Ah, yes!' said Mr Keith with a sigh. 'No wonder you hesitate. It is quite disheartening, all that drunkenness.'

CHAPTER 6

IT stands to reason that the Duchess was not a Duchess at all. She was American by birth, from some Western State, and her first husband had been an army man. Her second spouse – he, too, had died long ago – was Italian. In view of his passionate devotion to the Catholic Church and of a further payment of fifty thousand francs, he had been raised to the rank of Papal Marquis. He died relatively young. Had his life been spared, as it ought to have been, he might well have become a Papal Duke in course of time. He was carried off by an accident not of his own contriving – run over by a tramcar in Rome – before that further ducal premium was even expected to be paid. But for this, he ought to have died a Duke. He would have been a Duke by this time.

His widow, taking these things into consideration, felt it her duty to appropriate the more sonorous of the two titles open to her. Nobody contested her claim. All her friends, on the contrary, declared that she talked like a peeress and behaved like one; and in a world where the few remaining authentic specimens of that class fail to fulfil either the one or the other of these conditions, it was thought meet and proper that somebody should be good enough to carry on, if only in semblance, and if only in Nepenthe, the traditions of a race rapidly approaching extinction. It was pleasant to be able to converse with a Duchess at any hour of the day, and this one was nothing if not accessible so long as you were fairly well clothed, had a reasonable supply of small talk, and did not profess violent anti-papal sentiments.

Some people said she dressed like a Duchess, but there was less unanimity on this point. Her handsome oval face and towering grey hair induced her to cultivate an antique pose, with a view to resembling 'La Pompadour'. La Pompadour stood for something courtly and powdered. She certainly dressed better and on far less money than Madame Steynlin, whose plump figure, round sun-burnt cheeks, and impulsive manner would never have done for an old-world beauty, and who cared little what frocks she wore, so long as somebody loved her. The Duchess had all the aplomb of

La Pompadour, but not much of her French accent. Her Italian, too, was somewhat embryonic. That mattered little. The external impression, the grand manner, was everything. She was not lame, though she generally leaned on somebody's arm or a stick. It was rather a pretty stick. She would have worn a pomander in her hair, or on a chatelaine, if anybody had told her what a pomander was. As her friends were unable to enlighten her – Mr Keith even hinting that it was an object which could not be mentioned in polite society – she contented herself with a couple of patches.

Her rooms in that disused convent were an interminable suite of rectangular chambers, unpretentious but solidly built, with straight corridors running alongside. You beheld pretty pavements of old-fashioned tiles, not overmuch furniture, one or two portraits of the Pope, and abundance of flowers and crucifixes. The Duchess specialized in flowers and crucifixes. Everybody, aware of her fondness for them, gave her either the one or the other, or both. An elaborate arrangement for tea occupied one of the rooms; there was also a cold buffet for gentlemen – brandies and wines and iced soda-water and lobster sandwiches and suchlike.

A many-tongued conversation filled the air with pleasant murmurs. Various nationalities were represented, though the Russian colony was conspicuous by its absence. The Duchess, like Mr Freddy Parker, drew the line at Russians. If only they would not dress so oddly, with those open collars, leathern belts, and scarlet blouses! The judge, also, was never asked to come – he was too outspoken a freethinker, and too fond of spitting on the floor. Nor did Mr Eames put in an appearance. He avoided social obligations; his limited means prevented him from making any adequate return. But there was an ample display of ecclesiastics, together with a few other notabilities. Mr Heard encountered some familiar faces, and made new friends. He felt drawn towards Madame Steynlin – she had such a cheerful bright face.

'And how delightfully cool these rooms are!' he was saying to the Duchess. 'I wonder how you manage to keep the sirocco out?'

'By closing the windows, Bishop. English people will not believe that. They open their windows. In comes the heat.'

'If English people closed their windows they would die,' said Don Francesco. 'Half the houses in England would be condemned by law in this country and pulled down, on account of their low ceilings. Low ceilings have given the Englishman his cult of fresh air. He likes to be cosy and familiar and exclusive; he has no sense for broad social functions. There is something of the cave-dweller in every Englishman. He may say what he likes, but the humble cottage will always remain his dream. You can tell the ideals of a nation by its advertisements. This country is pastoral. That is why our advertisements are so apt to portray commercial conditions – enormous factories and engines and chimneys; we are dissatisfied with our agricultural state. The Frenchman's aspiration is woman; Paris hoardings will tell you that. England is a land of industrial troglodytes, where every man's cavern is his castle. Its advertisements depict either gross masses of food such as cave-dwellers naturally relish, or else quiet country scenes – green lanes, and sunsets, and peaceful dwellings in the country. Home, sweet home! The cottage! That means open windows or suffocation. ... I think I see the person who spoke to you on the steamer,' he added to Mr Heard: 'I don't like his looks. He is coming our way.'

'That must be Mr Muhlen,' exclaimed the Duchess. 'They say he played beautifully at the hotel last night. I wonder whether I could induce him to try my Longwood? It's rather an old model, I fear, and out of tune.'

The gentleman appeared, ostentatiously dressed, and escorted by Mr Richards, the Vice-President of the Alpha and Omega Club, who seemed to be fairly steady on his legs and was presently absorbed in an artistic examination of a number of silver ornaments, crucifixes, relics, and suchlike objects of virtue, which the Duchess had gathered together. He handled them like a connoisseur. Others of that institution had promised to attend the party but, on being overhauled by the conscientious Vice-President, were found to be unpresentable at the last moment.

The Duchess moved away to greet him. Mr Heard remarked to Don Francesco:

'That middle-aged colleague of yours, yonder – he has an unusual face.'

'Our parish priest. A sound Christian!'

The *parroco's* thin lips, peaked nose, beady eyes, and colourless cheeks proclaimed the anchorite, if not the monomaniac. He flitted about like a draught of cold air, refusing all refreshments and not daring to smell the flowers, lest he should derive too much pleasure from them. He was often called Torquemada, from his harsh and abstemious habits. The name had been given him, of course, by his brother priests, who knew about such matters, and not by the common people, to whom the word Torquemada would have suggested, if anything, a savoury kind of pudding. Torquemada was capable of any sacrifice, of any enormity, in

52

defence of the faith. A narrow medieval type, he was the only person on Nepenthe who would have been hewn in pieces for his God – nobody else allowing themselves to be even temporarily incommoded in so visionary a cause. He enjoyed a reputation of perfect chastity which differentiated him from all the remaining priests and contributed, more than anything else, to his unpopularity. It enraged the frankly carnal natives to such an extent that they made insinuations about his bodily health and told other horrible stories, swore they were true, and offered to give statistical figures in confirmation. They said, among other things, that after begging money from wealthy foreigners for alleged repairs to the parish organ and other godly purposes, he kept the proceeds himself on the principle that charity began at home and ought to end there. Nobody could deny his devotion to mother, sisters, and even distant relatives. So much was also certain, that the *parroco*'s family was poor.

Harp-like tinklings arose from an adjoining chamber; a general move took place in that direction. Mr Keith was there. He sat beside Madame Steynlin, who, being a fair performer herself, was listening with rapture to Muhlen's strains. During a pause he said:

'I wish I could make it out. It annoys me, Madame Steynlin, not to comprehend the charm of music. I would give almost anything to the person who can satisfy me that what I hear is not a succession of unnecessary noises.'

'Perhaps you are not musical.'

'That would not prevent my understanding the feelings of people like yourself. I don't want to be musical. I want to get a grip of this thing. I want to know. Tell me why you like it and why I don't. Tell me –'

The sounds began again.

'Ah!' said the Duchess, 'that wonderful *andante con brio*!'

Then, as the strains grew louder, she whispered to Don Francesco upon a subject which had always puzzled her.

'I would be glad to learn,' she said, 'why our parliamentary representative, Commendatore Morena, has never yet visited Nepenthe. Surely it is his duty to show himself now and then to his parishioners – constituents, I mean? This festival of Saint Dodekanus would have been such a good opportunity. His appearance would have been a discomfiture for the free-thinkers. Every year he promises to come. And every year he fails us. Why?'

'I cannot tell,' replied the priest. 'The animal has probably got other things to do.'

'The animal? Ah, don't say that! And such a good Catholic!'

53

'Foreigners, dear Duchess, I leave to your judgement. They are of little account, anyhow. But you will be guided by me in your appreciation of the worldly qualities of natives. Otherwise, with all your intelligence, it will be impossible for you to avoid mistakes. Let us leave it at that.'

'But why –'

'We will leave it at that, dear lady!'

'Indeed we will, Don Francesco,' replied the Duchess, who loved to be ruled in matters of this kind.

At this moment, the performer rose from the piano with unexpected suddenness, remarking *sotto voce* that if he had known he was to play on a spinet he would have brought some Lulli with him. He was beaming all over, none the less, and soon making arrangements with other guests for a series of picnics and boating excursions – getting on swimmingly, in fact, when the thoughtless Madame Steynlin captured him and began to talk music. He repeated that remark, too good to be lost, about the spinet; it led to Scarlatti, Mozart, Handel. He said Handel was the saviour of English music. She said Handel was its blight and damnation. Each being furnished with copious arguments, the discussion degenerated into technicalities.

Denis, meanwhile, was handing round tea-cakes and things, with the double object of making himself useful and of being as near as possible to Angelina, the hand-maiden of the Duchess, a bewitchingly pretty brunette, who was doing the same. Perhaps the existence of Angelina accounted for his respectful attentions and frequent visits to the Duchess. He felt he was really in love for the first time in his life.

He worshipped from afar. He would have liked to worship from a little nearer, but did not know how to set about it; he was afraid of troubling what he called her innocence. Hitherto he had scored no great success. Angelina, aged fifteen, with the figure of a fairy, a glowing complexion, and a rich southern voice, was perfectly aware of his idealistic sentiments. She responded to the extent of gazing at him, now and then, in a most disconcerting fashion. It was as though she cared little about idealism. She did not smile. There was neither love nor disdain in that gaze; it was neither hot nor cold, not yet lukewarm; it was something else, something he did not want at all – something that made him feel childish and uncomfortable.

And another pair of eyes were watching, all the time, her sinuous movements – those of Mr Edgar Marten. This young scientist, too, cherished loving thoughts about Angelina, thoughts of a more

54

earthly and volcanic tinge; certain definite projects which made him forget, at times, his preoccupation with biotite, perlite, magnetite, anorthite, and pyroxene.

'Denis,' said Keith, in his usual pompous fashion. 'Do put down that absurd tray and let people help themselves. Listen to me for a moment. How do you like this place? I am not asking out of vulgar curiosity; I am anxious to know the impressions of a person of your age and antecedents. You might collect them for me, will you? Not now. One day when you are in the mood. Somewhat terrestrial and palpitating, is it not, after the cloistered twilight of a University?'

'I came here from Florence,' observed Denis.

'And even after Florence! Do you know why? Because mankind dominates in Tuscany. The land is encrusted with ephemeral human conceits. This is not altogether good for a youngster; it disarranges his mind and puts him out of harmony with what is permanent. Just listen a moment. Here, if you are wise, you will seek an antidote. Taken in over-dose, all these churches and pictures and books and other products of our species are toxins for a boy like you. They falsify your cosmic values. Try to be more of an animal. Try to extract pleasure from more obvious sources. Lie fallow for a while. Forget all these things. Go out into the midday glare. Sit among rocks and by the sea. Have a look at the sun and stars for a change; they are just as impressive as Donatello. Find yourself! You know the Cave of Mercury? Climb down, one night of full moon, all alone, and rest at its entrance. Familiarize yourself with elemental things. The whole earth reeks of humanity and its works. One has to be old and tough to appraise them at their true worth. Tell people to go to hell, Denis, with their altarpieces and museums and clock-towers and funny little art galleries.'

Everybody is always giving me advice, thought Denis. And the worst of it is, it's often sound.

A melodious voice added:

'If, after that lecture, you still have some crotchety appreciation left for the works of man, you may be interested, when next you visit the Old Town, to look at some busts and other curiosities of mine. There is a little Greek bronze I would like to show you, though perhaps we had better not talk too openly about it. Pray come. You will extract pleasure from that statuette. And I will extract pleasure from your company. Obvious sources of pleasure, aren't they, Keith?'

It was Count Caloveglia. He was referring to the Locri Faun,

55

a wonderful antique which had recently been found on his property near the town of that name on the neighbouring mainland, and was about to be secretly smuggled out of Italy. He smiled in winning fashion as he spoke. Like everyone else, Denis had fallen under the spell of this attractive and courteous old aristocrat who was saturated to the very marrow in the lore of antiquity. There was sunshine in his glance -- a lustrous, gem-like grace; one realized from his conversation, from his every word, that he had discarded superfluities of thought and browsed for a lifetime, in leisurely fashion, upon all that purifies and exalts the spirit. Nothing, one felt, would avail to ruffle that deep pagan content.

'And how,' he continued addressing Denis, 'are your Italian studies progressing?'

'Fairly well, thank you. My French puts me out a little. And I can't yet conjugate properly.'

'That is certainly a drawback,' said Don Francesco, appearing on the scene. 'But don't let it trouble you,' he added in paternal tones. 'It will come in time. You are still young. You are learning Russian, Madame Steynlin?'

'Only a few words.' She blushed becomingly. 'There are certain sounds, like water being poured into a jug – neither easy nor pleasant. I am not as quick as some people. Mrs Meadows always speaks Hindustani to her old Sicilian woman. She comprehends perfectly.'

'So clever these people are, at languages!' said the Duchess.

Marten remarked:

'I don't bother to learn Italian. I talk Latin to them. They understand all right.'

'And what Latin, Marten!' laughed Denis. 'No wonder they understand. I'm coming to you on Thursday morning. Don't forget.'

'I have not had your public-school advantages. But I manage to get what I want out of them, generally speaking,' and he cast a fiery glance in the direction of Angelina, who returned it over her shoulder, unabashed. Denis, fortunately, was looking the other way.

'I wish I had enjoyed all your chances,' observed the Duchess, with a little mock-sigh. 'We were so carelessly brought up. I learnt practically nothing at school. It is a pity. Ah, Bishop! I forgot to tell you. Such a charming note from your cousin. She cannot come. The baby is teething and troublesome in this heat. You will have to drive up, I'm afraid. ... Mr Keith, I have not yet thanked you for those flowers and the book you sent. The flowers are quite

56

too lovely. Look at them! You are spoiling me – you really are! But I don't think I shall like the book. Lady Cecilia and her maid and that man, I forget his name – they do all sorts of things. They don't seem to be very nice people.'

'You have nothing but nice people round you, Duchess. Why should you want to read about them? There is so much goodness in real life. Do let us keep it out of our books.'

'That sounds a dreadful doctrine. I see the *parroco* is about to take his departure. Why does everybody leave so soon?'

She wandered away.

'The English are supposed to be bad linguists,' said Don Francesco. 'It is one of those curious international fallacies, like saying that the French are a polite nation –'

'Or that home-made marmalade tastes better than the stuff you buy in shops,' added Denis. 'I must help the Duchess to say good-bye to those people. She likes to have someone handy on such occasions. She needs an echo. I am becoming quite a good echo.'

'You are,' said Keith, rather sharply. 'Quite a pretty echo. And you ought to be a voice. Follow my prescription, Denis. The Cave of Mercury.'

Count Caloveglia remarked:

'What a pity that Latin, as scholars' language, for the definition and registration of ideas, was ever abandoned! It has the incalculable advantage that the meanings of words are irrevocably fixed by authority. New ones could be coined as occasion required. Knowledge would gain by leaps and bounds. There would be a cross-fertilization of cultures. As things now stand, half the intellectuals of this world are writing about matters which, unbeknown to themselves, have already been treated by the other half. One would think that Commerce, which has broken down geographical barriers, might have done the same to political ones. Far from it! In sharpening men's lust for gold, it has demarcated our frontiers with a bitterness hitherto unknown. The world of thought has not expanded; it has contracted and grown provincial. Men have lost sight of distant horizons. Nobody writes for humanity, for civilization; they write for their country, their sect; to amuse their friends or annoy their enemies. Pliny or Linnaeus or Humboldt – they sat on mountain-tops; they surveyed the landscape at their feet, and if some little valley lay shrouded in mist, the main outlines of the land yet lay clearly distended before them. You will say that it is impossible, nowadays, to gather up the threads of learning as did these men; they are too multifarious, too divergent. A greater mistake could not be imagined. For there

57

is a contrary tendency at work – a tendency towards unification. The threads converge. Medieval minds knew many truths, hostile to one another. All truths are now seen to be interdependent; never was synthesis easier of attainment. Conflict of nationality and language hinders the movement. Mankind at large is the loser. The adoption of a universal scholars' tongue would do much to remove the obstacle. When these Southern races coalesce to form the great alliance which I foresee, when the Mediterranean basin is once more the centre of human activity, as it deserves to be, some such plan will doubtless be adopted.'

'Your notion would suit me down to the ground,' said the bishop, who was a good Latinist. 'I would love to converse in the old style with a student from Salamanca or Bergen or Khieff or Padua or –'

Don Francesco gave utterance to some wholly unintelligible speech. Then he observed:

'The student might not be able to catch your meaning, Mr Heard. I was only talking Latin! You see, we would be obliged to standardize our pronunciation. I wonder, by the way, why the old scholars' language was ever discarded?'

'Patriotism destroyed it,' replied the Count. 'That narrow modern patriotism of the cock-on-the-dunghill type.'

Mr Keith began:

'It is an atavistic and altogether discreditable phenomenon – this recent recrudescence of monarchical principles –'

'What did you promise about long words?' playfully inquired the Duchess, who had just returned.

'I cannot help it, dear lady. It is my mother's fault. She was so very precise. I was carefully brought up.'

'That is a pity, Mr Keith.'

'Northern people are very precise,' said Don Francesco, folding his gown around his ample limbs. 'Particularly in love affairs. We down here, who live in this sirocco, are supposed to be calculating and mercenary in matters of the heart. We want dowries for our daughters – they say we are always coming to the point: money, money! The capacity of an English girl for coming to the point will take some beating. She paralyses you with directness. I can tell you a true story. There was a young Italian whom I knew – yes, I knew him well. He had just arrived in London; very handsome in the face, though perhaps a little too fat. He fell in love with an elegant young lady who was employed in the establishment of Madame Elise in Bond Street. He used to wait for her to come out at six o'clock and follow her like a dog, not daring to speak. He carried a costly bracelet for her in his pocket, and every day fresh flowers, which he was always too shy and too deeply enamoured to present. She was his angel, his ideal. He dreamt of her by day and night, wondering whether he would ever have the courage to address so tall and queenly a creature. It was his first English love affair, you understand; he learnt the proper technique later on. For five or six weeks this unhappy state of things continued, till one day, when he was running after her as usual, she turned round furiously and said: "What do you mean, sir, by following me about in this disgusting fashion? How dare you? I shall call the police if it occurs again." He was deprived of speech at first: he could only gaze in what you call dumb amazement. Then he managed to stammer out something about his heart and his love, and to show her the flowers and the bracelet. She said: "So that's it, is it? Well, of all the funny boys. Why couldn't you speak up sooner? D'you know of a place round here –"'

'Ha, ha, ha!'

It was a formidable explosion on the part of the Commissioner, in an adjoining room.

He was talking to some friends about Napoleon.

They wanted a fellow like that on Nepenthe – a fellow who got things done. Napoleon would have made no bones about the Wilberforce woman over there. It was a scandalous state of affairs. What was the use of a Committee for trying to keep her in order and getting her locked up in a sanatorium? Everybody knew what a Committee meant. Committee! It was a preposterous word. Committees were the same all the world over. Committee! He was in charge of that particular one; they were doing all they could, but what did it amount to? Nothing. To begin with, there was not enough money coming in, unless somebody could wheedle a cheque out of that rich old Koppen sensualist whose yacht might be arriving at any moment. And then her own pig-headedness! She refused to be talked over into doing what was in her own interests. Napoleon, he reckoned, might have talked her over – ha, ha, ha!

The lady in question, all unaware of these humanitarian designs, had taken up a strategic position in the neighbourhood of the drinks, and was glancing shyly round the room in search of a likely male who would fetch her a stiff glass of something from the buffet, and that soon. She was groggy, but not sufficiently primed to go there herself; she knew that everybody's eye would be fixed upon her; she had been much talked about of late. Drunk, she was impossible; dead sober, almost as bad – haughty, sullen, logical, with a grieved and surprised air suggestive of wounded dignity.

People avoided Miss Wilberforce. And yet you could not help liking her in those rare moments when she was just a little disguised. She had a pretty wit, then; a residue of gentle nurture; tender instincts and a winsomeness of manner that captivated you. Nor were appearances against her. That frail, arrowy figure was invariably clothed in black. She wore the colour by instinct. They said she had lost her sailor fiancé, who was drowned, poor lad, in the Mediterranean; and that she now wandered about at night looking for him, or trying to forget him and seeking oblivion in tipple.

The story happened to be true, for a wonder. She had received a twist for life. The death of this young lover gave to her impressionable being a shock which never passed off again. The world was turned inside out for Amy Wilberforce. She seldom spoke of his fate. But she was always talking about the sea. She tried to drown herself, once or twice. Then, gradually, she put on a new character altogether and relapsed into queer ancestral traits, stripping off, like so many worthless rags, the layers of laboriously acquired civilization. The refined and bashful girl became brusque, supercilious, equivocal. When sympathizing friends said that they had also lost lovers, she laughed and told them to look for new ones. There were better fish in the sea, etc, etc.

Soon she found herself abandoned, in spite of a full banking account. People had dropped her, right and left.

The years went by.

Calmly, without misgivings and without fervour, she took to the bottle.

Something drew her to Nepenthe – dim Mediterranean memories. Arrived there, she used to engulf three pints of Martell and Hennessy, one after the other, and then 'wash them out' – such was her phraseology – with a magnum of Perrier Jouet; a proceeding which, while it heightened her complexion and gave a sparkle to her poor flustered eye, was not conducive to the preservation of equilibrium in the lower limbs. There resulted those periodical 'nervous breakdowns' which necessitated seclusion and sometimes medical treatment. The collapses had become distressingly frequent within the last year or two. One of her many drawbacks was that she courted publicity in her cups. She was perfectly reckless as to what she then said, and had been known to bring a blush to the seasoned cheek of Don Francesco himself, who, unaware of her condition at one particular moment, politely ventured to inquire why she always wore black and was told that she was mourning, as everybody ought to mourn, for his lost innocence. Being an Englishwoman, she was a thorn in the side of her moral compatriot the Commissioner.

Her noctambulous habits often brought her into contact with the local police and sometimes with His Worship Signor Malipizzo. Greatly to the surprise of Mr Parker, the magistrate was observed to take a lenient view of the case. None the less, she had passed several nights in the local gaol. Staggering about the lanes of Nepenthe in the silent hours before dawn, she was liable to be driven, at the bidding of some dark primeval impulse, to divest herself of her raiment – a singularity which perturbed even the hardiest of social night-birds who had the misfortune to encounter her. Taxed with this freakish behaviour, she would refer to the example of St Francis of Assisi, who did the same, and brazenly ask whether he wasn't good enough for them? Whether she couldn't give her last shirt to a beggar, as well as anybody else? In short, there was nothing to be done with her.

The dear lady, as Keith often called her, was becoming a real problem.

And now her eye, roving round the room, fixed itself with the drunkard's divine unerring instinct upon Denis. What a nice, modest, gentlemanly-looking boy! Just what she wanted.

'This sirocco!' she sighed, groping dramatically for a chair. 'It makes me feel so funny. Oh dear! I shall go off in a faint. Ah, do be a kind young man and fetch me some brandy and soda. A large tumbler. Ah, do! And very little soda, please – on account of my heart. Only the smallest drop!'

She took two or three sips, paused awhile as though undecided whether she could possibly swallow such nasty stuff and then, with a fine show of reluctance, gulped it all down. Denis was spellbound; the dose, he artlessly imagined, was enough to kill a horse. Far from being damaged, Miss Wilberforce took a chair beside him, and began to converse. Charmingly she talked; all about England. As he listened he grew delighted, entranced. She was different, somehow, from all the other ladies he had lately met on the Continent. She was altogether different. Whence came it, he wondered?

Then, as the discourse proceeded, he began to realize what was the matter with them. It was odd, he thought, that he had not noticed it before. Miss Wilberforce made him realize wherein the difference lay. They spoke English, it was true; but they had all taken on a Continental outlook; alien phrases, expressions, affectations; cosmopolitan airs and graces that jarred on his frank, untarnished English nature. This one was otherwise. She was old England, through and through. The conversation cheered him to an unusual degree – among all those foreign people he felt strangely drawn towards this wistful lady who could talk so naturally and conjure up, by the mere power of words, a breath of his own home-stead in the Midlands. He might have been sitting with an elder sister just then, eating strawberries and cream and watching a ten-nis match on some shady green lawn. He was happy; happier still when Angelina once more floated into his ken and, noticing Miss Wilberforce, raised her eyebrows mischievously and gave him something that looked like a real smile, for a change.

She had another smile, however, for Mr Edgar Marten; and yet another one for Don Francesco, who, as she passed near him, profited by the occasion to give her a paternal semi-proprietary chuck under the chin, accompanying the indecorous movement with an almost audible wink.

Mr Heard had noticed everything. He frowned at first. It gave him a little twinge, and some food for thought. He was absurdly sensitive about women.

'A frolicsome child,' he mused. '*Lasciva puella*. Possibly wanton.'

What were this young man's relations with the girl? That con-tact of hand and chin – what did it imply? Was the action quasi-paternal, or pseudo-paternal? Regretfully he decided that it was only pseudo-paternal.

And yet – it was all so confoundly natural!

'Nobody but our *parroco* could keep his hands off that girl,' blithely remarked the priest.

Another little twinge. ...

CHAPTER 7

MR HEARD was not prone to wax enthusiastic over the delights of architecture or natural scenery. He called himself unexpansive and unromantic; he confessed to small understanding, small veneration, for artistic effects. The beauty of a man's character moved him more strongly than the beauty of any picture or any landscape. Yet, on arriving next afternoon at the upper plateau of Nepenthe, he could not help being struck by the strange and al-most compelling charm of the 'Old Town'. It was so different from the lower regions – so calm and reposeful.

Down below, in that more accessible modern settlement, everything was bright and many-tinted; there was movement and noise and colour; a dazzling spot! The subtle influence of the sea, though it lay four hundred feet lower down, was ever present; one felt oneself on an island. On reaching these heights that feeling evaporated. You were embowered in mighty trees, in the midst of which stood the Old Town.

Unlike that other one, it faced due North; it lay, moreover, a few hundred feet higher up. That alone could not have explained the difference in temperature, one might say in climate, between the two. To begin with, there was on this tiny upland basin exceptionally deep soil, borne down by the rains of unnumbered centuries from the heights overhead, and enabling those shady oaks, poplars, walnuts, and apples to shoot up to uncommon size and luxuriance and screen away the sunny beams. From above, meanwhile, a perennial shower descended. The moisture-laden sirocco, tearing itself to shreds against the riven summits of the high southern cliffs, dripped ceaselessly upon this verdant oasis in clouds of invisible dew. You could often enjoy the luxury of a shiver, at night-time, in the Old Town.

It was a stronghold originally; built on these heights for the greater security of the islanders against Saracenic inroads. When a more peaceful era drew nigh the population began to decline; they found it more convenient to establish themselves in the new settlement lower down. Then came the Good Duke Alfred – that potentate who, as Mr Eames was wont to say, *nihil quod tetigit non ornavit*. He took a fancy to this quaint old citadel which, before his day, could only be reached by a rough mule-track easily defended against invaders. After constructing a fine road of access with many twists and turnings, wide enough to admit the passage of two of his roomy state carriages driving abreast, he turned his mind to other improvements. Professing to be an admirer of the good old times, he decided to keep up its traditional character – it was to remain a fortress, in appearance if not reality. A massive crenellated rampart, furnished with four gateways and watch-towers at convenient intervals but serving no purpose in particular grew up around the place; every one of its houses which failed to fit in with the design of this battlemented structure – and there were a good many of them – was ruthlessly demolished. The Old Town was enclosed in a ring.

Desirous, next, of putting an end to the annoying exodus of the natives, he fixed by law the number of inhabitants; there were to be five hundred souls, neither more nor less. If in any one year the population exceeded that figure, the surplus was taken away, from among the adult males, to work as galley-slaves in his fleet; a deficiency in the requisite number was met by giving new husbands from the lower town, often three or four at a time 'with a view to ensuring good results', to those of the native women who had hitherto failed to produce offspring. The system worked well. With some trifling but reprehensible fluctuations, the birth-rate and death-rate remained even; things were at a standstill; a fact which caused His Highness to be compared, by a courtly panegyrist, to Joshua, who bade the sun arrest his march across the heavens. Another of these gentlemen calls the Duke's action a 'triumph of art over nature', adding, not without a grain of malice, that 'never have the generative capacities of mankind adapted themselves with more conspicuous success to the shape of an unnecessary wall'. Monsignor Perrelli, unfortunately, has nothing whatever to say on the subject. For reasons which will appear anon, he is remarkably silent on all that concerns the reign of his great contemporary.

Even so, the Prince was not satisfied. The fastness was yet imperfect; he disliked the variegated hues of the buildings – they reminded him of the garish brilliance in the lower town. Something different had to be contrived. He took thought and, being a man of taste and a decorist where picturesque effects were concerned, decreed that the entire place – walls, houses, the two convents (Benedictine and Carthusian), the church, and even stables and pigsties – were to be painted a uniform pink: 'pink,' he ordained, 'without the slightest admixture of blue.' He desired, in fact, a kind of rose or flesh colour, a particular tint which, he foresaw, would look well among the luscious verdure of the surroundings. His behest, as usual, was obeyed without much loss of time.

Then he surveyed his work, and saw that it was good. He had created a gem. The Old Town was a symphony in emerald and coral.

So it remained. The inhabitants grew to be proud of their rosy citadel; it was an unwritten law among them that every new house should adapt itself to this tone. For the rest, there was not much building done after his death, with the exception of a few isolated villas that sprang up, despite his old commands, in the neighbourhood. And the decline in population once more set in. Men forsook the place – all save the peasantry who tilled the surrounding fields. Towers and battlements crumbled to earth; roadways heaved uneasily with grassy tufts that sprouted in the chinks of the old paving-blocks. Sometimes at decline of day a creaking hay-wagon would lumber along, bending towards a courtyard in whose moss-grown recesses you discerned stacks of golden maize and pumpkins; apples and plum-trees, nodding drowsily over walls, littered the streets with snowy blossoms or fallen leaves. Commercial life was extinct. The few remaining shopkeepers wore an air of slumberous benevolence. The very stones suggested peace. A mellow and aristocratic flavour clung to those pink dwellings that nestled, world-forgotten, in a green content. ...

One of those few modern houses was the Villa Mon Repos. There was a curious history attached to the place. It had been built about a century ago at the orders of an eccentric French lady, a lyric poetess, who professed to be tired of life. She had heard that somewhere on Nepenthe was a towering precipice, unique of its kind and convenient for suicidal purposes. She thought she would like to live near that precipice – it might come in handy. There was nothing of the right sort in Paris, she declared; only five-storey hotels and suchlike; the notion of casting herself down from one of those artificial eminences did not appeal to her highstrung temperament; she craved to die like Sappho, her ideal. An architect was despatched, the ground purchased, the house built and furnished. That done, she settled up her affairs in France and established herself at Mon Repos. On the evening of her arrival she climbed the little height at the back of her domain and looked southward, down a sheer wall of rock eight or nine hundred feet high, over the wrinkled ocean. It made her feel queer. Further familiarity with the precipice did not breed contempt; her visits to the site became rarer and rarer. She died, at a patriarchal age, in her bed, after writing a scholarly pamphlet to prove that the tale of Sappho's leap over her famous silvery crag was a myth, the 'purest sensationalism', a fable of the grammarians 'hopelessly irreconcilable with what we know of that great woman's character'.

This much the bishop had learnt from Mr Keith. That gentleman liked the Sappho story; he called it absolutely true to human nature and so creditable to the old lady's intelligence that he would have insisted upon paying his respects to her had she not expired a good many years before his arrival on the island. And he, of course, got it from Eames, who, as annotator of Perrelli's *Antiquities*, was in the habit of garnering odd details anent private houses and so forth and had possessed himself, in the course of his researches, of this particular pamphlet, which he intended to reprint, together with others of its kind, in an appendix entitled 'Contemporary Social History'.

The driving road terminated at the Old Town. Mr Heard,

descending from his carriage, followed a pathway which had been described to him by Denis and soon found himself at the entrance of the Villa Mon Repos. It was an inconspicuous little place, surrounded by three or four chestnut trees and a rose-garden. A steep incline at the back of the property ended, abruptly, in air. He concluded that the precipice must be on the other side of that slope, and that if so, it was rather too near the house for his taste. Mr Heard thoroughly understood the feelings of the French poetess. He, too, was not fond of precipices. It was as much as he could do to look down from a church tower without growing dizzy.

On the house-steps, beside an empty cradle, sat a shrivelled hag – a gaunt, forbidding anatomy, with hooked nose and brown skin. Tousled grey hair, like that of a Skye terrier, hung over her forehead, half concealing a pair of coal-black eyes. She rose up, barred the entrance with one claw-like hand, and scrutinized him distrustfully.

'A Cerberus!' he thought. 'This must be the old lady who understands Hindustani. Now I wonder if she knows English?'

She seemed to understand that language too; or perhaps his kindly face disposed her in his favour. He was allowed to pass within.

The house was empty. Mrs Meadows had presumably gone out for a ramble, taking the child with her. He sat down and waited, glancing round the premises. It was a peaceful sort of abode, pervaded by a strong sense of home. It appealed to the bishop, who had domestic instincts and, despite his youth, was already a little weary of tossing about the world. He envied his cousin's happy married life. Would such an existence ever fall to his own lot? Although, like himself, she was only a bird of passage on Nepenthe, she had succeeded in impressing her personality upon those rather scantily furnished rooms and filling them with an atmosphere of England. Heavy bowls of fresh roses were ranged about. But what was she like, after all these years? Would she recognize him? Had she heard of his arrival on the island?

Mrs Meadows failed to return. Perhaps she had met some friend or neighbour who was keeping her to dinner together with the child. The old woman seemed unwilling or unable to give him any information as to her whereabouts. After waiting an hour, he scribbled a short note, left it on the writing-table, and took his leave. The eyes of that fierce creature followed him right out of the garden. So did the scent of roses. ...

The afternoon was drawing to its close, as Mr Heard, in a placid, contemplative frame of mind, once more drew nigh the pink ramparts of the Old Town, purposing to find his way home on foot.

He entered the most westerly of its four gateways. There were stone seats within the structure on either side of the road, convenient for sheltering from sun or rain. Passing under the vaulted roof he met Count Caloveglia, that handsome, soldier-like personality, who instantly recognized him and greeted him in friendliest fashion.

'Will you do me the pleasure of coming to my house, and allow me to offer you a cup of tea? It is visible from here – that rounded portal, do you see? With the fig tree leaning over the street. Only a hundred yards. Or perhaps we can rest awhile under this archway and converse. It is always pleasant to watch the movements of the country-folk, and there is a peculiar charm in this evening light. Well, let us sit down, then. I observe you are interested in those people. A singular illusion, is it not?'

He referred to a group of men and boys who, stripped to the waist, were bearing aloft immense masses of some argent-coloured rock.

'You've guessed my thoughts,' replied the bishop. 'How on earth are they able to support such a weight? They remind me of Atlas with the world on his shoulders.'

'It is pumice-stone – one of the old industries of the place. They excavate it on the hill-side yonder. Volcanic stuff. There are several suchlike indications of subterranean fires; a hot spring, for instance, which the people regard with a kind of superstitious awe. It is dedicated to Saint Elias and believed to stand in mysterious sympathy with the volcano on the mainland. You will observe too, sooner or later, something fiery and incalculable in the temperament of the natives. Perhaps it is due to the wine grown on these scorching slopes. If geologists are right, we are sitting at this moment on the crater of a volcano –'

'Dear me! That might be rather awkward. I suppose this pumice is very light?'

'Light as foam. But who can believe it? The bearers move within a few feet of us, and yet it resembles the most ponderous limestone or granite. Then you ask yourself: How is it possible! If their burden were what it seems to be, they would be crushed to earth instead of striding proudly along. Admirable figures! As you say, the spectacle takes one back into mythological times. Would you not call it a procession of Titans, children of the Gods, storing up mountain-blocks for some earth-convulsing battle? Your eyes deceive you. Like Thomas, the doubting apostle, you must

67

touch with your hands. And even then you are not wholly convinced. To me, who know the capacity of human bone and muscle, these men are a daily miracle. They mock my notions of what is permissible. How hard it is, sometimes, to trust the evidence of one's senses! How reluctantly the mind consents to reality! The industry is decaying,' he added, 'but I hope it will outlive my time.'

'Everything seems to decay up here in sober and gracious fashion. I am delighted, Count, with your Old Town. There is an autumnal flavour about the place. It is a poet's dream. Some philosopher might dwell here – some sage who has grown weary of disentangling life's threads.'

Rarely did Mr Heard use florid and sentimental language like this. The soft light, the reposeful surroundings, the homelike influence of the Villa Mon Repos – all had conspired to put him into an uncommonly idyllic mood of mind. He felt disposed to linger with the kindly stranger who seemed so much more communicative and affable than on the occasion of those theatricals. He lit a cigarette and watched, for a while, the flow of life through that gateway. Its passage was pierced, like the eye of a needle, with a slender shaft of light from the westering sun. Fine particles of dust, suspended overhead, enveloped the homeward-moving peasantry in a tender mist of gold.

'Yes,' replied the Count. 'This citadel is a microcosm of what the world might be, if men were reasonable. Not all men! A great proportion must be good enough to remain what they are. We could not live without those whose business it is to bring the reasonableness of the few into its proper relief. Were it otherwise, there would be no more reasonableness on earth, would there?'

'And that would be a pity,' observed Mr Heard. 'I was much interested, Count, in what you said yesterday. You spoke of the Mediterranean becoming once more the centre of human activity. There is an attraction in the idea, to one who, like myself, has been brought up on the classics and has never forgotten his spiritual debt to antiquity. But I question whether the majority of my countrymen would be moved by such considerations.'

The old man replied:

'I think we need not trouble about majorities. No one can expect a majority to be stirred by motives other than ignoble. Your English majority, in particular, is quite unaware of its debt to us: why should it turn eyes in our direction? But as for other Northern men, the enlightened ones – I cannot help thinking that they will come to their senses again one of these days. Oh yes! They will recover their sanity. They will perceive under what artificial and cramping conditions, under what false standards, they have been living; they will realize the advantages of a climate where nature meets you half-way. I know little of England, but the United States are pretty familiar to me; the two climates, I imagine, cannot be very dissimilar. That a man should wear himself to the bone in the acquisition of material gain is not pretty. But what else can he do in lands adapted only for wolves and bears? Without a degree of comfort which would be superfluous hereabouts he would feel humiliated. He must become strenuous if he wishes to rise superior to his inhospitable surroundings.'

'We think a good deal of strenuousness,' objected the bishop.

'Have you not noticed that whenever anything, however fantastic, is imposed upon men by physical forces, they straightway make a god of it? That is why you deify strenuousness. You dare not forgo it. The Eskimo doubtless deifies the seal-blubber; he could not survive without it. Yet nobody would be an Eskimo if he had a chance of bettering his condition. By all means let us take life seriously. But let us be serious about things that matter.'

'Things that matter, Count! Is it not creditable for a man to support his wife and family in the best conditions possible?'

'Assuredly. But chosen spirits will do this in regions where the same results can be obtained with a smaller outlay of vital force. We have only a certain amount of energy at our disposal. It is not seemly to consume every ounce of it in a contest with brute nature. Man is made for better things. Whatever fails to elevate the mind is not truly profitable. Tell me, sir, how shall the mind be elevated if the body be exhausted with material preoccupations? Consider the complex conditions under which a Northern family is obliged to live. Think of the labour expended upon that unceasing duel with the elements – the extra clothing and footwear and mufflers and mantles, the carpets, the rugs, the abundant and costly food required to keep the body in sound working condition, the plumbing, the gas, the woodwork, the paintings, and repaintings, the tons of fuel, the lighting in winter, the contrivances against frost and rain, the never-ending repairs to houses, the daily polishings and dustings and scrubbings, and those thousand other impediments to the life of the spirit! Half of them are non-existent in these latitudes; half the vitality expended upon them could therefore be directed to other ends. At close of day, your Northerner is pleased with himself. He has survived; he has even prospered. His family is adequately housed and clothed. He feels "presentable", as he calls it, in the eyes of those who share his illusions. He fancies he has attained the aim and object of existence. He is too dazed with the struggle to perceive how incongruous his efforts have been. What has he done? He has sacrificed himself on the altar of a false ideal. He has not touched the fringe of a reasonable life. He has performed certain social and political duties – he knows nothing of duties towards himself. I am speaking of men from whom better things might have been expected. As for the majority, the crowd, the herd – they do not exist, neither here nor anywhere else. They leave a purely physiological mark upon posterity; they propagate the species and protect their offspring. So do foxes. It is not enough for us. Living in our lands, men would have leisure to cultivate nobler aspects of their nature. They would be accessible to purer aspirations, worthier delights. They would enjoy the happiness of sages. What other happiness deserves the name? In the Mediterranean, Mr Heard, lies the hope of humanity.'

The bishop was thoughtful. There occurred to him various objections to this rather fanciful argument. Still, he said nothing. He was naturally chary of words; it was so interesting to listen to other people! And at this particular period he was more than usually reflective and absorbent.

Happiness – an honourable, justifiable happiness – how was it to be attained? Not otherwise, he used to think, than through the twofold agency of Christianity and civilization. That was his old College attitude. Imperceptibly his outlook had shifted since then. Something had been stirring within him; new points of view had floated into his ken. He was no longer so sure about things. The structure of his mind had lost that old stability; its elements seemed to be held in solution, ready to form new combinations. China had taught him that men can be happy and virtuous while lacking, and even scorning, the first of these twin blessings. Then had come Africa, where his notions had been further dislocated by those natives who derided both the one and the other – such fine healthy animals, all the same! A candid soul, he allowed his natural shrewdness and logic to play freely with memories of his earlier experiences among the London poor. These experiences now became fraught with a new meaning. The solemn doctrines he had preached in those days: were they really a panacea for all the ills of the flesh? He thought upon the gaunt bodies, starved souls, and white faces – the dirt, the squalor of it! Was that Christianity, civilization?

The Count, pursuing some other line of thought, broke out into a kind of Delphic rhapsody:

'Folly of men! The wits of our people have been blunted, their habits bestialized, their very climate and landscape ruined. The alert genius of the Greeks is clogged by a barbaric, leaden-hued religion – the fertile plains of Asia Minor and Spain converted into deserts! We begin, at last, to apprehend the mischief; we know who is to blame; we are turning the corner. Enclosed within the soft imagination of the *homo mediterraneus* lies a kernel of hard reason. We have reached that kernel. The Northerner's hardness is on the surface; his core, his inner being is apt to quaver in a state of fluid irresponsibility. Yet there must be reasonable men everywhere; men who refuse to wear away their faculties in a degrading effort to plunder one another, men who are tired of hustle and strife. What, sir, would you call the phenomenon of today? What is the outstanding feature of modern life? The bankruptcy, the proven fatuity, of everything that is bound up under the name of Western civilization. Men are perceiving, I think, the baseness of mercantile and military ideals, the loftiness of those older ones. They will band together, the elect of every nation, in god-favoured regions round the Inland Sea, there to lead serener lives. To those who have hitherto preached indecorous maxims of conduct they will say: "What is all this ferocious nonsense about strenuousness? An unbecoming fluster. And who are you, to dictate how we shall order our day? Go! Shiver and struggle in your hyperborean dens. Trample about those misty, rain-sodden fields, and hack each other's eyes out with antediluvian bayonets. Or career up and down the ocean, in your absurd ships, to pick the pockets of men better than yourselves. That is your mode of self-expression. It is not ours." And Mediterranean people will lead the way. They have suffered more than all from the imbecilities of kings and priests and soldiers and politicians. They now make an end of this neurasthenic gadding and getting. They focus themselves anew and regain their lost dignity. That ancient individualistic tone reasserts itself. Man becomes a personality once more –'

He continued for some time in this prophetic strain, the bishop listening with considerable approbation, though, at a certain point of the discourse, he would have liked to drop a word about Thermopylae and Marathon. He also knew something of the evils of Northern industrialism – how it stunts the body and warps the mind.

'What a charming dreamer!' he thought.

It was rather convenient for the Count to be able to pass, just then, for a dreamer.

As a matter of fact, he was an extremely practical old gentleman.

CHAPTER 8

'SANIDIN?' queried Denis almost flippantly, as he held up a fragment of rock.

He was not particularly eager to hear Marten's answer. He had thought, only a few days ago, that he would like to be a geologist; Marten had inspired him with a fancy for that science. The fit was already passing.

How quickly this geological mood had evaporated. How quickly everything evaporated, nowadays.

All was not well with Denis. Early that morning he had tried his hand at poetry once more, after a long interval. Four words – that was all the inspiration which had come to him.

Or vine-wreathed Tuscany...

A pretty turn, in the earlier manner of Keats. It looked well on the snowy paper. 'Or vine-wreathed Tuscany.' He was content with that phrase, so far as it went. But where was the rest of the stanza?

How easily, a year or two ago, could he have fashioned the whole verse. How easily everything was accomplished in those days. To be a poet; that was a fixed point on his horizon. Any number of joyous lyrics, as well as three plays not intended for the stage, had already dropped from his pen. He was an extraordinary success among his college friends; everybody liked him; he could say and do what he pleased. Was he not the idol of a select group who admired not only one another but also the satanism of Baudelaire, the hieratic obscenities of Beardsley, the mustiest Persian sage, the modernest American ballad-monger? He was full of gay irresponsibility. Ever since, on returning to his rooms after some tedious lecture, he announced to his friends that he had lost an umbrella but preserved, thank God, his honour, they augured a brilliant future for him. So, for other but no less cogent reasons, did his doting, misguided mother.

Both were disappointed. Those sprightly sallies became rarer; epigrams died, still-born, on his lips. He lost his sense of humour; grew mirthless, fretful, self-conscious. He suddenly realized the existence of a world beyond his college walls; it made him feel like a hot-house flower exposed to the blustering winds of March. Life was no longer a hurdle in a steeple-chase to be taken at a gallop; it was a tangle of beastly facts that stared you in the face and refused to get out of the way. With growing years, during vacation, he came in contact with a new set of people: men who smiled indulgently at mention of all he held most sacred – art, classics, literature; men who were plainly not insane and yet took up incomprehensible professions of one kind or another – took them up with open eyes and unfeigned zest, and actually prospered at them in a crude worldly fashion.

He shrank at first from their society, consoling himself with the reflection that, being bounders, it did not matter whether they succeeded or not. But this explanation did not hold good for long. They were not bounders – not all of them. People not only dined with them: they asked them to dinner. Quite decent fellows, in fact. Nothing was wrong with them, save that they held a point of view which was at variance with his own.

It was a rude awakening. Every moment he was up against something new. There were quite a lot of things, he discovered, which a fellow ought to know, and doesn't. Too many of them to assimilate with comfort. They crowded in upon him and unsettled his mind. He kept up a brave exterior, but his inner core was suffering; he was no longer certain of himself. He became easily swayed and changeful in his moods. That sure touch in lyrics, as in daily life, was deserting him. His dreams were not coming true. He was not going to set the Thames on fire with poetry or anything else. He would probably be a failure. Aware of this weakness, he looked up to what was strong. Everything different from himself, everything forceful, emphatic, and clear-cut, exercised a fascination upon him. He tried, in an honest, groping fashion, to learn what it was all about. That was why he had taken to Edgar Marten, the antithesis of himself, bright but dogmatic, a slovenly little plebeian but a man who after all had a determined, definite point of view.

Denis repeated:

'Sanidin?'

'Let's have a look at it, then,' said Marten, condescendingly, 'though I can't say I'm in a geological temper this morning. The south wind seems to rot one's intelligence somehow. Hand it here. Sanidin be blowed! It's specular iron. Now I wonder why you should hit upon sanidin? Why?'

He, too, did not pause for a reply. He turned his glance once more down the steep hill-side which they had climbed with a view to exploring some instructive exposure of the rock. Marten intended to utilize the site as a text for a lay sermon. Arrived at the spot they had sat down. As if by common consent, geology was forgotten. To outward appearances they were absorbed in the beauties of nature. Sirocco mists rose upwards, clustering thickly overhead and rolling in billowy formations among the dales. Sometimes a breath of wind would convulse their ranks, causing them to trail in long silvery pennants across the sky and, opening a rift in their gossamer texture, would reveal, far down below, a glimmer of olives shining in the sunlight or a patch of blue sea, framed in an aureole of peacock hues. Stones and grass were clammy with warm moisture.

'It's a funny thing,' said Marten, after a long pause. 'I've often noticed it. When I'm not actually at work, I'm always thinking about girls. I wish I could talk better Latin, or Italian. Not that I should be running after them all day long. I've got other fish to fry. I've got to catalogue my minerals, and I'm only half-way through. For the matter of that, I haven't come across half as many nice ones here as I thought I would.'

'Minerals?'

'Girls. I don't seem to take to these foreigners. But there's one –'

'Go on.'

'You're a queer fellow, Phipps. Don't you ever look at women? I believe you have the makings of a saint in you. Fight against it. A fellow can't live without vices. Here you are, with lots of money, stewing in a back bedroom of a second-class hotel and getting up every morning at five o'clock because you like lying in bed late. Is that your way of mortifying the flesh? Got a soul, eh? Get rid of it. The soul! That unhappy word has been the refuge of empty minds ever since the world began. You're just like a man I used to know at Newcastle. You can't think what an ass he was. A sort of eugenical crank, who talked about the City Beautiful where everybody would lead regenerated lives like a flock of prize sheep. Everything sanitary and soulful; nothing but pure men and pure women. An addle-headed theorist, he was, till a woman got hold of him – one of the other kind, you know – and gave him something practical to think about. That's what will happen to you, Phipps. I can see it coming.'

'I've been analysing myself lately. I find I have too much romance in my composition as it is.'

'What do you call romance?'

Denis thought awhile. Then he said:

'When a man invests ordinary people or objects or occurrences with an extraordinary interest. When he reads attributes into them which they don't possess, or exaggerates those which they do possess. When he looks at a person and can't help thinking that there is nobody on earth quite like her.'

74

'Too celestial for me, on the whole. But I'm glad you said that last part. Glad for your sake, I mean. It shows that you've perhaps got something better than a soul, after all.'

'What is that?'

'A body. Look here, Phipps. I also have my romantic moments, though you wouldn't believe it. I can be as romantic as ever you please. But not when I'm alone.'

'I should like to see you in that condition. And talking Latin, no doubt?' he added with a laugh.

'I daresay you would,' replied the scientist. 'Given the circumstances under which I become romantic, you'll find it a little difficult. But there's no knowing. Funny things happen sometimes!'

Denis had picked up another stone. He scrutinized it with close attention, and then began to turn it round and round in his hand in an absent-minded fashion. At last he remarked:

'We are not doing much mineralogy, are we? What do you think of chastity, Marten?'

'Chastity be blowed. It's an unclean state of affairs, and dangerous to the community. You can't call yourself a good citizen till you have learnt to despise it from the bottom of your heart. It's an insult to the Creator and an abomination to man and beast.'

'Perhaps you never gave it a fair trial,' suggested Denis.

'Perhaps I'm not quite such a damned fool as all that. A man needn't handle everything dirty in order to be doubly sure about it. If you tell me that a dead donkey smells bad, I'm quite prepared to believe you without poking my nose into it. Chastity is a dead donkey. No beating will bring it to life again. Who killed it? The experience of every sane man and woman on earth. It's decayed; it ought to be buried. You ask me to give it a trial. Perhaps I will, when I'm in the same mellow condition myself. Everything in its proper season. Don't let us reverse the natural order of things. When we cease to practise, then is the time to preach. A fellow of your size! And with your good looks, too. Who knows how many golden opportunities you've missed. Try to make up for lost time, Phipps. Get rid of conventional notions, if you value your health.'

'I will, when I find them wrong. What do you think of women – generally speaking, I mean?'

Marten replied, without a moment's hesitation:

'Thank God I'm a Jew. You must take that into consideration. I think the Mormons have made a good shot at solving the woman question, if the question exists at all. Mormonism is a protest
75

against monogamy. And please observe that it's a protest not on the part of man alone. It's a protest on the part of woman. Never forget that. In fact, I don't believe any woman would ever bind herself to one fool of a man if she had her own way. She wouldn't marry at all. She needn't, nowadays. She won't very soon. A man who marries – well, there may be some excuse for him, though a love-match is generally a failure and a money-match always a mistake. The heroes, the saints and sages – they are those who face the world alone. A married man is half a man.'

'Ahem!'

Marten was silent.

'I did not ask you to stop,' said Denis. 'You've got it very pat!'

'Plain sailing, my boy. It's the social reformers and novelists who create these artificial conundrums; they want to sell their rotten literature; they want to make us forget that the only interesting and important part of the business is what nobody talks or writes about. What does it all amount to? Man creates intellectually and physically. He classifies minerals or blasts out a tunnel. Woman creates physiologically; she supplies the essential, the raw material; her noblest product is a child. I get on splendidly with women, because we both realize the stupidity of the average sex-twaddle. We have no illusions about each other. We know exactly what we are after. We know exactly how to attain it. I tell you what, Phipps, Female Emancipation is going to do away with a lot of cant and idealism. Knock the silly male on the head. There'll be an end of your chastity-worship, once women are fairly started on the game. They won't put up with it.'

'Disgusting,' said Denis. 'Go on.'

'I'm done. What, sanidin again?'

Dennis still held the stone in his hand. He was thinking, however, of other things. He liked to collect fresh ideas, to be impregnated with the mentality of other people – he knew how much he had to learn. But he would have preferred his mind to be moulded gently, in artistic fashion. Marten's style was more like random blows from a sledge-hammer, half of them wide of the mark. It was not very edifying, or even instructive. Keith was the same. Why was everybody so violent, so extreme in their views?

Marten repeated:

'Sanidin?'

'It might be sanidin in places,' replied Denis. 'I do know a little something about crystals, Marten. I have read Ruskin's *Ethics of the Dust*.'

'Ruskin. Good God! He's not a man; he's an emetic. But you

76

never answered my first question. You always hit upon sanidin. Why?'

'Oh, I don't know. It's rather a pretty word, don't you think? It would do for a Christian name. Girls' names are so terribly commonplace. They are always Marjorie, or something. If I had a daughter, I should call her Sanidin.'

'You're not likely to find yourself in that position, at this rate. If I had a daughter, I know perfectly well what I should call her.'

'What?'

'Angelina.'

'You would?' asked Denis slowly. 'And why?'

'Oh, it's rather a pretty name, don't you think?'

'Not a bad name at all, now I come to think of it. But it sounds foreign. I thought you did not care about foreigners?'

'I don't. But there's one –'

'Go on,' said Denis.

Mr Marten winked.

The mists had fled from the hill-tops; rocks and vineyards, and the sea at their foot, lay flooded in sunshine. With one accord, the two young men rose from the ground and turned their steps homewards. The mineralogical lesson was over.

'Coming to Keith's tonight?' inquired Marten with a fine show of nonchalance.

'I don't know.'

'I would if I were you. They say he does things properly. There'll be an awful crowd – a regular bust-up. He only gives one of these entertainments a year. Dancing and Chinese lanterns and champagne in torrents. Won't you go?'

'Perhaps later in the evening.'

Denis was perturbed. He scented a rival in this brutalitarian, though it seemed hardly possible that Angelina should take much notice of him. Meanwhile he felt in need of some gentlemanly and soothing influence, after such an outpouring of vulgarity. He thought of the bibliographer. He liked Eames; he admired that scholarly detachment. He, too, might end in annotating some masterpiece – who knows? To be a bibliographer – what a calm, studious life!

'I think I'll go to Eames,' he remarked.

'Really? A colourless creature, that Eames. As dry as a stick; a typical don. I promised him a mineralogical map, by the way. You might tell him I haven't forgotten, will you? I wonder what you can see in the man?'

'I rather like him,' said Denis. 'He knows what he wants.'

77

'That is not enough, my young friend!' replied Marten with decision. 'A fellow must want something sensible.'

'What do you call sensible?'

'Sanidin, and things like that. Things with pretty names. Eh, Phipps?'

Denis said nothing.

His friend continued jovially:

'The tavern mood is upon me. I am going to Luisella's to get a drink. One gets sick of that Club. Besides, I've taken rather a fancy to that younger sister. The second youngest, I mean; the one with the curly hair – you know! I only wish I knew a bit more Latin.'

Luisella's grotto-tavern had become quite a famous rendezvous. You could drop in there at any hour and always find company to your liking. Don Francesco had a good deal to do with its discovery; he discovered, at all events, the second eldest of the four orphan sisters who managed the house. After a time, having convinced himself that they were all good penitents and being a kindly sort of man, he thought that other people might like to share in the seductions which the place afforded. He took foreign friends there from time to time, and none were disappointed. The wine was excellent. Russians, excluded from the Club by Mr Parker's severity, frequented the spot in considerable numbers. They were nicely treated there. Not many nights previously one of the Master's disciples, the athletic young Peter Krasnojabkin, who was credited with being a protégé of Madame Steynlin's, had distinguished himself by drinking sixteen bottles at a sitting. He afterwards smashed a few chairs and things, for which he apologized so prettily next morning that the girls would not hear of his paying for the damage.

'It's all in the family,' they said. 'Come and break some more!'

That was the way they ran the place, as regards drinks. The quality of the refreshments, too, was quite out of the common. As for the girls themselves – their admirers were legion. They could have married anyone they pleased, had it not been more in accordance with the interests of their business, to say nothing of their personal inclinations, to have only lovers.

As Marten disappeared under that hospitable doorway, it flashed through the mind of Denis that Eames was a confirmed recluse; he might not like being disturbed in the morning.

Besides, he was probably at work.

He thought of going to see the bishop. There was a glamour in the name. To be a bishop! His mother had sometimes suggested the Church, or at least politics as a career for him, if poetry should

78

fail. But this one was so matter-of-fact and unpretentious in his clothing, his opinions. A broken-down matrimonial agent, Don Francesco had called him. Mr Heard was not his ideal of a shepherd of souls; he was only a colonial, anyhow. A grey type of man – nothing purple about him, nothing glowing or ornate. He did not get on particularly well with him either.

Besides, he hardly knew him sufficiently to intrude at this hour of the day.

One thing was certain. He would go to the Cave of Mercury that very evening. Keith was right. He must try to 'find himself'. He wanted to be alone, to think things out. Or perhaps – no. He did not want to be alone with his thoughts. They were too oppressive just then. He required some kind of company.

Besides, Keith had said 'full moon'. The moon was not yet quite full.

No!

He would see what the Duchess was doing, and perhaps stay to luncheon. Eames could wait. So could the bishop. So could the cave. He was fond of the Duchess.

Besides, it was such a quaint place – that austere old convent, built by the Good Duke Alfred.

CHAPTER 9

'THAT is the worst of dining with a man. You have to be civil next morning. But surely, Eames, we two need not stand on ceremony? I am particularly anxious for you to come to-night. Can't you really manage it? I want you to meet Malipizzo and say a few nice words to him. You are too aloof with that man. There is nothing like keeping on the right side of the law.'

'What do you mean by that?'

'The right side of the judge,' said Keith. 'It is so easy to be polite to people, and so advisable in some cases. How would you like to spend a week or two in gaol? He will have you there one of these days, unless you have placed him under some kind of obligation. He represents justice here. I know you don't like him. But what would it cost you – just a friendly handshake?'

'He cannot touch me. I have nothing on my conscience.'

'Conscience, my dear fellow, is a good servant but a bad master. Your sentiments are English. They will never do in a country where the personal element still counts for something.'

'The personal element signifying favouritism and venality?' asked Eames. 'A pretty state of affairs!'

'The philosopher can only live under a venal government.'

'I disagree with you altogether.'

'You always disagree with me,' answered Keith. 'And you always find yourself in the wrong. You remember how I warned you about that little affair of yours? You remember what an ass you made of yourself?'

'What little affair?' inquired Eames, with a tinge of resignation in his voice.

The other did not reply. Mr Keith could be tactful, on occasion. He pretended to be absorbed in cutting a cigar.

'What little affair?' insisted the bibliographer, fearful of what was coming next.

It came.

'Oh, that balloon business. ...'

It was not true to say of Mr Eames that he lived on Nepenthe because he was wanted by the London police for something that happened in Richmond Park, that his real name was not Eames at all but Daniels – the notorious Hodgson Daniels, you know, who was mixed up in the Lotus Club scandal, that he was the local representative of an international gang of white-slave traffickers who had affiliated offices in every part of the world, that he was not a man at all but an old boarding-house keeper who had very good reasons for assuming the male disguise, that he was a morphinomaniac, a disfrocked Baptist minister, a pawnbroker out of work, a fire-worshipper, a Transylvanian, a bank clerk who had had a fall, a decayed jockey who disgraced himself at a subsequent period in connexion with some East End mission for reforming the boys of Bermondsey and then, after pawning his mother's jewellery, writing anonymous threatening letters to society ladies about their husbands and vice-versa, trying to blackmail three Cabinet Ministers and tricking poor servant-girls out of their hard-earned wages by the sale of sham Bibles, was luckily run to earth in Piccadilly Circus, after an exciting chase, with a forty-pound salmon under his arm which he had been seen to lift from the window of a Bond Street fishmonger.

All these things, and a good many more, had been said. Eames knew it. Kind friends had seen to that.

To contrive such stories was a certain lady's method of asserting her personality on the island. She seldom went into society owing to some physical defect in her structure; she could only sit at home, like Penelope, weaving these and other bright tapestries – odds and ends of servants' gossip, patched together by the virulent industry of her own disordered imagination. It consoled Mr

80

Eames slightly to reflect that he was not the only resident singled out for such aspersions; that the more harmless a man's life, the more fearsome the legends. He suffered, none the less. This was why he seldom entered the premises of the Alpha and Omega Club, where, quite apart from his objection to Parker's poison and the loose and rowdy talk of the place, he was liable to encounter the lady's stepbrother. Of course he knew perfectly well what he ought to have done. He ought to have imitated the example of other people who behaved like scoundrels and openly gloried in it. That was the only way to be even with her; it took the wind out of her sails. Keith often put the matter into a nutshell:

'The practical advantages of doing something outrageous must be clear to you. It is the only way of stopping her mouth, unless you like to have her poisoned, which might be rather expensive even down here, though you may be sure I would do my best to smooth things over with Malipizzo. But I am afraid you don't realize the advantages of ruffianism as a mode of art and a mode of life. Only think: a thousand wrongs to every right! What an opening for a man of talent, especially in a country like this, where frank and independent action still counts its admirers. You have done nothing of late, worthy to be recorded in the *chronique scandaleuse* of Nepenthe. Twelve years ago, wasn't it, that little affair of yours? Time is slipping by, and here you muddle along with your old Perrelli, in a fog of moral stagnation. It is not fair to the rest of us. We all contribute our mites to the gaiety of nations. Bethink yourself. Bestir yourself. Man! Do something to show us you are alive.'

To such speeches Mr Eames would listen with a smile of amused indignation. He was incapable of living up to the ideals of a man like Keith, whose sympathy with every form of wrong-doing would have rendered him positively unfit for decent society but for his flagrant good nature and good luncheons. He suffered in silence.

He had good reason for suffering. That 'little affair' of twelve years ago was a ghost which refused to be laid. Everyone on the island knew the story; it was handed down from one batch of visitors to the next. He knew that wherever his name was mentioned this unique indiscretion of his, this toothsome morsel, would likewise be dished up. It would never grow stale, though atoned for by twelve years of exemplary conduct. He felt guilty. There was a skeleton in his cupboard. He realized what people were saying.

'Know Eames? Oh, yes. That quiet man, who writes. One can't

swallow half those yarns about him; quite impossible to believe, of course. She overdoes things, the good woman. All the same, there's no smoke without fire. You know what actually did happen, don't you? Well! one really doesn't quite know what to make of a fellow like that, does one?'

What had happened?

The bibliographer had fallen in love, after the fashion of a pure-minded, gallant gentleman. It was his first and only experience of this kind – an all-consuming passion which did much credit to his heart but little to his head. So deeply were his feelings involved that during those brief months of infatuation he neglected, he despised, he derided his idol Perrelli. He put on a new character. While the dust was accumulating on those piles of footnotes, Mr Eames astonished people by becoming a society man. It was a transfiguration. He appeared in fancy ties and spats, fluttered about at boating parties and picnics, dined at restaurants, perpetrated one or two classic jokes about the sirocco. Nepenthe opened its eyes wide till the truth was made manifest. After that, everybody said he might have discovered a worthier object for his affection than the *ballon captif*.

She was a native of the mainland to whose credit it must be said that she did not pretend to be anything but what she was – an exuberant, gluttonous dame, with volcanic eyes, heavy golden bracelets, the *soupçon* of a moustache, and arms as thick as other people's thighs: an altogether impossible person. Nobody but a man of genuine refinement, scrupulous rectitude, delicate sense of honour, and kindly disposition would have risked being seen in the same street with such a horror; nobody but a real gentleman could have fallen in love with her. Mr Eames ran after her like a dog. He made a perfect ass of himself, heedless of what anybody thought or said of him. The men declared he was going mad – breaking up – sickening for an attack of G.P. 'Miracles will never cease,' charitably observed the Duchess. Alone of all his lady acquaintances, Madame Steynlin liked him all the better for this gaucherie. She was a true woman – friend of all lovers; she knew the human heart and its queer little vagaries. She received the couple with open arms and entertained them royally, after her manner; gave them a kind of social status. Under this friendly treatment Mr Eames grew thinner from day to day; he was visibly losing flesh. The dame prospered. Piloted by the love-sick bibliographer, she gradually waddled her way – it was uphill work, for both of them – into the uppermost strata of local society, where, owing to the rarefied atmosphere, her appetite, to say nothing of her person, soon gained notoriety. She was known, in briefest space of time, as 'the cormorant', as 'prime streaky', as 'Jumbo', as 'the phenomenon', and, by those who understood the French language, as the '*ballon captif*'.

The '*ballon captif*'... How things got about on Nepenthe! Somehow or other, this odious nickname reached her lover's ears. It embittered his existence to such an extent that, long after the idyll was over, he had serious thoughts of leaving the island, and would doubtless have done so but for his rekindled enthusiasm for Monsignor Perrelli. So sensitive did he remain on this point that the mere mention of balloons, or even aeroplanes, would make him wince and feel desirous of leaving the room; he always thought that people introduced the subject with malicious purpose, in order to remind him of this unforgettable peccadillo, the 'balloon business', his one lapse from perfect propriety. Mr Keith, who confessed to a vein of coarseness in his nature, prided himself upon it and, in fact cultivated insensitiveness as other people cultivate orchids, pronouncing it to be the best method of self-protection in a world infested with fools – Mr Keith sometimes could not resist the temptation of raking up the ashes surreptitiously, after an elaborate, misleading preamble. He loved to watch his friend's meekly perplexed face on such occasions.

Heaven knows how long the affair might have lasted but for the fact that a husband, or somebody, unexpectedly turned up – a husky little man with a cast in one eye, who looked uxorious to an alarming degree. He carried her off in the nick of time to save Mr Eames from social ostracism, mental dotage, and financial ruin. Her mere appearance had made him the laughing-stock of the place; her appetite had led him into outlays altogether incompatible with his income, chiefly in the matter of pastries, macaroons, fondants, ices, caramels, chocolates, jam tartlets, and, above all, meringues, to which she was fabulously destructive.

It took some living down, that episode. He feared people would talk of it to his dying day; he knew they would! He wished balloons had never been invented. None the less he stuck it out bravely, threw himself with redoubled zeal into Monsignor Perrelli, and, incidentally, became more of a recluse than ever.

'It had been a lesson,' he reflected. '*Semper aliquid haerebit*, I am afraid. ...'

Ernest Eames was the ideal annotator. He was neither inductive nor deductive; he had no axe to grind. His talent consisted in an ant-like hiving faculty. He was acquisitive of information for a set purpose – to bring the *Antiquities* up to date. Whatever failed to fit in with this programme, however novel, however interesting – it was ruthlessly discarded. In this and other matters he was the reverse of Keith, who collected information for its own sake. Keith was a pertinacious and omnivorous student; he sought knowledge not for a set purpose but because nothing was without interest for him. He took all learning to his province. He read for the pleasure of knowing what he did not know before; his mind was unusually receptive because, he said, he respected the laws which governed his body. Facts were his prey. He threw himself into them with a kind of piratical ardour; took them by the throat, wallowed in them, worried them like a terrier, and finally assimilated them. They gave him food for what he liked best on earth: 'disinterested thought'. They 'formed a rich loam'. He had an encyclopaedic turn of mind; his head, as somebody once remarked, was a lumber-room of useless information. He could tell you how many public baths existed in Geneva in pre-Reformation days, what was the colour of Mehemet Ali's whiskers, why the manuscript of Virgil's friend Gallus had not been handed down to posterity, and in what year, and what month, the decimal system was introduced into Finland. Such aimless incursions into knowledge were a puzzle to his friends, but not to himself. They helped him to build up a harmonious scheme of life – to round himself off.

He had lately attacked, in Corsair fashion, the Greek philosophers and had disembowelled Plato, Aristotle, and the rest of them, to his complete satisfaction, in a couple of months; at present he was up to the ears in psychology, and his talk bristled with phrases about the 'function of the real', about reactions, reflexes, adjustments, and stimuli. For all his complexity there was something so childlike in his nature that he never realized what an infliction he was, nor how tiresome his conversation could become to people who were not quite so avid of 'disinterested thought'. Living alone and spending too much time in unprofitable studies, his language was apt to be professorially devoid of humour – a defect he made heroic efforts to remedy by what he called the 'Falernian system'. It was the fault of his mother, he said; she was a painfully conscientious woman. A man's worst enemies are his parents, he would add.

So far as was known, Mr Keith had never written a book, a pamphlet, or even a letter to the newspapers. He maintained a good deal of correspondence, however, in different parts of the world, and the wiser of those who were favoured with his epistles preserved them as literary curiosities, under lock and key, by reason of the writer's rare faculty of expressing the most atrocious things in correct and even admirable English. Chaster than snow as a conversationalist, he prostituted his mother-tongue, in letter-writing, to the vilest of uses. Friends of long standing called him an obscene old man. When taxed with this failing – by Mr Eames, for instance, who shivered at what he called *praetextata verba* – he would hint that he could afford to pay for his little whims, meaning, presumably, that a rich man is not to be judged by common standards of propriety. Such language was peculiarly galling to Mr Eames, who held that the possession of wealth entails not only privileges but obligations, and that the rich man should set the example of purity in words and deeds, etc. etc. etc.

They were always disagreeing, anyhow.

'You exalt purity to a bad eminence,' Keith would remark. 'What did you say about the book I lent you the other day? You said it was morbid and indecent; you said that no clean-minded person would care to read it. And yet, after an unnecessary amount of arguing, you were forced to admit that the subject was interesting and that the writer dealt with it in an interesting manner. What more can you expect from an author? Believe me, this hankering after purity, this hypersensitiveness as to what is morbid or immoral, is by no means a good sign. A healthy man refuses to be hampered by preconceived notions of what is wrong or ugly. When he reads a book like that he either yawns or laughs. That is because he is sure of himself. I could give you a long list of celebrated statesmen, princes, philosophers, and prelates of the Church who take pleasure, in their moments of relaxation, in what you would call improper conversation, literature, or correspondence. They feel the strain of being continually pure; they realize that all strains are pernicious, and that there is no action without its reaction. They unbend. Only invertebrate folks do not unbend. They dare not, because they have no backbone. They know that if they once unbent, they could not straighten themselves out again. They make a virtue of their own organic defect. They explain their natural imperfection by calling themselves pure. If you had a little money –'

'You are always harking back to that point. What has money to do with it?'

'Poverty is like rain. It drops down ceaselessly, disintegrating the finer tissues of a man, his recent, delicate adjustments, and leaving nothing but the bleak and gaunt framework. A poor man is a wintry tree – alive, but stripped of its shining splendour. He is always denying himself this or that. One by one, his humane instincts, his elegant desires, are starved away by stress of circumstance. The charming diversity of life ceases to have any meaning for him. To console himself, he sets up perverse canons of right and wrong. What the rich do, that is wrong. Why? Because he does not do it. Why not? Because he has no money. A poor man is forced into a hypocritical attitude towards life – debarred from being intellectually honest. He cannot pay for the necessary experience.'

'There is something in what you say,' Eames would assent. 'But I fear you are overstating your case.'

'So did Demosthenes and Jesus Christ, and likewise Cicero and Julius Caesar. Everybody overstates his case, particularly when he is anxious to do something which he considers useful. I regard it as a real grievance, Eames, not to be allowed to assist you financially. Having never done a stroke of work in my life, I can talk freely about my money. My grandfather was a pirate and slave-dealer. To my certain knowledge, not a penny of his wealth was honestly come by. That ought to allay your scruples about accepting it. *Non olet*, you know. Let me write you out a cheque for five hundred, there's a good fellow. Solely as a means of smoothing over the anfractuosities of life and squeezing all the possible pleasure out of it! What else is money made for? They say you live on milk and salad. Why the hell –'

'Thanks! I have all I want; sufficient to pay for the minor pleasures of life.'

'Such as?'

'A clean handkerchief now and then. I see no harm in dying poor.'

'Where would I be, if my grandfather had seen no harm in it? Don't you really believe that money sweetens all things, as Pepys says?'

The diarist was one of Keith's favourite authors. He called him a representative Englishman and regretted that the type was becoming extinct. Eames would reply:

'Your Pepys was a disgusting climber. He makes me ill with his snobbishness and silver plate and monthly gloatings over his gains. I wonder you can read the man. He may have been a capable official, but he was not a gentleman.'

'Have you ever seen a gentleman, except on a tailor's fashion plate?'

'Yes. One, at all events; my father. However, we won't labour that point; we have discussed it before, haven't we? Your money would sweeten nothing for me. It would procure me neither health of body nor peace of mind. Thanks all the same.'

Mr Keith, true to his ancestral tenacity, was not easily put off. He would begin again:

'George Gissing was a scholar and a man of refinement, like yourself. You know what he says? "Put money in thy purse, for to lack the current coin of the realm is to lack the privileges of humanity." The privileges of humanity: you understand, Eames?'

'Does he say that? Well, I am not surprised. I have sometimes noticed gross, unhealthy streaks in Gissing.'

'I will tell you what is unhealthy, Eames. Your own state of mind. You derive a morbid pleasure from denying yourself the common emoluments of life. It's a form of self-indulgence. I wish you would open your windows and let the sun in. You are living by candlelight. If you analysed yourself closely –'

'I don't analyse myself closely. I call it a mistake. I try to see soberly. I try to think logically. I try to live becomingly.'

'I am glad you don't always succeed,' Keith would reply, with a horrible accent on the word 'always'. 'Heaven shield me from a clean-minded man!'

'We have touched on that subject once or twice already, have we not? Your arguments will never entangle me, though I think I can be fair to them. Money enables you to multiply your sensations to travel about, and so forth. In doing so, you multiply your personality, as it were: you lengthen your days, figuratively speaking; you come in contact with more diversified aspects of life than a person of my limited means can afford to do. The body, you say, is a subtle instrument to be played upon in every variety of manner and rendered above all things as sensitive as possible to pleasurable impressions. In fact, you want to be a kind of Aeolian harp. I admit that this is more than a string of sophisms; you may call it a philosophy of life. But it is not my philosophy. It does not appeal to me in the least. You will get no satisfaction out of me, Keith, with your hedonism. You are up against a brick wall. You speak of my deliberately closing up avenues of pleasure. They ought to be closed up, I say, if a man is to respect himself. I do not call my body a subtle instrument; I call it a damned nuisance. I don't want to be an Aeolian harp. I don't want my sensations multiplied; I don't want my personality extended; I don't want my outlook widened; I don't want money; I don't want aspects of life. I'm positive, I'm literal. I know exactly what I want. I want to concern myself with what lies under my hand. I want to be allowed to get on with my work. I want to bring old Perrelli up to date.'

'My dear fellow! We all love you for that. And I am delighted

87

to think you are not really clean-minded, in spite of all these lofty protestations. Because you aren't, are you?'

If, after such discourse, the bibliographer still remained mulishly clean-minded, Keith would return to the psychological necessity of 'appropriate reaction' and cite an endless list of sovereigns, popes, and other heroes who, in their moments of leisure, were wise enough to react against the persistent strain of purity. Then, *via* Alexander of Macedon, 'one of the greatest sons of earth', as Bishop Thirlwall had called him – Alexander, with whose deplorable capacity for 'unbending' a scholar like Eames was perfectly familiar – he would switch the conversation into realms of military science, and begin to expatiate upon the wonderful advance which has been made since those days in the arts of defensive and offensive warfare – the decline of the phalanx, the rise of artillery, the changed system of fortifications, those modern inventions in the department of land defences, sea defences, and, above all, aerial defences, parachutes, hydroplanes. ...

Whereupon a curious change would creep over the bibliographer's honest face. He knew what this talk portended. His features would assume an air of strained but polite attention, and he generally broke off the conversation and took his departure at the earliest moment consistent with ordinary civility. On such occasions he was wont to think his friend Keith an offensive cad. Sadly shaking his head, he would say to himself:

'*Nihil quod tetigit non inquinavit.*'

CHAPTER 10

MR KEITH was apt to be a bore, but he could do things properly when he wanted, as for example on the occasion of his annual bean-feast. There were no two opinions about that. The trees, arbours, and winding ways of his garden were festooned that evening with hundreds of Chinese lamps whose multi-coloured light mingled pleasingly with the purer radiance of the moon, shining directly overhead. It was like fairyland, the Duchess was wont to declare, year after year. And Don Francesco, who, on this particular night, clung closely to her skirts in view of that impending conversion to the Roman Church, replied laughingly:

'If fairyland is anything like this, I would not object to living there. Provided always, dear lady, that you are to be found somewhere on the premises. What do you say, Mr Heard?'

'I will gladly join your party, if you will allow me,' replied the bishop. 'This aspic could not be better. It seems to open up a new world of delights. Dear me, I fear I am becoming a gourmand, like Lucullus. Though Lucullus, to be sure, was a temperate man. No, thank you, Don Francesco; not a drop more! My liver, you know. I declare it's making me feel quite dizzy.'

As Marten had foretold, the wine flowed in torrents. There was a bewildering display of cold dishes, too, prepared under the personal supervision of the chef – that celebrated artist whom Keith had inveigled out of the service of a life-loving old Ambassador by the threat of disclosing to the police some hideously disreputable action in the man's past life which His Excellency had artlessly confided to him, under the seal of secrecy.

Mr Samuel, a commercial gentleman who had got stuck somehow or other at the Alpha and Omega Club, cast a practised eye over the wines, chaud-froids, fruits, salads, ices, the lanterns, and other joys of the evening and announced, after a rough computation, that Keith's outlay for that little show must have run well into three figures. Mr White agreed, adding that it did one good to get a mouthful of drinkable fizz after Parker's poison.

'Ah, but you ought to try the punch.'

'Come on, then,' said White.

They moved away and soon stumbled upon a cluster of bibulous mortals in their element. Miss Wilberforce was there. She liked to linger near the fountain-head; the fountain-head, on this occasion, being a cyclopean bowl of iced punch. The lady was in grand condition; festive, playful, positively flirtatious. She nibbled, between her libations, at a savoury biscuit (she hated solid food, as a rule) in order, she said, to staunch her thirst; she told everybody that it was her birthday. Yes, her birthday! In fact, she was quite a different creature from the bashful visitor at the Duchess's entertainment; she was hardly shy at all.

'Punch and moonlight!' she was saying. 'It's all as right as rain – birthday or no birthday.'

Miss Wilberforce had about forty birthdays in the year, each of them due to be worthily celebrated like this one.

It was a sad and scandalous business. Better things might have been expected of her. She was so obviously a lady. She had been so nicely brought up. While there was still an English Church on the island, she never failed to attend Divine Service, despite her Sunday headache. She was often the only member of the congregation – she and Mr Freddy Parker, whose official dignity and English origin, however questionable his Christianity, constrained him to put in an appearance. Mortal enemies, they used to sit in opposite pews, glaring across the vacant building to see if they could catch each other asleep, responding at irregular intervals out of sheer cussedness, and trying vainly to feel more charitable during those moments when the scraggy young curate – generally some social failure who raked together a few pounds from these hazardous continental engagements – recited the Gospel according to St John. Those days were over. She was definitely on the downward grade. Three members of the Club and two Russian apostles were even then engaged in tossing up who should have the privilege of seeing her home. The lot fell to Mr Richards, the excellent Vice-President, an elderly gentleman whose carefully parted hair and flowing beard made him the very picture of respectability. To look at him, one would have said that the dear lady could not be in better hands.

Mr Keith was a perfect host. He had the right word for everybody; his infectious conviviality made them all straightway at their ease. The overdressed native ladies, the priests and officials moving about in prim little circles, were charmed with his affable manner, 'so different from most Englishmen'; likewise that flock of gleeful tourists who had suddenly turned up, craving for admission without a single letter of introduction between them, and were forthwith welcomed on the strength of the fact that one of their party had been to Easter Island. Even the *parroco* could not help laughing as Keith, with irresistible good nature, seized him by the arm and thrust a *marron glacé* between his lips. An ideal host! The 'Falernian system' was in abeyance that day. It was the one evening in the year when, in the interests of his guests, he could be relied upon to remain absolutely sober to the last moment; a state of affairs which doubtless had its drawbacks, seeing that it made him, in longer conversational efforts, rather more abstruse and unintelligible than usual – 'blind sober', as Don Francesco once said. Even sobriety was forgiven him. He took the precaution, of course, to keep the house locked and to replace his ordinary services of plate by Elkington; people being pardonably fond of carrying away mementoes of so enjoyable an evening. Bottles, plates, and glasses were smashed by the dozen. He liked to see them smashed. It proved that everybody was having a good time.

A person unacquainted with Keith's nature could never have guessed what a sacrifice this entertainment was to him. He was an egoist, a solitary, in his pleasures; he used to contend that no garden on earth, however spacious, was large enough for more than one man. And this little Nepenthe domain, though he saw it for only a few weeks in the year, was the apple of his eye. He guarded it jealously, troubled at the thought that its chaste recesses might be profaned, if but for one day, by the presence of a motley assemblage of nonentities. But a man of his income is expected to do something to amuse his fellow-creatures. One owes certain duties to society. Hence this gathering, which had become a regular feature in the spring calendar of the island. Having once decided on the step, he did not propose to be bound by conventionalities which were the poison of rational human intercourse. Unlike the Duchess and Mr Parker, he refused to draw the line at Russians; the Club, too, was represented by some of its most characteristic members. He often descanted on the social intolerance of men, their lack of graciousness and generous instincts; he would have made room for the devil himself – at all events in his 'outer circle'. Such being the case, it stands to reason that he did not draw the line at free-thinkers. It was sometimes rather hard to know where he did draw the line.

The red-haired judge, with straw hat and Mephistophelean limp, was there, looking like an Offenbach villain out for a spree. After being effusively greeted by the host – they understood one another perfectly – and forced to eat a quantity of some pink-looking stuff which he could not resist although knowing it would disagree with him, His Worship, left to his own devices, hobbled along in pursuit of his new friend Muhlen. He found him, and was soon relating succulent anecdotes of his summer holidays – anecdotes, all about women, which Muhlen tried to cap with experiences of his own. The judge always went to the same place – Salsomaggiore, a thermal station whose waters were good for his sore legs. He described to Muhlen how, in jaunty clothes and shining shoes, he pottered about its trim gardens, ogling the ladies, who always ogled back; it was the best fun in the world, and sometimes –! Mr Malipizzo, for all his incredible repulsiveness, posed as an ardent and successful lover of women. No doubt it cost money. But he was never at a loss for that commodity; he had other sources of revenue, he hinted, beside his wretched official salary.

Wandering along arm in arm, they passed various contingents of the Russians, male and female, whose scarlet blouses shone brightly under the variegated globes of light. These exotics were happy as children, full of fun and laughter; none more so than the young giant Krasnojabkin, whose name had been coupled by scandal-mongers with that of Madame Steynlin. An admiring audience had gathered around him while he performed a frenzied cancan in an open moonlit space; he always danced when he had enough to drink. The judge looked on with envy. It sickened him to realize that those far-famed luncheons and dinners of Madame Steynlin were being devoured by a savage like this. And the money he doubtless extracted from her! Presently a loud guffaw from some bosky thicket announced that the friends had been joined by the Financial Commissioner for Nicaragua. The Trinity was complete. They were always together, those three, playing cards at the Club or sipping lemonade and vermouth on the terrace.

'Oh, Mr Keith,' said the Duchess in her sweetest accents, 'do you know what this entertainment makes me think?'

'Shall I guess?'

'Nothing of the kind! It makes me think that it is very, very wrong of a man like you to be a bachelor. You want a wife.'

'To want a wife, Duchess, is better than to need one. Especially if it happens to be only your neighbour's.'

'I am sure that means something dreadful!'

Don Francesco broke in:

'Tell me, Keith, how about your wives? What have you done with them? Is it true that you sold them at various Oriental ports?'

'They got mislaid, somehow. All that was before my Great Renunciation.'

'Is it true that you kept them locked up in different parts of London?'

'I made it a rule never to introduce my lady-friends to one another. They are so fond of comparing notes. Novelists try to make us believe that women delight in men's society. Rubbish! They prefer that of their own sex. But please don't refer to the most painful period of my life.'

The priest insisted:

'Is it true that you gave the plumpest of them to the Sultan of Colambarg in exchange for the recipe of some wonderful sauce? Is it true that you used to be known as the Lightning Lover? Is it true that you used to say, in your London days, that no season was complete without a ruined home?'

'She exaggerates a good deal, that lady.'

'Is it true that you once got so drunk that you mistook one of those red-coated Chelsea pensioners for a pillar-box and tried to post a letter in his stomach?'

'I'm very short-sighted, Don Francesco. Besides, all that was in a previous incarnation. Do come and listen to the music! May I offer you my arm, Duchess? I have a surprise for you.'

'You have a surprise for us every year, you bad man,' she said.

92

'Now do try and see if you can't get married. It makes one feel so good.'

Keith had a peculiar habit of vanishing for a day or two to the mainland, and returning with some rare orchid from the hills, a piece of Greek statuary, a new gardener, or something. Sowing his wild oats, he called it. During this last visit he had come across the tracks of an almost extinct tribe of gipsies that roamed up and down the glens of those mysterious mountains whose purple summits were visible, on clear days, from his own windows. After complex and costly negotiations they had allowed themselves to be embarked, for this one night only, in a capacious sailing-boat to Nepenthe, in order to pleasure Mr Keith's guests. And here they sat, huddled together in dignified repose and abashed, as it seemed, by the strangeness of their surroundings; a bizarre group stained to an almost negro tint by exposure to sun and winds and rain.

Here they sat – gnarled old men and sinewy fathers of families, with streaming black hair, golden earrings, hooded cloaks of wool, and sandals bound with leathern thongs. Mothers were there, shapeless bundles of rags, nursing infants at the breast. The girls were draped in gaudy hues, and ablaze with metal charms and ornaments on forehead and arms and ankles. They showed their flashing teeth and smiled from time to time in frank wonder, whereas the boys, superbly savage, like young panthers caught in a trap, kept their eyes downcast or threw distrustful, defiant glances round them. Here they sat in silence, smoking tobacco and taking deep draughts out of a pitcher of milk which was handed round from one to the other. Occasionally the older people would pick up their instruments – bagpipes of sheepskin, small drums, and gourd-like mandolines – and draw from them strange dronings, gurglings, thrummings, twangings; soon a group of youngsters would rise gravely from the ground and, without any preconcerted signal, begin to move in a dance – a formal and intricate measure, such as had never yet been witnessed on Nepenthe.

Something inhuman and yet troublingly personal lay in the performance; it invaded the onlookers with a sense of disquietude. There was primeval ecstasy in those strains and gestures. Giant moths, meanwhile, fluttered overhead, rattling their frail wings against the framework of the paper lanterns; the south wind passed through the garden like the breath of a friend, bearing the aromatic burden of a thousand night-blooming shrubs and flowers. Young people, meeting here, would greet one another shyly, with unfamiliar ceremoniousness, and then, after listening awhile to the music and exchanging a few awkward phrases, wander

93

away as if by common consent – further away from this crowd and garish brilliance, far away, into some fragrant dell, where the light was dim.

'What do you make of it?' asked Keith of Madame Steynlin, who was listening intently. 'Is this music? If so, I begin to understand its laws. They are physical. I seem to feel the effect of it in the lower part of my chest. Perhaps that is the region which musical people call their ear. Tell me, Madame Steynlin, what is music?'

'That's a puzzle,' said the bishop, greatly interested.

'How can I explain it to you? It is so complicated, and you have so many guests this evening. You are coming to my picnic after the festival of Saint Eulalia? Yes? Well, I will try to explain it then' – and her eye turned, with a kind of maternal solicitude, down the pathway to where, in that patch of bright moonshine, her young friend Krasnojabkin, gloriously indifferent to gipsies and everything else, was astounding people by the audacity of his terpsichorean antics.

'Let that be a promise,' Keith replied. 'Ah, Count Caloveglia! How good of you to come! I would not have asked you to such a worldly function had I not thought that this dancing might interest you.'

'It does, it does!' said the old aristocrat, thoughtfully sipping champagne out of an enormous goblet which he carried in his hand. 'It makes me dream of that East which it has never been my fortune, alas, to behold. What a flawless group! There is something archaic, Oriental, in their attitudes; they seem to be fraught with all the mystery, the sadness, of life that is past – of things remote from ourselves.'

'My gipsies,' said Keith, 'are not everybody's gipsies.'

'I think they despise us! And this austere regularity in the steps of the dancers, this vibrating accompaniment that dwells persistently on one note – how primitive, how scornfully unintellectual! It is like a passionate lover knocking to gain an entrance into our hearts. And he succeeds. He breaks down the barrier by the oldest and best of lovers' expedients – sheer reiteration of monotony. A lover who reasons is no lover.'

'How true that is,' remarked Madame Steynlin.

'Sheer monotony,' repeated the Count. 'And it is the same with their pictorial art. We blame the Orientals for their chill cult of geometrical designs, their purely stylistic decoration, their endless repetitions, as opposed to our variety and love of floral, human, or other naturalistic motives. But by this simple means they attain

94

their end – a direct appeal. Their art, like their music, goes straight to the senses; it is not deflected or disturbed by any intervening medium. Colour plays its part; the sombre, throbbing sounds of these instruments – the glowing tints of their carpets and tapestries. Talking of gipsies, do you know whether our friend van Koppen has arrived?'

'Koppen? A very up-to-date nomad, who takes the whole world for his camping-ground. No, not yet. But he'll turn up in a day or two.'

Count Caloveglia was concerned, just then, about Mr van Koppen. He had a little business to transact with him – he fervently hoped that the millionaire would not forgo his annual visit to Nepenthe.

'I shall be glad to meet him again,' he remarked carelessly. Then looking up he saw Denis, who moved under the trees alone. Observing that he seemed rather disconsolate, he walked up to him and said in a fatherly tone: 'Will you confer a favour, Mr Denis, on an old man who lives much alone? Will you come and see me, as you promised? My daughter is away just now and will not be back till midsummer. I wish you could have met her. Meanwhile, I am a little solitary. I have also a few antiquities that might interest you.'

While Denis, slightly embarrassed, was uttering some appropriate words, the bishop suddenly asked:

'Where is Mrs Meadows? Wasn't she coming down tonight?'

'Of course she was,' said Keith. 'Isn't she here? What can this mean? Your cousin is a particular friend of mine, Heard, though I have not seen her for the last six days or so. Something must be wrong. That baby, I expect.'

'I missed her once already,' said Heard. 'I'll write and make an appointment, or go up again. By the way, Count – you remember our conversation? Well, I have thought of an insuperable objection to your Mediterranean theory. The sirocco. You will never change the sirocco. The Elect of the Earth will never endure it all their lives.'

'I think we can change the sirocco,' replied the Count, meditatively. 'We can tame it, at all events. I do not know much about its history; you must ask Mr Eames –'

'Who is at home,' interrupted Keith, 'closeted with his Perrelli.'

'What has been, may be,' continued the old man, oracularly. 'I question whether the sirocco was as obnoxious in olden days as now, otherwise the ancients, who had absurdly sensitive skins,

95

would have complained of it more frequently. The deforestation of Northern Africa, I suspect, has much to do with it. Frenchmen are now trying to revive those prosperous conditions which Mohammedanism has destroyed. Oh, yes! I don't despair of muzzling the sirocco, even as we are muzzling that other Mediterranean pest, the malaria.'

Keith observed:

'Petronius, I remember, speaks of the North wind being the mistress of the Tyrrhenian. He would not use such language nowadays, unless alluding to its violence rather than its prevalence. Once I thought of translating Petronius. But I discovered certain passages in the book which are almost improper. I don't think the public ought to be put into possession of such stuff. I am rather sorry; I like Petronius – the poetical fragments, I mean; they make me regret that I was not born under the Roman Empire. People are leaving,' he added. 'I have said good-bye to about fifty. I shall be able to get a drink soon.'

'So you were born out of time and out of place, like many of us,' laughed the bishop.

Count Caloveglia said:

'It is an academic problem, and therefore a problem which does not exist for me, and therefore, Keith, a problem dear to your own metaphysical heart, to inquire whether a man is ever born at an inopportune moment. We use the phrase. If we took thought we would discard it. For what is the truth of the matter? The truth is that a man of whom we say this is born at exactly the right moment; that those with whose customs and aspirations he seems to be in discord have urgent need of him at that particular time. No great man is ever born too soon or too late. When we say that the time is not ripe for this or that celebrity, we confess by implication that this very man, and no other, is required. Was Giordano Bruno, or Edgar Poe, born out of time? Surely no generation needed them more imperiously than their own. Only fools are born out of time. And yet – no; not even they. For where should we be without them?'

He smiled suavely, as though some pleasant thought was passing through his mind.

'At any rate a good many people die too soon or too late,' said Mr Edgar Marten, who, after doing full justice to the food and drinks, had suddenly appeared on the scene. 'Often too late,' he added.

Keith, despite his professions of sanity and reason, had an inexplicable, invincible horror of death; he quailed at the mere

96

mention of the black phantom. The subject being not at all to his taste, he promptly remarked:

'The scholar Grosseteste was unquestionably born too soon. And I know one man who is born too late. Who? Yourself, Count. You were made for the Periclean epoch.'

'Thank you,' said that gentleman with a gracious wave of his hand. 'But forgive me for disagreeing with you. Had I lived in that age, I should be lacking in reverence for what it accomplished. I should be too near to its life; unable, as you say, to see the forest for the trees. I should be like Thucydides, a most sensible person who, if I recollect aright, barely mentions Ictinus and the rest of them. How came it about? This admirable writer imagined they were building a temple for Greece; he lacked the interval of centuries which has allowed mankind to see their work in its true perspective. He possessed traditional moral standards whereby to judge the actions of historical contemporaries; he could praise or blame his politicians with a good conscience. For the Parthenon creators he had no sure norm. The standards were not yet evolved. Pheidias was a talented fellow-citizen – a hewer in stone by profession; what could he know of the relations of Pheidias to posterity? Great things can only be seen at a proper distance. Pheidias, to him, may have been little more than an amateur, struggling with brute material in the infancy of his trade or calling. No, my friend! I am glad not to be coeval with Pericles. I am glad to recognize Hellenic achievements at their true worth. I am glad to profit by that wedge of time which has enabled me to reverence things fair and eternal.'

'Things fair and eternal,' echoed Keith, who was getting too thirsty and restless to discuss art matters. 'Come with me! I will show you things fair and eternal.'

He led the way to a distant arbour, overhung with a canopy of blood-red passion-flowers and girt about by their crimson blossoms. A lighted lantern of grotesque design dangled from the clustering foliage in its roof. Within, directly under the beams, all by itself, on an upright chair beside a small table, sat an incongruous, startling, awe-inspiring apparition – a grimy old man of Mongolian aspect. He might have been frozen to stone; so immobile, so lifeless were his features. Belated visitors passed near the entrance of the shrine, peered within as at some outlandish and sinister freak of nature, and moved on with jocular words. Nobody ventured to overstep the threshold, whether from religious fear or because of something repellent, something almost putrescent, which radiated from his person. A contingent of Little White

97

Cows, a kind of bodyguard, stood at a respectful distance beyond, intent upon his every movement. The Master never stirred. He sat there to be looked at – accustomed to homage almost divine; beatifically inane. Like the Christians of old, he wore no hat. The head was nearly bald. A long cloak, glistening with grease-stains, swathed his limbs and portly belly, on which one suspected multitudinous wrinkles of fat. Two filmy lidless eyes, bulging on a level with his forehead, stared into vacuity; his snub nose grew out of a flattened face whose pallor was accentuated by the reflection of the glittering leaves – it looked faded and sodden, like blotting-paper that has been left out all night in the rain. Sporadic greenish-grey hairs were scattered about his chin. The mouth was agape.

On Mr Keith's appearance he made no sign of recognition. Presently, however, his lips seemed to get out of control. They moved; they began to chatter and to mumble, in childish fashion, the inarticulate yearnings of eld, Keith said, as though displaying some museum curiosity:

'Mine is the only house on Nepenthe which the Master still deigns to enter. I'm afraid he has grown very groggy on his pins of late; if he sat on any but a straight-backed chair they would never get him up again. To think that was once a pretty little boy. ... Poor old fellow! I know what he wants. They've been neglecting him, those young idiots.'

He departed, and soon returned with a tumbler full of raw whisky, which he placed on the table within reach of the arm. A flaccid, unwholesome-looking hand was raised slowly, in a kind of deprecatory gesture; then allowed to fall again upon the belly, where it lay, with the five fingers, round and chalky-white, extended like the rays of a starfish. Nothing more happened.

'We must go away for a while,' said Keith, 'or else he won't touch it. He does not object to alcohol, you know. Whisky has not come out of a warm-blooded beast. But it's going into one. A kind of Asiatic Socrates, don't you think?'

'A Buddha,' suggested the Count. 'A Buddha in second-rate alabaster. A Chinese Buddha of a bad, realistic period.'

'It's odd,' remarked Mr Heard. 'He reminds me of a dead fish. Something ancient and fishlike – it's that mouth –'

'He's a beauty!' interrupted Edgar Marten, sniffing with disgust. 'Eyes like a boiled haddock. And that thing has the cheek to call itself a Messiah. Thank God I'm a Jew; it's no business of mine. But if I were a Christian, I'd bash his blooming head in. Damned if I wouldn't. The frowsy, fetid, fly-blown fraud. Or what's the matter with the Dogs' Home?'

'Come, come,' said Mr Heard, who had taken rather a liking to this violent youngster and was feeling more than usually indulgent that evening. 'Come! He can't help his face, I fancy. Have you no room in your heart for an original? And don't you think – quite apart from questions of religion – that we tourists ought to be grateful to these people for diversifying the landscape with their picturesque red blouses and things?'

'I have no eye for landscape, Mr Heard, save in so far as it indicates strata and faults and other geological points. The picturesque don't interest me. I am full of Old Testamentary strains; I can't help looking at men from the ethical point of view. And what have people's clothes to do with their religion? He can't help his face, you say. Well, if he can't help that greasy old mackintosh, I'll eat my hat. Can't a fellow be a Messiah without sporting a pink shirt or fancy dressing-gown or blue pyjamas or something? But there you are! I defy you to name me a single-barrelled crank. If a man is a religious lunatic, or a vegetarian, he is sure to be touched in some other department as well; he will be an anti-vivisectionist, a nutfooder, costume-maniac, stamp-collector, or a spiritualist into the bargain. Haven't you ever noticed that? And isn't he dirty? Where is the connexion between piety and dirt? I suggest they are both relapses into ancestral channels and the one drags the other along with it. When I see a thing like this, I want to hew it in pieces. Agag, Mr Heard; Agag. I must have another look at this specimen; one does not see such a sight every day. He is a living fossil – post-pleistocene.'

He drew off; Keith and the Count, engaged in some deep conversation, had also moved a few paces away.

Mr Heard stood alone, his back turned to the Master. Moonlight still flooded the earth, the lanterns were flickering and sputtering. Some had gone out, leaving gaps of darkness in the lighted walks. Many of the guests retired without bidding farewell to their host; he liked them to feel at their ease, to take 'French leave' whenever so disposed – to depart à l'anglaise, as the French say. The garden was nearly empty. A great quietude had fallen upon its paths and thickets. From afar resounded the boisterous chorus of a party of revellers loth to quit the scene; it was suddenly broken by a terrific crash and bursts of laughter. Some table had been knocked over.

Standing there, the bishop could not but listen to Keith, who had raised his voice in emphasis and was saying to the Count, in his best Keithean manner:

'I am just coming to that point. A spring-board is what humanity
99

needs. What better one can be contrived than this pure, unadulterated Byzantinism? Cretinism, I call it. Look at the Orthodox Church. A repository of apocalyptic nonsense such as no sane man can take seriously. Nonsense of the right kind, the uncompromising kind. That is my point. The paralysing, sterilizing cult of these people offers a far better spring-board into a clean element of thought than our English Church, whose *demi-vierge* concessions to common sense afford seductive resting-places to the intellectually weak-kneed. Do I make myself clear? I'm getting infernally thirsty.'

'I quite agree with you, my friend. The Russians have got a better spring-board than the English. The queer thing is, that the Russian won't jump, whereas the Englishman often does. Well, well! We cannot live without fools.'

Mr Heard was slightly perturbed by these words. A good fellow like Keith! '*Demi-vierge* concessions to common sense': what did he mean by that? Did his Church really make such concessions?

'I'll think about it tomorrow,' he decided.

The Master, when they returned to him, had not budged from his resting-place. The fingers still lay, starfish-wise, upon the folds of that soiled homespun; his eyes still stared out of the leafy bower; his face still wore its mask of placid imbecility.

The glass was empty.

Slowly, as on a pivot, his head turned in the direction of the bodyguard.

Forthwith some favourite disciple – not Krasnojabkin, who happened to be escorting Madame Steynlin to her villa just then – darted to his side; with the help of two lady-apostles known, respectively, as the 'goldfinch' and the 'red apple', they conveyed him out of that shelter into the deserted, moonlit garden. He leaned heavily on the arm of the youth; peevish sounds, quasi-human, proceeded from his colourless lips. And now he was almost speaking; desirous, it seemed, of formulating some truth too deep for human utterance.

'I bet I know what he is saying,' whispered Keith. 'It's something about the Man-God.'

CHAPTER 11

THE Russian Government is notoriously tender-hearted. But even the worm will turn. ...

Scholars who have treated of the life of the ex-monk Bazhakuloff, divide it into five clearly marked periods: the probationary, dialectical, political, illumined, and expiatory.

The first began in youth when, being driven from his father's house by reason of his vagrant habits and other incorrigible vices, he entered a monastery near Kazan. Despite occasional lapses prompted by the hot blood of his years and punished with harsh disciplinary measures, he seems to have performed his monkish duties with sufficient zeal. It was observed, however, that with increasing years he became unduly interested in questions of dogma. He talked too freely; he was always arguing. Being unable to read or write, he developed an astonishing memory for things he had heard and faces he had seen; he brought them up at inconvenient moments. He grew factious, obstreperous, declaring that there was much in the constitution of the Holy Russian Church which ought to be amended and brought up to date. What people wanted, he said, was a New Jerusalem. A violent altercation with his Superior touching the attributes of the Holy Ghost ended in a broken jaw-bone on the part of the older man, and the expulsion of the younger. The dialectical period had set in. The convent inmates, on the whole, were glad to see the last of him – particularly the Father Superior.

We next find him living in a large barn about fifteen miles from Moscow. The Superior being unwilling to publish the true facts of the broken jaw-bone, a certain fame, the fame of an earnest but misunderstood religious innovator, had preceded him. Adherents, barely twenty at first, gathered to his side. These disciples, humble analphabetics like himself, have left us no record of what passed at those long discussions. Certain it is that he now began to formulate the rules of his Revised Church. They were to live on charity, to go bare-headed, and to wear red blouses – like the Christians of old. The charm of these simple regulations spread abroad, and gained him fresh recruits. There were now some cultured folk among them, who collected his sayings into the *Golden Book*. He decided to limit his disciples to the 'Sacred Number 63', and to call them 'Little White Cows'. Asked why he chose this title, he answered that cows were pure and useful animals without which humanity could not live; even so were his disciples. The innate good sense of this speech increased his reputation. About this time, too, he would sometimes prophesy, and undergo long periods of motionless self-abstraction. At the end of one of these latter, after tasting no food or drink for three and a half hours, he gave utterance to what was afterwards known as the First Revelation. It ran to this effect: 'The Man-God is the Man-God, and not

101

the God-Man.' Asked how he arrived at so stupendous an aphorism, he answered that it just came to him. There were troubles in the neighbourhood over the audacity of this utterance; some called it a divine inspiration, to the majority it was known as the Unnamable Heresy. For a brief while the town was formed into two camps, and the Chief of Police, a prudent official, was at his wits' end what to do with these inflammable elements, seeing that the ex-monk's followers had now swelled to several hundreds and contained not a few of the more influential aristocrats of the city. In this dilemma, he applied for instruction to the Procurator of the Holy Synod. That gentleman, having considered the case, rashly decided that a visionary of this stamp might be useful for furthering certain projects of his own. He hoped, by placing him under an obligation, to fashion out of the young reformer an amenable instrument – a miscalculation which he lived (though not for long) to repent. Under the Procurator's aegis, Bazhakuloff was summoned to the Capital. The political period was beginning. Moscow, on the whole, was glad to see the last of him – particularly the Chief of Police.

There began the most brilliant epoch of his life. By steps which it is needless to trace, he fought and wormed his way into the favour of the Court. A good deal of his worldly success may well have been due, as his enemies assert, to an incredible mixture of cringing, astuteness, and impudence. It stands to reason, however, that a man of this type must have possessed sterling qualities of his own to be found occupying – all this was years and years ago – a suite of apartments in the Palace, where he lived in splendour, a Power behind the Throne, the Confidential Adviser of the Highest Circles. His monkish garb was soon encrusted with orders and decorations, no State function was complete without his presence, no official appointment, from the highest to the lowest sphere of government, was held to be valid without his sanction. Red blouses, one of several keys to his favour, could be counted by thousands. He crushed opposition with an iron hand. He wrought a miracle or two; but what chiefly accounted for the almost divine veneration in which he was held was a succession of lucky prophecies – none luckier than that wherein, during one of his moments of inspired self-abstraction, he foretold the early and violent death of his former protector, the man to whom he owed this rise to the pinnacles of fame. For even so it fell out. Not many day later the Procurator of the Holy Synod was found murdered in bed by an unknown hand. A certain journalist, writing from Switzerland, boldly states that the Procurator was murdered at the instigation of Bazhakuloff and claims to have heard, from an eye-witness whom he does not name, of a bitter quarrel between the two on the subject of a certain lady as to whose identity we are also left in doubt. It may be true; such things have happened ere now. This particular writer's credibility, however, is none of the best; he has been convicted over and over again of forcing the note in his diatribes against what he calls 'retrogression into idolatry'. There was certainly a good deal of unrest in the country during the period of the ex-monk's ascendency; no less than 13,783 persons had been banished to Siberia, and 3,756 executed at his orders. Yet nothing, it seemed, could shatter his position when, with appalling suddenness, a thunderbolt descended. Nobody knows to this day what took place. It was something Russian; some scandal in the Highest Spheres which may see the light of day, centuries hence, when the Imperial Archives are disclosed as musty Court history to the eyes of students curious in such matters. At this crisis, when 44,323 persons, mostly liberals, were awaiting trial in the prisons of the capital, the ex-monk would doubtless have been quietly removed after the fashion of Court favourites, had not his adherents, now numbering many hundred thousands, threatened a revolution. A secret compromise was effected. He was banished, with every outward mark of disgrace, to a monastery in the remote and inhospitable region of Viatka, there to meditate upon the instability of human affairs. The illumined period was drawing nigh. The Capital, on the whole, was glad to see the last of him – particularly the prisoners awaiting trial.

The diet and discipline nearly killed him at first. He was consoled by knowing that his fame had spread far and wide. The Court being unwilling to publish the true facts of his disgrace, he was regarded as a martyr, a victim of political intrigue, an injured saint. Disciples multiplied. The *Golden Book* was filled with priceless sayings – wise and salutary maxims which echoed from end to end of the country. The New Jerusalem took on a definite shape; the nucleus of the movement, the initiated among his followers, were retained as the 'Sacred 63'; he called them his apostles and himself their Messiah, which some people thought rather presumptuous of him. His reputation for sanctity became such that he was once more a power to be reckoned with; the Court, in fact, was on the verge of receiving him into favour again, when the Second Revelation was announced. It ran to this effect: Flesh and blood of warm-blooded beasts is Abomination to Little White Cows. Asked how he contrived to formulate so novel and tremendous a proposition, he answered that it just came to him. His

103

followers – there were about three million of them now – instantly refused to touch the Unclean Thing, and all would have gone well but for the fact that the Army was tinctured with the New Faith, and that the Grand Dukes had recently become involved in extensive and lucrative contracts for supplying the troops with meat. The soldiery refusing to eat either beef or mutton or pork, percentages declined. These leaders took up a firm patriotic attitude. The health and morale of the entire army, they declared, were dependent upon a sound nutritive diet obtainable only through the operation of certain radio-active oxydized magneto-carbon-hydrates which exist nowhere save in the muscular tissue of animals. This new heresy endangered the very foundations of Empire!

They were not people to compromise where questions of national prosperity were concerned. They suggested, privately, that he should cancel his Revelation. He refused. They then sent him a confidential messenger offering the choice of assassination or deportation within the space of three hours. He inclined to the latter alternative, and was straightway conveyed to the frontier by special train with as many rouble notes in his pocket as he had been able to scrape together in the flurry of departure. Some disturbances broke out when the news of his banishment became known; a few whiffs of grapeshot worked wonders. The majority of his adherents abjured their error; the rest of them, aided by charitable contributions from a secret committee of enthusiasts, found their way abroad to dwell under the shadow of the banished Messiah. The expiatory period was approaching. Russia, on the whole, was glad to see the last of him – particularly the Grand Ducal party.

A broken man, he decided to establish himself on Nepenthe, drawn thither partly on account of the climate but chiefly by the report of its abounding lobsters and fishes, an article of diet of which he was inordinately fond. Disciples followed singly, and in batches. Their scarlet blouses became a familiar object in the streets of the place; good-natured and harmless folks for the most part who, if they ran up bills with the local tradespeople which they failed to pay, did so not out of natural dishonesty, but because they had no money. They used to bathe, in summer-time, at a certain little cove near the foot of the promontory on which Madame Steynlin's villa was situated. She watched their naked antics at first with disapproval – what could you expect, she would say, from Russians? Then she observed them eating raw crabs and things. It struck her that they must be hungry. Being a lady of the sentimental type, childless, and never so happy as when feeding or mothering somebody, she took to sending them down baskets of

104

food or carrying it herself. They were so poor, so far from their homes, so picturesque in those red shirts and leathern belts!

Of late years Madame Steynlin had given up marrying, having at last, after many broken hopes, definitely convinced herself that husbands were only after her money. Rightly or wrongly she wanted to be loved for herself; loved, she insisted, body and soul. Even as the fires of Erebus slumber beneath their mantle of ice, she concealed, under a varnish of conventionality – the crust was not so thick in her case – a nature throbbing with passion. She was everlastingly unappeased, because incurably romantic. All life, she truly declared, is a search for a friend. Unfortunately she sought with her eyes open, having never grasped the elementary truth that to find a friend one must close one eye: to keep him – two. She always attributed to men qualities which, she afterwards discovered, they did not possess. Her life since the marrying period had been a breathless succession of love affairs, each more eternal than the last.

In matters such as these, Madame Steynlin was the reverse of the Duchess. True to her ideal of La Pompadour, that lady did not mind how many men danced attendance on her – the more the merrier. Nor did she bother about their ages; for all she cared, they might be, and often were, the veriest crocks. She was rather particular, however, about stiff collars and things; the appearance and conversation of her retinue, she avowed, should be of the kind to pass muster in good society. Madame Steynlin liked to have not more than one man escorting her at a time, and he should be young, healthy-looking, and full of life. In regard to minor matters she preferred, if anything, Byronic collars to starched ones; troubling little, for the rest, what costume her cavalier was wearing or what opinions he expressed. In fact, she liked youngsters to be frank, impetuous, extravagant in their views and out of the common rut. The two ladies had been likened to Divine and Earthly Love, or to Venus Urania and Venus Pandemos – a comparison which was manifestly unfair to both of them.

It was during this summer bathing that Madame Steynlin made the acquaintance of what was, at the time, the Master's favourite disciple. His name happened to be Peter – Peter Arsenievitch Krasnojabkin. He was a fine son of earth – a strapping young giant who threw himself into eating, drinking, and other joys of life with enviable barbaric zest. There was not an ounce of piety in his composition. He had donned the scarlet blouse because he wanted to see Nepenthe and, like the Christians of old, had no money. Driven by that roving spirit which is the Muscovite's heritage and by the desire of all sensible men to taste new lands, new wine, new women, he professed himself a Little White Cow. It was quite the regular thing to do. It brought you to the notice of that secret committee of enthusiasts who paid your travel expenses; it gave you a free trip to the sunny south. Everyone wondered how he had managed to rise so rapidly in the Master's graces. Madame Steynlin now stepped between them. She grew fond of Peter, and marked him for her own. He fulfilled every one of her conditions as to age, costume, and opinions. Besides, he was always so gloriously hungry! She invited him to luncheon once or twice, and then began to take Russian lessons from him. 'He is only a boy,' she would say.

Conversing, as best she could, with this child of nature, it dawned upon her that she had hitherto been mistaken in her estimate of the Russian character. She began to understand the inward sense of that brotherly love, that apostolic spirit, which binds together every class of the immense Empire – to revere their simplicity of soul and calm god-like faith. She revised her former narrow Lutheran views and openly confessed that she was quite wrong in declaring, as once she did, that what the Little White Cows needed was 'more soap and less salvation'. The magic of love! It softened, not for the first time, her heart towards all humanity and in particular, on this occasion, towards the rest of the saintly band; were they not her brothers and sisters? She even knitted six pairs of warm woollen socks and sent them with a polite message to the Master – a message which was left unanswered, though the socks were never returned. As to Peter – she called him her Little Peter or, in his more expansive moments, Peter the Great. Soon he was always coming to the villa at meal-times and staying for hours afterwards, while they wrestled with the complexities of Russian genders. He made no secret of the pleasure he derived from filling his healthy young stomach at her expense; everything supplementary to that prime condition he took as a gift from the gods. If he had not been so simple-minded he could have wheedled any amount of money out of her. The affair had now been going on for four months – quite a long while, as such affairs went.

Not for the first time did Madame Steynlin experience the drawbacks of her house, as regards natural situation. It was, as Don Francesco often pointed out, 'the most unstrategic villa on Nepenthe'. Ah, that peninsula, that isthmus, or whatever you called the thing – what on earth had attracted her to the place? What demon had tempted her to buy it? How she envied other people – Keith, for example, who, if he had been a man of that kind, could have allowed any visitor, in broadest daylight, to creep in or out of his mouldy old gateway in the wall without a soul being any the wiser! High-priced horticultural experts had been consulted as to the best means of thickening the vegetation and screening the approaches to the house. They had met with scanty success. The soil was of the most sterile, intractable rock; those few wind-blown olives were dreadfully diaphanous, and Peter's blouse visible from afar – even from the market-place. Everything got about on Nepenthe. People began to twit her about the progress of those 'Russian lessons'. It became quite a scandal. Signor Malipizzo was more annoyed than anyone else. He hated the whole brood of Russians, and had formed various projects for uprooting the association from the island. His friend the Commissioner thoroughly endorsed these views. Often he declared that something must be done about it.

The Master, despite his seclusion, had heard of the affair. He was grieved, but not unduly so; he had other disciples to choose from. Every new arrival from Holy Russia, regardless of sex or age, spent some hours or days, as the case might be, alone with the Master in his apartment, in order to be initiated into the Law and impregnated with its full signification; such was the way of the New Jerusalem. By this system of spiritual control he could be sure of finding a successor sooner or later. Besides, the defection of this favourite disciple was only a drop in the ocean of his griefs. What secretly preyed upon his mind was that, on the verge of returning to his former state of worldly prosperity, he had been inspired to issue that Second Revelation regarding warm-blooded beasts. He ought to have known about the Grand Dukes, and what a sacrilegious hot-tempered clique they were! 'This comes,' he would say, 'of placing the service of God above that of my earthly masters.' It kept him in exile on this island – the deadlock in the matter of that Second Revelation. The expiatory period was not yet over, though Nepenthe, on the whole, would have been glad to see the last of him – particularly Signor Malipizzo.

Meanwhile, the Little White Cows lived on: the richer in houses sleeping fifteen or twenty in one room, after the happy style of patriarchal Russia – the humbler folk in old ruins, sheds, cellars, or even caverns of the rock. You could do that sort of thing in a climate like Nepenthe, if you were not fastidious in the matter of owls, bats, lizards, toads, earwigs, centipedes, and an occasional scorpion.

CHAPTER 12

No Russians dwelt within the Cave of Mercury. It was inconveniently remote; it was difficult of approach; moreover, it was haunted. Dreadful rites had been performed there in olden times. The walls had dripped human gore. Death-groans of victims slain by the priestly knife resounded in its hollow entrails. Such had been the legend in the days of those monkish chroniclers in whose credulous pages Monsignor Perrelli, incredulous himself, had discovered a mine of curious information.

Then came the Good Duke Alfred. His Highness posed as a conservative in some matters; it pleased him to revive memories of the long-buried past. He cared little about ghosts. He liked to take things in hand. After remarking in his brisk epigrammatic fashion that 'not everything old is putrid', he devoted his attention to the Cave of Mercury and caused a flight of convenient stairs to be built, wide enough to admit the passage of two of his fattest Privy Councillors walking abreast, and leading down to this particular grotto through a cleft in the rock. Nobody knew what happened there under his superintendence. Mankind being ever prone to believe the worst of every great man, all kinds of stupid and even wicked things were said, though not during his lifetime. People vowed that he carried on the old traditions, the tortures and human sacrifices, and even improved upon them in his blithe Renaissance manner. They were ready to supply circumstantial and excruciating details of how, disguised, down to the minutest details of costume, in the semblance of the Evil One, he had sought to prolong his life and invigorate his declining health with the blood of innocent children, artfully done to death after fiendish, lingering agonies. Father Capocchio, needless to say, had some shocking pages on this subject.

Mr Eames, who had made a careful study of Duke Alfred's reign, came to the conclusion that such excesses were incompatible with the character of a ruler whose love of children was one of his most salient traits. In regard to those other and vaguer accusations, he contended that the Duke was too jovial by nature to have tortured any save those who, in his opinion, thoroughly deserved it. Indeed, he was sceptical about the whole thing. Monsignor Perrelli might have told us the truth, had he cared to do so. But, for reasons which will appear anon, he is remarkably silent on all that concerns the reign of his great contemporary. He says nothing more than this:

'His Highness deigned, during the same year, to restore, and put into its old working order, the decayed heathen rock-chapel vulgarly known as the Cave of Mercury.'

To put into *its old working order*; that would sound rather suspicious, as though to contain a veiled accusation. We must remember, however, that the historian of Nepenthe bore a grudge against his Prince (of which likewise more anon), a grudge which he was far too prudent to vent openly; so bitter and personal a grudge that he may have felt himself justified in making a covert innuendo of this kind whenever he could safely risk it.

Meanwhile, everything remained as before – shrouded in mystery. Being doubly haunted now, by the Duke's victims and by those earlier ones, the cave fell into greater neglect than ever. Simple folk avoided speaking of the place save in a hushed whisper. It became a proverb among the islanders when speaking of something outrageously improbable: 'Don't tell me! Such things only happen in the Cave of Mercury.' When someone disappeared from his house or hotel without leaving any trace behind – it happened now and then – or when anything disreputable happened to anyone, they always said, 'Try the Cave,' or simply, 'Try Mercury.' The path had crumbled away long ago. Nobody went there except in broad daylight. It was as safe a place as you could desire, at night-time, for a murder or a love-affair. Such was the Cave of Mercury.

Denis had gone to the spot one morning not long after his arrival. He had climbed down the slippery stairs through that dank couloir or funnel in the rock overhung with dropping maidenhair and ivy and umbrageous carobs. He had rested on the little platform outside the cavern's mouth, glancing down a rocky glen upon some patches of vineyard far below, and upwards, at the narrow ribbon of sky overhead. Then he had gone within, to examine what was left of the old masonry, the phallic column, and other relics of the past. That was ten days ago. Now he meant to follow Keith's advice and go there at midnight. The moon was full.

'This very night I'll go,' he thought.

All was not well with Denis. And the worst of it was, he had no clear notion of what was the matter. He was changing. The world was changing too. It had suddenly expanded. He felt that he, also, ought to expand. There was so much to learn, to see, to know – so much, that it seemed to paralyse his initiative. Could he absorb all this? Would he ever get things into order once more, and recapture his self-possession? Would he ever again be satisfied with himself? It was an invasion of his tranquillity, from within and

109

without. He was restless. Bright ideas never came to him, as of old; or else they were the ideas of other people. A miserable state of affairs! He was becoming an automaton – an echo.

An echo. ... How right Keith had been!

'It's rotten,' he concluded. 'I'm a ludicrous figure, a pathetic idiot.'

The novel impressions of Florence had helped in the disintegration. Nepenthe – its sunshine, its relentless paganism – had done the rest. It shattered his earlier outlook and gave him nothing in exchange. Nothing, and yet everything. That vision of Angelina! It filled his inner being with luxurious content; content and uncertainty. It was there, at the back of every dream, of every intimate thought and every little worldly phrase that he uttered. He was like a man who, looking long at the sun, sees its image floating in heaven, on earth – wherever he casts his eye. Angelina! Nothing else was of any account. How would it all end? He drifted along in blissful apprehension of what the next day might bring. She seemed to have become genuinely well-disposed towards him of late, though in rather a mocking, maternal sort of fashion.

The poetic vein had definitely run dry. Impossible to make things rhyme, somehow. Perhaps his passion was too strong for technical restraints. He tried his hand at prose:

'Your eyes bewilder me. I would liken you to a shaft of sunlight, a withering flame – a black flame, if such there be – for your grace and ardour are even as a flame. Your step is laughter and song. Your hair is a torrent of starless night. The sun is your lover, your god. He takes joy in your perfection. Your slender body palpitates with his imprisoned beams. He has moulded your limbs and kissed your smooth skin in the days when you ... nevermore will you whiten those kisses. ...'

'It won't do,' he sadly reflected, laying down the pen. 'The adaptation is too palpable. Why does everybody anticipate my ideas? The fact is, I have nothing to say. I can only feel. Everything went right, so long as I was in love with myself. Now everything goes wrong.'

Then he remembered Keith's pompous exhortation. 'Find yourself! You know the Cave of Mercury? Climb down, one night of full moon –'

'There is something in what he says. This very night I'll go.'

It was particularly hard for him, that evening. The Duchess was dining with a party at Madame Steynlin's; it was an open secret that the entertainment would end in a moonlit excursion on the water; she would not return till very late. Angelina would be alone, accessible. It was her duty to guard the house in the absence of its mistress. He might have gone there on some pretext and talked awhile, and looked into her elvish eyes, and listened to that Southern voice, rich and clear as a bell. Almost he yielded. He thought of the ineptitude of the whole undertaking and, in particular, of those slippery stairs; one might break one's neck there at such an hour of the night. Unless one wore tennis shoes –

Well, he would wear them. He would resist the temptation and approve himself a man. Everybody, even the Duchess, was always telling him to be a man. He would find himself. Keith was right.

The night came.

He descended noiselessly into the cool and dark chasm, resting awhile on a ledge about half-way down, to drink in the spirit of the place. All was silent. Dim masses towered overhead; through rifts in the rocky fabric he caught glimmerings, strange and yet familiar, of the landscape down below. It swam in the milky radiance of a full moon whose light streamed down from some undiscoverable source behind the mountain, suffusing the distant vineyards and trees with a ghostly tinge of green. Like looking into another world, he thought; a poet's world. Calmly it lay there, full of splendour. How well one could understand in such a place, the glamour, the romance, of night! Romance. ... What was left of life without romance? He remembered his talk with Marten; he thought of the scientist's crude notions of romance. He pitied the materialism which denied him joys like these. This moonlit landscape – how full of suggestion! That grotto down below – what tales it could unfold!

The Cave of Mercury. ...

How had Mercury, the arch-thief, come to be presiding genius here? Denis knew; his friend Eames had explained everything to him. Mercury had nothing whatever to do with the site. That name had been proved by the bibliographer to be the invention of some pedantic monk who liked to display his learning to a generation avid of antiquities, a generation which insisted on attaching a Roman deity to every cavern. It was a wilful fabrication, made in the infancy of archaeology when historical criticism was non-existent. And the same with all those stories about human sacrifices and tortures. There was not a word of truth in them. So Mr Eames had decided, after a systematic investigation both of the older authorities and of the grotto itself. The legends, too, were simply invented to give a zest to a locality whose original antique name had apparently been lost, though he had not yet abandoned all hope of stumbling across it by one of those lucky accidents

111

which reward the lover of old parchments and title-deeds. A pure invention. It was plain to Mr Eames, from what remained of ancient symbols on the spot, that the cave had been consecrated to older and worthier rites – to some mysterious, primeval, fecund Mother of Earth. Her name, like that of her habitation, had lapsed into oblivion.

'There is something grand in this old animistic conception,' Eames had said. 'Later on, under the Romans, the place seems to have been dedicated to Priapic rites. That is rather a depreciation, isn't it? It brings us down from fruitfulness to mere lasciviousness. But where are you going to draw the line? Everything tends to lose its hallowed meaning; it becomes degraded, bestialized. Still, the roots of the idea are sound. In giving sensual attributes to a garden god the ancients had in mind the recklessness, the spendthrift abundance, of all nature – not excluding our own. They tried to explain how it came about that the sanest man is liable, under the stress of desire, to acts of which he vainly repents at leisure. I don't suppose they meant to justify those acts. If they had, they would have given a less equivocal position to Priapus in their celestial hierarchy. Priapus, you know, was not wholly divine. I think they only wanted to make it quite clear that we cannot drive out nature with a fork. I wish we could,' he added.

And then he sighed. The poor fellow was thinking, at that moment, of balloons.

Denis remembered this conversation. Earth-worship: the cult of those generative forces which weld together in one mighty instinct the highest and lowliest of terrestrial creatures. ... The inalienable right of man and beast to enact that which shall confound death, and replenish the land with youth, and joy, and teeming life. The right which priestly castes of every age have striven to repress, which triumphs over every obstacle and sanctifies, by its fruits, the wildest impulses of man. The right to love!

Musing thus, he began to understand why men of old, who looked things squarely in the face, should have deified this friendly all-compelling passion. He reverenced the fierce necessity which drives the living world to its fairest and sole enduring effort. Be fruitful and multiply. He recognized for the first time that he was not a lonely figure on earth, but absorbed into a solemn and eternal movement; bound close to the throbbing heart of the Universe. There was grandeur, there was repose, in being able to regard himself as an integral part of nature, destined to create and leave his mark. He felt that he was growing into harmony with permanent things – finding himself. He realized now what Keith had meant.

112

It cost him quite an effort to tear himself away from that ledge. He began to descend once more.

Near the entrance of the Cave he paused abruptly. It seemed as if a sound had issued from the interior of the rock. He listened. It came again – a human sound, unquestionably, and within a few yards of his face. A whisper. There was something going on – Earth-worship. ...

Suddenly a succession of words broke upon the stillness – breathless words, spoken in a language which not everybody could have translated. He recognized the voice. It said:

'*Ego te amare tantum! Non volere? Non piacere? Non capire?* Oh Lord, can't you understand?'

It was Mr Marten's voice. Mr Marten was being romantic. No answer came to his fervent pleading. Perhaps they were not coherent enough. He began again, *tremolo agitato, con molto sentimento*:

'*O ego te amare tantum! Nemo sapit nihil. Duchessa in barca aquatica cum magna compania. Redibit tardissimo. Niente timor. Amare multissimo! Ego morire sine te. Morire. Moriturus. Capito? Non capire?* Oh, *capire* be blowed!'

There was a short pause. The language seems to have been understood this time. For, amid a ripple of laughter, a rich Southern voice was heard to say with a sigh of mock resignation:

'*Sia fatta la volontà di Dio!*'

Then silence. ...

Denis turned. He walked up the steps as in a dream neither slowly nor fast. No one was ever more unhappy, though he scarcely felt as yet the depths of his own humiliation. It was more like a stab – a numbing assassin-like stab. He could hear the beatings of his heart.

He reached the upper level of the town, he knew not how.

All lay quiet as he found his way among the familiar buildings. It was after midnight; most of the lamps had been extinguished. The streets were deserted. He heard, in the distance, the song of a drunken wayfarer reeling homewards from a tavern or from the Club.

In one of the little roadways that converge upon the market-place something was astir. It was a dun phantom of willowy outline, swaying capriciously to and fro, like a black feather tossed by the wind. Miss Wilberforce! She fluttered down upon a doorstep and began crooning a vulgar song about 'Billy had a letter for to go on board a ship'. Denis moved to the other side of the narrow path, hoping to escape unobserved. The light was too strong.

113

'My young friend,' she cried in quite a hoarse and altered tone of voice, 'we should know each other! We've had the pleasure, haven't we? Been down to the sea, have you? And what are the wild waves saying?'

Denis stood still, petrified with disgust. Was it possible? Was this the lady who had charmed him the other day? Who had spoken of England and conjured up memories of his own home in the Midlands? With a playful gesture she sent her hat careering across the street and began to fumble at her breast, unlacing or unbuttoning something. It was horrible, in the moonlight.

A boot, flying merrily over his head, recalled him to his senses. He turned to go, and had already made a few paces when the voice croaked after him:

'Does your mother know you're out?'

CHAPTER 13

SOME good genius took him by the hand next day and led him to the house of Count Caloveglia, in response to that friendly twice-repeated invitation. The old man saw at a glance that something serious was amiss. He plunged at once, with quick insight, into what he took to be extraneous topics of conversation.

'I am glad you like my fig-tree! It gave a distinctive tone to this quiet courtyard, don't you think? I could not have wished for anything more appropriate. Its shape, its associations, are alike pleasing. The fig is a legendary tree; a volume could be written about the stories and superstitions which have twined themselves around it. Some think it was the Biblical Tree of Knowledge. Judas Iscariot, they say, hanged himself on a fig-tree. It came from the East – Bacchus brought it on his journey as a gift to mortal men. How much we owe to those of the Greek Gods who were yet not wholly divine! The Romans, too, held it in veneration. You have doubtless heard about the *ficus ruminalis,* at whose feet the cradle of Romulus and Remus was stranded? Among many nations it became the outward symbol of generative forces. The Egyptians consecrated the fig to Isis, that fecund Mother of Earth. Statues of Priapus were carved out of its wood in allusion, possibly, to its reckless fertility or for some analogous reason; it was also held to be sacred, I know not why, to Mercury –'

Denis, during this little speech, had begun to look more troubled than ever. The other continued:

'There is something in the very twistings of that smooth trunk and those heavy-laden branches that suggests fruitfulness. How voluptuously they writhe! A kindly growth, lover of men, their dwellings and ordered ways. That is why we foster it. We are all utilitarians here, Mr Denis; we think of the main purposes of life. Besides food, it gives us welcome shade at this season; the leaves fall off in winter and allow the sunlight to percolate into our rooms. You will not find evergreen trees planted near our windows. We know the value of sunshine; where the sun enters, we say, the physician does not enter. In England the light is feebler and yet they made this mistake, during the Georgian period of architecture. They thought that houses were invented to be looked at, not to be lived in. Determined to be faithful to the tradition and regardless of the difference in climate, they planted the ilex about those mansions which must be dank and gloomy in winter-time, however charming, externally, to those who relish the chill Palladian outlines. You have lately been to Florence, I hear. Come! Let us sit indoors. The courtyard is rather too sultry to-day, in spite of the shade. My old servant will bring some tea, presently. Or perhaps you would prefer some wine and a biscuit? Or a glass of liqueur? ... Well? And Florence?'

'It has left me rather confused, so far,' replied Denis. 'Some of the things are overwhelming.'

'Overwhelming? That is perhaps because you do not see the movement in its continuity, because you have not traced the stream to its source. I can understand your feelings. But one need not be overwhelmed by these men. They were lovable folk, who played with their art like some child that has discovered a long-lost toy. It is a pity that their activities were so hampered by the conventions of religious dogma. Viewed by itself, the Renaissance may seem overwhelming; it shoots up like a portentous lily out of the blood-drenched soil of a thousand battlefields. Let me take you to its real source.'

He showed him that little statuette, the Locri Faun. Denis was enchanted with it.

'You have heard of Sir Herbert Street? He also thinks highly of this thing. He is now adviser in art matters to Mr van Koppen, who is a patron of mine and who, I hear, will arrive tomorrow or the day after.'

'Street? I met him at my mother's house. Wasn't he at South Kensington? A great man for dining out. You cannot pick up an evening paper without reading something about him. That kind of man! All the same, he wrote a good book on the Siena School. I liked it, didn't you?'

'It is a fair appreciation, from the collector's point of view. He

115

has stayed with me here once or twice, and given me reason to form a high opinion of his capacities. Now if you compare this Faun with your Florentine art, you will see what I mean by going to the fountain. There is a difference not only in technique, but in outlook. The man who wrought this did not trouble about you, or me, or himself. He had no moods. His art is purely intellectual; he stands aloof, like a glacier. Here the spring issued, crystal-clear. As the river swells in size it grows turbid and discoloured with alien elements – personality, emotions.'

'I have noticed that,' said Denis. 'It is what we call the malady of thought. This Faun, you say, was found on the mainland yonder?'

'Near the site of old Locri, on a piece of ground which still belongs to me. I suspect there are still a good many Greek relics to be excavated on the site. We discovered a Demeter some years ago; a mutilated head in marble; it is now in Paris. You can see the very place from my roof here, on bright days. These men, Mr Denis, were our masters. Do not be misled by what you are told of the wanton luxury of those shores; do not forget that your view of that age has filtered through Roman stoicism and English puritanism which speak with envy lurking at their hearts – the envy of the incomplete creature for him who dares express himself. A plague has infected the world – the plague of repression. Don't you think that the man who made this Faun was entitled to dine well?'

'I cannot quite make it out,' said Denis, still examining the statuette.

'Ah! How does it make you feel?'

'Uneasy.'

'You are aware of a struggle between your own mind and that of the artist? I am glad. It is the test of beauty and vitality that a beholder refuses to acquiesce at first glance. There is a conflict to be undergone. This thing thrusts itself upon us; it makes no concessions, does it? And yet one cannot but admire! You will seldom encounter that sensation among the masterpieces of the Renaissance. They welcome you with open arms. That is because we know what their creators were thinking about. They are quite personal and familiar; they had as many moods, one suspects, as a fashionable prima donna. They give pleasure. This Faun gives pleasure and something more – a sense of disquieting intimacy. While intruding upon our reserve with his solemn, stark, and almost hostile novelty, he makes at the same time a strange appeal – he touches upon chords in our nature of which we ourselves were

116

barely cognisant. You must yield, Mr Denis, to this stranger who seems to know so much about you. When you have done so, you will make a surprising discovery. You have gained a friend – one of those who never change.'

'I am trying to,' replied Denis. 'But it is difficult. We are not brought up that way, nowadays.'

'No. Men have lost their frankness, their self-assurance. Whoever yields must be confident of his own strength. Our contemporaries have lost that feeling. They dare not be themselves. They eke out lack of sincerity by profusion of commonplace. Unlike the heroes of Homer, they repress their tears – they repress everything, save their irrepressible flatulence of mind. They are expansive in unimportant matters and at wrong moments – blown about in a whirl of fatuous extremes. The impersonal note has vanished. Why has it gone, Mr Denis?' he suddenly asked. 'And when did it go?'

The other was rather puzzled what to reply.

'I suppose you could trace its disappearance to the days of which you spoke, when artists began to display their moods to the world. Perhaps further still. Some Roman writers were fond of talking about their own affairs. If they do, the public naturally becomes interested. People like Byron must have had a good deal to do with it. He was always harping on his private life.'

He paused, but the Count merely asked:

'No farther back than that?'

'I don't know. Christianity made us interested in other people's feelings. Brotherliness, you know. That must have helped. So did Socrates, by the way. Of course it lowers the general standard. Where everybody can read and write, there's an end of good taste. No, I don't mean that exactly,' he added, feeling that he was expressing himself very stupidly.

'Well?'

'Oh, everything! The telegraph and society papers and interviewing and America and yellow journalism... and all those family memoirs and diaries and autobiographies and Court scandals. ... They produce a new kind of public, a public which craves for personalities rather than information. They want to learn about our clothes and incomes and habits. Not a questioning public I mean; a prying public –'

'A cannibalistic public,' said the Count, quietly. 'Men cannot live, it seems, save by feeding on their neighbour's life-blood. They prey on each other's nerve-tissues and personal sensations. Everything must be shared. It gives them a feeling of solidarity, I

117

suppose, in a world where they have lost the courage to stand alone. Woe to him who dwells apart! Great things are no longer contemplated with reverence. They are hauled down from their pedestals in order to be rendered accessible to a generation of pigmies; their dignity is soiled by vulgar contact. This lust of handling – what is its ordinary name? Democracy. It has abraded the edge of that keen anthropocentric outlook of the Greeks which exalted whatever was distinctively human. Men have learnt to see beauty here, there, and everywhere – a little beauty, mark you, not much! They fail to realize that in widening their capacity of appreciation they dilute its intensity. They have watered their wine. There is more to drink. The draught is poorer.'

It seemed to Denis that the Count's wine had not been watered.

'Let me show you one or two other things,' said the old man.

They wandered about the premises awhile, looking at marbles, prints, intaglios, coins, till a serving-man entered – a clean-shaven and rather bony old creature whom the Count called Andrea – to announce tea. Denis was feeling calmer; he had fallen under the beguiling influence of this place. He realized that his host was different from the artist type he had hitherto encountered: more profound, more veracious. Already he formed the project of returning to listen to his melodious voice and learn some more about that Hellenic life, which had hitherto been a sealed book to him. Nobody ever spoke to him after the Count's fashion. He contrasted his address with the bantering, half-apologetic, supercilious tone of those other elderly persons who had heretofore deigned to enlighten him. He was flattered and pleased at being taken seriously and bidden to think in this straightforward, manly fashion; it unstrung his reserve and medicined to his wounded self-respect.

'So your mother would like to see you in Parliament?' asked the Count. 'Politics are apt to be a dirty game. One cannot touch dirt without soiling one's hands. We have a deputy here, the Commendatore Morena – well, one does not like to speak about him. Let me ask you a question, Mr Denis. Why do politicians exist?'

'I suppose the answer would be that it is profitable to mankind to be run by somebody.'

'Profitable, at all events, to those who do the running. Your good Sir Herbert Street has lately sent me a batch of books about the ideal public life of the future. Socialistic forecasts, and that kind of literature. He is a world-improver, you know, among other things. They have amused me more than I thought they would. That venerable blunder: to think that in changing the form of gov-

118

ernment you change the heart of man. And in other respects, too, these dreamers are at sea. For surely we should aim at simplification of machinery. Conceive, now, the state of affairs where everybody is more or less employed by the community – the community, that comfortable word! – in some patriotic business or other. Everybody an official, all controlling each other! It would be worse than the Spanish Inquisition. A man could live at Toledo by subscribing to certain fixed opinions; he could be assured of a reasonable degree of privacy. Nothing could save him under socialism. An insupportable world! When people cease to reflect they become idealists.'

'I suppose they do,' replied Denis, rather dubiously. Then it struck him that this might account for his own hazy state of mind – this lack of occupation or guiding principle. For the rest, he had not given much thought to such questions. To be a politician – it was one of the few projects which had never seriously entered his head. After a pause, he remarked:

'I can't help noticing that portrait over there. It's a very pretty thing.'

'The little pastel? It is a sketch of my daughter Matilda. I did it myself when she was here last Christmas. Poor child, she can only come for her holidays; there is no chance of a respectable education on this island. But I run over to see her every now and then. You will observe I am not much of a colourist!'

'You have been parsimonious with the tints. It reminds me of some of Lenbach's work which I saw at Florence; it is in the same manner.'

'It appears you like art,' said the Count. 'Why not devote yourself to it? But perhaps your English social conditions are not propitious. Here is a letter from a friend of mine which arrived this morning; you know his name – I will not mention it! A well-known Academician, whose life is typical of your attitude towards art. Such a good fellow. He likes shooting and fishing; he is a favourite at Court, and quite an authority on dress-reform. He now writes to ask me about some detail of Greek costume which he requires for one of his lectures to a Ladies' Guild. Art, to him, is not a jealous mistress; she is an indulgent companion, who will amiably close an eye and permit a few wayside flirtations to her lover – enthusiasms for quite other ideals, and for the joys of good society in general. That is the way to live a happy life. It is not the way to create masterpieces.'

'I would take myself seriously, I think,' said Denis. 'I would not dissipate my energies.'

119

He meant it. To be an artist – it dawned upon him that this was his true vocation. To renounce pleasure and discipline the mind; to live a life of self-denial, submitting himself humbly to the inspiration of the great masters. ... To be serene, like this old man; to avoid that facile, glib, composite, note – those monkey-tricks of cleverness. ...

Then, after this vision had passed before his eyes like a flash, he remembered his grief. The notion of becoming a world-famous artist lost all meaning for him. Everything was blighted. There was not a grain of solace to be found on earth.

The Count, meanwhile, was looking with concern upon his companion's grave face, whose flawless profile might have emerged into life under the thought-laden chisel of Lysippus. He wondered what he could say or do to drive away this melancholy. The youth had been so bright that day at the entertainment of the Duchess; he seemed to have stepped straight out of a sunny dialogue of Plato. Serious trouble now shone out of his eyes. Something had happened. Something was wrong with him; wrong, too – he reflected – with a world which could find no better occupation for such a person than to hand round buttered tea-cakes at an old woman's party to a crowd of cosmopolitan scandalmongers.

Denis rose, remarking:

'I wish I could stay a little longer! But it is getting so late. I'm afraid I must be going.'

He held out his hand.

'You have caught me in a somewhat sad and depressed mood, I fear,' replied the other, heaving a most artistic sigh. And his features suddenly looked quite careworn. As a matter of fact, he had not been so joyous for many long years – that news of Mr van Koppen's proximate arrival having made him feel fifty years younger and, but for his ingrained sense of Hellenic moderation, almost ready to dance with delight.

'I am sorry I have been so despondent,' he went on. 'Sometimes one cannot help oneself. It shall not occur again! I will try to be more amusing next time you come. If I thought it would help, I would communicate my sorrows and claim your sympathy. But what does it avail to unburden oneself? Friends will share our joys, but every man is a solitary in his griefs. One soon finds that out! One soon realizes the vanity of all those talks about the consolations of philosophy and the comforts of religion, doesn't one? I suppose even you have your moments of dejection?'

'One worries about things now and then. It is perfectly natural, I daresay.'

120

'Perfectly. We are not stones – least of all persons like yourself. I would not be at your age again, not for the wealth of Croesus! I suffered too much. All young people suffer too much; they bear it silently, like heroes. The eye of youth dilates and distorts the images. The focusing process is painful. Youth has no norm. It was in one of my worst fits of despondency, I remember, that my old teacher gave me certain advice which, after I had puzzled it out, did me some good. In fact, I have acted upon it to this very day; I recall it as plainly as if he were speaking now. Well, I am sorry you are leaving. I would keep you here if I could. But I hope you will not forget to come another day. You have cheered me up wonderfully! Shall Andrea find you a carriage?'

'What did he say?' asked Denis.

'The old teacher? Let me see. ... He said: Do not be discomposed by the opinions of inept persons. Do not swim with the crowd. They who are all things to their neighbours, cease to be anything to themselves. Even a diamond can have too many facets. Avoid the attrition of vulgar minds; keep your edges intact. He also said: A man can protect himself with fists or sword but his best weapon is his intellect. A weapon must be forged in the fire. The fire, in our case, is tribulation. It must also be kept untarnished. If the mind is clean, the body can take care of itself. He said: Delve deeply; not too deeply into the past, for it may make you derivative; nor yet into yourself – it will make you introspective. Delve into the living world and strive to bind yourself to its movement by a chain of your own welding. Once that contact is established, you are unassailable. Externalize yourself! He told me many things of this kind. You think I was consoled by his words? Not in the slightest degree. I was annoyed. It struck me, at the moment, as quite ordinary advice. In fact, I thought him rather a hypocrite; anybody could have spoken as he did! I was so disappointed that I went to him next day and told him frankly what I thought of his counsel. He said – do you know what he said?'

'I cannot even guess.'

'He said: "What is all wisdom save a collection of platitudes? Take fifty of our current proverbial sayings – they are so trite, so threadbare, that we can hardly bring our lips to utter them. None the less they embody the concentrated experience of the race, and the man who orders his life according to their teaching cannot go far wrong. How easy that seems! Has anyone ever done so? Never. Has any man ever attained to inner harmony by pondering the experience of others? Not since the world began! He must pass through the fire."'

'I had no teacher like that,' observed Denis. 'He must have been a man of the right kind.'

'Oh, he meant well, the old rascal,' replied the Count with a curious little smile.

CHAPTER 14

DENIS descended from the Old Town. At a turn of the road he overtook the bishop, who was moving slowly in the same direction.

'How is Mrs Meadows?' inquired the young man.

'Not particularly well, I'm afraid. And the Count?'

'Oh, quite all right.'

They walked along in silence, having little to say to each other. That visit had done Denis good; he would return soon again, if only for the purpose of cheering up the lonely old man, who at the last moment had given him a photograph of the Locri Faun, with a kindly inscription from himself. He was not to show it to anybody, the Count had said – not yet! The government must not hear about that relic – not yet! Later on, perhaps very soon, everything would be in order. Denis cherished that photo in his pocket. He was thinking, too, of the pastel – the face of Matilda, which seemed like a star shining through the mist. ... Then he remembered the bishop walking at his side. He felt he ought to say something more to this dry Colonial whom he could not help contrasting, greatly to his disadvantage, with the Count.

'Hasn't it been hot today?'

'Stifling,' replied Mr Heard. 'The warmest day we have had, so far. Not a breath of wind.'

'Not a breath. ...'

The conversation flagged once more. They did not hit it off, somehow; they seemed to drift further apart every time they met. Each was preoccupied with his own thoughts. The bishop was more taciturn than usual; the interview with his cousin had not been quite a success.

Denis, after a while, made another effort. He spoke of some of Count Caloveglia's antiquities and, one thing leading to another, told Mr Heard the story of a friend of his in Florence, who had excavated some wonderful early Italian pots, fragments of them, out of an old garden well. They were all lustred, he said.

'That must have been a very pleasant surprise,' observed the bishop, who had small use for lustred ware and lunatics who collected it. Feeling that it was his turn to say something, he remarked:

'I am dining with the Duchess tonight. Will you be there?'

'No,' replied the young man with an unwonted air of decision. Never again would he be seen in that austere old convent, built by the Good Duke Alfred. Never again! Promptly, however, he toned down the harshness of his answer by adding that the lady had very kindly asked him to come, but he couldn't manage it, that evening.

'I shall have to console her about the burglary,' continued the bishop.

'What burglary?'

Mr Heard explained that the premises had been entered while the Duchess was dining at Madame Steynlin's on the previous evening, the night of the water-party. Evidently the work of a man who knew his business. A man familiar with the ins and outs of the house. And a man of taste, into the bargain. All the sham articles had been left untouched; he had gone off with nothing but genuine things – a few precious crucifixes and *bonbonnières*. No one had the faintest idea who the thief was. Most mysterious! The disaster could hardly have occurred but for the fact that the young girl Angelina, who was supposed to sleep on the premises, had been called away late at night to look after a suffering aunt. The old woman, it appeared, was liable to sudden heart-attacks. She had been round to see the Duchess early in the morning with endless apologies, and had fortunately been able to corroborate her niece's story.

'I am glad of it,' concluded the bishop. 'Because that maid, when I saw her, struck me as rather a flighty young person – the sort of girl who would take advantage of her mistress's absence to have a little flirtation with a policeman round the corner. I am glad the aunt could explain things so satisfactorily. I was wrong about that girl. Shows how careful one must be in judging of other people, doesn't it? I must say she looked to me like a regular little coquette.'

Denis had so little sympathetic comment to make on this painful story that Mr Heard was quite surprised at his indifference. He always understood the young man to be a particular friend of the Duchess.

'These artistic people!' he thought. 'They have quite another way of looking at things. Dear me. I shall never live to understand them.'

The two separated at the market-place without much reluctance on either side.

During dinner, the Duchess was calm about her misfortune. She bore it well. She had been vigorously consoled by Don Francesco, who pointed out that such little things are trials of faith and that she ought to be thankful for the opportunity of proving how little she cared for earthly riches. While not exactly thankful, she was certainly as resigned as anybody could have been. Angelina had already been taken into grace again, at the charitable suggestion of the priest. Everyone was puzzling who the thief could be (it happened to be Mr Richards); the police had not discovered the faintest clue.

'It does not much matter if they do,' said Don Francesco. 'I don't think, my dear lady, that you will get the judge to take up your case very actively. You know how he hates the clericals. In fact, I fear he will not move a finger unless the culprit also happens to be a good believer. In that case, he might lock him up. He is so fond of imprisoning Catholics!'

'A bad state of the law,' commented the bishop.

'It is,' replied Don Francesco. 'And perhaps you do not know,' he added, turning to the company, 'that there has been another robbery as well, doubtless by the same hand. Yes! I only heard of it an hour ago. Poor Miss Wilberforce is the victim. She is terribly upset. A number of valuables have disappeared from her house; they must have been ransacked, she thinks, at the time of Mr Keith's party. I understand she was rather overcome on that occasion. The thief seems to have been aware of her condition, and to have profited by it.'

'Poor Miss Wilberforce!' said everybody. They were all sorry for poor Miss Wilberforce.

It was a rather dull dinner-party on the whole. Mr Heard left at half-past eleven.

Passing the Club on his way home, he remembered his intention of looking in there and perhaps doing good to a few of those fellows.

He climbed up the stairs. There was a fearful row going on. The place was crammed with members of various nationalities, drinking and arguing amid clouds of tobacco smoke. They seemed all to be at loggerheads with one another and on the verge of breaking out into violence, the south wind having been particularly objectionable all day long. A good deal of filthy and profane language was being used – it was worse than those hot places he had known in Africa. That pink-faced old drunkard known as Charlie was the only person who made any signs of recognizing him. He half rose from his chair with a genial: 'Hello, Bishop –' and instantly collapsed again. Mr Muhlen was there; he bowed rather distantly. A tremulous, pale-faced youngster invited him pressingly to a drink, and just as the bishop was on the verge of accepting with a view to getting the victim out of that den of vice, the lad suddenly remarked: 'Excuse me, won't you?' and tottered out of the door. They were too far gone to be spoken to with any prospects of success. Things might have been different if the restraining influence of Mr Freddy Parker could have made itself felt, but that gentleman was at home, his lady being not very well. In the Commissioner's absence Mr Richards, the respectable Vice-President, was making his voice heard. Sober or not, he was certainly articulate and delighted with himself as, stroking his beard placidly, he roared out above the crowd:

'I've no use for makeshifts. Honesty is a makeshift. A makeshift for saving time. Whoever wants to save time is not fit for the society of gentlemen.'

'Hear, hear!'

'Call yourself a gentleman?' inquired another.

'Just a makeshift. You won't hear honesty talked about in the great periods of the world's history. It's the small tradesman's invention, is honesty. He hasn't the brains to earn anything more than three and a half per cent! That's why he is always in such a hurry to finish his first little deal and get on with the next one. Else he'd starve. Hence honesty. Three and a half per cent! Who's going to pick that up? People who earn three hundred don't cackle about honesty.'

'Call yourself a gentleman? Outside!'

'I've no use for honesty. It's the small man's flap-doodle, is honesty. This world isn't made for small men! I am talking to you over there – the funny little bounder who made the offensive remark just now.'

'Are you? Well, take that!'

A glass tumbler, which Mr Richards dodged in quite a professional manner, came hurtling through the air and missed the bishop's forehead by about four inches.

That crowd was past his aid. He turned to go. As he did so, a curious idea flitted through his brain. This Mr Richards – was he, perhaps, the burglar? He was; but Mr Heard dashed aside the horrible suspicion, mindful of the mistake he had made about Angelina's character and how careful one must be in judging of other people. The voice, meanwhile, pursued him down the stairs:

'No, gentlemen! I've no use for an honest man. He always lets you down. Fortunately, he is rather rare –'

125

Mr Heard slept badly that night, for the first time since his arrival on Nepenthe. It was unbearably hot. And that visit to Mrs Meadows had also troubled him a little.

The Old Town looked different on this occasion. A sullen death-like stillness, a menacing stagnation, hung about those pink houses. Not a leaf was astir under the burning sirocco sky. Even old Caterina, when he saw her, seemed to be afflicted, somehow.

'*Soffre, la Signora*,' she said. The lady was suffering.

The bishop would not have recognized his cousin after all those years; not if he had met her in the street at least. She greeted him affectionately and they talked for a long time of family matters. It was true, then. Her husband's leave had been again postponed. Perhaps she would travel back to England with him, and there await the arrival of Meadows. She would let him know definitely in a day or two.

He watched her carefully while she conversed, trying to reconstruct, out of that woman's face, the childish features he dimly remembered. They were effaced. He could see what Keith had meant when he described her as 'tailor-made'. There was something clear-cut about her, something not exactly harsh, but savouring of decision. She was plainly a personality – not an ordinary type. The lines of her face told their story. They had been hammered into a kind of hard efficiency. But over that exterior of tranquil self-possession was superimposed something else – certain marks of recent trouble. Her eyes looked almost as if she had been weeping. She made a tremendous show of cheeriness, however, calling him Tommy as in olden days.

Just a little headache. This sirocco. It was bad enough when it blew in the ordinary fashion. But quite intolerable when it hung breathlessly about the air like this. Mr Eames – he once called it *plumbeus Auster*. That meant leaden, didn't it? Everybody had headaches, more or less.

Was she speaking the truth? The bishop decided that she had a headache and that this south wind was certainly unendurable. None the less, he suspected that she was employing the common subterfuge – telling the truth, but not the whole truth; perhaps not even the main part of it. She was holding back something.

'You haven't attended to those roses lately,' he said, observing that the flowers had not been changed and that their fallen petals strewed the tables. 'They looked so fresh when I was here alone the other day.'

'What a dreadful person you are, Tommy, for noticing things. First you discover my headache, and now those flowers! I see I shall have to be careful with you. Perhaps you would like to look at my precipice and tell me if there is anything wrong with that too? You have heard of the old French lady, I daresay. She ended, you know, in not approving of it at all. We can have tea when we come back. And after that perhaps you will let me know what is wrong with baby!'

'I can tell you that without looking at him. He is teething.'

'Clever boy! As a matter of fact, he isn't. But I had to make some excuse to the dear Duchess.'

They climbed up the short slope and found themselves looking towards the sea over the face of a dizzy cliff. A falcon, on their approach, started with rustle of wings from its ledge and then swayed crazily over the abyss. Watching this bird, the bishop felt a sudden void in his stomach. A sensation of blackness came before his eyes – sky and sea merged together – his feet were treading on air. He promptly sat down.

'Not an inch nearer!' he declared. 'Not for a thousand pounds. If you go along that edge again, I shall have to look the other way. It makes me feel empty inside.'

'I'm not in the least giddy,' she laughed. 'There was an English boy who threw himself over this cliff for a bet – you have heard the story? They never found his body. It's a good place for throwing oneself down, isn't it?'

She seemed to consider the idea quite seriously.

'Well?' she pursued. 'Have you any fault to find with my precipice?'

'I have. It ought to be railed in. It is dangerous. What a temptation this cliff must be to anyone who has an enemy to dispose of! It would be so simple,' he added, laughing.

'That advantage has never struck me before. ...'

These and other things passed through Mr Heard's mind as he lay in bed that evening. He came to the conclusion that he could not quite make his cousin out. Had something upset her? And what did she mean by that sudden conundrum:

'Do you know anything, Tommy, about our laws of illegitimacy?'

'Nothing,' he had replied, 'except that they are a disgrace to a civilized country. Everybody knows that.'

She seemed to be disappointed. Perhaps she mistrusted him. The thought gave him a little pain. He had done nothing to merit mistrust. He was frank and open himself; he liked others to be the same.

What was the use of thinking about it? He knew tantalizingly

127

little about his cousin – nothing but scraps of information gathered from his mother's letters to him. He would call again in a day or two and make some definite arrangements about their journey to England. Perhaps he had talked more dully than usual. ... Or could it be the south wind?

Neither of these explanations was wholly convincing.

CHAPTER 15

NOTHING was happening. For the first time since many years, the Nepenthe season threatened to be a failure. It was the dullest spring on record. And yet there was a quality in that heavy atmosphere which seemed to threaten mischief. Everybody agreed that it had never been quite so bad as this. Meanwhile, people yawned. They were bored stiff. As a source of gossip, those two burglaries were a negligible quantity. So was the little accident which had just happened to Mr Keith, who ruefully declared he had done it on purpose, in order to liven things up. No one was likely to be taken in by this kind of talk, because the accident was of an inglorious and even ludicrous kind.

Being very short-sighted he had managed to stumble backwards somehow or other, into a large receptacle of lime which was being slaked for patching up a wall. Lime, in that condition, is boiling hot. Mr Keith's trousers were rather badly scalded. He was sensitive on that point. He suffered a good deal. People came to express their sympathy. The pain made him more tedious, long-winded, and exhortatory than usual. At that particular moment Denis was being victimized. He had thoughtlessly called to express his sympathy, to see those celebrated cannas, and because he could not bear to be alone with his thoughts just then.

'Suffering!' exclaimed Mr Keith. 'That is what you young poets want. At present you are too unperplexed and glib. Suffering! It would enlarge your repertoire; it would make you more human, individual, and truthful. What is the unforgivable sin in poetry? Lack of candour. How shall there be candour if the poet lacks worldly experience? Suffering! That is what you people want. It would make men of you.'

Mr Keith was considerably denser than Count Caloveglia. But even he, during this oration, could not help noticing that it jarred on his listener's nerves; there was something wrong, he concluded.

Denis had not a word to say in reply. As if anyone could be more suffering than himself! He was full of a dumb ache. He marvelled at Keith's obtuseness.

'Come and see my cannas,' said the other with a kind of brutal tactfulness. 'There is a curious story attached to them. I must tell it you one of these days. It sounds like a fairy tale. You like fairy tales?'

'I do,' replied Denis.

'Then we have one point in common. I could listen to them for hours. There is something eternal about them. If you ever want to get anything out of me, Denis, tell me a fairy tale.'

'I must remember that,' replied Denis with a wan smile. 'There is one thing I should very much like to get out of you; the secret of your zest in life. You have so many interests. How do you manage it?'

'Heredity, I suppose. It has given me a kind of violent driving power. I take things by the throat. Have you ever heard of Thomas Keith, a soldier in a Highland regiment, who became governor of the Holy City of Medina? No, I suppose you have not. And yet he must have been a remarkable man, to obtain this unique position in the world. No interest in Arabian history? Why not? Well, Thomas Keith – that is my stock. Pirates and adventurers. Of course I live sensibly. Shall I give you my recipe for happiness? I find everything useful and nothing indispensable. I find everything wonderful and nothing miraculous. I reverence the body. I avoid first causes like the plague. You will find that a pretty good recipe, Denis.'

The young man wondered whether the prescription would be of any avail for his particular complaint.

Then they went into the garden, Mr Keith hobbling painfully with two sticks and indulging in very bad language. They paused awhile under some trellis-work covered with a profusion of Japanese convolvuluses, pale blue, slate colour, rose-tinted, purple, deep red, with white and coloured bands – a marvellous display of fragile beauty.

'I have never seen anything like it!' declared Denis.

'They die away in winter. I get fresh seeds every year from Japan, the latest varieties. How they cling for support to the wooden framework! How delicate and fair! One hardly dares to touch them. Are you always going to be a convolvulus, Denis?'

'Me? Oh, I see what you mean. Were you never a convolvulus, Mr Keith?'

His friend laughed.

'It must have been a good while ago. You don't like advice, do you? Have you ever heard of that Sparker affair?'

'You don't mean to say –'

'Yes. That was me. That was my little contribution to the gaiety of University life. So you see I am in the position to give advice to people like yourself. I think you should cultivate the function of the real, and try to remain in contact with phenomena. Noumena are bad for a youngster. But perhaps you are not interested in psychology?'

'Not exactly, I'm afraid,' replied Denis, who was more anxious to see those cannas.

'So I perceive. Wouldn't you get more fun out of life if you were? I am nearly done with psychology now,' he added. 'It was the Greek philosophers, before then. When I take up a subject this is what I do. I don't ask what are Aristotle's teachings or relations to his age or to humanity. That would lead me too far. I ask myself: what has this fellow got to say to me? To me, you understand. To me.'

'That must simplify matters.'

'It does,' replied Keith, quite unaware of the faint tinge of College irony in the other's words. 'Direct experience comes only from life. But you can get a kind of substitute out of books. Perhaps you are afraid of them? Take the fellows by the throat! See what they have to say. Make them disgorge. Get at their facts. Pull them to pieces. I tell you what, Denis. You must go through a course of Samuel Butler. You are moving in the same direction; perhaps he may be a warning to you. I took him up, I remember, during my biological period. He was exactly like yourself – bewildered by phenomena.'

Denis, meekly resigned, enquired:

'Was he?'

'I spent nearly a week over Butler. I found him interesting not for what he writes, but for what he is. A landmark. Think of when he wrote. It was an age of giants – Darwin and the rest of them. Their facts were too much for him; they impinged on some obscure old prejudices of his. They drove him into a clever perversity of humour. They account for his cat-like touches, his contrariness, his fondness for scoring off everybody from the Deity downwards, his premeditated irresponsibilities, his –'

'Did he not prove that the *Odyssey* was written by a woman?'

'He did. Anything to escape from realities – that was his maxim. He puzzled his contemporaries. But we can now locate him with absolute certainty. He personifies the Revolt from Reason. *Surtout, mon ami, point de zèle*. He talks about the Scylla of Atheism and the Charybdis of Christianity – a state of mind which, by the way, is not conducive to bold navigation. He was always

130

wavering between the two in an attitude of suburban defiance, reconciling what is irreconcilable by extracting funny analogies all round for the edification of "nice people" like himself. Oh, very English! He did not lack candour or intelligence. Nor do you. He understood the teachings of the giants. So do you. But they irked him. To revenge himself he laid penny crackers under their pedestals. His whole intellectual fortune was spent in buying penny crackers. There was something cheeky and pre-adolescent about him – a kind of virginal ferocity. That iridescent charm of sexlessness which somebody, one of these days, must be good enough to analyse for us! He lacked the male attributes of humility, reverence, and sense of proportion.'

Mr Keith paused, but it was only to take breath.

'Did he?' inquired Denis. 'The sense of proportion –'

'The tail of a cow was just as important to him as the tail of a comet; more important, if it could be turned into a joke. Look at the back of his mind and you will always see the same thing: horror of a fact. That is what lies before you, Denis, if, in a world of facts, you refuse to assimilate them. They will disagree with you, as they disagreed with Butler. They will drive you where they drove him – into abstractions. Read Butler! You will find him full of abstractions. Others went the same way. The painter Watts, for instance. He also suffered under the reign of the giants. He also took refuge in abstractions. Faith leading Hope towards Despair. Why don't you write a book about these things, Denis?'

'I am going to be an artist.'

'An artist? That is better than a poet. Verse-making is a little out of date, is it not? It corresponds to juvenile stages of human development. Poets are a case of genepistasis. If they would at least get a new stock of ideas! Their demonology is so hopelessly threadbare. But why an artist? I think you were made for a bank manager, Denis. Don't look so surprised. Everybody grows up, you know. Shelley, if he had lived long enough, would have become a passable gentleman farmer. You can take my word for that.'

'I suppose I shall have to,' replied the young man.

'Don't take Mr Keith's word for anything!' said a voice behind his shoulder.

It was Don Francesco, who had come upon them unawares. He now removed his hat and began to mop his forehead and various double chins with a many-tilted handkerchief as large as a table-cloth.

'My dear Don Francesco!' said Keith. 'You always interrupt me in the middle of my sermons. What shall we do with you?'

'Give me something to drink,' replied the priest. 'Else I shall evaporate, leaving nothing but a grease stain on this beautiful garden path.'

'To evaporate,' said Keith, with a tinge of sadness in his voice. 'What an ideal resolution!'

'I'll get you some wine out of the house,' suggested Denis politely. 'But first of all tell me this. Mr Keith has been giving me his recipe for happiness. What is yours?'

'Happiness is a question of age. The bachelor of forty – he is the happy man.'

'That does not help me much,' said Denis. 'But I'll get your wine, all the same.'

He went.

'A nice young fellow,' observed the priest. 'This little accident of yours,' he continued, 'does not reflect itself on your face. You always look like a baby, Keith. What is your secret? I believe you have concluded a pact with the devil for your soul.'

'To tell you the truth, Don Francesco, he never made me an offer for it.'

'Sensible devil! He knows he will get it sooner or later for nothing.'

They conversed awhile till Denis returned, bearing sundry bottles and glasses on a tray. The priest smiled at the sight. Light-hearted allusions to Ganymede rose to his lips, but were repressed. He swallowed down the rising inclination to be classical at the expense of good taste, and engulfed, on the top of it, as a kind of paper-weight, a vast tumblerful of red Nepenthe wine. The draught, instead of cheering, seemed to make him suddenly despondent. He wiped his lips and remarked, in a grave and almost conscience-stricken manner:

'I have some unpleasant news for you, gentlemen. The fountain of Saint Elias has ceased to flow. We heard it this morning from a sailor, an unusually trustworthy person – a man, I mean, who can be relied upon to tell the truth when there is nothing to be gained by concealing or distorting it. The thing must have happened last night. Yes, it has dried up altogether. What is to be done?'

'You don't say so,' remarked Keith. 'This is really interesting! I thought something was going to happen. I suppose your people are rather alarmed?'

Denis interrupted:

'I don't understand what you are talking about. Why should

132

not a fountain dry up if it wants to? And what does it matter to anybody?'

'What does it matter?' echoed the priest. 'This is no ordinary fountain, I am sorry to say. Have you never heard of Beelzebub?'

CHAPTER 16

Now, with regard to fountains, it is to be noted that Nepenthe, an islet of volcanic stone rising out of the blue Mediterranean, has never – for all its natural attractions – been renowned for cool springs and bubbling streamlets. There is, to be sure, a charming couplet in some old humanist about *lympha Nepenthi*; but modern scholars are disposed to think either that the text is corrupt and that the writer was picturing an imaginary *nympha* – some laughing sea-lady – or else that he merely indulged in one of those poetic flights which are a feature of the literature of his period. For whatever the cause may be – whether internal fires have scorched up the natural humours of the soil, or whether the waters of Nepenthe are of such peculiar heaviness that, instead of flowing upwards in the shape of fountains, they tumble downwards into caverns below the sea – the fact remains: Nepenthe is a waterless land. And this may well be the reason, as several thoughtful observers have already pointed out, why its wines are so abundant in quantity, so cheap in price, and of such super-excellent flavour. For it is a fact conformable to that law of compensation which regulates all earthly affairs, a fact borne out by the universal experience of mankind, that God, when He takes away with one hand, gives with the other. Lack of water, on the face of things, might be deemed a considerable hardship. There are tracts in Africa where people have been known to barter wives and children for a cupful of the liquid element. Of the inhabitants of Nepenthe it must be said to their credit that they endure their lot with equanimity, and even cheerfulness. Their wine costs nothing. Why grumble at the inscrutable ways of Providence? Why be thirsty, why be sober, when you can get as drunk as a lord for the asking?

For the rest, there are indications to show that such was not the original condition of affairs on the island. On the contrary, certain legends still current among the country-folk lead one to suspect that fountains once flowed on this arid rock. And more than legends. Monsignor Perrelli, in his *Antiquities of Nepenthe*, has gone into the subject with his usual thoroughness. The reader who takes the trouble to consult that work will find, in the twenty-sixth chapter of the third section dealing with the Natural

133

Productions and Water-Supply of the island, an enumeration of no less than twelve fountains still flowing during the author's lifetime. Some of them issued high up, in rocky clefts; others at the middle heights, among vineyards and orchards; the majority at, or near, the seashore. All of these springs, he tells us, had the following features in common: they were more or less hot, unpleasant to the taste, of foetid odour, and therefore unfit for culinary or other common uses. 'But let it be not supposed,' he hastens to add, 'that they were worthless, inasmuch as there is no such thing as a worthless gift of Providence. Whoever argues on such fallacious lines,' he says, 'will stand convicted both of folly and of irreverence, seeing that it is the business of mankind, when confronted by a phenomenon which seems to mock their intelligence, humbly to ponder the evidence – to investigate causes and ascertain results.' In the present case the utility of the waters, if not for cooking or drinking, then for other specific purposes, had been put to the proof time out of mind, in an empirical fashion; though it was not till the reign of the Good Duke Alfred that a series of classical experiments placed our knowledge of their medicinal properties on a sound scientific footing.

In a dissertation attached to this twenty-sixth chapter – a dissertation larded with illustrative extracts from Galen, Celsus, Avicenna, Antonius Musa, Oribasius and about fifty others of the ancients who professed the healing art – Monsignor Perrelli condenses for his readers the results of these classical experiments; he hands down the names of these springs and their manifold healing virtues.

The Fountain of Saint Calogero, described as one of the most famous, was lukewarm, of ammoniacal and alkaline flavour; a glassful of it produced the most violent retchings and vomitings. Properly applied, however, the water had been found to relieve the gout, the discomforts of child-bearing, leprosy, irritation of the mucous membrane of the nose, impetigo, strabismus, and ophthalmia. If the patient observed care in his diet, avoiding articles of calorific nature such as fried fish and boiled lentils, he would find himself greatly benefited by its use in the case of cornucoptic hydrocephalus, flatulence, tympanitis, and varicose veins. It was useful, furthermore, as a cure for the stings of scorpions and other venomous beasts.

The so-called 'Fountain of Paradise', of nitrous ingredients, spurted forth with a prodigious hissing noise, at a temperature of boiling lead, from so inaccessible a fissure in the rocks that little had been done to investigate its peculiar properties. It was held none the less to be efficacious for the distemper known as *plica polonica*, and the peasant folk, mixing its spray with the acorns on which their pigs were fattened, had observed that these quadrupeds prospered vastly in health and appearance.

The Fountain of Hercules, laxative and tartaric, had proved its efficacy in cases of enlarged spleen, hare-lip, vertigo, apoplexy, cachexia, cacodoria, cacochymia senilis, and chilblains. It was also considered to be a sovereign remedy for that distressing and almost universal complaint, the piles.

The Fountain known as 'La Salina', of arsenical nature, was frequented chiefly by women who found in its waters an alleviation for troubles which Monsignor Perrelli does not specify. It was recommended, moreover, as a sheep-dip.

The Fountain of the Virgin, purgative and blastopeptic, had given relief to sufferers from the quartan fever, herpes, elephantiasis, and to all persons of atrabiliary and lunatick temperament.

The so-called 'Old Fountain', of sub-acidulate and vitriolique flavour, chalybeate and cataplastic, was renowned for removing stains from household linen. Taken in minute doses, under medical advice, it gave relief to patients afflicted with the wolfe, *noli me tangere*, crudities, Babylonian itch, globular pemphlegema, fantastical visions, koliks, asthma, and affections of the heart. It also 'fortifies the stomach, comforts the bowels, reduces the gall-stone to sand, the sand to mud, the mud to water – water which can be passed out of the system by the usual channels'.

The Fountain of Saint Vulcan, anti-blepharous and amygdaloidal, was charged with such potent minerals that a single spoonful produced a diarrhoea more distressing to witness than cholera. None the less, applied externally, it was a wondrous remedy in cases of jaundice, toothache, and open wounds.

The Fountain of the Capon, sedative and scorbutic, was indicated for rheumatisms of every kind, not excluding sprained limbs, hydrophobia, lycanthropy, black choler, oppilations, and procrastinating catapepsia.

The Fountain known as 'Spina Santa' was resorted to by all persons suffering from maladies of the alimentary canal, such as dysentery, cloven palate, follicular hepatitis, and trabulated hyperaemia of the Bivonian passage.

The Fountain of Saint Feto had, by virtue of its smell alone, applied to her nose as she lay in her coffin, raised from the dead a certain Anna da Pasto.

The Fountain popularly called 'La Pisciarella' was peculiarly adapted to those ailments which are incidental to childhood and youth – to wit: chlorosis, St Vitus' Dance, constipation, ringworm, otootitis, and other perimingeal disturbances, urticaria, moon-sickness, scrofula, and incontinence of urine.

Lastly, the Fountain of Saint Elias, sulphurous and saponaceous, was renowned for its calming influence upon all who suffered from abuse of lechery or alcohol, or from ingrowing toe-nails.

This concludes the list.

'Whence we may safely infer,' said Monsignor Perrelli at the termination of this chapter, 'that our island is second to no part of the globe in this divine gift of salutary waters. And if some should ask why certain of these springs have recently undergone a marked diminution in volume we can but answer, simply and truthfully, that their virtues are no longer in as great demand as formerly. For is it not a fact that distempers like leprosy and *plica polonica* are now almost unknown on Nepenthe? It follows that the waters adapted to maladies such as these have performed their appointed task, so far as this island is concerned. They are doubtless flowing elsewhere, through mysterious channels of the earth, to carry their health-giving virtues into fresh regions for the saving of men's lives, to the glory of their Creator.'

Thus far the learned and ingenious Monsignor Perrelli. ...

It stands to reason that so remarkable a chapter should not have escaped the notice of the bibliographer, who, as already observed, had been engaged for the last quarter of a century in elucidating the text of the old historian and enriching it with footnotes for the better understanding of modern students. In the interval of three and a half centuries many changes had taken place in the physical aspect of Nepenthe; among other things, these twelve streams of pestilential odour had ceased to flow, all save the fountain of Saint Elias; their very sites had been forgotten, though traditions of their former existence still lingered among the populace.

Searching among the archives for whatever might bear on the ancient history of these springs, Mr Eames had accumulated abundant material for footnotes geological, hydrographical, and balneo-therapic. Furthermore, his personal explorations on the island had enabled him to locate the site of at least four of these old fountains, and to prove that if some of them had been covered up under the *débris* of landslides, the majority had disappeared in consequence of a general desiccation of the province.

Lastly and chiefly, his investigations had brought him in contact with that manuscript, already mentioned, of the Dominican monk Father Capocchio – a manuscript in which he alighted upon a curious but troublesome literary discovery anent these very fountains. The author, a contemporary of Monsignor Perrelli, a hater of Nepenthe, a cleric of lascivious and lecherous temperament, has in this parchment preserved what he calls a 'popular joke' – a saying which he declares to have been 'common property of the whole country' on the subject of Nepenthe and its evil-smelling waters. It was one of those scholarly, ponderous, and yet hopelessly straightforward jokes of the late Renaissance; a joke to which Monsignor Perrelli does not allude, both for reasons of local patriotism and of general decorum; some vulgar dictum, in short, connected with the name of the patron saint of Nepenthe who, he urged, was simply a local nature-god, christianized.

When the bibliographer's eagle eye first fell upon this passage he was staggered. Then, on reflection, he found himself in an awkward predicament – his natural modesty as a man contending with a no less natural and legitimate pride and desire as historian that the fruits of his labours should not be lost.

'These,' he said, 'are the dilemmas which confront the conscientious annotator.'

What position was he to take up? Should he exclude the miserable joke altogether from his amended and enlarged edition of Perrelli? He did not feel himself justified in this line of conduct. Some future investigator would be sure to unearth it and get the credit for his industry. Should he re-state it in such terms as to make it palatable to refined readers, diluting its primary pungency without impairing its essential signification? He was disposed to adopt that course, but, unfortunately, all attempts at verbal manipulation failed. Good scholar as Mr Eames was, the joke proved to be obdurate, uncompromising; vainly he wrestled with it; try as he would, it stood out naked and unashamed, refusing to be either cajoled or bullied into respectability. There was no circumventing that joke, he decided. Should he reproduce it therefore *in extenso*? Such, after mature deliberation and not without certain moral misgivings, he conceived to be his duty towards posterity. Veiled in the obscurity of a learned tongue, the joke was surreptitiously introduced into the company of a thousand chaste footnotes that could dispense with such covering devices.

Of the subsequent history of the Saint Elias Fountain, which alone still continued to flow, the bibliographer also learned much – how its fame had grown in the seventeenth and eighteenth centuries till it attracted invalids from the most distant provinces, necessitating the erection of a palatial pump-room for the better accommodation of visitors; how latterly again the waters had unaccountably fallen into disfavour with the public. And this, not-withstanding the fact that in 1872 the celebrated Privy Councillor Dr Saponaro, Director of the Montecitorio Home for Incurables, had written, at the urgent solicitation of the Nepenthe Town Authorities (who were alarmed at the decrease in their bathing-tax revenue), a pamphlet – a pamphlet which, by the way, cost them a mint of money in view of the author's deserved reputation as incorruptible scientist – a pamphlet extolling the virtues of the spring; proving, by elaborate chemical analysis, that its ingredients had not only not changed a whit since the days of Monsignor Perrelli but actually improved in quality; and concluding with the warm recommendation that they were as well adapted as ever for curing those ailments to which the island population was peculiarly liable – namely, the consequences of excessive lechery and alcohol, and the discomfort caused by ingrowing toe-nails.

The local deputy, Don Giustino Morena, had often promised his Nepenthean constituents to look into the matter and see that something was done. But he was a busy man. Up to the present he had apparently not moved a finger.

And now this fountain, the last survivor of the twelve health-giving springs, had suddenly run dry. ...

The bad news spread like wild-fire. It was regarded – for reasons which will presently appear – as a portent of gravest significance. The clergy met in unofficial but well-attended conclave to deliberate as to what attitude should be adopted towards the phenomenon, and what measures taken to allay popular apprehensions.

There was gossip, too, at the Club. Most of its members were of the *laissez-faire* or even rationalistic type, and one of them – an unobtrusive Hindu who was suspected of wearing stays – went so far in his indifference as to declare that the only result of the dry-ing-up of the fountain would be 'one smell the less on Nepenthe'. A small but compact minority, however, thought otherwise. Ob-sessed by vague forebodings, they found an able and eloquent in-terpreter of their fears in the Commissioner, who, rather redder in the face than usual, strode fussily up and down the premises, tugging at his disreputable briar pipe, drinking whisky with any-body who cared to pay for it, and declaring to all and sundry that something must be done. It was his panacea – his unvarying for-mula for every emergency, scandalous or otherwise. Something must be done, he avowed. And from the card-table came two ap-proving echoes – the voices of Mr Muhlen and Signor Malipizzo, who did not care tuppence about the fountain but never lost an

138

opportunity of expressing their public approval of Mr Parker's words and actions.

Something must be done and that soon, for in a few brief hours an atmosphere of gloom, a sense of impending calamity, had begun to hover over the sunny island. The natives called to mind, with consternation, that only once within the memory of their ancestors had the fountain behaved after this fashion. It was on the eve of that great volcanic outbreak on the mainland which, by a deadly shower of ashes, destroyed their crops and impoverished them to such an extent that for three consecutive months they could barely afford the most unnecessary luxuries of life. They opined with some show of reason that the little streamlet had been tempted by ancient and obscure bonds of sympathy to forsake its old home and creep away, under leagues of shimmering sea, towards the fiery heart of the volcano; there to undergo some chemical process of readjustment, some ordeal, some torrid nuptial rite which would result in the birth of a flaming monster and the ruin of mankind.

The terrace was crowded with folk; all eyes were turned towards the distant fire-mountain. But the volcano had never looked so placid, so harmless, so attractive; its shapely flanks suffused with the crimson light of evening, while wreaths of violet vapour ascended in lazy intermittent spirals from the cone. They rose into the zenith playfully, one after the other, as though the volcano were desirous of drawing attention to its pretty manners, and were wafted onwards, in delicate wisps of smoke, by the persistent South wind. The clergy now began to appear in goodly numbers upon the scene. They were in the best of humours and more ready than usual, it seemed, to take part in any conversation which might be going on. It had been decided, during their informal gathering, that the apprehensions of the faithful could not be better allayed at this preliminary stage than by a mild demonstration of this kind. Appearances were everything; so they had concluded, not for the first time. And it was precisely then that the simple-minded *parroco*, surrounded by a knot of devout believers, pointed to the playful cloudlets of smoke as they issued from the mouth of the crater, and made a remark which he thought not only cheerful and apposite, but calculated to calm the minds of his hearers. He said that no rosy schoolboy smoking his first cigarette ever looked more innocent. An ominous, fateful speech! Yet such was his holy simplicity that he failed to realize its import. He failed to perceive how inauspicious the metaphor had been till Don Francesco in a whisper, pointed out that appearances are apt to be deceptive

139

and, alluding to certain experiences of his own at the tender age of six years, affirmed that the smoking of a first cigarette, for all its seeming harmlessness, is liable to be followed by something in the nature of a cataclysm.

There was worse to come. For while the sun yet lingered on the horizon news of further portents came thick and fast. A plum-tree belonging to a farmer of good standing had unaccountably lost all its leaves. The Duchess arrived in a state of unusual trepidation, declaring that the tortoise-shell of her lorgnette gave forth a crackling sound. She appealed to Don Francesco to explain the meaning of this extraordinary circumstance; it crackled most distinctly, she declared. Not far from the little bay where only yesterday the streamlet of Saint Elias still trickled into the sea, a fisherman had caught a one-eyed lamprey – a beast unquestionably of ill repute. The bibliographer, strolling about with Denis, recollected that his fox-terrier that very morning had been violently sick. He seemed to attach no great importance to the affair; all the same, he said, it was rather queer; dogs are not like that; now if it had been Keith. ... The baby of the principal grocer had tumbled downstairs and thereupon proceeded to swallow eight of its elder brother's marbles which had been carelessly left on the floor – without experiencing, so far as could be ascertained, any appreciable injury. A mysterious disease, known as the scabies, had broken out among the Russian apostles. The yacht of the American millionaire, Mr van Koppen, arrived that day; there was nothing startling in this, since he visited the island year after year at the same season; but why should she collide with a fishing-boat at the moment of anchoring?

And from the Old Town came news of a portentous fowl which had suddenly assumed the plumage of the male sex. It was a hen renowned, hitherto, for her temperate and normal habits and, as it happened, known by sight to the local parish priest, who, horrified at the transformation of the feathered monster and mindful of the Papal Bull *ne nimis noceant nobis* which enjoins upon Christians the duty of destroying all unnatural productions, however generated, incontinently ordered it to be put out of the way. But the destruction of this androgyne proved an arduous task. It was reported that the creature fought for its life with the energy of a demon, crowing vigorously the while and laying, in the very act of death, an egg – an egg of spheroidal form, bluish in colour, and apparently hard-boiled – an egg which the Chief Medical Officer of Health had no great difficulty in recognizing as that of a cockatrice.

In view of these and other sinister occurrences it is not surprising that a sense of insecurity should have fallen upon the more credulous section of the natives. Even sceptical persons thought it rather provoking on the part of Providence, or whoever managed these things, that the disquieting of men's minds should take place during this particular fortnight, the most important of the whole year, midway between the great feasts of Saint Dodekanus and Saint Eulalia, when the island was crammed with visitors.

And there followed late at night yet another surprise. Mr Parker had been called away from his duties at the Club in hot haste by the news that his lady was seriously ill. A few days earlier she had been stung on the lip by a mosquito; no further attention was paid to the incident, though the disagreeable South wind provoked a rise in temperature and some discomfort. On this afternoon, however, her face had suddenly begun to assume strange tints and to swell in wondrous fashion. It was now already enlarged to twice its natural size and altogether – in the words of the physician who had been summoned to her villa – 'a thing to see'.

It had always been a thing to see. So, at least, said those who were privileged to know. There were tropical strains in her blood – strains from some flowery land in the Caribbean Sea – strains which refused to mingle in harmonious fashion with the white elements in her ancestry. She was neither lovely nor lovable, and it was regarded as a kindly dispensation of Heaven that some malformation of the lower limbs kept her confined to her boudoir, where no visitor ever called save a few misguided new-comers to the island who were unaware of her idiosyncrasies. These idiosyncrasies, due to the enforced inactivity of her feet, took the form of a grotesque activity of the tongue. Her infirmity preventing her from learning how things really stood, she let her phantasy run riot on the occasional reports which reached the villa; and that phantasy, nourished by lack of physical exercise, indulged in a love of scandalmongering which bordered, and sometimes trespassed, on the pathological. She distilled scandal from every pore, and in such liberal quantities that even the smiling and good-natured Don Francesco once spoke of her as 'the serpent in the Paradise'. But perhaps he only said that because Madame Parker was not over-fond of him – his rival the *parroco* being her friend and confessor.

Such being the case, the prospect of her possible demise was received with unconcern and even relief by all save a notable number of tradesmen who prayed fervently for her health because the lady, presuming on her connexion with the official representative

141

of the friendly state of Nicaragua, had contrived to owe them considerable sums of money. Knowing the Commissioner as they did, these victims feared that they would never be able to collect their due in the event of her death. Hence their prayers for her speedy recovery.

What would that gentleman do without her? For it was his redeeming feature that he felt, or professed to feel, affection for this graceless harridan who was the only person on earth that believed, or professed to believe, in the integrity of his motives. It is to be presumed that they saw through each other perfectly; she, at least, may well have appraised him at his true value. She must have known him for a dishonest fool. Yet this principle of mutual attachment was never relinquished. Wiser than her stepbrother, she knew that a house divided against itself must fall; she therefore approved, forcefully if without conviction, of his every word and deed. Such approval did him good. It created a fictitious self-esteem. And this was really rather unfortunate, since self-esteem, by giving him a sense of importance and consequence in the world, rendered him a good deal more objectionable to his fellow-creatures than he need have been.

Meanwhile she lingered on, and a small group of inquirers were gathered round the physician who was returning late at night from his third visit. The moralists among them saw the finger of God in the fact that her mouth, out of which had proceeded so much harm to strong men and women, should now be sealed by one of the frailest of His creatures. The doctor shrugged his shoulders at this kind of talk. He was no moralizer; he was a true Southerner, an aesthete – one of those who could appreciate the subtle beauty of a skin disease. He waxed discursive on the subject; said that the lady's face reminded him of the rainbow in a certain picture by a local genius; avowed that there were moments when even a doctor's hard life had its compensations, and that this was one of them.

His enthusiasm carried the audience off their feet. It converted the sternest preachers into artists. They forgot to talk about moral lessons. All congratulated the good Aesculapius on his choice of the medical profession as a career and his luck in beholding a spectacle such as this, especially when he added, with glowing eloquence, that it was astonishing how so small an insect, a mere mosquito, should be able to produce an eruption of this magnitude and in colours, moreover, which would have made Titian or Peter Paul Rubens burst with envy.

142

CHAPTER 17

DECIDEDLY, things were happening, as Mr Heard would have said.

Strange to say, that gentleman himself was probably the only person on Nepenthe who still remained in ignorance of all these praeternatural occurrences. In the early morning, after admiring the sea overhung by a cloudless sky and once more thanking the Duchess in his heart for such a delightful residence when he might have been boxed up in some stuffy hotel bedroom, he descended to the beach for his morning bathe. Such was his custom. The swim did him good, it freshened him up.

Then back to breakfast and a busy morning's work, to settle up arrears of correspondence. He wrote to various friends in England; he wrote a long letter – the third since his arrival – to his mother, telling her of all such things as might interest her; a nice gossipy letter, full of information about the entertainments of the foreigners on Nepenthe, about the obliging natives, the Russian colony, the persistent sirocco, his own domestic life, his improved health. Much as he liked the place and people, he said, he expected to be leaving in a week or so. He concluded with two pages describing his last visit to his cousin. She was rather poorly or troubled in mind, he thought; he would see her again ere long.

And that reminded him – he would write to Mrs Meadows as well. He did so, inquiring after her health, asking whether he could be of any assistance, and promising to call again shortly. 'Rather a formal epistle,' he concluded on reading it through. He was unable to force the note: he could never write or talk otherwise than he felt, and this cousin, after all, was rather remote, self-centred, and difficult of comprehension. 'It must go as it is,' he decided. 'To be quite frank, she's not exactly encouraging either. Asks such queer questions. What on earth did she mean by that conundrum about illegitimacy, I wonder?'

Then luncheon; then a long sleep till tea-time. Everyone slept at this hour during the days of sirocco-heat. What else was there to do? He had already learned to look forward to that calm post-prandial hour of slumber. One owes something to oneself, *n'est-ce pas?* as Muhlen had said.

On waking he bethought him of an invitation to tea with Madame Steynlin. He would have listened gladly to her music and her instructive and charitable talk about Nepenthe and its inhabitants. But he was afraid of meeting Russians there. The lady seemed to be specializing in Muscovites just then, and Mr Heard was not in the Russian mood. He would take what he called 'a day off' from social duties.

Slipping his field-glasses into his pocket, he rambled upwards by now familiar paths, past white farmhouses nestling in a riot of greenery, till he reached the barer regions. The vines were more sparsely cultivated here, and soon all trace of human handicraft was at an end. He found himself on a little plateau of volcanic cinders and lava-blocks. The spare grasses and flowers that grew between fuliginous masses of stone were already losing their bright enamel under the withering heat; a peculiar odour, acrid but stimulating to the nostrils, rose from the parched ground. Here he rested awhile. He scanned the landscape through his glasses – a wine-coloured sea at his feet, flecked with sailing-boats innumerable; confronting him the volcano whose playful antics were even then attracting the attention of a crowded Piazza. And his eye roved along the serrated contours of the mainland, its undulating shore-line, its distant peaks throbbing in the sunset glow; they rested upon many villages, coral-tinted specks of light, so far away they seemed to belong to another world. It was a pleasure to breathe on these aerial heights, surrounded by sky and sea; to survey the world as a bird might survey it. Like floating in air. ...

He sat and smoked and pondered. He tried to get himself into perspective. 'I must straighten myself out,' he thought. Assuredly it was a restful place, this Nepenthe, abounding in kindly people; his affection for it grew with every day. Rest without; but where was that old rest within, that sense of plain tasks plainly to be performed, of tangible duty? Whither had it gone? Alien influences were at work upon him. Something new had insinuated itself into his blood, some demon of doubt and disquiet which threatened his old-established conceptions. Whence came it? The effect of changed environment – new friends, new food, new habits? The unaccustomed leisure which gave him, for the first time, a chance of thinking about non-professional matters? The South wind acting on his still weakened health? All these together? Or had he reached an epoch in his development, the termination of one of those definite life-periods when all men worthy of the name pass through some cleansing process of spiritual desquamation, and slip their outworn weeds of thought and feeling?

Whatever it was he seemed to be no longer his own master, as in former days. Fate had caused his feet to stray towards something new – something alarming. He was poised, as it were, on the brink of a gulf. Or rather, it was as if that old mind of his, like a boat sailing hitherto briskly before the wind, had suddenly encountered a bank of calm, of utter and ominous calm; it was a thing spellbound; a toy of circumstances beyond human control. The canvas hung in the stagnant air. From which quarter would the quickening breeze arrive? Whither would it bear him?

And his glance fell upon a slender coquettish vessel, a newcomer, lying in the sunny harbour under the cliff. He knew it from hearsay. It was the *Flutterby*, van Koppen's yacht. He recollected all he had ever heard about the millionaire; he tried to conjure up some idea of his features and habits from gossip overheard at odd moments.

This man, he concluded, must be intelligent beyond ordinary standards. It would be worth while making his acquaintance. America is notoriously the land of youthful precocity. But it is not every American who, as a stripling of fourteen summers, puzzling in callow boyish perplexity upon the thousand ills that afflict mankind and burning with desire for their betterment, makes a discovery in Malthusian methods destined to convulse the trade and the social life of a continent. Not everybody is like young Koppen – he attached a van to his name on reaching his seventy-fifth million – who, possessed at that time of barely three dollars in the world and not even the shadow of a moustache, had both the wit to realize the hygienic importance of a certain type of goods and the pertinacity to insist on cheapening their price, in the interests of public health, to such an extent that – to quote from subsequent advertisements – they should be 'within reach of the humblest home'. It is not everybody – no, not every American – who, after revolutionizing the technique of manufacture and shattering the Paris monopoly, dares boldly to advertise the improved article across the length and breadth of the land, and to thrust his commodity upon a reluctant market in the teeth of popular prejudice and commercial rivalry. Van Koppen had done all this. And it was noted that he had done it without ever for a moment losing sight of his dual aim – mercantile and philanthropic; for if he was a humanitarian by natural disposition, he became what is called 'a tradesman by force of circumstance' – and not a bad tradesman either. He had done all this and more. Unlike most self-made men who remain yoked like oxen to their sordid affairs (in harness, they aptly call it), he had been shrewd enough to retire from business in the heyday of his age, on a relatively modest competence of fifteen million dollars a year. He was spending his time at present in the gratification of personal whims, and leaving the remaining millions to be picked up by whoever cared to take the trouble. Manifestly an unusual type of millionaire – this man who had lived down half a century of obloquy and was now hailed, in well-informed circles, as the saviour of his country.

Nor was this all. Van Koppen was described as a brisk, genial, talkative old fellow, rather fat, with a clear complexion, sound teeth, scrubby grey beard, a twang barely sufficient to authenticate his transatlantic descent, and the digestion of a boa-constrictor. He was tremendously fond of buttered tea-cakes – so the Duchess said; a man who, in the words of Madame Steynlin, 'really appreciated good music' and who, as the *parroco* never ceased to declare, could be relied on to give a handsome contribution towards the funds for supporting the poor and repairing a decrepit parish organ. (The parish poor were never in such dire distress, the parish organ never so hopelessly deranged, as during that annual week when the *Flutterby* rode at anchor.)

In fact there was no doubt about it; van Koppen had the gift of making himself beloved. But nobody's company was more markedly to his taste than that of Count Caloveglia. The two old men spent hours together in Caloveglia's shady courtyard, eating candied fruits, sipping home-made liqueurs of peaches or mountainherbs and talking – ever talking. Between them there existed some strong and strange bond of friendship or interest. Speculation was rife as to its origin, its meaning, its end.

What was all the talk about?

Andrea, the devoted retainer, however, artfully approached on the subject, was ambiguous to a distressing degree. It was understood, none the less, that Count Caloveglia was perhaps of use to the other in the accumulation of classical relics which – the Italian Government forbidding the export of antique works of art – were smuggled at night-time on board the *Flutterby* to be incorporated in a magnificent museum somewhere out West, a museum which was destined to be presented by van Koppen as a gift to the great American people. Again, it might be inferred that these two elderly gentlemen, choice representatives of two conflicting civilizations, widely experienced and profoundly versed, each in his own way, in the knowledge of mankind, took a sincere and childlike pleasure in one another's society, going over past times and anxious, to the very end of life, to add something fresh to their store of learning.

Both these explanations were sufficiently plausible to be straightway dismissed by the majority as inadequate to account for the phenomenon. They inclined, rather, to adopt an alternative and alluring theory propounded by the Commissioner's lady. This

146

theory laid it down that the American was bargaining for the Count's daughter, a pretty girl whom the old ruffian had shut up in a convent somewhere in anticipation of the day when a purchaser, rich enough to content his inordinate lust of gold, should present himself. Van Koppen was that purchaser. They had now been haggling, she said, for two or three years; a *dénouement* might be expected at any moment. If the Count's avarice could be appeased the unhappy child might expect to find herself, with as little delay as possible, an inmate of the floating harem on board the *Flutterby*.

No visitor was safe from her lively tongue, and alas, certain little details, insignificant in themselves, gave ground for the ungenerous hypothesis that van Koppen, like all the rest of them, had his cloven hoof. There was the usual 'dark side' to this otherwise charming and profitable stranger, the usual mystery, the usual fly in the ointment. In the first place, it was a singular fact, much commented on, that nobody had ever been invited on board the yacht. That alone was suspicious. *If you want to get anything out of old Koppen* – so ran a local saying – DON'T *propose a visit to the Flutterby*. More curious still was the circumstance that nobody, save the owner and certain bearded venerables of the crew, had ever been known to land on the island. How about the other passengers? Who were they? The millionaire never so much as mentioned their existence. It was surmised, accordingly, that he voyaged over the seas with a bevy of light-hearted nymphs; a disreputable mode of conduct for a man of his advanced years, and all the more aggravating to other people since, like a crafty and jealous old sultan, he screened them from public view. Impropriety could be overlooked – it could pass, where a millionaire was concerned, under the heading of unconventionality; but such glaring selfishness might end in being fatal to his reputation.

Confirmatory evidence of this scandalous state of affairs was obtained, one sunny morning in the most unexpected fashion. A fisherman named Luigi, paddling about the stern of the *Flutterby*, where, in consequence of the kitchen refuse thrown overboard, marine beasts of every shape and kind were wont to congregate, cast down his spear at what looked like a splendid caerulean flatfish of uncommon size and brilliance. The creature shivered and collapsed at that contact in the most unnatural, unfishlike manner; and Luigi drew up, to his amazement, a fragment of a lady's dress – to wit, a short length of sky-blue *crêpe de Chine*. Bitterly disappointed, he nevertheless took the matter with characteristic Southern philosophy. 'This will do for my little Annarella,' he decided. And doubtless the child, arrayed in these celestial tints, would have been the envy of all her girl companions at the next festival of the patron saint but for the fact that Mr Freddy Parker was strolling on the beach at the very moment of the man's return to land. By a piece of rare good luck, as he himself phrased it, his eye fell upon the dripping fabric; by a stroke of intuition not rare but unique, he divined its worth as a sociological document. Promising the man a reasonable sum of money (the Commissioner happened to have no loose change in his pocket just then) he carried the incriminating morsel in triumph to the Residency, where it was displayed by his lady, to all and sundry, in corroboration of her theory.

'That settles it,' she used to say. 'Unless indeed he dresses up his cabin-boy as a girl; and in that case ...'

Mr Heard, reposing on the rough pumiceous ground with his eye fixed upon the naughty *Flutterby*, whose virginal whiteness, with declining day, had assumed a tell-tale crimson blush, pieced together these and sundry other little bits of information. They made him more than usually thoughtful; they chimed in with his momentary mood of self-analysis.

One thing was dead certain. To circumnavigate the globe in the arms of a dozen chorus-girls was not his ideal. He was not built on those lines. He purposed, God willing, to spend the evening of his days in another and more respectable manner. A vision arose before his imagination – a vision of a peaceful homestead among the green lanes of England, where he would lead a life of study and of kindly, unostentatious acts, with family and friends; old friends of College days, and London days, and African days; new friends from among the rising generation – straightforward and decent-minded youngsters, whom he would take to his heart like a father.

Why could not van Koppen see the beauty of such dreamings?

And yet, he argued, if the man does seclude them in this fashion – supposing they really exist – who can blame him? No woman is safe on Nepenthe with persons like Muhlen about. From chance meetings in the street, from stray conversations overheard, he had been led to take an unreasoning dislike to this foreigner, whose attitude towards the gentle sex struck him as that of a cur. Muhlen, if the yacht were his, would flaunt these ladies about the streets. The American, in keeping them secluded on board, betrayed a sense of shame, almost of delicacy; a sense of his obligations towards society which, so far as it went, was rather a laudable trait of character than otherwise.

And then – the difference between himself and the millionaire in life, training, antecedents! A career such as van Koppen's called for qualities different, often actually antagonistic, to his own. You could not possibly expect to find in a successful American merchant those features which go to form a successful English ecclesiastic. Certain human attributes were mutually exclusive – avarice and generosity, for instance; others no doubt mysteriously but inextricably intertwined. A man was an in-dividual; he could not be divided or taken to pieces; he could not be expected to possess virtues incompatible with the rest of his mental equipment: however desirable such virtues might be. Who knows! Van Koppen's doubtful acts might be an unavoidable expression of his personality, an integral part of that nature under whose ferocious stimulus he had climbed to his present enviable position. And Mr Heard was both shocked and amused to reflect that but for the cooperation of certain coarse organic impulses to which these Nepenthe legends testified, the millionaire might never have been able to acquire the proud title of 'Saviour of his Country'.

'That's queer,' he mused. 'It never struck me before. Shows how careful one must be. Dear me! Perhaps the ladies have inevitable organic impulses of a corresponding kind. Decidedly queer. H'm. Ha. Now I wonder. ... And perhaps, if the truth were known, these young persons are having quite a good time of it –'

He paused abruptly in his reflections. He had caught himself in the act; in the very act of condoning vice. Mr Thomas Heard was seriously concerned.

Something was wrong, he concluded. He would never have argued on similar lines a short time ago. This downright sympathy with sinners, what did it portend? Did it betray a lapse from his old-established principles, a waning of his respect for traditional morality? Was he becoming a sinner himself?

Thomas – the doubting apostle. He wondered whether there was anything in a name.

Then he called to mind how he had approved – yes, almost approved – of Don Francesco's deplorable act of familiarity towards the little serving-maid. An absurdly small matter, but symptomatic. Things like that had happened in Africa lately. He remembered various instances where he had intervened on behalf of the natives, despite the murmured protests of the missionaries. They were such laughing, good-natured animals – so fine and healthy! What was it, this excessive love of erring humanity, and

149

whither trending? Mr Heard began to vex his soul, to stray about in a maze of doubts. It was so miserably complex, this old, old problem of right and wrong; so unreasonably many-sided. Anon, he pulled himself together with characteristic bluntness.

'The whole question,' he concluded, 'is plain as a pikestaff. Am I becoming more of a Christian, or less?'

As though to learn an answer to his riddle he gazed from his eyrie over the wide horizon, upon leagues of sea rising upward to blend their essence, under the magic touch of evening, with the purple dome overhead.

The elements, as is their wont upon such occasions, gave forth no clear reply.

CHAPTER 18

AND now, in the sunlit hour of dawn, he was bathing again. An excellent habit. It did him good, this physical contact with nature. Africa had weakened his constitution. Nepenthe made him feel younger once more – capable of fun and mischief. The muscles were acquiring a fresh tone, that old zest of life was coming back to him. His health, without a shadow of doubt, had greatly improved.

While disporting himself in amphibious joy among the tepid waves he seemed to cast off that sense of unease which had pursued him of late. It was good to inhale the harsh salty savour – to submit himself to these calming voices – to float, like a careless Leviathan, in the blue immensity; good to be alive, simply alive.

Another hot and clammy day was in store for the island. No matter. This sirocco, of which older inhabitants might well complain, had so far exerted no baleful influence upon him. Quite the reverse. Under its tender moistening touch his frame, desiccated in the tropics, seemed to open out, even as a withered flower uncloses its petals in water. In Africa all his thoughts and energies had been concentrated upon a single point. Here he expanded. New interests, new sensations, seemed to lie in wait for him. Never had he felt so alert, so responsive to spiritual impressions, so appreciative of natural beauty.

Lying in motionless ecstasy on the buoyant element he watched the mists of morning as they soared into the air. Reluctantly, with imperceptible movement, they detached themselves from their watery home; then clambered aloft in spectral companies, drawn skyward, as by some beckoning hand, under the stealthy compulsion of the sun. They crept against the tawny precipices, clinging to their pinnacles like shreds of pallid gauze, and nestling demurely among dank clefts where something of the mystery of night still lingered. It was a procession of dainty shapes wreathing themselves into gracious attitudes; mounting – ever mounting. As he beheld their filmy draperies that swayed phantom-like among the crags overhead, he understood those pagan minds of olden days for whom such wavering exhalations were none other than sea-nymphs, Atlantides, offspring of some mild-eyed god of Ocean rising to greet their playfellows, the Oreads, on the hills.

The wildest stretch of Nepenthe coast-line lay before him. Its profile suggested not so much the operation of terrestrial forces as a convulsed and calcined lunar landscape – the handiwork of some demon in delirium. Gazing landwards, nothing met his eye save jagged precipices of fearful height, tormented rifts and gullies scorched by fires of old into fantastic shapes, and descending confusedly to where the water slept in monster-haunted caverns.

Not a sign of humanity was visible save one white villa, far away. It was perched on a promontory of heliotrope-tinted trachyte; struck by the morning beams it flashed and glowed like a jewel in the sunshine. He knew the place: Madame Steynlin's abode. The sight of it reminded him of a promise to attend her picnic next week; all Nepenthe would be invited, after the feast of Saint Eulalia. And hard by the shore, at its foot, he discerned certain minute scarlet specks.

What could they be?

Why, of course! They were recognizable, even at this distance, as the blouses of the Sacred Sixty-three, who frequented this somewhat public spot for bathing purposes, blandly indifferent, or resigned, to the gaze of inquisitive onlookers. Mr Heard, among others, had witnessed their aquatic diversions.

The Messiah was hindered by age and growing infirmities from taking part in the proceedings; moreover, he had been sickening lately, it was said, for some new Revelation – a Revelation of which the island was to become cognizant that very morning. But others of the Muscovite band were fond of congregating at this spot and hour for their lustral summer rites – white-skinned lads and lasses, matrons and reverent elders, all in a state of Adamitic nudity, splashing about the water of this sunny cove, devouring raw fish and crabs after the manner of the fabled Ichthyophagi, laughing, kissing, saying nice things about God, and combing out

151

each other's long tow-coloured hair. Madame Steynlin, a spectator by necessity if not deliberate choice of these patriarchal frolics, disdained to controvert certain frivolous folk who resorted to the same beach to gratify a morbid curiosity, under the pretext that it was a delectable entertainment and one of the sights of Nepenthe. She disdained, nowadays. It had not ever been thus. Things were different before Peter the Great came upon the scene. In those unregenerate times her Lutheran upbringing condemned, in no measured terms, this frank exhibition of animal nature. A warm friendship with the good-looking apostle had now opened her eyes to the mystic sense of what went on. Earthly love had given an unearthly tinge to her mind. The veil had fallen; she saw through external appearances into the Symbolic Beyond. Deeply penetrated of its inner meaning, she would say that the spectacle called up visions of the Age of Innocence, when the world was young. ...

An elegant rowing-boat suddenly swept into Mr Heard's field of vision. It had approached from round the entrance of the small bay and was already within a few yards ere he caught sight of it. He dived skilfully, and on returning to the surface beheld Mr Keith smiling upon him, with owlish benevolence, through his spectacles.

'How pretty you look,' he said. 'Just like a mermaid that's lost its tail.'

'You flatter me!'

'Not at all. Climb in and I'll take you for a row.'

'Hadn't I better get some clothes on?'

'As you please. We can take you off that boulder if you want to dress.'

'You're very kind.'

Kind indeed. To admit a friend into one of his yachts or rowing-boats was an act of rare self-sacrifice on the part of Mr Keith, who maintained that no vessel, not even an Atlantic liner, was large enough for more than one passenger.

'You are comfortable in here,' the bishop remarked, as he presently stepped on board, and looked around him. 'Cleopatra's barge must have been something like this.'

'There will be no breeze worth talking about all day. We must row.'

An awning of red silk screened off the rays of the sun; the appointments of the small boat – the polished wood of rare texture, morocco leather cushions, and elaborate fittings – bespoke the taste or at least the income of a Sybarite. A grizzly brown sailor

152

and his curly-pated son were the oarsmen; in the stern sat a couple of Keith's attendants, whom Mr Heard might have mistaken for two Greek genii but for the fact that between them lay an enormous and hideously modern receptacle of wicker-work which impaired the illusion. It troubled the bishop, both by reason of its incongruity and because he could not divine what its purport might be, till Keith solved the mystery by saying,

'I thought I would like to see for myself about this fountain of Saint Elias and, incidentally, enjoy a little al fresco luncheon by the shore. Now I wonder whether there will be enough food for both of us in the basket?'

'That thing? Dear me. I thought it might contain a cottage piano. What fountain?'

'You haven't heard anything? Nothing at all?'

He outlined the events of the preceding day.

'What?' he continued. 'They didn't even tell you about Miss Wilberforce? Well, whether she thought it was her birthday, or whether all these omens upset her nerves – Oh, the usual thing, only rather more so. Decidedly more so. It was late at night, you see, and she insisted on singing "Auld Lang Syne", and even on translating it, for the benefit of the constable who arrested her, into her own particular brand of Italian. In fact, there was a good deal of trouble, till somebody let down a blanket from a window. It happened to be a new policeman unaccustomed to her ways, and he has had a bad shock. His wife complained to the judge, who sent round word to me this morning that she was in the lock-up.'

'In prison. An English lady!'

'It is not the first time by any means. But I feel exactly as you do about it. I've bailed her out, and stopped his mouth with a fifty-franc note. Please keep this between ourselves.'

Mr Heard was not pleased to learn this incident. It seemed a discordant note on Nepenthe. He observed:

'Miss Wilberforce apparently can be relied upon to create a diversion of a scandalous nature. I wish I could do something to help such a poor creature!'

'The dear lady! I don't know what we should do without her. By the way, have you seen Denis lately? We must be friendly to that young fellow, Heard. I don't think he is altogether happy in this clear pagan light. He seems to be oppressed about something. What do you make of him?'

'Of Denis? Nothing at all.'

'You interest me.'

153

'How so?'

'Because your values appear to be perverted. Your heart remains dead to Denis, but goes out to a worthless and incurable drunkard. The one is supremely happy, the other plainly troubled in mind. It leaves you cold. How do you explain it?'

Mr Heard began to wonder. Were his values really vitiated? Had he done anything to justify self-reproach? He remembered meeting Denis lately, in a fit of dejection, as it seemed; they had passed each other with a few words of greeting. Perhaps he might have been a little more friendly. Well, he would atone for it on the next occasion. He asked:

'Has he no relations?'

'A mother, at present in Florence. There have been misunderstandings, I suspect. He has probably found her out, as he found out our Duchess; as he will find out both you and me, if we give him the chance. Meanwhile he gropes about in a wistful fashion, trying to carve out a scheme of life for himself and to learn something from all of us. What can a person of that kind have in common with a mother of any kind?'

'Everything,' said Mr Heard enthusiastically.

'Nothing at all. You are thinking of your own mother. You forget that you never see her. Any son can live with any mother under those conditions. The fact remains: nobody can misunderstand a boy like his own mother. Look around you, and see if it is not true! Honour thy father and mother. Perhaps. But we must civilize our mothers before we can expect any rational companionship between them and their sons. Girls are different. They are more cynical and less idealistic, they can put up with mothers, they can laugh at them. I am speaking in a general way. Of course there are shining exceptions. Mothers at present can bring children into the world, but this performance is apt to mark the end of their capacities. They can't even attend to the elementary animal requirements of their offspring. It is quite surprising how many children survive in spite of their mothers. Ask any doctor.'

'If that is the case there must be something wrong with our social system. You may be sure that the female cat or canary bird is just as efficient in her department as the male in his. Speaking from my own experience among the London poor, I should say that the father is often a mere parasite on his wife and children –'

'We may both of us be right. But I wish you would take Denis in hand a little. Will you? Perhaps you misread his character. He may be afraid of you.'

'Have you any particular reason –?'

154

'I don't like his looks. There is something tragic about him lately.'

Mr Heard was slightly nettled. After all, he was not on Nepenthe for the purpose of doling out consolations to melancholy undergraduates.

'I should be sorry to think myself singled out for his distrust,' he replied. 'At the same time, I don't notice that he has much to say to certain other people – to the Commissioner, for instance, or to Mr Muhlen.'

'Muhlen? He is quite right to leave Muhlen alone. Quite right. It proves his intuition. I have learnt all about that man. A beastly character. He has a bad record. Lives on blackmail and women. His real name is Retlow.'

And Mr Keith lit a cigar, as though to dismiss the subject.

'Retlow, you say? That's queer.'

The name sounded familiar to the bishop. Where had he heard it before? He racked his memory. Where could it have been? Retlow. ... It was not a common name. Long ago, obviously. Where? In African days, or earlier?

His searchings were interrupted by the voice of the old boatman who, relinquishing an oar, pointed to a swart precipice near at hand and said in tolerable English (the older generation of natives all spoke English – their children were learning Russian):

'The suicides' rock, gentlemens. Ah! Many is the poor Christian I have pick up there. He throw down hiself. Him dead. Often in small pieces. Here blood. Here brain. Here leg and boot. Here finger. Ah! The poor Christian. That so, gentlemens.'

The bishop scanned with a shudder this frowning cliff of basalt, and turned to address his companion.

'Do people really throw themselves over here?'

'Very few. Not more than three or four in a season, I'm told. The local suicides, as a rule, are not as spectacular as they might be considering the landscape. They shoot themselves or take poison, which shows a certain consideration for other people. It is not a pleasant job, you know, to row to this remote spot and scramble about the cliff at the risk of a broken neck, collecting shattered fragments of humanity into a potato sack.'

'Not at all pleasant!'

'As compared with England,' Keith pursued, 'life here is intense, palpitating, dramatic – a kind of blood-curdling farce full of irresponsible crimes and improbable consequences. The soil is saturated with blood. People are always killing themselves or each other for motives which, to an Englishman, are altogether outside

155

the range of comprehensibility. Shall I tell you about one of our most interesting cases? I happened to be on the island at the time. There was a young fellow here – an agreeable young fellow – an artist; he was rich; he took a villa, and painted. We all liked him. Then, by degrees, he became secretive and moody. Said he was studying mechanics. He told me himself that much as he liked landscape painting he thought an artist – a real artist, he said – ought to be versed in ancillary sciences; in fortification, wood-carving, architecture, and so on. Leonardo da Vinci, you know. Well, one day they could not get into his bedroom. They broke open his door and discovered that he had constructed a perfectly formed guillotine; the knife had fallen; his head lay on one side and his body on the other. You may well be surprised. I went carefully into that case. He was in the best of health, with a creditable artistic record behind him. He had no troubles, financial or domestic.'

'Then what on earth –?'

'The scenery of Nepenthe. It got on his nerves; it unstrung him. Does that surprise you too? Don't you feel its effect upon your-self? The bland winds, the sea shining in velvety depths as though filled with some electric fluid, the riot of vegetation, these extrava-gant cliffs that change colour with every hour of the day? Look at that peak yonder – is it not almost transparent, like some crystal of amethyst? This coastline alone – the sheer effrontery of its mineral charm – might affect some natures to such an extent as to dislocate their stability. Northern minds seem to become fluid here, impressionable, unstable, unbalanced – what you please. There is something in the brightness of this spot which decom-poses their old particles and arranges them into fresh and unex-pected patterns. That is what people mean when they say that they "discover themselves" here. You discover a mechanism, you know, when you take it to pieces. You catch my meaning?'

'I catch it.'

He nodded. He understood perfectly. Some analogous process was going on within him at that moment. He, too, was discovering himself.

'Have you discovered yourself, Keith?'

'Yes, by other methods, elsewhere. I am only here for a short time in the spring and another ten days in September. That is hardly enough, even supposing I were the sort of person to be accessible to these externals. I have passed that stage. I am too old, too unemotional. I prefer devouring a partridge *en casserole* or listening to your conversation ('listening to my conversation!'

156

thought Mr Heard) to all the scenery in the world. But I watch other people; I make it my business to study their condition; I put myself in their places. *Je constate*, as the French say. To them, the landscape of Nepenthe is alive, often malignantly alive. They do what you cannot so effectually do in the North; they humanize it, identifying its various aspects with their own moods, its features with their own traditions.'

Mr Heard thought of those tremulous mists he had seen only an hour ago – the daughters of old Ocean.

'They humanize it,' he echoed. 'The mythopoetic faculty!'

'Perhaps this capacity of Southern scenery to hear a mortal interpretation accounts for the anthropomorphic deities of classical days. I often think it does. Even we moderns are unaccountably moved by its varying facets which act sometimes as an aphrodisiac, and sometimes by their very perfection, their discouraging spell, their insolent beauty, suggest the hopelessness of all human endeavour. .... Denis! I should think him capable of anything just now. Do you imagine a person like this could possibly remain insensible to the beguiling influence of these surroundings?'

'I never thought about him.'

'Really? You interest me, Heard. If you deny the susceptibility of a temperament like his, you deny the whole operation of externals upon character and action. You deny, for example, the success of the Roman Catholic Church, which relies, for its moral effects, upon such optic appeals to the senses, and upon the ease with which transitory feelings can be transmuted into axioms of conduct. Do you deny this?'

'Not at all. I have seen enough of their system to realize its extreme simplicity.'

'And then think of the peculiar history of this island and its situation as a converging point for men of every race and every creed. All these things stimulate to rapid nervous discharges; that is, to inconsidered, foolish actions –'

'All fools!' the boatman interrupted. 'All foreigners! We people don't do these things. Only dam-fool foreigners. That so, gentlemens. They have trouble themselves, then they come to this rock and, boom! make trouble for their friends.'

'Boom!' echoed his son, who had apparently caught the drift of the old man's speech. Whereat the two Greek genii in the stern laughed immoderately; knowing, as they did, that the boy had not the slightest idea of what his father was talking about.

'Boom!' they repeated, in derisive chorus.

At that moment all the occupants of the boat pricked up their

157

ears. A sound had reached them, a similar sound – a sound that recalled the distant firing of a big gun. Boom! It reverberated among the rocks. The rowers dropped their oars. Everyone listened.

The sound came again. This time there was no question as to its origin. It was artillery, beyond a doubt.

The old sailor had grown preternaturally grave.

'*Il cannone del duca*,' he said.

The cannon of the Good Duke Alfred, never used save on urgent or solemn occasions, was being discharged.

Then the boatman made another remark, in Italian, to Keith.

'What does he say?' asked Mr Heard.

'He thinks they must be calling out the militia.'

Something was very wrong, up yonder, on the market place.

CHAPTER 19

THE cannon, to be hereinafter described, is not the sole surviving relic of the Good Duke's rule. Turn where you please on his island domain, memories of that charming and incisive personality will meet your eye and ear; memories in stone – schools, convents, decayed castles, and bathing chalets; memories in the spoken word – proverbs attributed to him, legends and traditions of his sagacity that still linger among the populace. *In the days of the Duke*: so runs a local saying, much as we speak of the 'good old times'. His amiable, laughter-loving ghost pervades the capital to this hour. His pleasantries still resound among those crumbling theatres and galleries. That gleeful devilry of his, compounded of blood and sunshine, is the epitome of Nepenthe. He is the scarlet thread running through its annals. An incarnation of all that was best in the age, he identified, for well-nigh half a century, his interests with those of his faithful subjects.

He meditated no conquests. It sufficed him to gain and to retain the affection of men in whose eyes he was not so much a prince, a feudal lord, as an indulgent and doting father. He was the ideal despot, a man of wide culture and simple tastes. 'A smile,' he used to say, 'will sway the Universe.' Simplicity he declared to be the keynote of his nature, the guiding motive of his governance. In exemplification whereof he would point to his method of collecting taxes – a marvel of simplicity. Each citizen paid what he liked. If the sum proved insufficient he was apprised of the fact next morning by having his left hand amputated; a second error of judgement – it happened rather seldom – was

158

rectified by the mutilation of the remaining member. 'Never argue with inferiors,' was one of His Highness's most original and pregnant remarks, and it was observed that, whether he condescended to argue or not, he generally gained his point without undue loss of time.

'It's so simple,' he would say to those perplexed potentates who flocked to him from the mainland for advice on administrative questions. 'So simple! One knock to each nail. And keep smiling.'

It was the Good Duke Alfred who, with a shrewd eye to the future prosperity of his dominions, made the first practical experiments with those hot mineral springs – those healing waters whose virtues, up till then, had been unaccountably neglected. Realizing their curative possibilities, he selected fifty of the oldest and wisest of his Privy Councillors to undergo a variety of hydro-thermal tests on their bodies, internal and external. Seven of these gentlemen had the good luck to survive the treatment. They received the Order of the Golden Vine, a coveted distinction. The remaining forty-three, what was left of them, were cremated at night-time and posthumously ennobled.

He was the author of some mighty fine dissertations on falconry, dancing, and architecture. He wrote furthermore, in the flamboyant style of his period, two dozen pastoral plays, as well as a goodly number of verses addressed, for the most part, to ladies of his Court – a Court which was thronged with poets, wits, philosophers, and noble women. The island was a gay place in those days! There was always something doing. His Highness had a trick of casting favourites into dungeons, and concubines into the sea, that endeared him to his various legitimate spouses; and the rapidity with which these self-same spouses were beheaded one after the other, to make room for what he mirthfully called 'fresh blood', struck his faithful subjects as an ever-recurring miracle of state-craft. 'Nothing,' he used to say to his intimates, 'nothing ages a man like living always with the same woman.' Well aware, on the other hand, of the inequality of social conditions and keenly desirous of raising the moral tone of his people, he framed iron laws to restrain those irregularities of married life which had been a disreputable feature of local society prior to his accession.

Not in vain had he pondered in youth the political maxims of the great Florentine. He cultivated assiduously the friendship of Church and Mob; he knew that no throne, however seemingly well-established, can weather the blasts of fortune save by resting on these twin pillars of security. So it came about that, while all Europe was convulsed in savage warfare, his relations with other

159

rulers were marked by rare cordiality and simplicity of intercourse. He never failed to conciliate his more powerful neighbours by timely gifts of local delicacies – gifts of dark-eyed virgins to grace their palaces, and frequent hampers of those succulent *langoustes* for which the coastal waters of the island are renowned, both items of the finest quality obtainable. A born statesman, he extended this ingratiating demeanour even to those minor sovereigns from whom, to all appearances, he had nothing to fear, supplying them likewise with periodical consignments of pretty maidens and well-flavoured crayfish, only of somewhat inferior quality – the crustaceans often too young, the damsels occasionally over-ripe.

His high aspirations made him the precursor of many modern ideas. In educational and military matters, more especially, he ranks as a pioneer. He was a pedagogue by natural instinct. He took a sincere delight in the school-children, limited their weekly half-holidays to five, designed becoming dresses for boys and girls, decreed that lute-playing and deportment should become obligatory subjects in the curriculum, and otherwise reformed the scholastic calendar, which, before his day, had drifted into sad confusion and laxity. Sometimes he honoured the ceremony of prize-giving with his presence. On the other hand, it must be admitted that, judged by modern standards, certain of his methods for punishing disobedience smack of downright pedantry. Thrice a year, on receiving from the Ministry of Education a list containing the names of unsatisfactory scholars of either sex, it was his custom to hoist a flag on a certain hill-top; this was a signal for the Barbary pirates, who then infested the neighbouring ocean, to set sail for the island and buy up these perverse children, at purely nominal rates, for the slave-markets of Stamboul and Argier. They were sold ignominiously – by weight and not by the piece – to mark his unqualified disapproval of talking and scribbling on blotting-pads during school hours.

It is recorded of the Good Duke that on one occasion he returned from this scene looking haggard and careworn, as though the sacrifice of so many young lives weighed on his fatherly spirit. Presently, envisaging his duties towards the State, he restrained these natural but unworthy emotions, smiled his well-known smile, and gave utterance to an apophthegm which has since found its way into a good many copy-books: 'In the purity of childhood', he said, 'lie the seeds of national prosperity.' And if it be inquired by what arts of Machiavellian astuteness he alone, of all Christian princes, contrived to maintain friendly relations

160

with these formidable Oriental sea-rovers, the answer lies at hand. His device was one of extreme simplicity. He appealed to their better natures by sending them, at convenient intervals, shiploads of local delicacies, girls and lobsters – of indifferent quality, it is true, but sufficiently appetizing to attest his honourable intentions.

His predecessors, intent only upon their pleasures, had given no thought to the possibility of a hostile invasion of their fair domain. But the Good Duke, despite his popularity, was frequently heard to quote with approval that wise old adage which runs 'In peace, prepare for war.' Convinced of the instability of all mundane affairs and being, moreover, a man of original notions as well as something of an artist in costumery, he was led to create that picturesque body of men, the local Militia, which survives to this day and would alone entitle him to the grateful notice of posterity. These elegant warriors, he calculated, would serve both for the purpose of infusing terror into the minds of potential enemies, and of acting as a decorative body-guard to enhance his own public appearances on gala days. He threw his whole soul into the enterprise. After the corps had been duly established, he amused himself by drilling them on Sunday afternoons and modelling new buttons for their uniforms; to give them the requisite military stamina he over-fed and starved them by turns, wrapped them in sheepskin overcoats for long route-marches in July, exercised them in sham fights with live grapeshot and unblunted stilettos and otherwise thinned their ranks of undesirables, and hardened their physique, by forcing them to escalade horrible precipices at midnight on horseback. He was a martinet; he knew it; he gloried in the distinction. 'All the world loves a disciplinarian,' he was wont to say.

Nevertheless, like many great princes, he realized that political reasons might counsel at times an abatement of rigour. He could relent and show mercy. He could interpose his authority in favour of the condemned.

He relented on one celebrated occasion which more than any other helped to gain for him the epithet of 'The Good' – when an entire squadron of the Militia was condemned to death for some supposed mistake in giving the salute. The record, unfortunately, is somewhat involved in obscurity and hard to disentangle; so much is clear, however, that the sentence was duly promulgated and carried into effect within half an hour. Then comes the moot question of the officer in command who was obviously destined for execution with the rest of his men and who now profited, as events proved, by the clemency of the Good Duke. It appears that this individual, noted for a childlike horror of bloodshed (especially when practised on his own person), had unaccountably absented himself from the ceremony at the last moment – slipping out of the ranks in order, as he said, to bid a last farewell to his two aged and widowed parents. He was discovered in a wine-shop and brought before a hastily summoned Court-martial. There his old military courage seems to have returned to him. He demonstrated by a reference to the instructions laid down in the Militiaman's Year-book that no mistake in saluting had been made, that his men had therefore been wrongfully convicted and illegally executed, and that he, *a fortiori*, was innocent of any felonious intent. The Court, while approving his arguments, condemned him none the less to the indignity of a double decapitation for the offence of leaving his post without a signed permit from His Highness.

It was at this point that the Good Duke interposed on his behalf. He rescinded the decree; in other words, he relented. 'Enough of bloodshed for one day,' he was heard to remark, quite simply.

This speech was one of his happiest inspirations. Instantly it echoed from mouth to mouth; from end to end of his dominions. Enough of bloodshed for one day! That showed his true heart, the people declared. Enough of bloodshed! Their enthusiasm grew wilder when, in an access of princely graciousness, he repaired the lamentable excess of zeal by pinning the Order of the Golden Vine on the offending officer's breast; it rose to a veritable frenzy as soon as they learned that, by Letters Patent, the entire defunct squadron had been posthumously ennobled. And this is only one of many occasions on which this ruler, by his intimate knowledge of human nature and the arts of government, was enabled to wrest good from evil, and thereby consolidate his throne. ...

It is passing strange, on the face of it, that this vivid personality, one of the most arresting figures in the history of the country, should be so briefly dealt with in the pages of Monsignor Perrelli. Doubly strange, and a serious disappointment to the reader, in view of the fact that the two men were contemporaries, and that the learned writer must have enjoyed exceptional facilities for obtaining first-hand knowledge of his subject. Almost inexplicable indeed, when one remembers those maxims which he himself, in the Introduction to his *Antiquities*, lays down for the writing of history; when one calls to mind his own gleams of exotic scholarship, those luminous asides and fruitful digressions, those statesmanlike comments on things in general which make his work not so much a compendium of local lore as a mirror of the polite learning of his age. It is no exaggeration to say that, compared with the ample treatment meted out to inconspicuous rulers like Alfonso the Seventeenth or Florizel the Fat, his account of the Good Duke Alfred is the baldest, the most perfunctory and conventional of chronicles. Neither good nor evil is related of him. There is nothing but a monotonous enumeration of events.

It was the bibliographer who, poring over the pages of the rival monk Father Capocchio, that audacious and salacious friar already mentioned – it was the bibliographer who hit upon a passage which suggested a solution of the mystery and proved that, though Monsignor Perrelli lived during the reign of the Good Duke, it would be stretching unduly the sense of a plain word to say that he 'flourished' under his rule. Other persons may have flourished; not so the kindly prelate.

'Nothing whatever,' says this implacable enemy of Nepenthe, 'is to be recorded to the credit of the sanguinary brigand – so he terms the Good Duke – nothing whatsoever: save and except only this, that he cut off the ears of a certain prattler, intriguer, and snuff-taking sensualist called Perrelli, who, under the pretence of collecting data for an alleged historical treatise, profited by his priestly garb to play fast and loose with what little remained of decent family life on that God-abandoned island. Honour to whom honour is due! The ostensible reason for this unique act of justice was that the said Perrelli had appeared at some palace function with paste buckles on his shoes, instead of silver ones. The pretext was well chosen, inasmuch as the tyrant added to his other vices and absurdities the pose of being an extravagant stickler for etiquette. We happen to know, nevertheless, that the name of a young dancer, a prime favourite at Court, cropped up persistently at the time in connexion with this malodorous but otherwise insignificant episode.'

It were idle, at this hour of the day, to pursue the inquiry; the mutilation of Monsignor Perrelli's person, however, would explain better than anything else his equivocal attitude as historian. Nor is the incident altogether inconsistent with what we know of the Duke's cheerful propensities. 'Nose after ears!' was one of his blithest watchwords. Faced with so dispiriting a prospect and aware that His Highness was as good as his princely word, the sympathetic scholar, while too resentful to praise his achievements, may well have been too prudent to disparage them. Hence his reticence, his circumspection. Hence that monotonous enumeration of events.

This microscopic blot on the Duke's escutcheon, as well as other more commendable details of his life, were duly noted down by the zealous Mr Eames, who, in addition, had the good fortune to receive as a gift from his kindly but unassuming friend Count Caloveglia a quaint portrait of the prince, hitherto unknown – an engraving which he purposed to reproduce, together with other fresh iconographical material, in his enlarged and fully annotated edition of the *Antiquities*. The print depicts His Highness full face, seated on a throne in the accoutrements of Mars, with a gallant wig flowing in mazy ringlets from under the helmet upon his plated shoulders; overhead, upon a canopy of cloud, reclines a breezy assemblage of allegorical females – Truth, Mercy, Fame with her trumpet, and so forth. His nervous clean-shaven features do not wear the traditional smile; they are thoughtful, almost grim. On his left is portrayed a huge *cannon*, astride of which can be seen a chubby angel; the Duke's hand reposes, in a paternal caress, on the cherub's head – symbolical doubtless of his love of children. His right elbow rests upon a table, and the slender be-jewelled fingers are listlessly pressing open a lettered scroll of parchment on which can be deciphered the words '*A chi t'ha fig-liato*' (to her who bare thee) – a legend which the bibliographer, whose acquaintance with the vernacular was not on a level with his classical attainments, conjectured to be some fashionable courtly toast of the period.

The mention of artillery recalls the fact that His Highness was an amateur of ordnance. He established a gun-foundry on the island, and what he did not know about the art of casting pieces, as practised in his day, was plainly not worth knowing. Had it not been for his passionate love of testing new processes and new com-binations of metal, he might have attained to a European reputa-tion in that department. But he was always experimenting, and the consequence was that his cannons were always splitting. One, however, a monster of its kind, remained intact, to outward ap-pearances. It was fired on every conceivable occasion – to sum-mon the Militia, for example, from remote corners of the island at any hour of the day or night, a considerable hardship to those who lived at a distance of two or three miles, seeing that according to the instructions set forth in the Militiaman's Year-book, the sternest penalties were imposed upon all who failed to appear in their ranks at the Palace gates within five minutes after the signal had been sounded.

It was a perilous gun to handle. Owing to some undiscoverable flaw of construction or imperfection in the alloy, the monster soon developed a disconcerting knack of back-firing, hazardous to life and limb. It stands to reason that the Good Duke attached no undue importance to any trifling disaster accruing therefrom. On the contrary, in order to be sure of a thunderous detonation, he often deigned to superintend in person the loading of this particular piece.

'More powder,' he would then command. 'More powder! Ram it in! Never mind her little caprices! A good salute is worth a good soldier! More powder! Fill her up to the brim! She's only playful, like her master.' Those who lost fingers or hands or arms received the Order of the Golden Vine. Whenever a major portion of the anatomy, a head or so forth, went astray, the victim was posthumously ennobled.

Since his day, thanks to the science of a Paduan engineer, this defect has been almost completely overcome, and the gun can still be heard on great occasions, such as the Duke's birthday, the Festival of the Patron Saint, or the visit to the island of some foreign sovereign; it is also discharged, as of yore, to summon the Militia for the purpose of quelling any popular disturbance. But even now it occasionally relapses into its old humours – with this difference, that instead of being decorated with a coveted distinction, the disabled man is sent to the hospital and told not to make a fool of himself next time.

This was the gun whose sound attracted the strained attention of Mr Keith and his companions, far away, on the sea, under the cliffs.

CHAPTER 20

THE firing had ceased; the boat began to glide forwards once more. But Mr Heard's eye remained fixed upon the ill-omened black rock. The sun's rays had already licked dry the moisture on its surface; it shone with a steady dull glow. Some malefic force seemed to dwell here. Some demon haunted the place, peering out of its crevices or rising up from the turquoise-tinted water at its foot. The suicides' rock!

That vague sense of apprehension, of impending disaster, once more invaded him. Suddenly it revealed itself in definite terms. A ghastly notion flitted through his mind.

'You think it possible that Denis –?' he began.

His friend seemed to have lost all interest in that subject. It was a way he had.

'Denis? I really could not tell. I'm not sufficiently in his confidence. ... Honour thy father and thy mother,' he proceeded, reverting to his former theme. 'What think you, Heard, of this old injunction? Is it not altogether obsolete? Was it not written for quite other conditions? Honour thy father and mother. Why? The State educates children, feeds them, investigates and cures their complaints, washes and weighs them, reports on their teeth and stomachs, prescribes when they may begin to smoke and enter public-houses: where does parental authority come in? The State provides old folks with refuges and pensions: how about the former obligations of children? Child and parent alike now thank the community for what they once received from each other. And the geographical elements that went to the making of a home are also dispersed. Rich and poor roam like gipsies from one country to another, from one flat into the next; the patriarchal board is replaced by clubs and grill-rooms and fried-fish shops. Many a man who thinks to found a home discovers that he has merely opened a tavern for his friends. Note, too, that the family has outgrown its ecclesiastical sanction; the oil of supernaturalism which once greased the wheels has run dry; the machinery is creaking. Industrial conditions have killed the old home. *Requiescat!* Honour thy father and mother. Industrialism has killed that commandment. Thou shalt not steal. Consider this injunction, Heard, and ask yourself whether industrialism does not split its sides with laughing at it. If we are to galvanize that old collection of laws into some semblance of life, every one of them must be rewritten and brought up to date. They are inappropriate for modern life; their interest is purely historical. We want new values. We are no longer nomads. Industrialism has killed the pastoral and the agricultural points of view. And how the modern Jews smile at our infatuation for those queer doctrines and legends which they themselves have long ago outgrown. A propos, what has become of Marten?'

'Left the island, I hear.'

'Quick work. Now I wonder why?'

Everybody wondered at Marten's precipitate departure. Even Angelina wondered.

She just wondered.

Had he known that she wondered, and just wondered, he might have been tempted to prolong his stay. But Marten was too young to be a practical psychologist. He had lived for half a day in terror of what he called 'the inevitable reaction', unaware of the fact that certain people do not suffer from reactions and too engrossed in mineralogy to have learnt, from a study of other sciences, that Angelina was one of them. She had passed that stage, with Homeric laughter, long before his appearance on Nepenthe. She just wondered, nowadays.

166

Scared, as though the avenging Furies were at his heels, he quitted the scene of his nocturnal romance, leaving half his geological projects incomplete. Had he taken the amiable Don Francesco into his confidence he might have heard something to his advantage. But the scientist could not endure the sight of a Christian priest. Like other intolerant folk, he was now paying for his prejudices.

'An erotic little beast,' Keith went on. 'And a typical Hebrew—a scoffer. Have you noticed what a disruptive and irreverential brood they are? They move up and down society like some provocative fluid, insensible to our ideals; they take a diabolical pleasure in shattering our old-established conceptions of right and wrong. I confess I like them for that; they need shattering, some of those conceptions. And they have their weaknesses too, their Achilles heel – music, for instance, or chess. When next you are in town don't forget to go to that little chess club of theirs over Aldgate East station. It is better than a play to watch their faces. And with all this materialism they have a mysterious feminine leaven of enthusiasm and unworldliness. What pecuniary advantage could Marten expect to gain from his minerals?'

'A professorship.'

'Why, possibly. He had the professorial temperament; there was not much poetry in his composition. If you were to ask him, "What are those wonderful rocks over there, shaped like some Titanic organ and glowing with a kind of violet flame?" he would say, "Organ be blowed. It's columnar lithoidite." I learnt a little from him, but not enough. I wish we had him here. He could have told us something.'

And Mr Keith, ever avid of fresh things, regretted his lost opportunities. He was in one of his acquisitive, Corsair moods. He said:

'I could take geology by the throat just now. It's disgusting, not to know things!'

His companion, meanwhile, beheld the panorama in all its nightmarish splendour, as it drifted past him. He saw the bluffs of feathery pumice, the lava precipices – frozen cataracts of white, black, blood red, pale grey, and sombre brown, smeared over with a vitreous enamel of obsidian or pierced by oily, writhing dykes that blazed with metallic scintillations. Anon came some yawning cleft or an assemblage of dizzy rock-needles, fused into whimsical tints and attitudes, spiky, distorted, over-toppling; then a bold tufa rampart, immaculate in its beauty, stainless as a curtain of silk. And as the boat moved on, he looked into horrid dells which the rains had torn out of the loose scoriae. Gaping wounds, they wore the bright hues of corruption. Their flanks were blotched with a livid nitrous efflorescence, with flaring sulphur, unhealthy verdure of pitchstone, streaks of arsenical vermilion; their beds — a frantic maze of boulders.

He beheld this crazy stratification, this chaos of incandescent nature, set in a frame of deep blue sky and sea. It lay there calmly, like some phantasmagoric flower, some monstrous rose that swoons away, with upturned face, in a solar caress.

He saw it with the eye. His mind was elsewhere. He was trying, in honest and relentless fashion, to discover himself. What if his human values were really wrong!

Thomas, the doubting apostle. ...

Africa had made him think; had made him more silent and reflective than ever. And now this sudden strange stimulus of Nepenthe — it was driving his thoughts headlong, out of their old grooves.

Here was Keith, a man of altogether different stamp, drawing conclusions which he dared not formulate for himself. How far were they applicable, those old Hebrew precepts, to modern conditions? Were they still availing as guides to conduct?

'You are a candid person, Keith, and I think I am. I sincerely try to be. Will you tell me what you think? You seem to have a quarrel with Moses and his commandments, which we are taught to regard as the keystone of ethics. I don't want to discuss things. I want to listen to the opinions of a man so different from myself as you are. It may do me good. And I think I could stand almost anything,' he added, with a laugh, 'in this landscape — in this clear pagan light, as you call it.'

'I used to be interested in such things as a boy. I suppose all respectable boys are; and I was respectable even at that tender age. Nowadays, though I still pick up an Oriental rug now and then, I have no further use for Oriental gods.'

'What is your objection to them?'

Mr Keith paused before replying. Then he said:

'The drawback of Oriental gods is that they have been manufactured by the proletariat for the use of the aristocracy. They act accordingly; that is, they distil the morality of their creators, which I consider a noxious emanation. The classic gods were different. They were invented by intellectualists who felt themselves capable of maintaining a kind of comradeship with their deities. Men and gods were practically on a level. They walked hand in hand over the earth. These gods belonged to what one might call the horizontal or downstairs variety.'

'And those others?'

'Oh, they are the upstairs or vertical type. They live overhead. Why overhead? Because they have been created by the proletariat. The proletariat loves to humiliate itself. Therefore they manufacture a god who approves of grovelling, a god who can look down upon them. They exalt this deity to an infinite degree in point of goodness and distance, and in so doing they inevitably abase themselves. Now, I disapprove of grovelling. That means I disapprove of upstairs gods.'

'Upstairs gods –'

'If you walk into my front door as a distinguished visitor I am happy to show you the place. You can prowl about the garden, poke your nose into the pantry, and learn, if it amuses you, all about my private life. But if you rent a high attic overlooking my premises and stare out of your window all day long, watching my movements and noting down everything I do, why, damn it, I call that vulgar. Staring is bad form. Vertical gods are inquisitive. I don't like to be supervised. I don't care about this *dossier* business. My garden is for you and me to walk about in, not for outsiders to stare into. Which reminds me that you have not been to see me lately. You ought to come and look at my cannas; you really ought. They are in magnificent bloom just now. When shall it be?'

Mr Keith seemed to be already tired of the subject. In fact he was as near being bored as ever he allowed himself to be. But the other refused to let the conversation be side-tracked. He wanted to know.

'Vertical and horizontal gods. ... Dear me. Sounds rather profane.'

'I have not heard that word for quite a long time.'

'You don't feel the need of any kind of superior being to control human affairs?'

'Not up to the present. I can find no room in my Cosmos for a deity, save as a waste product of human weakness, an excrement of the imagination. If you gave me the sauciest god that ever sat on a cloud or breakfasted with the Village Idiot – 'pon my word, I shouldn't know what to do with him. I don't collect bric-à-brac myself, and the British Museum is dreadfully overstocked. Perhaps the Duchess could make some use of him, if he specialized in lace vestments and choral mass. By the way, I hear that she is going to be admitted into the Roman Church next week; there is to be a luncheon after the ceremony. Are you going?'

'Vertical and horizontal gods. ... I never heard that distinction made before.'

'It is a difference, my dear Heard. Mankind remains in direct contact with the downstairs variety. That simplifies matters. But the peculiar position of those others – perpendicularly overhead at a vast distance – necessitates a troublesome code of verbal signals, unintelligible to common folk, for the expression of mutual desires. You cannot have any god of this kind without some such cumbrous contrivance to bridge over the gulf and make communication possible. It is called theology. It complicates life very considerably. Yes,' he pursued, 'the vertical-god system is not only vulgar; it is perplexing and expensive. Think of the wastage, of the myriads of people who have been sacrificed because they misinterpreted some enigmatical word in the code. Why are you intent on these conundrums?'

'Well, partly at least, it's quite a practical matter. You know that American millionaire, van Koppen, and the scandal attached to his peculiar habits? It made me wonder, only yesterday –'

But at this juncture the tiresome old boatman lifted up his voice once more.

'See that high cliff, gentlemens? Funny thing happen there, very funny. Dam-fool foreigner here, he collect flowers. Always collecting flowers on bad rocks; sometimes with rope round him, for fear of falling; with rope, ha, ha, ha! Nasty man. And poor. No money at all. He always say, "All Italians liars, and liars where go? To Hell, sure. That's where liars go. That's where Italians go." Now rich man he say liar to poor man. But poor man, he better not say liar to rich man. That so, gentlemens. One day he say liar to nice old Italian. Nice old man think: "Ah, you wait, putrid puppy of bastard pig, you wait." Nice old man got plenty good lot vineyards back of cliff there. One day he walk to see grapes. Then he look to end of cliff and see rope hanging. Very funny, he think. Then he look to end of rope, and see nasty-man hanging. That so, gentlemens. Nasty-man hanging in air. Can't get up. "Pull me up," says he. Nice old man, he laugh – ha, ha, ha! laugh till his belly hurt. Then he pull out knife and begin to cut rope. "See knife?" he shout down. "How much to pull up?" Five hundred dollar! "How much?" Five thousand! "How much?" Fifty thousand! Nice old man say quite quiet: "You no got fifty thousand in the world, you liar. Liars where go? To Hell, sure. That's where liars go. That's where you go, Mister. To Hell." And he cut rope. Down he go, patatrac! round and round in air, like firework wheel, on to first rock – paff! second rock – paff! third rock – paff! fifty rock – pa-pa-pa-paff! Six hundred feets. After that he arrive, all messy, in water. That so, gentlemens. Gone where to?

170

Swim to Philadelphia? I don't think! Him drownded, sure. Ha, ha, ha! Nice old man, when he come home that morning, he laugh. He laugh. He just laugh. He laugh first quiet, then loud. He laugh all the time, and soon family laugh too. He laugh for ten days, till he nearly die. Get well again, and live plenty good years after. In Paradise today, God rest his soul! And never found out, no never. Fine judge on Nepenthe. Always find judge here. He know everything, and he know nothing. Understand? All nice peoples here. That so, gentlemens.'

He told the tale with Satanic gusto, rocking himself to and fro as though convulsed with some secret joy. Then, after expectorating violently, he resumed the oars which had been dropped in the heat of gesticulation.

The bishop was pensive. There was something wrong with this story – something fundamentally wrong. He turned to Keith:

'That man must be a liar too. If, as he says, the thing was never found out, how can he have learnt all about it?'

'Hush, my dear fellow. He thinks I don't know, but I do. It was his own father to whom the adventure occurred.'

'The adventure!' said Mr Heard.

'The adventure. Surely you are not going to make a tragedy of it? If you cannot see the joke of that story, you must be hard to please. I nearly died of laughing when I first heard it.'

'What would you have done?'

'If I had been the botanist? I would not have made myself disagreeable to the natives. Also, I would not have got myself into a tangle with that rope.'

'You think he ought to have cut it?'

'What else could the poor fellow do? It strikes me, Heard, you attach inordinate importance to human life.'

'It's all rather complex,' sighed the bishop.

'Now that is really interesting!'

'Interesting?'

'Why should you find it complex, when I find it simple? Let me see. Our lives are perfectly insignificant, aren't they? We know it for a fact. But we don't like it. We don't like being of no account. We want something to make us feel more valuable than we are. Consequently we invent a fiction to explain away that insignificance – the fiction of a personality overhead everlastingly occupied in watching every single one of us, and keenly engrossed in our welfare. If this were the case, we would cease to be insignificant, and we might try to oblige him by not killing each other. It happens to be a fiction. Get rid of the fiction, and your feeling of

171

complexity evaporates. I perceive you are in an introspective mood. Worrying about some pastoral epistle?'

'Worrying about my values, as you would say. Up to the present, Keith, I don't seem to have had time to think; I had to act; there was always something urgent to be taken in hand. Now that I am really lazy for the first time, and in this stimulating environment, certain problems of life keep cropping up. Minor problems, of course; for it is a consolation to know that the foundations of good conduct are immutable. Our sense of right and wrong is firmly implanted in us. The laws of morality, difficult as they often are to understand, have been written down for our guidance in letters that never change.'

'Never change? You might as well say, my dear Heard, that these cliffs never change. The proof that the laws of good conduct change is this, that if you were upright after the fashion of your great-grandfather you would soon find yourself in the clutches of the law for branding a slave, or putting a bullet through someone in a duel. I grant that morality changes slowly. It changes slowly because the proletariat, whose product it is, does the same. There is not much difference, I imagine, between the crowds of old Babylon and new Shoreditch; hence their peculiar emanations resemble each other more or less. That is why morality compares so unfavourably with intellectuality, which is the product of the upper sections of society and flashes out new lights every moment. But even morality changes. The Spartans, a highly moral people, thought it positively indecent not to steal. A modern vice, such as mendacity, was accounted a virtue by the greatest nation of antiquity. A modern virtue, like that of forgiving one's enemies, was accounted a vice proper to slaves. Drunkenness, reprobated by ancients and moderns alike, became the mark of a gentleman in intermediate periods.'

'I see what you are driving at. You wish me to think that this fictitious value, as you would call it – this halo of sanctity – with which we now invest a human life, may be blown away at any moment. Possibly you are right. Perhaps we English do exaggerate its importance. They don't take much account of life in my part of Africa.'

'And then, I disagree with what you say about the difficulty of understanding the laws of morality. Any child can grasp the morality of its period. Why should I pretend to be interested in what a child can grasp? It is a positive strain to keep one's mind at that low level. Why should I impose this strain upon myself? When a grown-up man shows an unfeigned interest in such

172

questions I regard him as a case of arrested development. All morality is a generalization, and all generalizations are tedious. Why should I plague myself with what is tedious? Altogether the question that confronts me is not whether morality is worth talking about, but whether it's worth laughing at. Sometimes I think it is. It reminds me of those old pantomime jokes that make one quite sad, at first, with their heart-breaking vulgarity; those jokes, you know, that have to be well rubbed in before we begin to see how really funny they are. And, by Jove, they do rub this one in, don't they? You must talk to Don Francesco about these things. You will find him sound, though he does not push his conclusions as far as I do – not in public, at least. Or to Count Caloveglia. He is a remarkable Latin, that old man. Why don't you drive up one day and have a look at his Locri Faun? Street, the South Kensington man, thinks very highly of it.'

'I would like to listen to you just now. I am listening, and thinking. Please go on. I'll preach you my sermon some other day.'

'Will you? I wonder! I don't believe, Heard, that you will preach another sermon in your life. I don't think you will ever go back to Africa, or to any other episcopal work. I think you have reached a turning point.'

The bishop was thoughtful for a moment. Those words went home. Then he said lightly:

'You are in better vein than you were a short while ago.'

'That story of the botanist has revived me. He tells it rather well, doesn't he? It is good to inhabit a world where such things can still happen. I feel as if life were worth living. I feel as if I could discuss anything. What were you going to say about the American millionaire?'

'Ah, yes,' replied Mr Heard. 'I wondered, supposing these reports about the ladies are true, how far you and I, for example, should condone his vices.'

'Vices. My dear bishop! Under a sky like this. Have a good look at it; do.'

Mr Heard, barely conscious of what he was doing, obeyed the counsel. Raising his hand, he pushed the silken awning to one side. Then he peered skyward, into the noonday zenith; into an ocean of blue, immeasurable. There was no end to this azure liquid. Gazing thus, his intelligence became aware of the fact that there are skies of different kinds. This one was not quite like his native firmament. Here was no suggestion of a level space overhead, remote, but still conceivable – a space whereon some god might have sat, enthroned, note-book in hand, jotting down men's virtues and vices, and what not. A sky of this kind was obviously not built to accommodate deities in a sitting posture.

Instead of commenting on this simple observation he remarked:

'I mean, whether one should publicly approve of van Koppen's ladies, supposing they exist.'

'Why should I approve or disapprove? Old Koppen's activities do not impinge on mine. Like a sensible fellow, he cultivates a hobby. He indulges himself. Why interfere? Tell me, why should I disapprove of things?'

'Look here, Keith! Not long ago you were disapproving of vertical gods.'

'That is different. They do impinge on my activities.'

'Are the peculiar hobbies of their votaries distasteful to you?'

'Not at all. Their hobbies do not clash with mine. To feel righteous, or to feel sinful, is quite an innocent form of self-indulgence –'

'Innocent self-indulgence? Dear me! You seem to be taking morality by the throat for a change. Is that your conception of sin? How should Moses have come to inscribe some particular form of wrong-doing into his Code, if it had not proved harmful to the community at large?'

His friend paused before replying. He took out another cigar, bit off its end, and lighted it. Then he sent a few fragrant whiffs over the sea. At last he said:

'Moses! I have a clear portrait of Moses in my mind; a clear and favourable portrait. I imagine him gentle, wise, and tolerant. Picture to yourself such a man. He is drawing up a preliminary list of the more noteworthy forms of misconduct, with a view to submitting it for Divine approval, to be welded later into the so-called Ten Commandments. He is still puzzling, you perceive, which sins ought to be included and which left out. Now that particular offence of which our millionaire is accused happens to have been left out of consideration so far.'

'Why has it been left out?' inquired the bishop.

'Nomadic habits. And besides – Moses, don't forget, is a kindly old fellow, who likes people to have as much harmless amusement as possible; he is not always sniffing about to discover evil. But Aaron, or some other old family friend of his, thinks differently. He is a person such as we all know – a sour-faced puritan who has lost the vigour which people, rightly or wrongly, attribute to van Koppen. This man forgets what he used to do in his own youthful days; he comes up to Moses, professing to be horrified at this particular offence. "These young people," he says, "the way they go on! It's a sin, that's what it is. And you, Moses, I'm ashamed of you. This sort of thing ought to be stopped. It ought to be publicly reprimanded in those blessed Tables of yours." "A sin?" says gentle Moses. "You surprise me, Aaron. I confess it never struck me in that light before. But I think I see your point. We have a conference to-night on the Holy Mountain; I may be able to get a clause inserted –" "Do, there's a good fellow," says the other. "But aren't you a little hard on the youngsters?" asks Moses. "You wouldn't believe it, but I was a boy myself once and I should have got into a lot of rows if such an enactment had been in existence then. Moreover (and here his eyes assume a rapt, prophetic look), I seem to see, rising out of the distant future, a personage of royal line, beloved of God – one David who, if your proposal were to come into force, would be classed as a pretty hot sinner." "Oh, bother David! Look here, I'm not asking for a loan of money, old man. Just see to it that my New Sin is inscribed in the Tables. Hang it all! What's that, to a man of your influence up there? You can't think how it annoys me nowadays to see all these young people – all these young people – need I go into particulars?" "You needn't. I'm not altogether a fool," says gentle Moses. "And I'll see what I can do to oblige you, if only for the sake of your dear mother." '

The bishop, at the end of this narration, could not help smiling.

'That,' continued Keith, 'is how Moses gets talked over by the Pharisees. That is how sins are manufactured and classified. And from that preposterous old Hebrew system of right and wrong they jump straight into our English penal code. And there they sit tight,' he added.

'Is that your quarrel with what you call the upstairs god system?'

'Precisely! It does not affect me by its insanitary tendency to multiply sins. It affects me when it impinges on my own activities; that is to say, when it transforms those sins into legal crimes. How would you like to be haled before a Court of law for some ridiculous trifle, which became a crime only because it used to be a sin, and became a sin only because some dyspeptic or impotent old antediluvian was envious of his neighbour's pleasure? Our statute-book reeks of discredited theories of conduct; the serpent's trail of the theologian, of the reactionary, is over all.'

'It never struck me in that light before,' said Mr Heard.

'No? Our reverence for inspired idiots: has it never struck you? Don't you realize that we are still in the stage of that *enfant terrible* of Christianity, Paul of Tarsus, and his gift of tongues? In the

175

stage of these Russians here, with their decayed Messiah? What do you think of them?'

'I must say they look pretty, all bathing together. Rather improper. But decidedly apostolic. You know I am not easily shocked in such matters. When you have lived in Africa among the M'tezo! Lovely fellows. I assure you they could give points to anyone on this island. And your friends the Bulanga! To think that I once baptized three hundered of them in one day. And the very next week they ate up old Mrs Richardson, our best lady preacher. The poor dear! We buried her riding-boots, I remember. There was nothing else to bury.... It's getting warm, isn't it? Makes one feel sleepy.'

'Sleepy? I don't agree with you at all. That Russian sect, Heard, had between two and three million followers out there. But I fancy our little contingent will not be on this island much longer. The judge tells me that he means to make short work of them when he gets a chance. If the militia have really been called out, I should not be surprised to learn that the Messiah has been up to some new tomfoolery.'

'Really? H'm. The militia. ... I find it very warm all of a sudden.'

Mr Heard had listened enough for the time being. Now he leaned back and rested.

But Keith was wide awake.

'You are a disappointing person, Heard. First you inveigle me into a religious discussion and then, when I begin to wake up, you go to sleep.'

'I don't want to argue, my dear fellow. It's too hot to argue. I wanted to hear your opinion.'

'My opinion? Listen, Heard. All mankind is at the mercy of a handful of neurotics. Neurotics and their catchwords. Catchwords like duty, charity, purity, sobriety. Sobriety! In order that Miss Wilberforce may not come home drunk – listen, Heard! – all we other lunatics forgo the pleasure of a pint of beer after ten o'clock. How we love tormenting ourselves! Listen, Heard. I'll tell you what it is. We are ripe for a new Messiah, like these Russians. We are not Europeans. We are Indian fakirs, self-torturers. We are a pack of masochists. That is what upstairs gods have done for us. Listen, Heard!'

The bishop failed to catch the import of this peroration. Its sound alone reached him like an echo from far away. He was unaccountably drowsy.

'Fakirs. I quite understand –'

The boat seemed to move more slowly than before. Perhaps the oarsmen were weary, or suffering from the heat. The glare pierced the awning. Mr Heard, as he reclined about his cushions, felt the perspiration gathering on his forehead. A spell had fallen upon him – the spell of a Southern noon. It lulled his senses. It laid chains upon his thoughts.

There was a long silence, broken only by the splash of the oars and by a steady flow of conversation on the part of the two Greek genii, who seemed impervious to the midday beams and entirely absorbed in one another. In decorous undertones they chattered and laughed. Mr Heard opened his drooping eyelids from time to time to take pleasure in their merry play of features, wondering dreamily what could be the subject-matter of this endless polite conversation.

CHAPTER 21

BOTH the old boatman and Mr Keith were correct in their surmises. There was trouble in the market-place, serious trouble; so serious that for the first time in five years – ever since that deplorable scandal of the Irish lady and the poodle – the militia were being called out. And it was entirely the fault of the Sacred Sixty-three.

The Messiah, personally, was not to blame. That poor old man had much declined of late; he was enfeebled in health and spirits. A French artist who was specially despatched from Paris to do an original sketch of him for the enterprising journal *L'Illustration* had, at the end of several sittings, uncharitably declared him to be '*complètement ga-ga*'. The voluptuous surroundings of Nepenthe, the abundant food, adoration of disciples, alcoholic and carnal debaucheries, had impaired his tough Moujik frame and blunted his wit, worked havoc with that energy and peasant craftiness which once ruled an Emperor's Court. His body was obese. His mind was in a state of advanced putrefaction. Even his personal cleanliness left something to be desired. Sitting there, puffy and pasty, in a darkened room, he looked more than ever like some obscene vegetable that has grown up in the shade.

He moved seldom and with difficulty; he hardly ever opened his mouth save to eat – for his appetite, thanks to certain daily exertions on the part of the communal doctor, was still fairly satisfactory. When he spoke at all it was in scattered monosyllables which even the most devoted of his disciples were unable to arrange into such coherence as to justify their inclusion in the *Golden Book*.

177

All this, though hidden from the world at large, had been observed with dismay by the initiated. It was an open secret among them that the last twenty-one sayings ascribed to him in that volume had never issued from his lips at all. They had been concocted by a clique of young extremists, who were now masters of the situation. These fanatics edited the *Golden Book* and held the old man completely in subjection, ousting his former and more moderate collaborators.

An ill-considered action on the part of this group led to the disaster and eclipsed the light of holiness on Nepenthe by bringing the apostles into conflict with the secular arm of the law. Fretting at the Master's prolonged inactivity and eager, after the fashion of disciples, to improve on his maxims, they decided upon a bold step. They decided that the time was ripe for a new Revelation.

The Messiah's last authentic one, it will be remembered, ran to the effect that 'flesh and blood of warm-blooded beasts is Abomination to Little White Cows'. He had been inspired to insert the word *warm-blooded* because fish, for example, was an article of diet of which he was inordinately fond, and he could not bring himself to deprive the faithful of this gift of God.

With misplaced zeal, and little thinking that it would cost many of them their lives and liberties, these enthusiasts gave it out that the new Revelation ran as follows: 'everything derivable from dead beasts is Abomination to Little White Cows'. They had been inspired to insert the word *dead* because sheep's wool, for example, was an article of clothing in which they greatly delighted, and they could not bring themselves to deprive the faithful of this gift of God.

Even as it stood, the Commandment entailed severe sacrifices on the part of the Sacred Sixty-three. No boot-leather, no picturesque belts, no bone knife-handles or combs, no tallow candles. ... They were prepared, none the less, to carry out to the letter this injunction since it gave them what all religious people require – something to torment themselves with; and this is how matters stood when, on that morning, a stalwart batch of new-comers from the wilds of Muscovy, burning with the ardour of abnegation and wholly ignorant of local laws and customs, sauntered across the market-place in freshly purchased hempen sandals.

Tobacco being derivable neither from warm-blooded beasts nor yet from dead ones, a member of the band bethought himself of the fact that he had run out of cigarettes. Knowing not a word of Italian, he entered the shop of a tobacconist and imitated the gesture of smoking with such success that the proprietor straightway

178

understood and supplied him with a packet. Then he remembered that he also needed matches. This called for a gesture'rather more complex; so complex, indeed, that perhaps nobody but a Nepenthean – gifted, as all his nation is, with alert intuition – could have divined the Apostle's want. The tobacconist was equal to the occasion. With a friendly smile of comprehension he laid on the counter a diminutive box of wax vestas, price two sous.

There the matter might have rested but for the new Revelation, which prompted the sturdy stranger to investigate the composition of the article tendered. He took out one match and examined it carefully. Then, triturating its substance between his fingers, he applied his nose to the product and sniffed critically. The outcome was suspicious in the highest degree. There was no perceptible odour of beeswax; the object had been compounded, only too plainly, of the fat of dead animals; it was the Abomination, the Unclean Thing. Devout, and gifted with the hot impulse of youth, he acted precisely as he would have acted in Russia under a similar provocation. With a third gesture, one of abhorrence and ungovernable fury, he threw the box in the tobacconist's face.

And there the matter, once more, might have rested, had the salesman been a Russian. Russians understand frank dealing.

He happened to be a native.

Fully to appreciate what followed, it is necessary to bear in mind that local tobacconists are in a somewhat anomalous position. They occupy a social status superior to those of many other countries. They are not private merchants or ordinary citizens; they are, in a manner, servants of the State. A native tobacconist is empowered to dispense *carta bollata*, which is the official stamped paper used for contracts and other legal documents requiring registration; he deals in tobacco and postage stamps – government monopolies; he sells, by special licence, wax vestas, on each box of which there is a duty so minute as not to be felt by the individual purchaser and yet, in its cumulative effect, so great as to enable the State to pay, out of this source of revenue alone, for the upkeep of all its colonial judges at a monthly salary of forty-five francs apiece. It is a reasonable tax. Don Francesco, who had notions of political economy and knew something of English life, having preached to thousands of Catholic miners in Wales and confessed hundreds of Catholic ladies in Mayfair – an occupation in which he might still be engaged but for a little *contretemps* which brought him into collision with the Jesuits of Farm Street – Don Francesco, who could voice the Southerner's one-sided point of view, often adverted to this match-tax when

179

proving the superiority of his country's administrative methods over those of England. This is what he would say to his intimate friends:

'The Russian has convictions but no principles. The Englishman has principles but no convictions – cast-iron principles, which save him the trouble of thinking out anything for himself. This is as much as anyone can ever hope to grasp concerning this lymphatic, unimaginative race. They obey the laws – a criminal requires imagination. They never start a respectable revolution – you cannot revolt without imagination. Among other things they pride themselves on their immunity from vexatious imposts. Yet whisky, the best quality of which is worth tenpence a bottle, is taxed till it costs five shillings; ale, the life-blood of the people, would be dear at threepence a gallon and yet costs fivepence a pint; tobacco, which could profitably be sold at twopence a pound, goes for fivepence an ounce. They will submit to any number of these extortions, being persuaded, in the depths of their turbid intelligence, that such things are devised for the good of the nation at large. That is the Englishman's method of procuring happiness: to deny himself pleasure in order to save his neighbour's soul. Ale and tobacco are commodities out of which a man can extract pleasure. They are therefore appropriate objects for harassing restrictions. But nobody can extract pleasure out of lucifer matches. They are therefore pre-eminently unfitted for exploitation as a source of governmental revenue. So keen is their sense of pleasure and non-pleasure, and such is their *furor phlegmaticus* on this particular question, that when it is proposed to establish a tax on matches – an imperceptible duty which would enrich the Exchequer to a vast extent – they will form a procession ten miles long to protest against the outrage, and threaten to batter down the Houses of Parliament. Why? Because there is no ethical purpose to be served by taxing matches, seeing that only a madman would give himself the guilty pleasure of either drinking or smoking them. In short, these English reason after the fashion of paranoiacs – logically, but from a wrong premise. Not that I dislike their women. ...'

The action of the quick-tempered Apostle can now be appraised in its full enormity. A local tobacconist is a person in authority, a State official, and the nation safeguards the interests and the fair name of those who serve it faithfully. When it is remembered that according to § 43 of the 16th Section of their Penal Code any person speaking disrespectfully to, or of, a Government official renders himself liable to a term of cellular confinement not exceeding thirty-one years, ten lunar months, and eighteen days, it may be imagined what penalties are applicable to the crime of actual personal violence towards such a sacrosanct individual – a crime of which the Russian was unquestionably guilty.

Now this particular tobacconist, though tremulously sensitive, like all Southerners, on a point of honour, was as good-natured and forgiving as might be consistent with his rank of Government official. He passed for a respectable married man with an eligible daughter and a taste for the quiet life; he did not want trouble. The purchase of an additional packet of cigarettes, accompanied or unaccompanied by a frank apology, would have more than satisfied his sense of honour.

There the matter might have rested. The second packet might have been bought and even the apology tendered, but for the ill-considered action of a young farmer who entered the shop at that moment to procure a couple of postcards. This worthy lad was one of several dozen aspirants to the hand of the tobacconist's daughter, whose dowry was reputed to be considerable. He witnessed the insult and, desirous of standing well in the graces of a prospective father-in-law, dealt the offending alien so masterly a punch in the region of the solar plexus that he not only doubled up, but forgot to straighten himself out again. Two or three lusty Apostles came to the rescue without delay. They threw the youth down, stamped on his face, pounded his abdomen, pulled his hair out in handfuls, and otherwise treated him exactly as if the thing were happening in Russia. This spectacle was too much for the tobacconist's sense of honour. With unwonted sprightliness he vaulted over the writhing cluster and summoned a municipal policeman. The officer was on the spot in a twinkling, sword and trumpet in hand. And there, in all conscience, the matter ought to have rested – with the identification and bestowal in custody of the turbulent parties.

But frenzy hung in the air; a red cloud of insanity was hovering over Nepenthe. Although the volcano continued to behave in exemplary fashion, although the clergy had done their utmost to allay popular apprehension, the native mind had not calmed down since the news concerning the Saint Elias fountain and those other portents had been disseminated. The inhabitants were in a state of suppressed alarm and ready, at the least provocation, to burst out into some fiendish act of folly. And the Russians especially those latest arrivals, could not withdraw themselves from the subtle influence of the South wind, the frank stimulation of a cloudless sky; it made them feel, after their gloomy forests and lowering horizons, like wild beasts that rush from darkened cages into some sunny arena. Everyone lost his wits. The appearance of a constable, far from restoring order, was the signal for an uproarious tumult; the *fracas*, as the French artist was heard to declare, promptly developed into a *mêlée*. Nobody troubled about the merits of the case further than that it was a question of Apostles *versus* Gentiles.

The former were in sad minority. But they constituted a serried rank of muscular Christians; they laid about them like those old monks of Alexandria. All Russians are born fighters – if not on the battlefield, then at least in the lanes and taverns of their natal villages. The Little White Cows, wholly ignorant of the difference between their own law and that of Italy on questions of assault and battery, used their fists with such force that thirty natives were stretched out in almost as few seconds. Their Faith was at stake; moreover, and as a matter of fact, they were enjoying themselves hugely. The occasion reminded them of a Sunday at home.

Then numbers began to tell – numbers and knives. For your sun-scorched Nepenthean, when duly roused, confesses to an expert knowledge of anatomy; he can tell you, to the fraction of an inch, where the liver, the spleen, kidneys, and various other coy organs of the human frame are located. Blood, the blood of the Sacred Sixty-three, began to flow. At that sight the women, as their manner is, set up a scream.

The Palace of Justice abutted on the market-place, and up to that moment His Worship Signor Malipizzo might have been lost to the world, so deeply immersed was he in threading the labyrinthine mazes of an exceptionally intricate affiliation case – a warm document, after his own heart. The sound of the scream suspended his labours. Like a gouty parrot he hopped down from his seat of judgement, spat on the floor, limped to the window, and took in the situation at a glance. That is to say, he understood the cause of the disturbance as little as did anyone else; it would have required a divine inspiration to guess that a box of wax vestas was at the bottom of the affair; but he knew enough, quite enough, more than enough, for the purpose in hand. He knew, to begin with, that Apostles were involved in the brawl. He knew, what was equally important, the provisions of the Penal Code. It sufficed. His chance for dealing with the Russian colony had at last arrived. Allowing himself barely time to smack his lips at this providential interlude, he gave orders for the great cannon of Duke Alfred to be sounded. It boomed once or twice over Nepenthe and reverberated among the rocks.

In times of yore a certain interval was wont to elapse before the militia could be assembled, living as they did in distant regions of the island. But nowadays, as befitted a laborious rural population, they were spending their morning in the wine-shops of the town, gambling, drinking, or playing skittles. This enabled a sufficient number of them to foregather, in an incredibly short space of time, at the outskirts of the market-place (occupied by a seething, howling tangle of humanity) – there to receive the plainest of instructions. They were to quell the disorder and to single out for punishment, whenever possible, the strangers, the obvious authors of the rebellion, easily discernible by their scarlet blouses. Not that the judge was particular about the lives or deaths of a few natives; he knew that any injuries received by his countrymen would strengthen his case against the outsiders. But an order couched in such terms would look well in the records of the Court.

Within ten minutes the market-place was cleared. The militia had used their weapons with such precision that four school-children, seven women, eleven islanders, and twenty-six Apostles were wounded – about half of them, it was believed, mortally. Order reigned in Nepenthe.

The warm affiliation case having been laid on ice for the nonce, the next few minutes were occupied by His Worship in issuing warrants of arrest against the Messiah's followers. They were lodged by batches in gaol, and in supplementary gaols – disused cellars and so forth. Once under lock and key they were safe from mischief for an indefinite length of time, since, according to the statutes of the Code of Criminal Procedure, there is no reason on earth why an Italian lawsuit should ever end, or indeed, why it should ever begin. They might, and probably would, remain incarcerated for life, pending the commencement of a trial which could only be set in motion by the Judge himself – a most improbable conjuncture – or, failing that, by an extravagant bribe to his official superior, the President of the Court of Cassation. How were poor Apostles to find the necessary sixty or seventy francs for such a venture?

His Worship retired to luncheon, reasonably satisfied with the morning's work. And yet not altogether delighted. Both the Messiah and Peter the Great had eluded his wrath. Peter was able to prove, beyond the shadow of a doubt, that he had spent the last twenty-four hours on Madame Steynlin's premises and knew nothing whatever of occurrences in the outside world. In the face of such a fact – so comfortable to common knowledge, so inherently probable–Malipizzo gave way. He was too good a lawyer

183

to spoil his case. Sooner or later, he foresaw, that bird would be caged with the rest of them. Regarding the Messiah, an unexpected and breathless appeal for mercy was lodged by the Communal doctor, atheist and freemason like the judge, who implored, with tears in his eyes, that the warrant for his arrest should be rescinded. By means of a sequence of rapid and intricate Masonic signs, he explained that Bazhakuloff was a patient of his; that he was undergoing a daily treatment with the stomach-pump; that the prison diet being notoriously slender, he feared that if he, the Messiah, were confined in captivity, then it, the stomach-pump, would be no longer required and therefore he, the physician, a family man, deprived of a small but regular source of income. Again the astute judge relented. This is how the Messiah and his disciple escaped.

They escaped, but not for long.

And all this happened while Mr Keith and his companion, drowsily ensconced among the morocco cushions of their boat, were being wafted over the blue sea, far away, under the cliffs.

CHAPTER 22

'THE Devil's rock, gentlemens! The rock of the Devil. Where the young English lord jump over. Everyone know that story.'

The word 'devil' caused the bishop to wake up from his pleasant dreams with something of a start.

'You had better take a good look at that cliff,' suggested Mr Keith. 'It is not only the finest on the island but, I fancy, the finest on the whole Mediterranean. Those on the Spanish coast and on Mount Athos lack the wonderful colour and the clean surface of this one. Looks as if it had been done with a knife, doesn't it? Alpine crags seem vertical but are nearly always inclined; their primary rock, you know, cannot flake off abruptly like this tufa. This is a genuine precipice. Plumb!'

'Terrific,' said Mr Heard. 'What was that about the English lord?'

'Two young fellows who rented the villa at the back of it for a summer. They used to bathe and booze all day long. I was not on the island at the time, but of course I heard about it. One day the younger one jumped over the edge of the cliff for a bet; said he was going to dive. They never recovered his body. There is a strong current at this point. That's so, isn't it, Antonio?'

'That so, gentlemens. Drink branty all the time, both of them. But little one – everybody smile at him. Pretty boy. Swim and dive, something lovely. One evening both get drunk and walk along the edge of cliff up there. Then little one, he say: I good diver, eh, what, friend? Big one say: You dive prettier than dolphin. – What bet, over cliff here, now? – Six bottle branty. – Done! Clothes off, over he go, like a sea-bird. All finished. That so, gentlemens. Next morning they bring clothes to big one into house. Big one, when he wake up and see clothes lying there, with no friend inside, he very angry with servants and everybody else, and drink no more branty for three days. Dam-fool foreigners.'

'That's a tragedy, anyhow,' said the bishop.

'You are right. It is quite artistic – that touch about bringing back the clothes, the empty shell, next morning. Quite artistic!'

Mr Heard looked up at the crag. It made him dizzy to picture some human body hurtling through the air from that awful height. Its surface was of perfect smoothness. But what struck him even more was the uncommon and almost menacing coloration. The rock was bluish-black, spattered with maculations of a ruddy sanguine tint, as though drops of blood had oozed out, in places, from its stony heart.

'I remember Mrs Meadows telling me that story,' he said to Keith. 'Isn't her villa at the back?'

'The very place. By the way, when next you call, would you please say something particularly nice *de ma part*? I don't see half enough of that lady, considering how much I like her. How is she?'

'Complains of headache.'

'Headache? That is very unlike Mrs Meadows. I always look upon her as a bundle of steel springs. Perhaps something is wrong with the baby.'

'Maybe,' replied the bishop. 'She seems to dote on it.'

Then that last visit to his cousin suddenly recurred to him; he remembered her conversation – he thought of the lonely woman up there. Strange! Somehow or other, she had been at the back of his mind all the time. He decided to call again in a day or two.

Keith said:

'I should not like to come between her and the child. That woman is a tiger-mother. ... Heard, there has been something on your mind all day long. What is it?'

'I believe there has. I'll try to explain. You know those Japanese flowers –' he began, and then broke off.

'I am glad you are becoming terrestrial at last. Nothing like Mother Earth! You cannot think how much money I wasted on

185

Japanese plants, especially bulbs, before I convinced myself that they cannot be grown on this soil.'

'Those paper flowers, I mean, which we used to put in our finger-bowls at country dinner-tables. They look like shrivelled specks of cardboard. But in the water they begin to grow larger and to unfold themselves into unexpected patterns of flowers of all colours. That is how I feel – expanding, and taking on other tints. New problems, new influences, are at work upon me. It is as if I needed altogether fresh standards. Sometimes I feel almost ashamed –'

'Ashamed? My dear Heard, this will never do. You must take a blue pill when we get home.'

'Can it be the South wind?'

'Everybody blames the poor sirocco. I imagine you have long been maturing for this change, unbeknown to yourself. And what does it mean? Only that you are growing up. Nobody need be ashamed of growing up. ... Here we are, at last! We will land at the little beach yonder, near the end of that gully. You can go ashore and have a look at the old thermal establishment. It used to be a gay place with a theatre and ballrooms and banqueting rooms. Nobody dare enter it nowadays. Haunted! Perhaps you will see the ghost. As for me, I mean to take a swim. I always feel as if I needed a bath after talking about religion. You don't mind my saying so, do you?'

Mr Heard, climbing upwards from the beach, felt as though he did not mind what anyone said about anything.

With the Devil's rock the most imposing tract of Nepenthean cliff-scenery came to an abrupt end. That mighty escarpment was its farthest outpost. Thereafter the land fell seawards no longer precipitously, but in wavy earthen slopes intersected by ravines which the downward-rushing torrents of winter had washed out of the loose soil. It was at the termination of one of these dry stream-beds that Mr Heard set foot on shore. Panting under the relentless heat, he wound his way along a path once carefully tended and engineered, but now crumbling to decay.

Before him, on a treeless brown eminence, silhouetted against the blue sky, stood the ruin. It was a fanciful, woe-begone structure, utterly desolate. The plaster, gnawed away by winds laden with searching sea-moisture, had fallen to earth, exposing the underlying masonry of cheap construction whose rusty colour was the same as that of the ground from which it had arisen, and into which it now seemed ready and eager to descend. Everything useful or portable, everything that spoke of man's occupation, everything that suggested life and comfort – the porcelain tiles, wood-work, window-panes, roofings, mosaic or marble floors, leaden pipes – all this had been carried away long ago. It stood there stark, dismantled, dehumanized, in the midday heat. Here was nothing to charm the eye or conjure up visions of past glory; nothing elegant or romantic; nothing savouring of grim, warlike purposes. It was a modern ruin; a pile of rubbish; a shameless, frivolous skeleton. Those hastily built walls and staring windows wore an air of faded futility, almost of indecency – as though the mouldering bones of some long-forgotten lady of pleasure had crept out of their tomb to give themselves an airing in the sun-shine.

Mr Heard, after glancing at what remained of a pretentious façade, stepped within.

Deep shade was here, in those of the chambers whose roofs re-mained intact; shade, and a steamy heat, and the noxious odour of some mineral product – the healing waters. He strayed in the twilight through halls and corridors, past ample saloons and rows of cells which had apparently served for convenience of disrobing. Everywhere that noisome smell accompanied his footsteps; the place was reeking with it. And all was in decay. Gaudy paper hung in tatters from the ceilings; the dust lay thick, undisturbed for generations. Unclean things littered in musty corners. Through gaping skylights a sunny beam would penetrate; it played about the mildewy stucco partitions encrusted, in patches, with a poisonous lichen of bright green. Wandering about this dank and mournful pile of wreckage, he could understand why simple folk should dread to enter so ghoul-haunted a spot.

Gladly he issued, by way of an obscure passage, into what had once been a trim garden. No trace of flowers or shrubs remained; the walks, the ornamental stone seats and artificial terraces, were merging into brown earth. Here, in the centre of this ruined pleasaunce, the health-giving fountain had lately flowed, bubbling up in a conch-shaped basin of cement. It was now dry. But a damp warmth still clung to its rim, whereon the mineral had left a comely deposit of opaline texture. Lowering his hand, he felt an intermittent stream of hot air rising out of the ground, feeble as the breath of a dying man. Still some mysterious gusts of life down there, he concluded, in the dark earth. How curious that volcanic connexion with the mainland, of which Count Caloveglia had spoken!

Soon he found himself beside the shattered framework of a small pavilion, built in a grotesque Chinese style and looking woefully out of place in this classic landscape, with the blue Tyrrhenian at its foot. And here he rested. He surveyed the traces of the old path leading down from the higher lands in serpentine meanderings; that path – once, doubtless, bordered by shady trees – whereby all those worldly invalids had once descended. He pictured the lively caravan afoot, on mule-back, in sedan chairs, seeking health and pleasure at this site, now so void of life. Lower down, almost within a stone's throw, lay the beach. The sailors, father and son, had drawn the boat up to the shore and were sitting huddled up on its shady side, with some food between them on a coloured handkerchief. That Brobdingnagian luncheon-basket had also been disembarked. Keith was swimming, together with his two genii; he looked like a rosy Silenus. They seemed to be enjoying themselves vastly, to judge by the outbursts of laughter. Mr Heard thought of going to join the fun, but gave up the idea; there was something astir that clogged his energies.

He knew them – these Southern noons. If no ghost resided in the melancholy ruin hard by, there might well be some imponderable hostile essence afloat in the still air of midday. Anything, he felt, could happen at this unearthly hour. The wildest follies might be committed at the bidding of this unseen Presence.

He tried to recollect what Keith had told him concerning Muhlen, that corrupt personality. Retlow ... where had he heard that name before? In vain he flogged his memory. There was an alien power in this brightness; a power as of a vampire that drained away his faculties, his vitality; a spirit of evil, exhaling from the sunny calm. It made a mock, a mirage, of the landscape which danced before his eyes; it distorted the realities of nature, the works of man. ...

Presently he observed that Keith and his companions were clothed and occupied in dragging things out of the preposterous food-receptacle. They called up to him. The spell was released.

He descended.

'Nice bathe?' he enquired.

'Rather! And now these fellows will make a passable omelette, to begin with. I don't fancy cold luncheons, do you? They seem to lie like lead on one's stomach.'

'Are those sailors not coming with us?'

'No. They are well paid for their work. No doubt they would like to be in my service too. But I never employ islanders, except for casual jobs; it saves me all kinds of local trouble and family intrigues. Nor yet older people. They are so apt to think; and once a servant begins to think he ceases to be of use. I believe in the outsider, for all purposes of human intercourse. If you want a thing done, go to the outsider, the intelligent amateur. And when you marry, Heard, be sure to select a wife from another class, another province, another country – another planet, if possible. Otherwise you will repent it. Not that I see any objection, on principle, to incest; it strikes me as the most natural proceeding in the world –'

'Dear me!'

'And yet – that inexplicable prejudice. It is probably artificial and of modern origin. I suspect the priestly caste. Royal Families kept up the custom and do so still, like that of Siam. Odd, how anachronisms linger longest at the two poles of society. What do you say,' he went on, 'to climbing a little up that gorge, into the shade? I cannot digest properly with the sun staring at me. And tell me, as we go along, your impressions of the ruin. ... I perceive drawbacks to incest; grave practical drawbacks – sterility, inbreeding. Yes, there is obviously something to be said for exogamy. *Audi alteram partem*, as Eames might say, though God knows why he thinks it sounds better in Latin. Seen the ghost?'

The bishop remembered a certain answer given him by Madame Steynlin, to whom he had once spoken of the 'tonic' effects of Keith's conversation.

'A tonic?' she had said. 'Very likely! But not a tonic for men and women. A tonic for horses.'

After luncheon they improvised a shelter in order to repose awhile. It was the right thing to do on Nepenthe at that hour of the day, and Mr Keith tried to conform to custom even under unusual circumstances such as these. Protected by the boat's scarlet awning from the rays of the sun, they slumbered through the flaming hours.

CHAPTER 23

THE Duchess was a good sleeper, as befitted a person of regular habits and pure life.

It was her custom to retire for the night at about eleven o'clock. Angelina, who reposed in an adjoining room, would enter softly at nine in the morning, draw up the blinds, and deposit a cup of tea at the bedside of her mistress. Up to that moment she would slumber like a child. Rarely did she suffer from insomnia or nightmare. On this particular night, however, her rest was troubled by a strange and disquieting dream.

She was a little girl once more, at her parental home out West. All the old memories were around her. It was winter time. She was alone, out of doors. Snow, the familiar snow, was falling from a sombre sky; already it lay deep on the boundless plains. It fell without ceasing. The sky grew darker. Hours seemed to pass, and still the flakes descended. It was not cold snow. It was warm snow – warm and rather suffocating. Very suffocating. It began to choke her. Suddenly she found she could breathe no more. She gave a wild cry of despair –

Her maid was standing beside the bed, a lighted candle in her hand. Otherwise the room was in pitch darkness. Angelina looked like a Tanagra statuette. Draped in nothing but a clinging night-gown that reached two inches below the knee and accentuated the charm of her figure, with the candle-light throwing playful gleams upon her neck and cheeks, Angelina was an apparition to gladden the heart of man.

The heart of the Duchess was not gladdened by any means.

'What is the meaning of this, girl?' she inquired sternly, in what she took to be the language of the country. 'And in the middle of the night!'

'It's nine o'clock, Madam.'

'Nine o'clock? Then draw the blinds.'

'I've drawn them.' She stepped to the window and tapped on the glass panes by way of confirmation. 'All dark outside,' she added. 'Ashes are falling from heaven. The volcano is very, very angry.'

'Ashes? The volcano? I must dress at once. Light two more candles. No, three! We can't have three candles burning. Don Francesco may be here at any moment.'

The Duchess often laughingly described herself as 'only a weak woman'. A certain number of persons concurred in that opinion. Just then she was the most self-possessed inhabitant of Nepenthe. The disturbance of nature left her undisturbed. Her intellect was naturally incurious as to the habits of volcanos; her soul, more-over, in good hands, her conscience in excellent working order, as befitted a potential convert to Catholicism. She could rely on a spiritual adviser who had instilled into her mind a lofty sense of obedience and resignation. Don Francesco would never desert her. He would arrive in due course, explaining why God had allowed the volcano to behave in this unseemly fashion, and brimming over with words of consolation for his daughter-to-be. God, if so disposed, could work a miracle and drive away the plague, even as he had sent it. Ashes or no ashes, all was for the best. Calmly she waited.

Out of doors, meanwhile, the shower went on without ceasing.

It had begun shortly after midnight; the ground was covered to the depth of two inches. Nepenthe lay veiled in Cimmerian gloom, darker than starless midnight – a darkness that could be felt; a blanket, as it were, hot and breathless, weighing upon the land-scape. All was silent. No footfall could be heard in the streets; the powdery ashes, softer than snow, absorbed every sound. And still they fell. Those few scared natives whom necessity forced to go abroad crept about in fear of their lives. They thought the end of the world had come. Terror-stricken, they carried knives and revolvers in their pockets; they passed each other distrustfully in the streets holding, in one hand a lighted torch or lantern, and in the other a handkerchief pressed to the face for fear of suffocation. In one or two of the shop windows could be discerned a light glim-mering feebly as through the thickest fog. All the ordinary sights and sounds of morning – the vehicles plying for hire, the cracking of whips, the cries of the fish and fruit vendors – all were gone. The deathly stillness was broken only by the clangour of the town clock, tolling the hours into a darkened world.

Half a dozen adventurous spirits had gathered together at the Club. They called themselves adventurous. As a matter of fact they were scared out of their wits and had gone there merely with a view to leaning on each other for mutual support and courage. There was no whisky-drinking that morning, no cards, no scan-dal-mongering. They sat round a table under an acetylene lamp, anxiously listening to a young professor from Christiania who claimed to be versed in the higher mathematics and was then occu-pied in calculating, by means of the binomial theorem, how long it would take for the whole town of Nepenthe to be submerged under ashes up to the roofs – presuming all the buildings to be of equal height. He was a new-comer to the place and, for that rea-son, rather a cheerful pessimist. He thought it quite possible that before the second floors of the houses had been reached – granted, of course, that none was higher or lower than the other – the wind might change and carry the ashes elsewhere. His demonstration had a depressing effect on the hearts of those who had lived longer on the island. They rose from the table and sadly shook their heads, prepared for the worst. They knew their sirocco.

As morning wore on other stragglers entered the premises, muffled up to the ears; they scattered ashes from their cloaks and hastily closed the door behind them. More lamps were lighted. The news was not inspiriting. It was dark as ever outside; you could not see your hand before your face; the shower had accu-mulated to an alarming extent. Some roofs had fallen in under the weight of ashes; telegraphic communication with the mainland was interrupted owing, it was supposed, to the snapping of the cable in some submarine convulsion; a man had stumbled in the market-place over the dead body of a woman – choked, no doubt; two of the judge's Russian prisoners, unaccustomed to volcanic phenomena, had gone stark staring mad and disembowelled one another with a carving-knife. Mr Muhlen, who presently turned up in anything but his usual sprightly humour, was furnished with a full and corrected version of this last affair, to the effect that there were not two, but fourteen, of these victims; that prior to their frenzied act they had partaken of bread and salt and sung the national anthem; that the instrument chosen was not a carving knife but a rusty chisel. None of his listeners seemed to be greatly moved by what, in ordinary circumstances, would have been a valuable contribution to the entertainment. They were waiting for the appearance of their president, the Commissioner, the life and soul of the place, who would be able to give them an official apology for this scandalous outbreak of nature. The Commissioner, for once in his life, failed to perform his duty.

That unfortunate man was sitting at home, in the remote villa known as the 'Residency', profoundly troubled in mind. He leaned over his study table, which was lighted by a lamp; his eyes peered dejectedly through the windows beyond, into the gloom. Before him lay the skeleton draft of his annual report to the Nicaraguan Minister of Finance, a gentleman who developed a passionate craving, once a year, to be informed of the condition of Nepenthe in regard to matters such as shipping and trade returns, zymotic diseases, and the methods locally employed for combatting beri-beri.

The elaboration of this report had hitherto given Mr Freddy Parker no trouble whatever. It was an understood thing between himself and his protector, Señor Pomponio dei Vergara y Puyarola, that his labours need not be otherwise than purely formal. To every one of the intelligent queries on the part of a paternal government it had been his custom, therefore, to append the magic word *nil*. Banking system – *nil*. Meat export – *nil*. Cotton industry – *nil*. Agriculture – *nil*. Canal traffic – *nil*. Teak trade – *nil*. Emery mines – *nil*. Fisheries – *nil*.

He could trust Señor de Vergara to arrange matters, in the event of any complaint arising as to the unwarranted ambiguity or succinctness of the Nepenthean Report.

Bad news had just reached him; very bad news indeed. His friend and protector had been stabbed to death, after the approved fashion of Nicaraguan politicians, by a couple of assassins in the pay of that minister's rival, a bankrupt tradesman who, desirous of bettering his fortunes, conceived that he would make as good a Finance Minister as anyone else and had, in fact, already usurped that post. Worse news could hardly be imagined. The prognosis was most unfavourable. For Mr Parker shrewdly argued that a rival of the late Don Pomponio would look askance at those whom His Excellency had exalted – at himself, for instance. And what then? However conscientiously he might henceforward edit the report, he realized that his position was no longer secure; he was liable to be recalled at any moment – to cede his place to some candidate of the opposing faction. Those damned republics! Or the post, being a purely honorary one created expressly for himself by the obliging and now defunct Don Pomponio, might be permanently abolished. It was not a pleasant prospect. Mr Freddy Parker was rather too old to start knocking about the world again. He was losing what he called his 'nerve'. What was to be done?

He tugged at his beard and puffed furious clouds of smoke out of his briar pipe. He thought of another grief – another source of anxiety. The quarterly remittance forwarded to him by certain obscure but respectable relatives in England, under the condition that he should never again set foot in that land of honest men, had not arrived. It was two weeks overdue. What had happened? Had they decided to cancel it? They had threatened to do so ere now. And if so, how was he going to live? It was a facer, that was. The equivalent of fifteen pounds sterling was urgently necessary at that very moment. Fifteen pounds. Who would lend him fifteen pounds? Keith? Not likely. Keith was a miser – a Scotchman, ten to one. Koppen? He had once already tried to touch him for a loan, with discouraging results. A most unsympathetic millionaire. Almost offensive, the old bounder had been. Perhaps somebody had let on about that bit of *crêpe de Chine* preserved at the Residency, and its uses as a sociological document. How things got about on Nepenthe! Where the hell, then, was money to come from?

Both these troubles, great in themselves, faded into insignificance before a new and overwhelming sorrow.

In a room directly overhead lay the dead body of his lady. She had breathed her last on the previous midday, and it is more than likely that the noise of the cannon-shots, reverberating through her chamber, had accelerated her end; not the noise as such, for she was naturally a rowdy woman and never felt comfortable save

193

in an atmosphere of domestic explosions and quarrels with servants, but the noise in its social significance, the noise as demonstrating to her exhausted consciousness that there was something wrong, something at the same time of considerable importance – something she might never live to comment on – happening in the market-place. In other words, it is highly probable that her death had been hastened by the moral rather than the physical shock of the noise; by disappointment; by the bitter reflection that she would never survive to learn what this new scandal, evidently an interesting one, was about.

The doctor, for reasons which he deemed sufficient, had recommended a speedy interment; it was fixed for that morning. The fall of ashes had put the ceremony out of the question. There she lay. And in the room below sat her bereaved stepbrother, distractedly gazing out of the window upon the darkness of Erebus.

It harmonized with the darkness of his mourning trousers, newly creased but not newly purchased; and of his soul. He saw his worldly existence menaced – tottering to its fall. All these catastrophes, so crushing, so unexpected, filled him with a kind of primeval terror. Mr Parker was neither a devout believer nor the reverse. He was a fool and liable, as such, under the stress of bodily or mental disturbance, to spasmodic fits of abject fright which he mistook for religion. An attack of indigestion, the failure of some pecuniary speculation, the demise of a beloved step-sister – these various happenings, so dissimilar to one another, had yet this feature in common, that they put the fear of God into the otherwise empty brain of Mr Parker.

He had been in many tight corners, but never in so tight a corner as this. Hardly ever. He thought of the lady lying dead upstairs and all she had done towards establishing and consolidating their social position; how she had economized for him, yes, and lied for him – better, far better, than he could ever hope to lie. For she possessed that most priceless of all gifts; she believed her own lies. She looked people straight in the face and spoke from her heart; a falsehood, before it left her lips, had grown into a flaming truth. She was a florid, improvident liar. There was no classical parsimony about her mis-statements. They were copious, baroque, and encrusted with pleasing and unexpected tricks of ornamentation. That tropical redundancy for which her person was renowned reflected itself likewise in her temperament – in nothing more than the exuberance of her untruths, which were poured out in so torrential a flood, with such burning conviction and opulence of detail that persons who knew her well used to stand aghast

194

(Catholics had been known to cross themselves) at the fertility of her constructive imagination, while the most hardened sceptics protested that, even if her facts were wrong, there could be no doubt as to her sincerity, her ingenuousness. Ah, she was a woman in a thousand! Often had Mr Parker sat at her feet, a respectful disciple, listening spellbound and striving to acquire that secret – a secret which was, after all, not so much art as nature. He could never hope to rival her technique.

That was because he could not look you in the face; because he disbelieved not only his own lies, but those of other people – and not only their lies, but their truths; because he distrusted everything and everybody, and was duly distrusted in his turn. Nobody believed a word he said, and some rude persons went so far as to tell him exactly what they thought of him. They called him a liar, in public and in private. Such experiences are trying to one's nerve; they end in giving you a shifty look. People who knew him well never took his word for granted, and the more casual acquaintances would say that even if his facts were correct now and then he could not help being a fraud all the same.

And now she was gone, this lady who had saved him from countless small annoyances, who had given him self-esteem and a kind of social backbone. He stared into the darkness. Where was money to come from – those miserable fifteen pounds, for example? What would happen?

He almost decided upon praying, only he could not think of appropriate words in which to appeal for this loan; it might seem to the Deity a contemptuously small sum, not worth bothering the angels about. On the other hand, he dared not apply for more than he actually needed – not to that quarter, at least – for fear of being found out. He was always being found out, even by his earthly creditors. Besides, there lingered at the back of his mind all the time certain doubts as to the efficacy of applying to God for money or anything else. The whole thing might be a farce. He remembered, with pain and grief, that he had already on several occasions tried the prayer-system, like most other systems. And alas, the result had invariably been *nil*. ...

A visit from His Reverence the *parroco* was announced.

This heroic priest, accompanied by two acolytes bearing torches, had braved the downpour of ashes. He never shirked his duty. It was his duty that morning to confer with Mr Parker anent the delayed funeral and other painfully material matters. For the deceased lady had not deserted the creed of her fathers; she was an ardent Catholic – so ardent that she professed great pain at her

195

stepbrother's alien leanings and had taken considerable trouble to convert him to her own way of thinking. She used to say, in her flowery language, that his contumacious attitude towards the true Faith gnawed at her vitals – meaning, presumably, that it annoyed her. Often she pointed out how many social and other advantages they would gain – living in a Catholic country – if he, too, could bring himself to enter the fold of believers. In vain! The Commissioner had a knack of being ultra-protestant on such occasions.

Not that he greatly cared to what Church he belonged. But if nobody made it worth his while – why, he remained an Englishman. He knew perfectly well that the *parroco*, his lady's confessor, was anxious to do something in the proselytizing line which might lower the prestige of Don Francesco. And he was clever enough to realize that, by embracing Catholicism at Torquemada's hands, he, the Official Representative of Nicaragua, would be putting a feather in the priest's cap. He was not going to put a feather in anybody's cap – not for nothing. It was not good enough. Some strong leader of nations had once remarked 'Every man his price.' Mr Parker liked that phrase; he was deeply convinced of its veracity. He also had his price, and once, in a moment of extreme financial embarrassment, he had delighted his stepsister by announcing that he was prepared to consider the question of conversion. He then named his price. It was a condition not to be expressed by such terms as a gratified church might have been able to concede by some elevation to a higher sphere or influence or other worldly favour; it was a figure baldly commercial, expressible, that is, in pounds, shillings, and pence.

'You've got some cheek, Freddy,' was all she could bring herself to say.

'My dear Lola, he can take it or leave it,' the Commissioner had replied, sulkily.

His Reverence never found himself in the odious dilemma of either taking or leaving it, for the lady was wise enough not to divulge so ignoble a proposition.

But now, while the good priest uttered a few parting platitudes of condolence, the other was revolving in his mind how negotiations – direct negotiations, this time – could be opened up. He needed fifteen pounds; well, one might be able to do a little juggling with the Club money for that part of the business. It was necessary, above all, to devise some means whereby the Nicaraguan Government might be induced to keep him at his old post. Here was Torquemada. How could that fellow be turned to account?

196

'The Nuncio!' he suddenly thought. A Catholic republic like Nicaragua was sure to have a Papal Nuncio, whatever that might be; and if he became a convert to the official faith of that country, the Nuncio would be delighted and might whisper in the ear of the President a few words commending his act and requesting that so good a servant of the Church should not be despoiled of his post. And if the President, himself a Catholic, could be brought to share this view, then he, Freddy Parker, could snap his fingers at the machinations of Señor de Vergara's successor.

He decided to show some signs of devotion to what he had been accustomed to call the grossest of superstitions; to reveal symptoms of latent Roman proclivities. Grief seemed to have sharpened his wits, for an inspiration came to him. After the sordid and melancholy details of the funeral had been discussed yet again – it was to take place as soon as ever the state of the sky would allow of it – Mr Parker, pointing to the blackened world outside, made an oracular remark.

'Something must be done,' he said.

His companion agreed, very heartily. But soon he drew a deep sigh. How could a volcanic eruption be stopped? In other words, what must be done?

'Let me suggest something, *parroco*. Why not organize a procession at once, a penitential procession? Such things take place during eruptions on the mainland. Why not here?'

It was the most tactful and diplomatic proposal that the Commissioner had ever made. A thundering good tip, in fact. How proud his Lola would have been had she heard him make it! A flash of inspiration – and he was actually following it up. The effect was instantaneous. At the sound of that word 'procession' the other's thin lips relaxed and into his ferrety eyes there came a gentler look. He was pleased, infinitely pleased. The Protestant Commissioner betraying only too plainly the heart of a Catholic – that augured well. But difficulties, apparently insurmountable, presented themselves.

'That thought, Signor Parker, coming from you, gives me pleasure beyond words. But I question whether a procession can be formed. Even the priests, most of them, would not care to attend. As to the populace – who is going to risk his life in the midst of this calamity? We might all be choked to death. Not that I would hesitate to play my becoming part!'

'You know your people – how inquisitive they are. If you toll the church bells, a certain number are sure to gather in the market-place in order to learn, even at risk of their lives, what is happening. When they see a torch-lit procession being formed, you will obtain a sufficient quantity, I feel sure, to carry the Holy Image of the Saint; and some to spare. Also I see no reason why the priests should be present in full strength. Toll the bells, *parroco*! You will get your men.'

His Reverence was thinking hard. At last he said:

'Your project appeals to me. It does credit to your heart. It would do credit to our island. I will try to arrange it. But if –'

'You mean, don't you, if the ashes continue to fall, notwithstanding our expiatory demonstration? Let me see. There was that disgraceful tumult in the town yesterday. Saint Dodekanus is perhaps too deeply vexed against his people to concede them a grace under such circumstances. I imagine him to be very displeased with us just now. That being the case, the fall of ashes might well be permitted to continue for our castigation, despite the penitential act. What do you think?'

Nobody knows what the *parroco* thought. It was not his habit to think aloud, much less to express opinions on ticklish arguments such as these. But he could corroborate the fact with a clear conscience.

'It was indeed enough to anger a saint in Heaven! Seven more of the wounded have succumbed to their injuries; three of them little children. Ah, these deeds of violence and bloodshed, for which Nepenthe was ever infamous! When will the peace of God descend upon our island?'

Mr Parker had no idea when that might happen. He was not particularly keen about the peace of God – he was keen about keeping his job. None the less, he managed to move his head up and down, in a decidedly becoming fashion.

'And now,' concluded the *parroco*, 'with your kind permission, I will take my leave, to confer with the clergy, if I can discover any of them, as to what can be done towards forming a procession. I confess that the more I think upon your idea, Signor Parker, the more I like it. If only we can find a sufficient number to participate!'

'Have no fear of that. Only toll the bells. You will get your men. This eruption is enough to make anybody religious. I mean – you know what I mean, *parroco*.'

The acolytes having rekindled their torches, His Reverence, a happier man, stepped boldly out of doors and was swallowed up in the murk. ...

This is a succinct and faithful account of the genesis of that procession which was to become famous in Nepenthean annals.

However much, in later years, certain envious folk might claim to be the originators of the project, it was from first to last the Commissioner's idea. Honour to whom honour is due. He deserved, and took, all credit for it. Meanwhile he sat down at his table once more, and stared into the pitchy darkness.

Not long afterwards, the sound of bells announced that something was being done. Men looked out of their windows and saw flickering lights moving about the gloom. The flames grouped themselves into definite arrangement; a procession was being formed. As the *parroco* had foretold, it was but sparsely attended in the beginning; out of sixty-five priests and canons of the Church, only fourteen found it convenient to attend; another dozen, however, were presently shamed into taking their places in the ranks. The same with the followers. Their number gradually increased. For the bells did the work of arousing curiosity; they tolled plangently into the night.

Stranger pageant never trod Nepenthe. Some thoughtful person had discovered that umbrellas might be used with advantage. Umbrellas were therefore utilized by all save the priests, the choristers, torchbearers, and those carrying the statue of the Saint, who, for reasons of personal dignity or expediency, preferred the other method. They chanted their psalms and litanies through handkerchiefs, knowing full well that their music would be none the less pleasing to the Saint for being more than usually nasal in tone. Thus, with soundless footfalls, they perambulated the streets and outskirts of the town, gathering fresh recruits as they went.

And still the ashes fell.

Viewing this cortège of awe-struck innocents braying into the blackness under their umbrellas at the heels of a silver-plated idol (not yet paid for), an intelligent God might well be proud of his workmanship. So thought the *parroco*. He was undismayed. Come what might, he had an explanation ready. Saint Dodekanus, if the ashes continued to fall, was only showing his displeasure; he was perfectly justified in letting his wrath be known for the better guidance of mankind. Certain of the younger priests, on the other hand, were growing nervous at the prospect of a possible failure of the procession. They began to blame His Reverence for what he had given them to understand was his own idea. For two hours they had now been in movement; they had swallowed a hatful of ashes. And yet no sign from Heaven. The sky appeared darker than ever. Many of the followers, exhausted, dropped out of the procession and returned sadly to their homes. They thought the speculation was going to turn out badly. The others deemed it not

199

impossible that the Saint could not see them through so thick a curtain. Well then, he might hear them. They chanted more furiously.

The sound must have reached Heaven at last, for a miracle occurred. The gloom decreased in density. Men looked up and beheld a sickly radiance overhead – it was the sun, ever so far away; it shone as when seen through thickly smoked glasses. Then a veil seemed to be withdrawn. The light grew clearer – the song of the penitents jubilant with hope. Sullen gleams, now, pierced the murky air. Outlines of trees and houses crept furtively into their old places. The fall of ashes had almost ceased. With a wrench, as it seemed, the final covering was drawn away. The land lay flooded in daylight.

That paean of joy and thanksgiving which ought to have greeted this divine largesse, died on the lips of the beholders when they saw the state of their island. Nepenthe was hardly recognizable. The Saint had lifted a mantle from Heaven only to reveal the desolation on earth. Ashes everywhere. Trees, houses, the fertile fields, the mountain slopes – all were smothered under a layer of monotonous pallor. They knew what it meant. It meant ruin to their crops and vineyards. None the less, they raised a shout, a half-hearted shout, of praise. For Nepentheans are born politicians and courteous by nature. It is their heritage from the Good Duke Alfred to 'keep smiling'. A shout was expected of them under the circumstances; it costs nothing and may even do good, inasmuch as Saint Dodekanus could remove the ashes as easily as he had sent them. Why not shout?

'A miracle, a miracle!' the cry went up. 'Long life to our patron!'

A poor tribute; but the Saint took note of it. Half an hour had barely passed ere the sky grew cloudy. Moist drops began to fall. It was the first rain for many weeks, and foreign visitors, accustomed to think of Nepenthe as a rainless land, were almost as interested in the watery shower as in that of ashes. Mud, such mud as the oldest midwife could not remember, encumbered the roofs, the fields, the roadways. It looked as if the whole island were plastered over with a coating of liquid chocolate. Now, if the shower would only continue –

Suddenly it ceased. The sky grew clear.

Saint Dodekanus had often been accused of possessing a grain of malice. Some went so far as to say he had the Evil Eye. It was by no means the first time in his long career that the natives had found cause to complain of a certain rancour in his temperament

200

– of certain spiteful viperish acts to which the priests, and they alone, were able to give a benevolent interpretation. Now their wrath blazed out against the celestial Patron. 'He's not fit for his job,' said some; 'let's get a new saint! The ruffian, the son of an impure mother – up to his tricks, was he? Ah, the cut-throat, the Saracen, the old paederast: into the ditch with him!'

During a brief moment his fate hung in the balance. For it was plain that the ashes, if unwetted, might ultimately have been blown away by the wind. But what was going to happen when all this mud, baked by the sun into the hardness of brick, covered the island?

Perhaps the Saint was only putting their tempers to the test. The experiment of another shout was worth trying. One could always punish him later on.

So feeble was the noise that Saint Dodekanus must have had uncommonly good ears. He had. And soon showed his real feelings. Rain fell once more. Instead of diminishing it grew more violent, accompanied by warm blasts of wind. There was sunshine overhead, but the peaks were shrouded in scudding vapours, trees bent under the force of the wind; the sea, a welter of light and shade, was dappled with silvery patches under the swiftly careering clouds. Soon there came a blinding downpour. Gullies were blocked up with mud; rills carried tons of it into the sea. Then the gale died down; the sun beamed out of a bright evening sky. The miraculous shower was over.

Men walked abroad and recognized their beloved Nepenthe once more. It glowed in tenderest hues. The events of morning and midday were like a bad dream. Everything sparkled with unaccustomed brilliance; the land was refreshed – swept clean; the sea alone remained discoloured to a dingy brown. Truly, as the Commissioner – once more a sound Protestant – remarked in later years: 'The old rotter came up to the scratch that time.' So clear and pleasant was the air that it seemed as if the wind had actually veered to the north. But no. It still blew from the other quarter – the old familiar sirocco. Which proved that the shower of ashes had not been 'carried elsewhere', as the youthful teacher of mathematics had prognosticated. It had not been carried anywhere. It simply ceased to fall, the volcano having momentarily run out of its stock of objectionable materials.

The Clubmen therefore, calling to mind the discussion of the morning, were led to revise their opinion as to that gentleman's intelligence. They remembered one or two things. They remembered that even when Heavenly Powers are not known to be directly interested in the event, eruptions now and then come to an end quite irrespective of the wind – a contingency which had not been foreseen in the acute young Scandinavian's computations.

'That comes,' they said, 'of studying the higher mathematics. ...'

For their miraculous deliverance from a shower of volcanic ashes the islanders gave all credit, as might have been expected, to their patron saint. And this proves how inadequately causes and effects are understood here on earth. For the priests, the most intelligent section of the populace, knew perfectly well that but for the orders of the *parroco* no procession could have taken place. The Saint would have remained locked up in his musty shrine, without the faintest chance of performing a miracle of any kind. They argued, consequently, that Saint Dodekanus got the credit for what was really the *parroco*'s notion. And Torquemada, thinking over the day's proceedings, was driven to confess that he was indebted for the suggestion to the fertile brain of the Nicaraguan Representative; in other words, that he, the *parroco*, was praised for what was really the Commissioner's idea. And it is evident that if Mr Parker's lady had not died from the effects of a mosquito-sting, that gentleman would never have been in such a complex funk as to suggest a procession to the worthy priest.

Thus it came about that the Commissioner, the Parish Priest, and the Patron Saint, got the credit for what was really an insect's work.

Which shows how a mosquito can cure an eruption.

CHAPTER 24

EVERYBODY was drunk that night in honour of the Saint's bounty, though Miss Wilberforce reached the climax of her activities at the early hour of 4 p.m. – during the torchlight procession.

An uproar had been generated at the Club; chairs were broken, bottles smashed, and sporting prints kicked about – all on account of a comical but rather scurrilous speech contrasting Europe with Australasia by a new-comer, a member of the New Zealand House of Representatives, who limped home not long afterwards with a damaged shin-bone and black eye. The more violent parties had been ejected during that incident, or carried to their lodgings. Only about half the usual number was left – all moderates, so far as drinking was concerned, but all more or less screwed that day as befitted the occasion. There was the card-table group, where

Mr Muhlen, with heightened colour in his cheeks, was losing money in so brilliant a fashion that everyone swore he must be on the verge of coming into a legacy or making some *coup* with a rich woman. In another room the so-called bawdy section, presided over by the dubious Mr Hopkins, were discussing topics not adapted to polite ears. The artistic group, sadly thinned by the ejection of four of its more imaginative and virile members who had distinguished themselves in the fray, now consisted solely of two youngsters, a black-and-white man and a literary critic; they sat in a corner by themselves, talking about colour-values in maudlin strains.

The ordinary club-group had, as usual, installed themselves in the most comfortable chairs on the balcony. They were boozing steadily, like gentlemen, and having no end of fun with the poor little Norwegian professor and his miscalculations. One of them – a venerable toper of Anacreontic youthfulness known as Charlie, who turned up on Nepenthe at odd intervals and whom the oldest inhabitant of the place had never seen otherwise than in a state of benevolent fuddle – was saying to him:

'Instead of filling yourself up with whisky in that disgusting fashion, my friend, you ought to travel. Then you wouldn't make such an exhibition of yourself as you did this afternoon over those ashes. Talk about volcanoes! Ever seen the Lake of Pitch in Trinidad? Queer place, Trinidad. You never know where you are. Though I can't say I saw much of it myself. I was asleep most of the time, gentlemen, and often tight. Mostly both. All angles and things, as you sail along. To get an idea of that place, you must take a banana, for instance, and cut it in half, and cut that in half again, and that half in half again – the banana, mind you, must always remain the same size – or suppose you keep on peeling a potato, and peeling, and peeling – well, Mr Professor, what are you laughing at now?'

'I was thinking what an interesting map one could draw of Trinidad if it's like that.'

'Interesting? That's not the word. It's hell. I wouldn't care to take on that job, not even to oblige my poor old mother, who died fifty years ago. Ever been to Trinidad, Mr Richards? Or you, Mr White? Or anybody? What, has nobody been to Trinidad? You ought to travel more, gentlemen. How about you, Mr Samuel?'

'Never farther West than the Marble Arch. But a friend of mine kept a ranch somewhere down there. One day he shot a skunk. Yes, Mr White, a skunk.'

'A skunk? I'm blowed. What on earth ever for did he do that? What did he want with a skunk? I thought they were protected by law to keep down rattlesnakes. That's so, isn't it, Charlie?'

'Snakes. You should see them in Trinidad. Snakes. Great Scot! It's a queer place, is Trinidad. All angles and things –'

'I don't think one can talk about a place being all angles and things, unless –'

'Tell me, Charlie, what did the fellow on the ranch want to do with that rattlesnake?'

'Couldn't say, my son. Maybe he thought of sending it to his mother. Or perhaps he did not want the skunk to get hold of its tail: see?'

'I see.'

'They're very sensitive about their tails. As ticklish as any young girl, I'm told.'

'As bad as all that, are they?'

'I don't think one can talk about angles when describing an island or even a continent, except in a figurative and flowery fashion. As teacher of geometry, it is my business to dwell among angles; and the thirty-five boys in my class will bear witness to the fact that my relations with angles, great and small, are above reproach. I admit that there are angles everywhere, and that a man who really likes their company will stumble against them in the most unexpected places. But they are sometimes hard to see, unless one deliberately looks for them. I think Charlie must have been looking for them in Trinidad.'

'I said angles *and things*, and I always stick to what I say. *And things*. You will be good enough, Mr Professor, to draw your map accordingly.'

'Gentlemen! I rise to a point of order. Our Indian friend here is greatly annoyed. He has been accused of wearing stays. At his urgent request I have convinced myself, by personal inspection, that he wears nothing of the kind. He is naturally slim-waisted, as befits a worthy representative of the noble Hairyan race. It has also been suggested that he loses caste by his present mode of conduct. He begs me to say that, being a Jamshi-worshipper, he doesn't care a brass farthing about caste. Thirdly, he has been blamed in certain quarters for his immoderate indulgence in Parker's poison. Let me tell you, gentlemen, in my capacity as Vice-President, that for the last four thousand years his family has enjoyed a special dispensation from the Great Mogul, authorizing the eldest son to drink whatever he damn well pleases. Our friend here happens to be the third son. But that is obviously not his fault. If it were, he would have come forward with an apology long ago. Gentlemen! I can't speak fairer than that. Whoever says I'm not a gentleman – why, he isn't one either.'

'Hear, hear! I never knew you were an ornithologist, Richards.'

'Nor did I – not till this moment. But when it's a question of defending the honour of a Club-member I always rise to the occasion. Some things – they simply make my blood boil. Look at this *Referee*: two weeks out of date! How the blazes is a man –'

'I say, Charlie, what did the fellow on the ranch want to do with that skunk? Something about tickling, wasn't it?'

'Hush, my boy. We can't talk about it here. You're not old enough yet. I don't think I ought to tell you. It's too funny for words. ...'

'You're a black-and-white man and I'm a writer, and really, you know, we're a cut above all those sots on the balcony. Now just be reasonable for a moment. Look here. Have you ever thought about the impossibility of realizing colour description in landscape? It's struck me a good deal lately, here, with this blue sea, and those orange tints on the mountain, and all the rest of it. Take any page by a well-known writer – take a description of a sunset by Symonds, for example. Well, he names all the gorgeous colours, the yellow and red and violet, or whatever it may be, as he saw them. But he can't make you see them – damned if he can. He can only throw words at your head. I'm very much afraid, my dear fellow, that humanity will never get its colour-values straightened out by means of verbal symbols.'

'I always know when a man is drunk, even when I'm drunk myself.'

'When?'

'When he talks about colour-values.'

'I believe you're right. I'm feeling a bit muzzy about the legs, as if I couldn't move. A bit fuzzy –'

'Muzzy, I think you said.'

'Fuzzy.'

'Muzzy. But we needn't quarrel about it, need we? I shall be sick in a minute, old man.'

'It's rather hard on a fellow to be always misunderstood. However, as I was saying when you interrupted me, I am feeling slightly wobblish in the peripatetic or ambulatorial department. But my head's all right. Now do be serious, for a change. You don't seem to catch my drift. This blue sea, and those orange tints on the mountains, I mean to say – how are they going to be held fast by the optic apparatus? The lens, you understand. I want to be able to shove them into a sketch-book, like you fellows. Well, how? That's what I want to know. How to turn my retina into a canvas.'

'Rot, my good sir.'

'It may be rot to you, but it strikes me as rather unfortunate, all the same, when you come to think of it. This blue sea, I mean, and those orange tints and all that, you know. Take a sunrise by John Addington. Of course, as a matter of fact, we ought both to have been born in another age – an age of sinecures. Why are sinecures extinct? I feel as if I could be Governor of Madagascar at this moment.'

'I feel as if you were getting slightly intoxicated.'

'That's me. But it's only my legs. My head is astonishingly clear. And I do wish you would try, just for once in a way, to follow my meaning. Be reasonable, for a change! I mean to say that a man has talents for all sorts of things. I, for example, have pronounced views upon agriculture. But what's the use of farming without capital? What I mean to say is this: we see the blue sea and the orange tints on the mountains, and all that, I mean, and we don't seem to realize, I mean, that we may die at any moment and never see them again. How few people grasp that simple fact! It's enough to make one sick. Or do you think it's a laughing matter?'

'Bally rotten, I call it. You're quite right. People don't realize things the way they ought, except in a few selected moments. They live like animals. I shall be sick in a minute, old man.'

'Like animals. Good Lord! You've hit the nail on the head this time. How true that is! Like animals. Like animals. Like animals.'

'I know what we want. We want fresh air. No more Parker's poison for me. Let's take a stroll.'

'I would if I could. But I can't get off this chair, damn it. I shall fall down if I move an inch. I can hardly turn my head round, as it is. Awfully sorry. You don't mind, do you?'

'Gad! That's awkward. Couldn't we take your chair along with us, somehow? I'm going to be sick, I tell you, this very minute.'

'Not here, not here! Third on the left. But surely, my dear fellow, you can put it off a little longer? Can't you be reasonable, for once in your life? Just for once in your life? Do listen to what those inebriated lunatics are saying on the balcony. ...'

'What did you do to that skunk, Charlie?'

'Not if I know it, young man. I promised my mother I'd never tell. Another day, perhaps, when I've got a little whisky inside me. It's too funny for words.'

'You oughtn't to go tickling young girls, Charlie. It's not polite, at your age. ...'

They all cleared out, as it seemed, after midnight; some on all fours, many of them fairly perpendicular. But when the serving-lad entered the premises, in the sober light of morning, to clear up the *débris*, he was surprised to perceive a human form reclining under a table. It was the young Norwegian professor. He lay there wide awake, with dishevelled hair and an inspired gleam in his eye, tracing on the floor, with the point of a corkscrew, what looked like a tangle of parallelograms and conic sections. He said it was a map of Trinidad.

CHAPTER 25

As to Miss Wilberforce – she was becoming a real problem.

Once again she had shocked the Faithful. She had misconducted herself by interrupting the torchlight procession with some of those usual or unusual antics, a detailed description of which, while entertaining to a few lost souls, would certainly mortify the majority of decent folk. The cup of endurance was full, over-brimming. Once again she had passed the night in the lock-up. Questioned as to her motives for this particular incident, she artlessly blamed the darkness, which misled her, she said, into the regrettable delusion that it was night; 'and at night, you know ...'

This, as Signor Malipizzo observed with his usual legal acumen, might pass for an explanation but nevermore for an excuse. How much longer, he continued, with a fine Ciceronian gesture of eloquent indignation – how much longer would the foreign colony on Nepenthe endure the presence in their midst of such a disgrace to womanhood?

Thus spake the judge, well aware of what was expected from a man in his position. In his heart he desired nothing less than her departure; he was charmed with her disturbing influence; he hoped she would live a hundred years on the island. In the first place, he received occasional gifts in kind from various grocers and wine-merchants who enriched themselves by supplying her at preposterous prices with intoxicants, and who thought by these subtle tactics to retain him as an ally in their cause. Secondly and chiefly, every new scandal of this nature gave him a fresh opportunity of consigning her, temporarily, to the lock-up. Only temporarily. Because Mr Keith would be sure to bail her out again in the morning, which meant another fifty francs in his pocket.

That is exactly what had just taken place. Mr Keith had bailed her out, for the thirty-fourth time. She was at liberty once more, sobering down.

Both the Duchess and Madame Steynlin pitied her, as only one woman can pity another. Often they prayed to their respective Gods, Lutheran and High Church, that she might be led to see the error of her ways or, failing that, removed by some happy accident from the island or, failing that, run over by a passing vehicle and injured – injured not dangerously, but merely to such an extent as to necessitate her permanent seclusion from society. Other careless folk were maimed by the furious driving of the Nepentheans; it was a common form of accident. Miss Wilberforce – the eye-sore, the scandal of her sex – remained intact. Some impish deity seemed to guide her wayward footsteps.

Had she been a person of low extraction there would have been no difficulty in dealing with her. But she was so obviously a lady – she had such obviously rich and influential connexions in England! These people, however glad to have her out of the way, might object if violent measures were taken by persons who, after all, had no right to interfere in her affairs. And the situation was rendered none the less complex by the attitude of Miss Wilberforce herself. She was a Tartar. She felt that all men's hands were against her. She used her tongue to good purpose and, at a pinch, her teeth and claws. The policemen of Nepenthe could bear witness to that fact. Drunk, she had a perfectly blistering flow of invective at command. Sober, she was apt to indulge in a dignified bestiality of logic that cut like a knife. It was only in the intermediate stage that she was affable and human. But to catch her in that intermediate stage was extremely difficult. It was of such very brief duration.

They tried to tempt her with the prospect of being repatriated. Strenuously she opposed the notion, on grounds of health. She argued that she had come to the South at the bidding of her English doctor – which was true enough, that grave personage having been urgently pressed by the family to make the suggestion; a return to England, she declared, would be the death of her. If any attempt were made to interfere with her liberty in this manner, she would appeal to the local Court for protection.

Then the project of sending her to an Inebriates' Home on the mainland was mooted. A sprightly young clergyman, not long resident on Nepenthe, volunteered for the delicate task of persuading the lady to take this step; it would be given out that she was merely undergoing a 'rest cure'. The sprightly young clergyman started on his mission full of bright expectations. He returned anon, looking prematurely aged. Nobody could get a word out of him at first; he seemed to have become afflicted with a partial paralysis of the tongue. After babbling childishly for an hour or so he fell silent altogether, and it was not till next morning that he recovered full powers of speech. Wild horses, he then announced, would not drag from his lips what had passed at the interview.

As a last resource it was decided to inaugurate a sanatorium on the island for her especial benefit, with a trained nurse permanently in attendance; during her ever-decreasing spells of sobriety the place, together with the nurse, could be utilized for needle-classes and so forth. Money was required. A committee of ladies and gentlemen collected a certain small amount, but their hopes did not rise high till the day when the Duchess broached the subject to her countryman, Mr van Koppen, after inveigling him into what she called 'a friendly teat-a-teat'. Surfeited to bursting-point with his favourite tea-cakes, the millionaire was in a lovely humour. He declared his readiness, then and there, to subscribe half a million francs to the scheme if – if his good friend Mr Keith would make himself responsible for a similar sum, or even a thousandth part of it.

'Half a million francs – what's that, Duchess, as the price of a smile from yourself? Cheap. Dirt cheap!'

'Another one?' queried the lady.

'Well, just one. I can't swallow any more. But I can still chew.'

So fatuously fond was he of this particular variety of condiment that, on their account alone, he would have imported the Duchess and her entire establishment into America. For all that, old Koppen was no fool. Half a million buttered tea-cakes could not impair the lively workings of a brain which had long ago mapped out a swift and sure path to worldly success. He had wind of this project; his answer was carefully prepared. It was a mathematical certainty that not one cent of those half-million francs would ever leave his pocket. For he knew what the Committee did not know – the real character of his friend Keith. Keith was a good fellow but a hopeless crank; Keith was perfectly capable of impoverishing himself in order to keep Miss Wilberforce out of prison. As to subscribing to the schemes of a pack of meddling fools who proposed to intern the dear lady – Keith would see them all damned first. This is how Mr van Koppen, a profound student of human nature, would have argued, had he lacked the opportunity of discussing the question with his good friend. As a matter of fact he had enjoyed that opportunity only a few days ago. He had warned Keith of what was coming, and had found him equally alert to the plans of the Committee and more desirous than himself, if possible, of frustrating them. They had chuckled vastly over a bottle of dry sparkling Nepenthe in anticipation of the event.

'Trust me,' said Keith. 'I'll talk their heads off.'

'I'm glad I shan't be there!' thought the American.

He knew his good friend. Keith could be decidedly fatiguing, especially when dead sober. He had all the Scotchman's passion for dissecting the obvious, discovering new facets in the commonplace, and squeezing the last drop out of a foregone conclusion.

It was a thousand pities that the Duchess, in the exuberance of her triumph, spread abroad the news of the millionaire's promise. For that news had an unfortunate and unexpected result. The Committee, which up till then had consisted of eight reputable members, now swelled, rapidly and mysteriously, to fourteen. Six new gentlemen, including the unspeakable Mr Hopkins, got themselves enrolled, and all six of them, as was afterwards made manifest, were persons of questionable integrity. By dint of small donations to the fund varying from five to fifteen francs, they had contrived to have their names put down; it was worth while, they thought, to risk a small sum on the chance of getting a slice out of old Koppen's half-million which could not possibly be used up in the rent or purchase of a three-roomed Sanatorium.

A committee of ladies and gentlemen, formed for charitable purposes, should be like Caesar's wife. This one had come to resemble the spouse of Claudius. Had the upright and intelligent Mr Freddy Parker still been its guiding spirit, he would soon have weeded out these undesirable elements and kept the pickings for himself. But Mr Parker, since his lady's illness, seemed to be withdrawn from all worldly concerns. He had become invisible. And now that the lady was dead he would presumably grow more invisible than ever. It was a severe blow to all concerned; to nobody more than to the Commissioner himself when, on emerging into society from his mourning retirement, he divined what a chance he had missed.

Every single member of the small sub-committee who came, in rather a formal group, to communicate to Mr Keith the terms of the millionaire's offer and to solicit his participation in the scheme purposed to attend the funeral of Mr Parker's lady. It was the right thing to do. That impressive function, already a day overdue, had been irrevocably fixed for 10.30 a.m., at the instance of the Chief Medical Officer of Health. Accordingly they reached the Villa Khismet at the matutinal hour of 9 a.m., convinced that the short interval would suffice to cajole out of Mr Keith a sum sufficient to bind old Koppen to his promise.

It struck them afterwards that this was their flagrant initial mistake. They ought to have controlled their impatience and waited for a more opportune occasion.

And they would have waited, but for the fact that Mr Hopkins, a person of dubious motives and antecedents, had insinuated himself into the deputation not without a purpose of his own. This gentleman insisted that delay was fatal. Mr Keith, he argued, would understand their impatience. The millionaire was sailing in a day or two. One might never get that cheque cashed, or even signed, before he left Nepenthe. And then? Why, then the scheme might fall through and – he added to himself – how was he going to get his share of the plunder?

The others, the respectable ones, gave way. Vainly they remonstrated. Vainly they pointed out that old Koppen was not a man to go back on his word: that a cheque could be made out in America as well as anywhere else; that the crux of the question was not the millionaire but his good friend Keith; that they might spoil all their chances by approaching the latter at such an unseasonable hour of the day. It was weak of them.

They ought to have waited. For Keith was fond of solitude at all times, and any one of his dozen gardeners could have told them that, like every other self-respecting scholar, he was in the habit of breakfasting not earlier than 9.30, and dangerous to approach before that meal. Or they might have made inquiries concerning his mode of life among his fellow-countrymen on Nepenthe. The bibliographer, for instance, would have informed them that Keith was 'generally sick about eleven' – meaning, by his playful nonsense, to insinuate that it was not safe to disturb him till after that hour. Be that as it may, he was certainly irritable before breakfast-time on every single day of the year and, as it happened, irritable beyond the common measure on this particular morning, because the downpour of the previous afternoon had dashed to pieces – among other material damage – the tender blooms of certain priceless ipomaeas. That alone was enough to infuriate an archangel. Moreover, like everybody else – he always conformed to custom – he had been slightly tipsy overnight. This had the singular effect of making him glum, ceremonious, and ready to take offence.

Here, now, was this pack of officious idiots blundering in upon him. Under ordinary circumstances he would have tried to be polite. As it was, he could hardly bring himself to give them a civil word of welcome. They caught him on his way from the bath to the garden – to a succulent breakfast under his favourite pine-tree within view of the Tyrrhenian; and his own flowered silk dressing-gown and gold-embroidered Turkish slippers contrasted oddly with the solemn vestments, savouring of naphthaline, which they had donned for the funeral. After the barest of apologies for a costume which, he ventured to think, was as suitable as any other for a gentleman at that hour of the morning, he bade them be seated and listened to what the speaker had to say – blinking ominously the while through his spectacles, like an owl with the sun in its eyes.

CHAPTER 26

It was a long and rambling exposition.

Miss Wilberforce must be protected against herself. They came to him for a contribution, however small, which would enable Mr van Koppen to fulfil his promise. It was not a question of meddlesomeness. It was a question of putting an end to a crying public scandal. Miss Wilberforce spent her days in sleeping and her nights in shocking the population of Nepenthe. The lady should be temporarily secluded in her own interests; she was not fit to be left alone; it was an act of charity to do what one could towards improving her health and prolonging her life. They were out for a philanthropic object – to assist in helping a fellow-creature. Miss Wilberforce must be protected against herself. Mr van Koppen's half-million would enable them to compass this end. His own contribution, however small, would enable Mr van Koppen to fulfil his promise. Miss Wilberforce must be protected –

He quite understood. Miss Wilberforce must be protected against herself. And he disagreed heartily. Nobody must be protected against himself. The attitude of a man towards his fellows should be that of non-intervention, of benevolent egotism. Every person of healthy digestion was aware of that cardinal truth. Unfortunately persons of healthy digestions were not as common as they might be. That was why straight thinking, on these and other subjects, was at a discount. Nobody had a right to call himself well-disposed towards society until he had grasped the elementary fact that the only way to improve the universe was to improve oneself, and to leave one's neighbour alone. The best way to begin improving oneself was to keep one's own bowels open, and not trouble about those of anybody else. Turkey rhubarb, in fact. The serenity of outlook thereby attained would enable a man to perceive the futility of interfering with the operation of natural selection.

The speaker, he went on, had dropped the word charity. Had the tribe of Israel cultivated a smattering of respect for physiology or any other useful science instead of fussing about supernatural pedigrees, they would have been more cautious as to their diet. Had they been careful in the matter of dietary, their sacred writings would never have seen the light of day. Those writings, a monument of malnutrition and faulty digestive processes, were responsible for three-quarters of what was called charity. Charity was responsible for the greater part of human mischief and misery. The revenues of the private charities of London alone exceeded five million sterling annually. What were these revenues expended upon? On keeping alive an incredible number of persons who ought to be dead. What was the result of keeping these people alive? A deterioration of the whole race. Charity consisted in setting a premium on bodily ill-health and mental inefficiency. Charity was an Oriental nightmare; an endeavour to raise the weak to the level of the strong; an incitement to improvidence. Charity disturbed the national equilibrium; it lowered the standard of mankind instead of raising it. Charity was an unmitigated nuisance which had increased, was increasing, and ought to be diminished.

By way of varying the phraseology, but not the thing, they had called themselves philanthropists. The meaning of that venerable word had decayed of late in characteristic fashion. Prometheus, the archetype, brought fire from Heaven to comfort certain people who had the wit to appreciate its uses. He did not waste his time wet-nursing the unfit, like a modern philanthropist. What was a modern philanthropist? He was a fellow who was always bothering you to do something for somebody else. He appealed to your purse for the supposed welfare of some pet degenerate. Prometheus appealed to your intelligence for the real welfare of rational beings. A rich man found it extremely simple, no doubt, to sign a cheque. But an act was not necessarily sensible because it happened to be simple. People ought to dominate their reflexes. Prometheus did not choose the simplest course – he chose the wisest, and found it a pretty tough job, too. That alone proved him to have been a man of sound digestion and robust health. Had it been otherwise, indeed, he would never have endured that vulture-business for so long.

The deputation exchanged glances, puzzled by this pompous and peevish exordium. It did not promise well; it sounded quite

213

unlike Mr Keith's usually bland address. Perhaps he had not yet breakfasted. 'We ought to have waited,' they thought. One of the listeners was so annoyed that he began:

'A paradox, Mr Keith, is not necessarily sensible, because it happens to be simple' – but was overborne by that gentleman, who proceeded calmly:

'So much for generalities. Now, Miss Wilberforce is a lady of independent means and of a certain age. She is not an infant, to be protected against herself or against others; she has reached years of indiscretion. Like a good many sensible persons, she lives in this country. Of course a residence here has its drawbacks – very grave drawbacks, some of them. But the drawbacks are counterbalanced by certain advantages. In short, what applies to one country does not always apply to the other. Yet you propose to treat her exactly as if she were living in England. That strikes me as somewhat unreasonable.'

'Mr van Koppen has promised us –'

'He may do what he likes with his money. But I don't see why I should become the pivot for making my good friend do what strikes me as a foolish action. I am too fond of him for that. Mr van Koppen and myself have many points in common; among other things this feature, that neither of us is of aristocratic birth. I suspect that this is what made you count on me for a subscription. You thought that I, having a little money of my own, might be tempted by certain sycophantic instincts to emulate his misplaced generosity. But I am not a snob. From the social point of view I don't care a tuppenny damn for anyone. On the other hand, my origin has given me something of Dr Samuel Johnson's respect for what he calls his betters. I like the upper classes, especially when they behave according to their old traditions. That is why I like Miss Wilberforce. She conducts herself, if report be true, with all the shamelessness of a born lady. Born ladies are not so common that we should hide them away in nursing homes. All forceful seclusion is dishonouring. Every little insect, drunk or sober, enjoys its freedom; and if you gentlemen were not philanthropists I would try to point out how galling your proposal must be, how humiliating to a high-spirited woman, to be placed under lock and key, in charge of some callous attendant. But to what purpose? Turkey rhubarb –'

'I am afraid, Mr Keith, that we have come at an inopportune moment?'

'It's quite possible. But I won't keep you much longer – you must be dying to attend that funeral! In fact, I would not detain you at all if I did not feel that you expected some kind of explanation from me. What were we saying?'

'Turkey rhubarb.'

'Ah, yes! I was trying to be fair-minded, which, by the way, is generally a mistake. It struck me that perhaps I over-emphasized its advantages just now. Because, of course, there is something to be said against the use of such drugs. In fact, now I come to think of it, there is a good deal to be said in favour of constipation. It is the cause of our English spleenfulness, and this spleenfulness, properly directed, has its uses. It engenders a certain energetic intolerance of mind. I think the success of our nation is largely due to this particular quality. If I were an historian I would amuse myself with proving that we owe not only Magna Charta, but our whole Empire – Canada, Australia, and all the rest of them – to our costive habits of body. What befits a nation, however, does not always befit a man. To crush, in a fit of chronic biliousness, the resistance of Bengal, and add its land to the British Empire, may be a racial virtue. To crush, in a fit of any kind, the resistance of our next-door neighbour Mr Robinson and add his purse to our own, is an individual vice. No! I fail to discover any personal advantage to be gained from excess of bile. The bilious eye sees intensely, no doubt, but in a distorted and narrow fashion; it is incapable of a generous outlook. Cloudy, unserene! A closing-up, instead of a widening-out. The bowels of compassion: what a wonderful old phrase! They ought to be kept open. I look around me, and see extraordinarily little good-will among my fellow-creatures. Here is Miss Wilberforce. What she yearns for is the milk of human kindness – gentle words, gentle dealing, from all of us. Instead of that, everyone is ready to cast stones at her. She is treated like a pariah. For my part I do not pass her by; I am not ashamed to consort with sinners, if such they be; I would like, if I could, to make her free and happy instead of imprisoning her in a place of self-reproach. A healthy man is naturally well disposed, not on principle or from any divine inspiration but because his bodily organs are performing their proper functions. His judgement is not warped by the black humours of indigestion. He perceives that natural laws, however harsh they seem, are never so harsh as our amateurish attempts to circumvent them. Modern philanthropy is an attempt of this nature. It is crass emotionalism. Regarded from the point of view of the race, your philanthropy is a disguised form of brutality.'

'Mr Keith!'

'All sentimentalists are criminals.'

215

This perverse balderdash was getting on the nerves of the deputation. It had one good effect, however. They had been afraid, at first, of wasting Mr Keith's time; now they began to realize that he was wasting theirs.

'Speaking for myself, Mr Keith, I should say that you are spoiling your case by over-statement, and that these reflections of yours are libels upon a class of men and women who devote their time and money, often their lives, to alleviating the distress of others. However that may be, they are generalities. We came to you about a practical matter, and an urgent one. We want to remove a crying scandal from the island. The habits of Miss Wilberforce, as I think I pointed out, are shocking to all decent folks. I suppose you won't deny that?'

'I remember your using those words. They struck me as remarkable because, for my own part, I have not yet discovered any man, woman, or child who could shock me. Some persons make a profession of being scandalized. I am profoundly distrustful of them. It is the prerogative of vulgarians to be shocked. If I ever felt inclined to blush, it would not be at the crooked behaviour of men, but at their crooked intellectual processes. Whenever a so-called scandal comes my way, I thank God for the opportunity of seeing something new and learning something to my advantage.'

'There is nothing very new about the scandalous conduct of Miss Wilberforce, save her unfortunate habit of divesting herself –'

'Please to note that there is a good deal of loose and exaggerated talk going on here. But one thing is quite certain. These exhibitions, supposing they really take place, have never been known to occur until after midnight – with the lamentable exception of yesterday afternoon, when it was even darker than midnight. If your decent folks are so squeamish, what are they doing in the streets at that unearthly hour? I am asleep then, as they ought to be. This may account for the fact that I have never seen the lady in a state of alcoholic exhilaration. But if I had the good luck to stumble upon her, I would certainly not be shocked.'

'And what, may I ask, would you do?'

'My feelings towards the spectacle would depend upon the momentary state of my mind. I might, for example, be in a frolicsome Elizabethan mood. In that case I would appreciate the humour of the situation. If only half of what I hear is true, she must be extremely funny at such moments. I would probably laugh myself into an apoplexy. I wish the English still possessed a shred of the old sense of humour which Puritanism, and dyspepsia, and newspaper reading, and tea-drinking have nearly extinguished. It ought to be revived afresh. Nothing like a good drunkard for that purpose. As a laughter-provoking device it is cheaper and more effective than any pantomime yet invented; and none the worse, surely, for being a little old-fashioned?'

'I must say, Mr Keith, I don't think God created anybody to be laughed at.'

'Maybe he didn't. But a fellow can't help laughing, all the same. On the other hand, I might be in that interfering humanitarian mood which is liable to beset even the wisest of us. I would then be tempted to lead her homewards gently but firmly, simulating intoxication, if I could bring myself to do it – pretending, you understand, to be in the same state as herself, if I could manage it with any prospect of success – in order to make her feel thoroughly at her ease. I should not dream of ruffling her state of mind by a single word of reproach; the private feelings and self-respect, even of a drunkard, should never be violated. Again, if I were in my ordinary reflective condition, I should doubtless stand aside and muse, as I have often mused, upon the folly of intemperance. Drunkenness – that shameful vice! How many estimable men and women have succumbed to it; men I have known, women I have loved and even respected! This makes me think that we ought to be grateful to have so glaring an example of insobriety before our eyes. We ought to regard Miss Wilberforce, if your account of her be true, as a Divine warning. Warnings are not sent for nothing. And you, gentlemen – you propose to hide away this heaven-sent warning in a sanatorium. That strikes me as flying in the face of Providence.'

'Our project would at least secure her from the risk of being run over by some vehicle.'

'Pray, why should the dear lady not choose to be run over? Surely she can please herself? It would be an appropriate ending to a brief and merry career. It would be more than this. We spoke, just now, of her example as a deterrent to others. Well, this example, so far as we spectators are concerned, would lose its point and pungency if she died as you propose – a half-reclaimed inebriate in some home. She must be run over, or otherwise violently destroyed, if we are to have the full benefit of the example. It is only then that we shall be able to say to ourselves: Ah, we always thought it was risky to drink strong waters, but *now we know*.'

'A fatal accident of this kind, quite apart from other considerations, would involve her relatives in all kinds of trouble with the legal authorities of this country.'

'I am glad you mentioned the legal aspects of the case; I had nearly forgotten them. They are most important. In electing to be crushed under a vehicle she acts on her own initiative. What you propose is nothing less than a curtailment of her liberty of action. How do you think the local authorities would envisage such an arbitrary step? I imagine it may cost you dear to arrogate to yourselves a power which, in this country at least, is vested in the proper authorities. You may well find yourselves in collision with the penal code of Italy, which has been framed, and is now administered, by men of uncommonly wide views – men who reverence personal freedom above gold and rubies. I should not be surprised if our magistrate on Nepenthe were to take, on legal grounds, the same view of the case as I take on purely moral ones, namely, that your action towards Miss Wilberforce would amount to an unwarranted persecution. He would regard it, very likely, as the unjustifiable incarceration of a perfectly harmless individual. Signor Malipizzo, I may say, has pronounced views as to his duties towards society.'

This was too much for one of the respectable members of the deputation. He asked:

'Are you referring to that blackguard, that pestilential hog, who calls himself a judge?'

'Perhaps you do not know him as well as I do. I wish you knew him better. I wish you knew him as well as I do! He is worth knowing. Let me tell you something about him – something new and characteristic. Like many natives, he is scrupulously fairminded and honest. Now I can get on, at a pinch, even with an upright man. That is because I always try to discover the good side of my fellow-creatures. But other people cannot. Accordingly, being an incorruptible magistrate, he is liable to encounter hostility among a certain disreputable section of the populace. His conscientious methods expose him to the accusation of harsh dealing. This has happened more than once. It happened only two days ago, when he sentenced to prison a batch of Russian lunatics who were responsible, among other damage, for the deaths of three innocent school-children. I commend his action. He erred, if at all, on the side of leniency; for we really cannot have a pack of raving wolves at large here. It is different in Russia. You can go mad there – indeed, that country, with its vast plains and trackless forests, seems to have been especially created for the purpose of running amok. But this island is really too small; there are so many glass windows and babies about – don't you think so, gentlemen?'

'Nepenthe is certainly a small place, Mr Keith.'

'Note, now, how differently he treats Miss Wilberforce, who not only never killed three school-children but has never, to the best of my knowledge, injured a living creature. I am informed on good authority that, after spending a tumultuous night in gaol, she had already regained her liberty. And this, if I am not mistaken, is the second or third occasion at least on which our judge has behaved in a similar manner towards her. Once more I commend his action. Why has Signor Malipizzo set the lady free? Because, unlike a modern philanthropist, he is aware of the wider issues involved; he acts not with the severity of a fanatic, but with the understanding, the tolerance, the mellow sympathy of a man of the world. I said that everyone on Nepenthe treated Miss Wilberforce as a pariah. That was a mistake. I ought to have allowed for one exception – our admirable judge! It strikes me as significant that an official who is bound to her by no ties of blood-relationship or nationality and who enjoys, moreover, a reputation – however undeserved – for harshness, should be the one person on Nepenthe to stretch a point in her favour; the one person who extends to her the hand of friendship, whose heart throbs in sympathy with her sad case. Significant, and not altogether creditable to us, her compatriots. Now who, I wonder, is the friend of man, the modern Prometheus; you who incarcerate her, or this alien lawyer who sets her free? To be perfectly frank, I find your attitude contrasts unfavourably with his own. You are the rigorists, the harsh ones. He is the humanitarian. Yes, gentlemen! In my humble opinion there is not a shadow of doubt about it. Signor Malipizzo is the true philanthropist. ...'

The deputation, wending to the market-place rather hurriedly in order to take their places in the funeral cortège, said to themselves:

'We ought to have waited.'

Thinking it over as they marched along, the respectable members came to the conclusion that the others, the Hopkins section, were really to blame for the discomfiture of the expedition. It was they who had insisted with specious arguments upon an interview at this unreasonable hour of the morning; as for themselves, they would gladly have waited for a more suitable occasion. In undertones, low but venomous, they commented upon the undue haste of Mr Hopkins and its probable motives. Later on they understood everything. Then they called him a thief and a rogue, loudly – but not to his face.

Which shows yet again how inadequately causes and effects are appreciated here on earth. The dubious Mr Hopkins may well

have been moved by mercenary considerations. But this fact had
nothing to do with the unsatisfactory issue of the affair. In other
words, even as the Saint, in the matter of that volcanic eruption,
had previously gotten the praise for what was not his merit, so
now this sinner was blamed for what was not his fault. Had the
sub-committee waited till the crack of doom, it would have made
no difference whatever to the general trend of Mr Keith's sen-
tentious irrelevancies.

Perhaps, if they had caught him in a better humour, he might
have had the decency to invite them to luncheon after the funeral.

Even this was problematical.

CHAPTER 27

THE funeral was a roaring success. The display of ecclesiastics and
choristers was unusually fine. Torquemada had seen to that part
of the business. It was his duty henceforward to cherish the bereaved representative of Nicaragua – a possible convert, at his
hand, to the true faith. The Clubmen, headed by the excellent Mr
Richards, wore their gravest faces. Furthermore, in view of the
lady's quasi-official position, the authorities of the island were
present in full numbers; the militia, too, looked superb in their
picturesque uniforms. And so large was the unofficial attendance,
so deafening the music, so brilliant the sunshine, so perfect the
general arrangements that even the deceased, captious as she was,
could hardly (under other circumstances) have avoided expressing
her approval of the performance.

There was an adequate display of fictitious grief among her
social equals. Madame Steynlin, in particular, carried it off – to
outward appearances – with remarkable success. She looked really
quite upset, and her hat, as usual, attracted the attention of all the
ladies. Madame Steynlin's hats were proverbial. She was always
appearing in new ones of the most costly varieties. And never, by
any chance, did they accord with her uncommon and rather ripe
style of beauty. Madame Steynlin was too romantic to dress well.
She trimmed her heart, and not her garments. A tidy little income,
however, enabled her to eke out lack of taste by recklessness of
expenditure. This particular hat, it was observed, must have cost
a fortune. And yet it was a perfect fright; it made her look fifteen
years older, to the delight of all the other women.

What cared Madame Steynlin about hats? Her distressful appearance was not feigned; she was truly upset, though not about
the death of the Commissioner's lady. With an effort whose vio-

lence nobody but herself could appreciate she had managed to extricate herself from the lion-like embraces of Peter the Great – to what purpose? To perform an odious social duty; to waste a fair morning in simulating grief for the death of a woman whom she loathed like poison. Nobody would ever understand what a trial in altruism it had been. Nobody, in fact, ever gave her credit for a grain of self-abnegation. And yet she was always trying to please people – denying herself this and that. How harshly the world judged!

She was also troubled in mind, though in a lesser degree, about the fate of the remainder of the Russian colony. Were they not all her brothers and sisters – these laughing, round-cheeked primitives? The magistrate, that caricature of a man, that vindictive and corrupt atheist, that tiger in human form, was doubtless thirsting for the blood of those still at liberty on Nepenthe. How much longer would Peter escape his malice? The dear boy! Her lambkin, her little soul – she had learnt to babble a few words of Russian – her playful, harmless, ever-hungry Peter! On this lovely island, where all men should be at peace – how harshly they dealt with one another!

The rest of the foreign colony, undisturbed by such bitter personal reflections, appeared to bear the loss of the lady with praiseworthy equanimity. They were, in truth, considerably relieved in mind. Death is the great equalizer. In his pale presence they forgot their old squabbles and jealousies; they forgot their numberless and legitimate complaints against this woman. All honoured the defunct who had now lost, presumably for ever, the capacity of mischief-making.

There was undisguised sorrow among the tradespeople and Residency servants. They flocked to the procession in crowds, desiring by this last mark of respect to attract the benevolent notice of the Commissioner and to be remembered in the event of some future settling-up of accounts. To their tear-stained eyes, it looked as if this happy event were receding farther and farther away into the dim distance. Hoping against hope, they mourned sincerely. And none wept more convincingly than the little maid Enrichetta, an orphan of tender years whom the lady had taken into her service as an act of charity and forthwith set to work like a galley-slave. The child was convulsed with sobs. She foresaw, with the intuition of despair, that instead of being paid her miserable wages for the last five months she would have to content herself with a couple of her deceased mistress's skirts, thirty-eight inches too wide round the waist.

There were wreaths – abundance of wreaths. Noticeable among them was an enormous floral tribute from the owner of the *Flutterby*. It attracted the most favourable comment. People said that nobody but a multi-multi-multi-millionaire could afford to forgive an affront like that affair of the *crêpe de Chine*. As a matter of fact, old Koppen would have been the last person on earth to forgive an injury of this particular kind. He was a good American; he never permitted loose talk about women, least of all if they were in any way connected with himself; he would get purple in the face, he would ramp and rage and hop about like a veritable Sioux, in the face of any suggestion of improprieties on board his yacht. No, Cornelius van Koppen had acted in all innocence, from natural kindliness of heart. The legend had never reached his ears, nobody (for a wonder) having dared to mention it to him.

Another wreath, from Count Caloveglia – an uncommonly pretty one, with a simple but heartfelt inscription – created legitimate surprise. Those white camellias, people reckoned, could not have cost less than twenty francs, and everybody knew that the dear old boy was as poor as a church mouse and that, moreover, he had enjoyed nothing but a bowing acquaintance with the deceased lady. He had indeed only spoken to her once in his life. But her face – her face had left an indelible impression on his sensitive and artistic mind.

There was something Greek about Count Caloveglia. His pedigree, uncontaminated by Moor or Spaniard, went back to hoariest antiquity. Many people said he was a reincarnation of old Hellas. Elbowing his way through crowded cities or chatting with sunburnt peasant lads among the vineyards, he received thrills of pleasurable inspiration – thrills to which grosser natures are inaccessible. He loved to watch the bodily movements of his fellow-creatures and all the eloquent gestures of Southern life – the lingering smile, the sullen stare of anger, the firm or flaccid step. Within this world of humdrum happenings he created a world of his own, a sculptor's paradise. Colour said little to him. He was enamoured of form, the lively passion of the flesh, the tremulous play of nerve and muscle. A connoisseur of pose and expression, he looked at mankind from the plastic point of view, peering through accidentals into what was spiritual, preordained, inevitable; striving to interpret – to waylay and hold fast – that divinity, fair or foul, which resides within one and all of us. How would this one look, divested of ephemeral appurtenances and standing there, in bronze or marble; what were the essential

222

qualities of those features – their aesthetic mission to men like himself; to what type or relic of the classic age might they be assimilated? He was for ever disentangling the eternal from mundane accessories. And there was an element of the eternal, he used to declare, in every creature of earth.

His was an enviable life. He dwelt among masterpieces. They were his beacons, his comrades, his realities. As for other things – the social accidents of time and place, his cares and his poverty – he wore them lightly; they sat upon his shoulders with easy grace, like his own threadbare coat. When he walked among men he could not help contriving imaginary statuary in his head, historical portraits or legendary groups; the faces and attitudes of those he encountered – each one found a place in the teeming realm of his creative phantasy, each one beckoned to him, from afar, as a joyous and necessary revelation.

An enviable life; and never more enviable than on the occasion when he was introduced, at some absurd tea-party, to the lady known as the Commissioner's step-sister. That face! It took possession of him! It haunted his artistic dreamings from the same day onwards. He had always cherished ambitious designs – none more ambitious than a certain piece of work conceived in the bold Pergamene manner, a noble cluster of women to be entitled 'The Eumenides'. ... Her face! That wonderful face proclaimed itself the keynote of the group. If he lived a thousand years he would never behold its like again. What would he not have given to model the lady, then and there!

But modelling was out of the question for the present. It must never be known that he was still capable of such an effort; it might spoil all his chances for the business in hand. He must continue to pose as heretofore for a harmless antiquarian, a dreamer. Nobody, save old Andrea the servant, must know the secret of his life. Yet he was not without hopes of being able to reveal himself ere long in his true character of creator. The day was perhaps not far distant when a pecuniary transaction between himself and his respected American friend, Mr van Koppen, would ease the burdensome poverty of his life. Then – then he would return to the golden projects of his youth; to the 'Eumenides' first of all. Light-hearted with bright expectancy, he saw the financial deal well-nigh concluded; the cheque might be in his pocket within a week; and now already he saw himself, in imagination, donning his faded frock-coat and wending his way down to the Residency to lay the foundations of his heart's desire. He would broach the subject with that insinuating Southern graciousness which was

223

part and parcel of his nature; the lady's vanity could be trusted to do the rest. He knew of old that no woman, however chaste and winsome, can resist the temptation of sitting as model to a genuine Count – and such a handsome old Count, into the bargain.

And now suddenly she had died – died, it might be, only a few days too soon. That face, the peerless face, was lost for ever to the world of art – his ideal snatched away by the relentless hand of fate. He mourned as only a sculptor can mourn. Thus it came about that something stronger than himself impelled him to manifest his grief. Despite Andrea's respectful but insistent remonstrances as to the appalling outlay, the wreath of camellias was ordered, and dispatched. An artist's tribute.

It created both surprise and a most excellent impression. What a gentleman he was! Always doing the right thing. How splendid of him! So they reasoned, though the wiser ones added that if he had known the deceased lady a little better he might have hit upon a more sensible way of spending his money.

The fact that there was a good deal of social gossip like this, that appointments for picnics and other functions were being made, would go alone to prove the advantages of a funeral of this kind, quite apart from the universal relief experienced when the coffin was lowered into the earth, and bystanders realized that the lady was at last definitely transferred into Abraham's bosom.

CHAPTER 28

ALL Nepenthe had stood by the side of the grave – all, save only Mr Keith. He remained at home. And this was rather odd, for it is the right thing to attend people's funerals, and Mr Keith prided himself upon always doing the right thing. It was his boast to pass for a typical Anglo-Saxon, the finest race on earth, when all is said and done; and he used to point out that you could not be a typical Anglo-Saxon unless you respected yourself, and you could not respect yourself unless you respected simultaneously your neighbours and their habits, however perverse they might sometimes appear. Now, a funeral, being unavoidable, cannot by any prestidigitations of logic be called perverse. All the more reason for being present. But for a strange twist or kink in his nature, therefore, he would have been on the spot. He would have turned up in the market-place to the minute, since he prided himself likewise upon his love of punctuality, declaring that it was one of the many virtues he possessed in common with Her Majesty Queen Victoria.

He disliked funerals. For all his open mind and open bowels,

Mr Keith displayed an unreasoning hatred of death, and what was still more remarkable, not the least shame in confessing it.

'The next interment I purpose to attend,' he would say, 'will be my own. May it be far off! No; I don't care about funerals and the suggestion they convey. A cowardly attitude? I think not. The coward refuses to face a fact. Death is a fact. I have often faced him. He is not a pretty fellow. Most men only give him a shy glance out of the corner of their eye. It scares them out of their wits and makes them say all sorts of snobbishly respectful things about him. Sheer flummery! It is with Death as it is with God – we call them good because we are afraid of what they can do to us. That accounts for our politeness. Death, universal and inevitable, is none the less a villainous institution. Every other antagonist can be ignored or bribed or circumvented or crushed outright. But here is a damnable spectre who knocks at the door and does not wait to hear you say "Come in". Hateful! If other people think differently it is because they live differently. How do they live? Like a cow that has stumbled into a dark hole, and now spends its time wondering how it managed to get such a sore behind. Such persons may well be gladdened by the approach of death. It is the best thing they can do – to depart from a world which they call a dark hole, a world which was obviously not made for them, seeing that they are always feeling uncomfortable about one thing or another. Good riddance to them and their moral stomach-aches.'

Mr Keith professed never to feel uncomfortable. Oh, no! He had no moral stomach-aches. Unlike other folk, he 'reacted to external stimuli in appropriate fashion', he cultivated the 'function of the real', he always knew how to 'dominate his reflexes'. His neural currents were 'duly co-ordinated'. Mr Keith was in love with life. It dealt fairly with him. It made him loth to bid farewell to his gracious earth and the blue sky overhead, to his cooks and his books, his gardeners and roses and flaming cannas; loth to exchange these things of love, these tangible delights, for a hideous and everlasting annihilation.

That was why, having got rid of the committee of exasperating buffoons, he was now prolonging breakfast far beyond the usual hour. The meal was over at last; and still he felt disinclined to move. Those people had disquieted his composure with their mephitic rant about philanthropy; they had almost succeeded in spoiling his morning. And now this funeral! Would he go into the house and do some reading or write a few letters? No. He could not write letters just then. He was not feeling sufficiently Rabelaisian. Epicurus was his God for the moment. In a mood of heathen

225

wistfulness he lit a cigar and leaned back in the chair, trying to recapture his serenity.

It was his favourite corner of the domain – a kind of projecting spur or platform shaded by a few grandiose umbrella pines. Near at hand, on a slightly lower level, rose a group of flame-like cypresses whose shapely outlines stood out against the sea, shining far below like a lake of pearl. The milky sheen of morning, soon to be dispelled by the breeze, still hung about the water and distant continent – it trembled upon the horizon in bands of translucent opal. His eyes roved round the undulating garden, full of sunlight and flowers and buzzing insects. From a verbena hard by came the liquid song of a blackcap. It gave him pleasure; he encouraged the blackcaps, delighting in their music and because they destroyed the spiders whose troublesome webs were apt to come in contact with his spectacles. The gardeners had severest instructions not to approach their nests. It was one of the minor griefs of his life that, being so short-sighted, he could never discover a bird's nest; no, not even as a child. Memories of boyhood began to flit through his mind; they curled upwards in the scented wreaths of his Havana. ...

The golden oriole's flute-like whistle poured down from some leafy summit in a sudden stream of melody. A hurried note, he thought; expressed without much feeling – from duty rather than inclination; not like the full-throated ease of other orioles in other lands he knew. His orioles and bee-eaters were invariably in a hurry. And so were the nightingales. They profited by his hospitality for a day or two and then, uttering a perfunctory little tune, some breathless and insincere word of thanks – just like any human visitor – betook themselves elsewhere, northwards.

Northwards!

He glanced into the mazy foliage of the pine tree overhead, out of which a shower of aromatic fragrance was descending to mingle with the harsher perfume of the cypress. How they changed their faces, the conifers – so fervently and friendly at this hour, so forbidding at night-time! Rifts of blue sky now gleamed through its network of branches; drenched in the sunny rays, the tree seemed to shudder and crackle with warmth. He listened. There was silence among those coralline articulations. Soon it would be broken. Soon the cicada would strike up its note in the labyrinth of needles – annual signal for his own departure from Nepenthe. He always waited for the first cicada.

Northwards!

To his little place in the Highlands, at first. The meagre soil and parsimonious culture, the reasonable discourse of the people, their wholesome disputatiousness, acted as a kind of purge or tonic after all this Southern exuberance. Scotland chastened him; its rocks and tawny glinting waters and bleak purple uplands rectified his perspective. He called to mind the sensuous melancholy of the birches, the foxgloves, the hedgerows smothered in dog-roses; he remembered the nights, full of fairy-like suggestions and odours of earth and budding leaves – those wonderful nights with their silvery radiance, calm and benignant, streaming upwards from the luminous North.

Then, after strolling aimlessly elsewhere, on sea or land, visiting friends – no matter whom or where – he would return to Nepenthe to indulge his genius to the full in the vintage bacchanals. He owned a small plantation that lay high up, among the easterly cliffs of the island. It produced that mountain wine which was held to be the best on Nepenthe. The vines grew upon a natural platform, surrounded by rugged lava crags that overhung the sea.

Hither he was wont to repair with certain of his domestic staff and three or four friends from out of his 'inner circle', to superintend the pressing of the grapes. There was a rude structure of masonry on the spot – a vaulted chamber containing winepress and vats and hoes and other implements of the husbandman's time-honoured craft; a few chairs and a table completed the furniture. Nobody knew exactly what happened up there. People talked of wild and shameless carousals; the rocks were said to resound with ribald laughter while Mr Keith, oozing paganism at every pore, danced faun-like measures to the sound of rustic flutes. Certain it was that the party often got riotously tipsy.

So tipsy that sometimes their host was unable to be moved down to his villa. On such days he was put to bed on the floor between two wine barrels, and the chef hastily advised to come up with some food and a portable kitchen range. In earliest morning he would insist upon tottering forth to watch the sun as it rose behind the peaks of the distant mainland, flooding the sea with golden radiance and causing the precipices to glitter like burnished bronze. He loved the sunrise – he saw it so seldom. Then breakfast; a rather simple breakfast by way of a change. It was on one of these occasions that the chef made a mistake which his master was slow to forgive. He prepared for that critical meal a dish of poached eggs, the sight of which threw Mr Keith into an incomprehensible fit of rage.

'Take those damned things away, quickly!' he commanded. It was the celebrated artist's one and only *lâche*.

As a rule, however, he did not sleep on the spot. Peasants, climbing to their work on the hillsides in the twilit hour of dawn, were wont to encounter that staggering procession headed by Mr Keith, who, with spectacles all awry and crooning softly to himself, was carried round the more perilous turnings by a contingent of his devoted retainers.

He found it pleasant to live like this. And now another spring was nearing its end. For how many more years, he wondered. ... That confounded funeral. ...

There was a rustle at his back. The southerly breeze had struck Nepenthe on its morning ripple over the Tyrrhenian, setting things astir; it searched a passage through those mighty canes which sprouted in a dank hollow where the rains of winter commingled their waters. The leaves grew vocal with a sound like the splash of a rivulet. Often he had listened joyfully to that melody which compensated, in some small degree, for the lack of the old Duke's twenty-four fountains. Legendary music! Now it made him sad. What was its burden? *Midas has asses' ears*. Midas, the fabled king, whose touch turned everything to gold. And gold, and jewels – of what avail were these against the spectre?

The gardeners, moving with bare feet among the sinuous paths, were quick to perceive that a cloud had fallen upon his spirit. They divined his moods with the tactfulness of natural sympathy. On some horticultural pretext one of them drew near and craftily engaged his thoughts and conversation. At last he said something that made him smile. One or two more appeared upon the scene, as if by accident. It was evident that the master needed cheering up. They began to tell him the fairy-tales he loved; tales of robbers and witches and pirates – grand old tales that never wearied him. To arouse his interest they joked among themselves, as though unaware of his existence. One of them, and then another, sang some wild song of love and war which he had picked up while wandering with his flock among the craggy hills of yonder mainland. He was laughing now; outdoing their songs and stories. It kept him young – to unbend, to play the fool in company such as theirs and relax the fibres stiffened by conventionality; it refreshed him to exchange the ephemeral for the eternal, the tomfoolery of social life for Theocritus and his deathless creatures. How fair it was, this smiling earth! How blithely the young voices went aloft!

They failed to drown those other strains, vagrant wraiths that now floated upwards over fields and houses on the tepid wings of the sirocco – fragmentary snatches, torn from the brazen measure of the municipal band as it marched with the funeral procession.

He cursed the sounds from the bottom of his heart. They reminded him of that infamous apparition, of all he most ardently desired to forget. His laughter died down. Wanly he looked at his mirthful pagans, the embodiment of joy. Yes; these were his distraction, his playmates, his elixir of life, his antidote against the only disease, the only sin, crime, vice which he recognized on earth – a vice none the less, because it happened to be the inevitable – the vice of old age. And all the time that pallid swarm came crowding on: messengers from the inexorable spectre. He felt them creeping about with ghostly tread, blighting the radiance of his life, tainting the very air he breathed. Hateful intruders! They wailed among his lilies. The garden was full of their horrid footsteps.

In their presence Mr Keith began to experience an uncomfortable sensation, a kind of chill – as though something evil had stepped between himself and the brave light of the sun. It was a feeling which he would have diagnosed, in other people, as perilously akin to a moral stomach-ache.

CHAPTER 29

ONLY one other person on Nepenthe found cause to complain of the municipal music. It was Mr Heard. Altogether, he was not greatly edified by this, the first funeral of its kind he had ever witnessed. A rowdy-dowdy business, he called it. The music was too lively and blatant for so solemn an occasion; the gorgeous vestments of the clergy, the loud chattering among the mourners, the violent gestures that accompanied Torquemada's well-meant and carefully prepared oration (Don Francesco, a born speaker, would have done it better, but the defunct was no friend or even client of his) – all these things savoured slightly of irreverence. Everyone was talking and laughing as they marched along. It was more like a polonaise than a funeral. In his African period the sight of such a burial would have affected him unpleasantly. But Mr Heard was changing, widening out.

'These people live gaily,' he said to himself. 'Why not? A funeral is supposed to be nothing but a friendly leave-taking. Why not be cheerful about it? We are all going to see each other again, sometime, somewhere, I suppose. ...'

The problem gave him no trouble whatever.

He found himself walking side by side with Mr Eames, who ventured to remark, in a seemly whisper, that he attended the funeral not so much out of respect for the lamented lady – every

229

cloud, he fancied, had a silver lining – as because he hoped to gather, from among so representative a concourse of natives and foreigners, the 'popular impression' of yesterday's eruption, with a view to utilizing it in his appendix of *Recent Volcanic Phenomena of Nepenthe*.

'Really?' replied the bishop. 'A chapter on Volcanic Phenomena? It is sure to be interesting.'

Mr Eames warmed to his subject.

It might be made interesting, he agreed, but for his own ignorance of geology. As it was the business gave him a vast deal of trouble. Monsignor Perrelli had dealt with geological matters in a fashion far too summary for present-day requirements. The old scholar was not to blame, of course, seeing that geology was quite a modern science; but he might at least have been a little more painstaking in his record of those showers of ashes and lapilli which were known to have covered the island from time to time. His account of them was lamentably defective. It was literally bristling with – with – with lacunae, which had to be filled up by means of laborious references to contemporary chronicles. Altogether one of the most unsatisfactory sections of an otherwise admirable work. ...

'I wish I could help you,' said Mr Heard.

'I wish you could. I wish anyone could. There was that young Jew, Marten, who understood more about these things than most people. A coarse little fellow, but quite a specialist. He promised to supply me with an up-to-date statement, accompanied by a map of the geological structure of the island. I said to myself: Just what I wanted! Well, this confounded statement has never reached my hands. Now I hear he has left the place. Gone away altogether. Didn't have the decency to say good-bye or leave his address. Too bad. Who knows when the next mineralogist will turn up? These fellows are not as common as blackbirds. Meanwhile I have to rely on my own efforts. It's wonderful, by the way, how much a person can pick up of odds and ends of information when forced, by a hobby of this kind, to delve into recondite departments of knowledge which he would otherwise not have dreamt of exploring. One grows quite encyclopaedic! Minerals, medicine, strategy, heraldry, navigation, palaeography, statistics, politics, botany – what did I know or care about all these things before I stumbled on old Perrelli? Have you ever tried to annotate a classic, Mr Heard? I assure you it opens up new vistas, new realms of delight. It gives one a genuine zest in life. Enthralling!'

And thereupon the bibliographer fell silent, all at once. He had

succumbed, yet again, to his besetting sin: talking too enthusiastically to outsiders of what was nearest his heart. Why on earth
should a globe-trotting bishop be bothered about the mineralogy
of Nepenthe? It was absurd: tactless of him.

He tried to atone for the blunder by some mundane trivialities.

'What are you doing afterwards?'

'Going up to see Mrs Meadows.'

'Are you? Do remember me very kindly! Or perhaps – no. Better not. Fact is, she cut me dead two days ago. At least, it looked
uncommonly like it. I confess I was rather upset, because I'm not
conscious of having done anything to annoy her. Indeed, I've always felt a kind of weakness for Mrs Meadows; there is something so fine and womanly about her. Will you try to find out
what it's all about? Thanks. Perhaps she may not have noticed
me. She was walking very fast. And I must say she was not looking herself at all. Not at all. White and scared. Looked as if she
had seen a ghost.'

The bishop was troubled by these words.

'Is that so?' he asked. 'You alarm me. I think I'll be off this
minute. She is my cousin, you know; and I've been rather concerned about her lately. Yes; I won't wait for the end of this
funeral; I'll be off! Perhaps we shall meet this evening. Then I can
tell you her news. As to deliberately cutting you – don't you believe that for a minute.'

'I shall be down here about seven o'clock. ....'

'People like her,' thought Mr Heard, as he fell out of the procession. He would make a point of having a good long chat, and
perhaps stay to luncheon.

He dreaded the coming heat of midday. It was quite warm
enough already, as he climbed slowly upward by the short cuts
that intersected the driving road, availing himself of every little
patch of shade that fell from trees or cottages athwart the pathway.

The country seemed deserted, the funeral ceremony having attracted all the natives from far and near. Yet one figure was moving rapidly up the road in front of him. Muhlen! Even at this distance he was recognizable; he looked, as usual, overdressed. What
was he doing there, at this hour? Mr Heard remembered seeing
him go up, once before, at the same time of the day.

He called to mind what he had heard from Keith in the boat.
He was quite prepared to believe that this man lived on blackmail
and women; that was precisely what he looked like. A villainous
personality, masquerading under an assumed name. The sight of

the fellow annoyed him. What business had he to transact up there? Retlow? Once more he began to puzzle where he had heard that name. It conjured up, dimly, some unpleasant connotation. Where? Long ago; so much was clear. For a brief moment he felt on the verge of remembering. Then his mind became blank as before; the revelation had slipped away, past recall.

He was glad to enter the shady garden of the villa Mon Repos. Old Caterina sat, sphinx-like, on the stones at the house entrance. There was some knitting-work on her lap, with brown wool and curiously shaped needles; one foot rested on the base of the cradle, which she rocked from time to time. At his approach she rose up, stark and hieratic, without a trace of a friendly smile on her countenance. Was the lady indoors? No, she was out. Out! Where? There was a definite but enigmatical movement of her withered brown arm; it appeared to embrace the universe. And when would she be back? No reply whatever. Only a slight upward movement of the eyes as much as to say: God knows!

'I'll wait,' thought Mr Heard.

He walked past the forbidding hag who seemed to exhale a positive hostility towards him and entered his cousin's sitting-room. He would wait. He waited. He glanced through a pile of illustrated newspapers that lay about. And still he waited. The room looked different somehow; almost untidy. There were no roses about. An hour passed. And still no sign of his cousin.

Out. Always out. What could this mean? Where could she be? It was all rather mysterious and unsatisfactory.

At last he took out his watch. Ten minutes to one! No use waiting any longer. He scribbled a hasty note, left it on the writing-table, and walked into the garden past the impenetrable Caterina, who barely deigned to glance up from her knitting. He would look for a carriage, and give himself the luxury of a drive down. It was too hot to walk at that hour.

Strolling along he espied a familiar courtyard that gave upon the street; Count Caloveglia's place. On an impulse he entered the massive portal which stood invitingly ajar. Two elderly gentlemen sat discoursing in the shade of the fig-tree; there was no difficulty in recognizing the stranger as Mr van Koppen, the American millionaire, a frequent visitor, they said, of Count Caloveglia.

A bronze statuette, green with age, stood on a pedestal before them.

'How kind of you to come and see me!' said the Italian. 'Pray make yourself as comfortable as you can, though these chairs, I fear, are not of the latest design. You are going to do me the

232

honour, are you not, of sharing my simple luncheon? Mr van Koppen is staying too.'

'Very good of you!'

'Delighted to make your acquaintance,' said the millionaire. 'Keith was talking about you only yesterday – such nice things! Do stay. Count Caloveglia has been touching on most interesting subjects – I would come from the other end of the world to listen to him.'

The Count, manifestly shy of these praises, interrupted by asking:

'What do you think of that bronze, Mr Heard?'

It was an exquisite little thing.

Perfect to the finger-tips and glowing in a lustrous patina of golden-green, the Locri Faun – so called from the place of its discovery – was declared to be stamped with that hall-mark of individual distinction which the artificers of old Hellas contrived to impress upon every one of the rare surviving bronzes of its period. It was perhaps the finest of the whole group. No wonder the statue had created wild excitement among the few, the very few, discreet amateurs who had been permitted to inspect the relic prior to its clandestine departure from the country. And much as they might deplore the fact that it was probably going to adorn the museum of Mr Cornelius van Koppen, an alien millionaire, not one of them found it in his heart to disapprove of Count Caloveglia's action. For they all liked him. Everyone liked him. They all understood his position. He was a necessitous widower with a marriageable daughter on his hands, a girl whom everybody admired for her beauty and charm of character.

Mr van Koppen, like all the rest, knew what hard times he had gone through; how, born of an ancient and wealthy family, he had not hesitated to sell his wonderful collection of antiques together with all but a shred of his ancestral estates, in order to redeem the gambling debts of a brother. That amounted to quixotism, they declared. They little realized what anguish of mind this step had cost him, for he concealed his true feelings under a cloak of playful worldliness. Excess of grief, he held, is an unlovely thing – not meet to be displayed before men. All excess is unlovely. That was Count Caloveglia's classic point of view. Measure! Measure in everything.

People revered him, above all else, for his knowledge in matters of art. His connoisseurship was not one of mere learning; it was intuitional. Astonishing tales were told of him. By the sense of touch alone, and in the dark, he could appraise correctly any

233

piece of plastic work you liked. He had a natural affinity with such things. They held it quite likely that the blood of Praxiteles or his compeers may still have flowed through his veins – certain, at all events, that there hung about his person the traditions of the versatile colonists on the shores of Magna Graecia, who, freed by legions of slaves from the trivial vexations which beset modern lives, were able to create in their golden leisure those monuments of beauty which are the envy and despair of our generation. On all that concerned the history and technique of ancient bronzes, more especially, he was *facile princeps* in the land, and it was hinted, after the sale of his property, that Count Caloveglia would not be slow to retrieve the fortunes of his family by putting into exercise those talents for metal-working of which, as a gifted boy, he had already shown himself to be possessed.

In this they were disappointed. He spoke of these things as 'sins of his youth', professing an invincible distaste, in these latter years, for the drudgery of work. He called himself an old dreamer. There was a shed, it is true, attached to the house, a shed which went by the name of a studio. All visitors were taken to see this *atelier*. It was smothered in dust and cobwebs. Clearly, as the Count himself would explain with a honeyed smile, it had not been in use for twenty years or more.

Mr van Koppen knew all this.

He knew about that strip of land which the old man had reserved for himself at the sale of his ancestral domain. It lay among the hills, some twenty or thirty miles above the classic site of Locri. On this spot, people were given to understand, fragments of old marbles and vases had been picked up by the peasantry within the last years. Things of small worth – pottery mostly; they lay about Count Caloveglia's Nepenthe courtyard and were given by him, as keepsakes, to any visitor who showed an interest in them. He attached no value to these trifles.

'From my little place on the hills,' he would say. 'Pray take it as a memento of the pleasure which your visit has given me! Oh, it is quite a small property, you know; just a few acres, with a meagre soil; in good years it produces a little oil and a barrel or two of wine. And that is all. I only kept back this morsel from the general ruin of my property – well, for sentimental reasons. One likes to feel that one is still tied – by a slender thread, it is true – to the land of one's ancestors. There is certainly no wealth to be obtained above ground. But it is quite possible that something might emerge from below, given the energy and the means to make systematic excavations. The whole country is so rich in remains of

Hellenic life! The countrymen, ploughing my few fields, often stumble upon some odd trifle of this kind. There was that De-meter you may have heard about; sadly mutilated, alas!'

Before the discovery of the Locri Faun on this site the only find of any value had been a battered head – a Demeter, presumably. It was sold to a Paris collector for a few thousand francs, and had thereafter attracted no further attention. It was not worth talking about.

Now, when this dazzling Faun came to light and Mr van Kop-pen announced his intention of purchasing the masterpiece for his collection, his art-expert, Sir Herbert Street – the eminent con-noisseur whom he had filched from the South Kensington Museum with the bribe of a Cabinet Minister's salary – thought it his duty to compare the disfigured Demeter with this new and marvellous thing. Sir Herbert Street was an inordinately vain man, but conscientious at the same time and, in matter of art-criticism, sufficiently reliable. Not every art-expert would have done what he did. In the interests of his employer he took the trouble of journeying to Paris and carefully examining the poor Demeter fragment. Then, viewing the Locri Faun at Nepenthe in the pre-sence of Count Caloveglia, he made rather a subtle remark.

'Does it not strike you, Count, that there is a curious, an evasive kind of resemblance between this Faun and the Demeter?'

The old man beamed with joy at these words.

'My dear Sir Herbert, allow me to congratulate you on your keen artistic perception! I believe you are the only person, besides myself, who has hitherto been struck by those definite but un-definable traits of similarity. Mr van Koppen may well be proud of your penetration –'

'Thank you,' said the other, immensely flattered. 'That is what I am paid for, you know. But now, how do you account for the likeness?'

'I will tell you my own hypothesis. I hold, to be brief, that they both came from the same workshop.'

'The same workshop! You amaze me.'

'Yes, or at all events from the same school of craftsmen, or some common fountain of inspiration. We know lamentably little of the art history of even a great centre like Locri, but, judging by the hints of Pindar and Demosthenes, I think there may well have been – there must have been – consummate local masters, now forgotten, who propagated certain methods of work, certain fashions in form and feeling and treatment which ended, naturally enough, in a kind of fixed tradition. This would suffice to explain

235

the resemblance which your sagacity has enabled you to detect between these two pieces. That is what I mean by saying that they came from the same workshop. What do you think of my theory?'

'I think it accounts for the fact in a most satisfactory manner,' the expert had replied, thoroughly convinced.

Mr van Koppen knew all this.

But he only believe half of it. ...

'You were saying, Count?'

The Italian shifted his glance from the dainty outlines of the Locri Faun and smiled upon his interlocutor and then upon Mr Heard, who had at last taken a seat, after walking approvingly round and round the statuette.

'I was going to tell you of another point which occurred later on to Sir Herbert; a man, by the way, of unusual acumen. We agreed that Locri was the indubitable place of origin both of the Demeter and of the Faun. Well, said he, granting this – how came they to be unearthed up in the hills, on your property, twenty-five miles away? I confess I was at first nonplussed by this question. For, to the best of my knowledge, there are no indications of any large Hellenic settlement up there. But it struck me that there may well have been a villa or two – indeed, there must have been, to judge by the miscellaneous ancient material found on my little place. This is what makes me think that these two relics were deliberately carried there.'

'Carried?'

'Carried. For although the summer season at Locri was undoubtedly more endurable then than it now is, yet the town must have been sufficiently hot in the dog-days; whereas my vineyard is situated among the cool uplands –'

'A kind of climatic station, you mean?'

'Precisely. Don't you think that richer people had domiciles in both places? The ancients, you know, were so sensitive in the matter of temperatures that in summer time they travelled only by night, and some of their toughest generals had underground chambers built for them during their campaigns. I can imagine, for instance, some young and ardent lover of art, in the days when Pythagoras taught under the glittering colonnades of Croton, when the fleet of Metapontum swept the blue Ionian and Sybaris taught the world how to live a life of ease – I can almost see this youth,' he pursued enthusiastically, 'flitting from a hot palace on the plain towards these breezy heights and, inflamed with an all-absorbing passion for the beautiful, carrying up with him one or

236

two, just one or two, of those beloved bronzes from which he could not, and would not, be parted – no, not even for a short summer month – to be a joy to his eyes and an inspiration to his soul among the mountain solitudes. These men, I take it, had a sense in which we their descendants are wholly deficient – the sense of the solace, of the pleasurable companionship, to be derived from works of art. That sense has been destroyed. The Japanese alone, of all moderns, still foster an ingenuous affection which prompts them to cling closely to these things of beauty, to press them to their hearts as loving friends; the rest of us, surrounded by a world of sordid ugliness, have become positively afraid of their fair but reproachful shapes. Ah, Mr van Koppen, that was the age of true refinement, the age of gold! Nowadays – nowadays we only carry our troubles about with us.'

The bishop was touched by these moving words.

Mr van Koppen, wearing a benevolent twinkle in his eye, said to himself:

'What a lordly liar! Almost as good as myself!'

Luncheon was announced.

CHAPTER 30

'YOU are quite right,' the Count was saying to Mr Heard. 'The ideal cuisine should display an individual character; it should offer a menu judiciously chosen from the kitchen-workshops of the most diverse lands and peoples – a menu reflecting the master's alert and fastidious taste. Is there anything better, for instance, than a genuine Turkish pilaff? The Poles and Spaniards, too, have some notable culinary creations. And if I were able to carry out my ideas on this point I would certainly add to my list of dishes a few of those strange Oriental confections which Mr Keith has successfully taught his Italian chef. There is suggestion about them; they conjure up visions of that rich and glowing East which I would give many years of my remaining life to see.'

'Then why not do what I have proposed several times already?' queried the millionaire. 'I am in the East every winter; we reckon this year to reach Bangkok the first fortnight in November. We can find room for you on board. We'll make room! Your company would give me more pleasure than I can say.'

Count Caloveglia was probably the only male person on earth to whom the owner of the *Flutterby* would have extended such an invitation.

'My dear friend!' replied the other. 'I shall never be able to repay your kindness, as it is. Alas, it cannot be done, not now. And don't you think,' he went on, reverting to his theme, 'that we might revive a few of those forgotten recipes of the past? Not their over-spiced entremets, I mean – their gross joints and pasties, their swans and peacocks – but those which deal, for example, with the preparation of fresh-water fishes? A pike, to my way of thinking, is a coarse, mud-born creature. But if you will take the trouble, as I once did, to dress a pike according to the complicated instructions of some obsolete cookery-book, you will find him sufficiently palatable, by way of a change.'

'You would make an excellent chef!'

'It is plain,' added Mr Heard, 'that the Count does not disdain to practise his skill upon the most ancient and honourable of domestic arts.'

'Indeed I don't. I would cook *con amore* if I had leisure and materials. All culinary tasks should be performed with reverential love, don't you think so? To say that a cook must possess the requisite outfit of culinary skill and temperament – that is hardly more than saying that a soldier must appear in uniform. You can have a bad soldier in uniform. The true cook must have not only those externals, but a large dose of general worldly experience. He is the perfect blend, the only perfect blend, of artist and philosopher. He knows his worth: he holds in his palm the happiness of mankind, the welfare of generations yet unborn. That is why you will never obtain adequate human nourishment from a young girl or boy. Such persons may do for housework, but not in the kitchen. Never in the kitchen! No one can aspire to be a philosopher who is in an incomplete state of physical development. The true cook must be mature; she must know the world from her social point of view, however humble it be; she must have pondered concerning good and evil, in however lowly and incongruous a fashion; she must have passed through the crucible of sin and suffering or, at the very least – it is often the same thing – of married life. Best of all, she should have a lover, a fierce and brutal lover who beats and caresses her in turns; for every woman worthy of the name is subject and entitled to fluctuating psychic needs – needs which must be satisfied to the very core, if the master is to enjoy sound, healthy fare.'

'We don't always allow them to fulfil that last condition,' observed Mr Heard.

'I know we don't. That is precisely why we are so often poisoned or starved, instead of being cheered with wholesome food.'

'You were speaking of woman-cooks?' asked van Koppen.

'I was. But it stands to reason that no woman can be trusted with so responsible a task – so sacred a mission, I ought to call it – in regions south of Bordeaux or east of Vienna. Among many other reasons the whole sex is too drowsy, outside that radius. And if she drinks a little –'

'Drinks a little?'

'If she drinks a little, why, it is all to the good. It shows that she is fully equipped on the other side of her dual nature. It proves that she possesses the prime requisite of the artist; sensitiveness and a capacity for enthusiasm. Indeed, I often doubt whether you will ever derive well-flavoured victuals from the *atelier* of an individual who honestly despises or fears – it is the same thing – the choicest gift of God. Andrea, my man here, is abstemious to the last degree; not, I am glad to say, from conviction or ill-health – it is the same thing – but because he is incurably desirous of saving my money. What is the consequence? You can taste his self-imposed asceticism in the very *zabaione*, for which I must really apologize! It speaks to the eye, but not to the heart. Let us hope the coffee will be more harmonious.'

'Would you not include some of our American dishes in your bill of fare?'

'To be sure I would; a fine selection. I have most pleasant recollections of the cuisine of Baltimore.'

'You can get all those things in New York.'

'No doubt; no doubt. But one thing invariably distresses me in transatlantic dinners: the unseemly haste in rising. One might really think the company were ashamed of so natural and jovial a function as that to which a dining-room is consecrated. And then, have you not noticed that, sitting at table, a certain intellectual tone, an atmosphere of a definite kind, is insensibly generated among the guests, whatever the subject of conversation may be? They are often quite unaware of its existence, but it hangs none the less about the room and binds the inmates together for the time being. Suddenly we are bidden to rise and betake ourselves elsewhere; to sit on other chairs in a different temperature among different surroundings. It is a wrench. That peculiar atmosphere is dissipated; the genius of the earlier moment driven out beyond recapture; we must adapt ourselves to other conditions and begin anew, often with a good deal of trouble – often, how often, against our inclination! I call that a perverse custom. Every state of the mind, whether we are in society or alone, should be pressed to the last drop, irrespective of whether we happen to have swallowed a final mouthful of food or not. When the conversation has died, as

239

everything must die, from sheer inability to draw further breaths of life, then is the time to break up that old encircling dome of thought; to construct a fresh one, if need be, in a fresh environment.'

'I confess,' said the American, 'it has always struck me as rather barbarous – this running away. I like to linger. But the ladies don't. They know that their dresses show off better in a parlour than under the boards of a mahogany table; perhaps their conversation, too, sounds better among arm-chairs and rugs. So we run after them, as we generally do; instead of making them run after us' ('as I do' he added to himself).

'But, Count! If you like our American dishes, why not get this man of yours to learn a few from the Duchess? I know she would gladly teach him; she is not jealous of her knowledge like a professional chef.'

'I would have asked her that favour long ago, if Andrea had been a born cook, like Keith's man. Unfortunately he is quite different. The philosopher is represented in his nature, but not the artist. He is only a devoted Arcadian, overflowing with good in- tentions.'

'And are they of no avail?' queried the bishop.

'I have been told that, in art and literature, they will atone for deficiency of natural talent. It may be so; some persons, at least, have been able to cajole their brain into believing this. However that may be, I do not think the rule can be extended into the domain of cookery. Good intentions – no. Nobody need attempt such an imposture on his stomach, an upright and uncompromis- ing organ, which refuses to listen to nonsense. Or let them try the experiment. Gastritis will be the result of good intentions. ...'

Mr Heard stretched out his legs. He was beginning to feel at ease. He liked this comely old man; he detected an abiding quality in his outlook and person. And he felt at home in these surround- ings. There was an air of simplicity and refinement in that calm ground-floor chamber, with its subdued light filtering through windows that opened upon the courtyard, groined vaulting of noble proportions, stucco frieze stained with age to an ivory hue, and those other decorations which the Count, loyal to the tradi- tions of old-world peasant architecture, had piously left unaltered – or, it may be, adapted to modern needs by touches so deft as not to reveal his own consummate artistry. Through the open door by which they had entered came breathings of warm wind laden with the suave odour of a tuft of Madonna lilies that grew, half neg- lected, in a shady corner. He had noticed them on his entry – how they stood in proud clusters, bending forward with mighty effort to reach the light.

His eye strayed into the courtyard and moved about the green penumbra created by the fig-tree's massy foliage; it glanced over fragments of statuary half buried under a riot of leaves and nodding flowers, and rested with complaisance upon the brickwork flooring of herring-bone pattern, coloured in a warm, velvety Indian-red. It was worn down here and there by tread of feet, and pleasantly marked with patches of emerald-green moss and amber-tinted streaks of light that played about its surface wherever the sunbeams could pierce the dense leafage overhead.

From where he sat he could see the Locri Faun on its pedestal. The figure was drowned in twilight. It seemed to slumber.

Meanwhile Andrea, looking uncommonly ceremonious in white tie and white cotton gloves, was handing round the coffee. It was pronounced an unqualified success. 'Absolutely harmonious,' declared the bishop, who had no hesitation, after a critical sip or two, in extending his approval to a curiously flavoured liqueur of unknown ingredients.

'From my little property on the mainland,' the Count explained. 'If it were a clear day I would take you up to my roof and show you the very site, although it is leagues and leagues away. But the South wind always casts a haze over the mainland at this time of day – a kind of veil.'

Mr van Koppen, connoisseur of cigars, opened his capacious case and offered its contents, without disclosing the fact that they were specially manufactured for him at a fabulous price.

'You will find them smokable, I hope. As a matter of fact it's no use trying to keep a cigar in good condition on the yacht. And it must be the same on an island like this. So far as tobacco is concerned, Nepenthe can be nothing but a ship at anchor.'

'True,' said the Count. 'The moist sirocco is injurious to the finer growths.'

'This South wind!' exclaimed Mr Heard. 'This African pest! Is there no other wind hereabouts? Tell me, Count, does the sirocco always blow?'

'So far as I have observed it blows constantly during the spring and summer. Hardly less constantly in autumn,' he added. 'And in winter, often for weeks on end.'

'Sounds promising,' observed the bishop. 'And has it no influence on the character?'

'The native is accustomed, or resigned. Foreigners, sometimes, are tempted to strange actions under its influence.'

241

The American said:

'You spoke of amalgamating our cuisine with yours, or vice versa. It can doubtless be done, to the profit of both parties. Why not go a step further? Why not amalgamate our respective civilizations?'

'A pleasant dream, my friend, with which I have occasionally beguiled myself! Our contribution to human happiness, and that of America – are they not irreconcilable? What is yours? Comfort, time and labour saving contrivances; abundance; in a word, all that is summed up under the denomination of utility. Ours, let us say, is beauty. No doubt we could saturate ourselves with each other's ideals, to our mutual advantage. But it would never be an amalgam; the joints would show. It would be a successful graft, rather than a fusion of elements. No; I do not see how beauty and utility are ever to be syncretized into a homogeneous conception. They are too antagonistic to coalesce.'

'But there is abundant beauty and grandeur in modern American life,' said the millionaire, 'quite apart, I mean, from that of the natural scenery. A fine steam-engine, for instance – I call that a beautiful thing, perfectly adapted to its end. Is its beauty really so antagonistic to that of your civilization?'

'I know that some excellent persons have been writing lately about the beauty of a swift-gliding motor-car and things of that kind. They are right, in one sense of the word. For there is a beauty in mechanical fitness which no art can enhance. But it is not the beauty of which I spoke.'

'And therefore,' observed the bishop, 'we ought to have another word for it.'

'Precisely, my dear sir! We ought to have another word. All values are continually being revised, and tested anew. Are they not? We have been restating moral values within the last half-century; it is the same with artistic ones. New canons of taste, new standards, are continually being evolved; there is a general widening and multiplying of notions. This, I think, ought to make us careful as to the words we employ, and ready to coin new ones whenever a new idea is to be expressed. If we enlarge our concepts, we should likewise enlarge our vocabulary. When I spoke of beauty, I used the word in its narrow classical meaning, a meaning which may be out of fashion, but which has the great advantage that it happens to be irrevocably fixed and defined for us by what the ancients themselves have handed down in the way of art and criticism. This particular beauty, I say, is irreconcilable with that other beauty of which you spoke.'

242

'How so?' asked the millionaire.

'There resides, for example, in Hellenic sculpture a certain ingredient – what shall we call it? Let us call it the factor of strangeness, of mystery! It is a vague emanation which radiates from such works of art, and gives us a sense of their universal applicability to all our changing moods and passions. That, I suppose, is why we call them ever young. They beckon to all of us familiarly and yet, as it were, from an unexplored world. They speak to us at all seasons in some loving and yet enigmatical language, such language as we may read, at times, in the eyes of a child that wakes from sleep. Now the swiftest and fairest steam-engine in the world is not for ever young; it grows obsolete and ends, after a short life, on the scrap-heap. That is to say, where usefulness enters, this spirit of mystery, of eternal youth, is put to flight. And there is yet another element of classical beauty which is equally at variance with your modern conception of it: the element of authority. Beholding the Praxitelean Eros, the veriest ruffian feels compelled to reverence the creator and his work. "Who was the man?" he asks; for he acknowledges that such things impose themselves upon his untutored mind. Now a certain Monsieur Cadillac builds the most beautiful motor-cars. Who is this man? We do not care a fig about him. He is probably a Jewish syndicate. Such being the case, I cannot bring myself to reverence Monsieur Cadillac and his cars. They are comfortable, but that factor of authority, which compels our homage to the Eros, is wholly lacking. Yet both things are called beautiful. That we should apply the same word to products so different, so hopelessly conflicting, as those of Praxiteles and Monsieur Cadillac – what does it prove? It proves our poverty of invention. And what does it explain? It explains our confusion of thought.'

The millionaire remarked:

'I suppose the human outlook has shifted with the years. Democracy has changed your old point of view.'

'Assuredly. No American, no modern of any race, I fancy, can divest himself of the notion that one man is as good as another; in the eyes of God, they add – meaning in their own eyes. No Greek, no ancient of any race, I fancy, could have burdened himself with so preposterous a delusion. Democracy has killed my point of view. It has substituted progress for civilization. To appreciate things of beauty, as do the Americans, a man requires intelligence. Intelligence is compatible with progress. To create them, as did the Greeks, he requires intelligence and something else as well: time. Democracy, in abolishing slavery, has eliminated

243

that element of time – an element which is indispensable to civilization.'

'We have some fine slavery in America at this moment.'

'I am using the word in the antique sense. Your modern slavery is of another kind. It has all the drawbacks and few of the advantages of the classic variety. It gives leisure to the wrong people – to those who praise the dignity of labour. Men who talk about the Dignity of Labour had better say as little as possible about civilization, for fear of confusing it with the North Pole.'

The American laughed.

'That's one for me,' he remarked.

'On the contrary! you are an admirable example of that happy graft which we mentioned just now.'

'Progress and civilization!' exclaimed Mr Heard. 'One uses those words so much in my walk of life that, thinking it over, I begin to wonder whether they mean more than this: that there are perpetual readjustments going on. They are supposed to indicate an upward movement, some vague step in the direction of betterment which, frankly, I confess myself unable to perceive. What is the use of civilization if it makes a man unhappy and unhealthy? The uncivilized African native is happy and healthy. The poor creatures among whom I worked, in the slums of London, are neither the one nor the other; they are civilized. I glance down the ages, and see nothing but – change! And perhaps not even change. Mere differences of opinion as to the value of this or that in different times and places.'

'Pardon me! I was using the words in a specific sense. What I mean by progress is the welding together of society for whatever ends. Progress is a centripetal movement, obliterating man in the mass. Civilization is centrifugal; it permits, it postulates, the assertion of personality. The terms are, therefore, not synonymous. They stand for hostile and divergent movements. Progress subordinates. Civilization co-ordinates. The individual emerges in civilization. He is submerged in progress.'

'You might call civilization a placid lake,' said the American, 'and the other a river or torrent.'

'Exactly!' remarked Mr Heard. 'The one is static, the other dynamic. And which of the two, Count, would you say was the more beneficial to humanity?'

'Ah! For my part I would not bring such considerations to bear on the point. We may deduce, from the evolution of society, that progress is the newer movement, since the State, which welds together, is of more recent growth than the individualistic family or

244

clan. This is as far as I care to go. To debate whether one be better for mankind than the other betrays what I call an anthropomorphic turn of mind; it is therefore a problem which, so far as I am concerned, does not exist. I content myself with establishing the fact that progress and civilization are incompatible, mutually exclusive.'

'Do you mean to say,' asked the millionaire, 'that it is impossible to be progressive and civilized at the same time?'

'That is what I mean to say. Now, if America stands for progress, this old world may be permitted – with a reasonable dose of that flattery which we accord to the dead – to represent civilization. Tell me, Mr van Koppen, how do you propose to amalgamate or reconcile such ferociously antagonistic strivings? I fear we will have to wait for the millennium.'

'The millennium!' echoed Mr Heard. 'That is another of those unhappy words which are always cropping up in my department.'

'Why unhappy?' asked Mr van Koppen.

'Because they mean nothing. The millennium will never come.'

'Why not?'

'Because nobody wants it to come. They want tangible things. Nobody wants a millennium.'

'Which is very fortunate,' observed the Count. 'For if they did, the Creator would be considerably embarrassed how to arrange matters, seeing that every man's millennium differs from that of his neighbour. Mine is not the same as yours. Now I wonder, Mr van Koppen – I wonder what your millennium would be like?'

'I wonder! I believe I never gave it a thought. I have had other things to puzzle out.'

And the millionaire straightway proceeded to think, in his usual clear-cut fashion. 'Something with girls in it,' he soon concluded, inwardly. Then aloud:

'I guess my millennium would be rather a contradictory sort of business. I should require tobacco, to begin with. And the affair would certainly not be complete, Count, without a great deal of your company. The millennium of other people may be more simple. That of the Duchess, for example, is at hand. She is about to join the Roman Catholic Church.'

'That reminds me,' said Mr Heard. 'She gave me some remarkable tea-cakes, not long ago. Delicious. She said they were your speciality.'

'You have found them out, have you?' laughed the American. 'I always tell her that once a man begins on those tea-cakes there is no reason on earth, that I can think of, why he should ever stop

245

again. All the same, I nearly overate myself the other day. That was because we had a late luncheon on board. It shall never occur again – the late luncheon, I mean. Have you discovered, by the way, whether the business of Miss Wilberforce has been settled?'

Mr Heard shook his head.

'Is that the person,' enquired the Count, 'who is reported to drink to excess? I have never spoken to her. She belongs presumably to the lower classes – to those who extract from alcohol the pleasurable emotions which we derive from a good play, or music, or a picture gallery.'

'She is a lady.'

'Indeed? Then she has relapsed into the intemperance of her inferiors. That is not pretty.'

'Temperance!' said the bishop. 'Another of those words which I am always being obliged to use. Pray tell me, Count, what you mean by temperance.'

'I should call it the exercise of our faculties and organs in such a manner as to combine the maximum of pleasure with the minimum of pain.'

'And who is judge of what constitutes the dividing line between use and abuse?'

'We cannot do better, I imagine, than go to our own bodies for an answer to that question. They will tell us exactly how far we may proceed with impunity.'

'In that case,' said the millionaire, 'if you drink a little too much occasionally – only occasionally, I mean! – you would not call that intemperance?'

'Certainly not. We are not Puritans here. We do not give wrong names to things. What you suggest would be by the way of a change, I presume – like the eating of a pike; something we do not indulge in every day. If I were to come home a little joyful now and then, do you know what these people would say? They would say: "The old gentleman is pleased to be merry tonight. Bless his heart! May the wine do him good." But if I behaved as Miss Wilberforce is reported to do, they would say: "That old man is losing self-control. He is growing intemperate. Every evening! It is not a pretty sight." They never call it wrong. Their mode of condemnation is to say that it is not pretty. The ethical moment, you observe, is replaced by an aesthetic one. That is the Mediterranean note. It is the merit of the Roman Church that she left us some grains of common sense in regard to minor morals.'

The bishop remarked:

246

'What I have seen of the local Catholicism strikes me as a kind of pantomime. That is the fault of my upbringing, no doubt.'

'Oh, I am not referring to externals! Externally, of course, our Church is the purest rococo –'

Mr Heard was expanding in this congenial atmosphere; he felt himself in touch with permanent things. He glanced at the speaker. How charming he looked, this silvery-haired old aristocrat! His ample and gracious personality, his leisurely discourse – how well they accorded with the environment! He suggested, in a manner, the secret of youth, and all that is glad, unclouded, eternal; he was a reflection, a belated flower, of the classic splendour which lay in ruins about him. Such a man, he thought, deserves to be happy and successful. What joy it must have been to a person of his temperament – the chance discovery of the Locri Faun!

A great stillness brooded upon the enclosure beyond. The shadows had shifted. Sunny patches lay, distributed in fresh patterns, upon the old brickwork flooring. An oval shaft of light, glinting through the foliage, had struck the pedestal of the Faun and was stealthily crawling up its polished surface. He looked at the statue. It was still slumbering in the shade. But a subtle change had spread over the figure, or was it, he wondered, merely a change in the state of his own mind, due to what the Count had said? There was energy, now, in those tense muscles. The slightest touch, he felt, would unseal the enchantment and cause life to flow through the dull metal.

Mr van Koppen was slightly ruffled.

'Are you not a little hard on the Puritans?' he asked. 'Where would we have been without them in America?'

'And after all,' added the bishop, 'they cleared up an infinity of abuses. They were temperate, at all events! Too temperate in some matters, I am inclined to think; they did not always allow for human weakness. They went straight back to the Bible.'

The Count shook his head slowly.

'The Bible,' he said, 'is the most intemperate book I have ever read.'

'Dear me!'

Mr van Koppen, a tactful person, scented danger ahead. He remarked:

'I did not know Italians read the Bible. Where did you become acquainted with it?'

'In New York. I often amused myself strolling about the Jewish quarter there and studying the inhabitants. Wonderful types, wonderful poses! But hard to decipher, for a person of my race. One

247

day I said to myself: I will read their literature; it may be of assistance. I went through the Talmud and the Bible. They helped me to understand those people and their point of view.'

'What is their point of view?'

'That God is an overseer. This, I think, is the keynote of the Bible. And it explains why the Bible has always been regarded as an exotic among Greco-Latin races, who are all pagans at heart. Our God is not an overseer; he is a partaker. For the rest, we find the whole trend of the Bible, its doctrinal tone, antagonistic to those ideals of equanimity and moderation which, however disregarded in practice, have always been held up hereabouts as theoretically desirable. In short, we Southerners lack what you possess: an elective affinity with that book. One may wonder how the morality of those tawny Semites was enabled to graft itself upon your alien white-skinned race with such tenacity as to influence your whole national development. Well, I think I have at last puzzled it out,' he added, 'to my own satisfaction at least.'

The bishop interposed with a laugh:

'I may tell you, Count, that I am not in the episcopal mood today. Not at all. Never felt less episcopal in my life. For that matter, it is our English ecclesiastics who have dealt some of the most serious blows at Biblical authority of late, with their modern exegesis. Pray go on!'

'I imagine it is nothing but a matter of racial temperament.'

'Goth and Latin?'

'One does not always like to employ such terms; they are so apt to cover deficiency of ideas, or to obscure the issue. But certainly the sun which colours our complexion and orders our daily habits, influences at the same time our character and outlook. The almost hysterical changes of light and darkness, summer and winter, which have impressed themselves on the literature of the North, are unknown here. Northern people, whether from climatic or other causes, are prone to extremes, like their own myths and sagas. The Bible is essentially a book of extremes. It is a violent document. The Goth or Anglo-Saxon has taken kindly to this book because it has always suited his purposes. It has suited his purposes because, according to his abruptly varying moods, he has never been at a loss to discover therein exactly what he wanted – authority for every grade of emotional conduct, from savage vindictiveness to the most abject self-abasement. One thing he would never have found, had he cared to look for it – an incitement to live the life of reason, to strive after intellectual honesty and self-respect, and to keep his mind open to the logic of his five

248

senses. That is why, during the troubled Middle Ages when the oscillations of national and individual life were yet abrupter – when, therefore, that classical quality of temperance was more than ever at a discount – the Bible took so firm a hold upon you. Its unquiet teachings responded to the unquiet yearnings of men. Your conservatism, your reverence for established institutions, has done the rest. No! I do not call to mind any passages in the Bible commending the temperate philosophic life; though it would be strange if so large a miscellany did not contain a few sound reflections. Temperance,' he concluded, as though speaking to himself – 'temperance! All the rest is embroidery.'

Mr Heard was thoughtful. The American observed:

'That side of the case never struck me before. How about Solomon's Proverbs?'

'Maxims of exhaustion, my dear friend. It is easy to preach to me. I am an old man. I can read Solomon with a certain patience. We want something for our children – something which does not blight or deny, but vivifies and guides aright; something which makes them hold up their heads. A friend, an older brother; not a pedagogue. I would never recommend a boy to study these writings. They would lower his spirits and his self-respect. Solomon, like all reformed debauchees, has a depressing influence on the young.'

'Do you know England well?' asked Mr Heard.

'Very little. I have spent a few days in Liverpool and London, here and there, on my periodical journeyings to the States. Kind friends supply me with English books and papers; the excellent Sir Herbert Street sends me more than I can possibly digest! I confess that much of what I read was an enigma to me till I had studied the Bible. Its teachings seem to have filtered, warm and fluid, through the veins of your national and private life. Then, slowly, they froze hard, congealing the whole body into a kind of crystal. Your ethics are stereotyped in black-letter characters. A gargoyle morality.'

'It is certainly difficult,' said Mr van Koppen, 'for an Anglo-Saxon to appraise this book objectively. His mind has been saturated with it in childhood to such an extent as to take on a definite bias.'

'Like the ancients with their Iliad. Where is a truer poet than Homer? Yet the worship of him became a positive bane to independent creative thought. What good things could be written about the withering influence of Homer upon the intellectual life of Rome!'

The bishop asked:

'You think the Bible has done the same for us?'

'I think it accounts for some Byzantine traits in your national character and for the formlessness and hesitancy which I, at least, seem to detect in the demeanour of many individual Anglo-Saxons. They realize that their traditional upbringing is opposed to truth. It gives them a sense of insecurity. It makes them shy and awkward. Poise! That is what they need, and what this unbalanced Eastern stuff will never give them.'

'The withering influence of Homer: surely that is a bad sign?' asked the American.

'And that of the Bible?' added Mr Heard.

'How shall a plant survive, save by withering now and then? If the ancients had not exhausted themselves with Homer, the soil might not have been ready for our Renaissance. A bad sign? Who can tell! Good and bad – I question whether these are respectable words to use.'

'You are content, as you observed before, to establish a fact?'

'Amply content. I leave the rest to the academicians. And the only fact we seem to have established is that your notions of morality resemble my notions of beauty in this one point: neither of them are up to date. You will have me admire a steam-engine. Why? Because of its delicately adjusted mechanism, its perfect adaptation to modern needs. So be it. I will modify my conception of what is fair in appearance. I will admire your steam-engine, and thereby bring my ideals of beauty up to date. Will you modify your conception of what is fair in conduct? Will you admire something more adapted to modern needs than those intemperate Hebrew doctrines; something with more delicately adjusted mechanism? The mendicant friar, that flower of Oriental ethics – he is not up to date. He resembles all Semites. He lacks self-respect. He apologizes for being alive. It is not pretty – to apologize for being alive!'

The American observed:

'I should say that even our greatest bigots, nowadays, don't take those old doctrines as seriously as you seem to think.'

'I daresay they don't. But they profess to reproach themselves for not doing so. And that is more contemptible. It adds insincerity to imbecility.'

A sunny smile played about his face as he spoke these words. It was evident that his thoughts were already far away. The bishop, following the direction of his glance, saw that it rested upon the statuette of the Faun whose head and shoulders were now enveloped in a warm beam of light. Under that genial touch the old relic seemed to have woken from its slumber. Blood was throbbing in its veins. It was in movement; it dominated the scene in its emphatic affirmation of joy.

Mr Heard, his eyes fixed upon the statuette, now realized the significance of what had been said. He began to see more clearly. Soon it dawned upon him that not joy alone was expressed by the figure. Another quality, more evasive yet more compelling, resided in its subtle grace: the element of mystery. There, emprisoned in the bronze, dwelt some benignant oracle.

Puzzle as he would, that oracle refused to clothe itself in words. What could it be?

A message of universal application, 'loving and enigmatical', as the old man had called it. True! It was a greeting from an unknown friend in an unknown land; something familiar from the dim past or distant future; something that spoke of well-being – plain to behold, hard to expound, like the dawning smile of childhood.

CHAPTER 31

TOWARDS evening Mr van Koppen drove the bishop down in the carriage which he usually hired for the whole of his stay on Nepenthe. They said little, having talked themselves out with the Count. The American seemed to be thinking about something. Mr Heard's eye roamed over the landscape, rather anxiously.

'I don't like that new cloud above the volcano,' he observed.

'Looks like ashes. Looks as if it might drift in our direction, doesn't it, if the wind were strong enough to move it? Do you see much of the Count?' he inquired.

'Not as much as I should like. What excellent veal cutlets those were! So white and tender. Quite different from the veal we get in England. And that aromatic wine went uncommonly well with them. It was his own growth, I suppose.'

'Very likely. From that little vineyard which produces so many good things.' He chuckled softly. 'As to English veal – I never yet tasted any worth eating. If you don't slaughter a calf till it's grown into a cow – why you're not likely to get anything but beef.'

'They say the English cannot cook, in spite of the excellence of their prime materials.'

'I think the prime materials are at fault. They sacrifice everything to size. It's barbaric. Those greasy Southdown sheep! It's the same with their fowls; they're large, but insipid – very different from the little things you get down here. Now a goose is capital fodder. But if you grow him only for his weight, you destroy his quality and flavour; you get a lump of blubber instead of a bird.'

'Apple-sauce?'

'I don't like apples in any shape. A sour kind of potato, I call them. They eat an awful lot of apples in our country. That is what makes so many of our women as flat as boards, in front and be-hind – especially in the Eastern States. It's apple-eating. Apples ought to be taxed. They ruin the female figure. I'm not sure that they don't sour the character as well.'

'Don't you care about our English vegetables?'

'Can't say I'm much in love with them, Mr Heard. Brussels sprouts, for instance – I'm very partial to Brussels sprouts. But the things they give you over there are the size of a bath-sponge, and much the same taste, I reckon. And the carrots! A carrot ought to be small and round and yellow, it ought to melt in the mouth like a plum. Those carrots aren't carrots at all. They're walking-sticks. And the peas! No, I don't care about English peas. Too large and too lively for me.'

'Lively?'

'That's it. Lively. I shall never forget my first experience of them,' he went on, laughing. 'There were two or three in the dish; just two or three; filled it up nicely. Looked like cannon-balls. What do they expect me to do with these things? I wondered. I didn't like to ask the waiter. One doesn't care to be taken for an ignorant stranger. Well, I landed one on my plate and began carv-ing at it, to see if there was anything eatable inside the shell, when the durned thing slipped away from my knife and crashed on to the floor. Bounced up like a marble. I called for a nutcracker – "I shall want the largest you've got," I said. They couldn't find one. Now, I'm not the sort of man, Mr Heard, to be beaten by a vege-table, if it really was a vegetable. Because, you see, it behaved more like a blamed mineral. I sent for the head waiter, and took him into my confidence. I tried to talk English, like I'm talking to you. "What d'ye call these things?" I asked. "Marrowfats, Sir." "Ah, I thought they weren't peas. You've got *petits pois* down on the bill of fare. Better get that put right. And now, how d'ye eat them?" "You bite them, Sir." "What's that?" "You just bite them!" That's what he said. "You bite them." Of course I didn't believe him. I thought it was just a bit of English humour, especi-ally as the other waiter was looking the opposite way all the time. Well, like a fool, I said to myself: "No harm in trying!" I've got pretty sharp teeth, you know, for a boy of my age. That's how I
252

managed to do what a lot of you younger fellows couldn't have done. I got them fixed into the softest of that bunch of marrowfats. But as to pulling them out again! The head waiter, you bet, had disappeared. And the other fellow was standing at the window with his back to me. Looking up the street, I should say, to see if it was going to rain.'

After this little outburst, the millionaire seemed to have nothing more to say.

He was thinking. ...

Cornelius van Koppen loved a good liar. He knew something about the gentle art. It was an art, he used to say, which no fool should be allowed to cultivate. There were too many amateurs knocking about. These bunglers spoiled the trade. Without doing any good to themselves, they roused distrust; they rubbed the fine bloom off human credulity. His puritan conscience was enraged at petty thefts, petty forgeries, petty larcenies. That was why he despised that otherwise excellent person, the Financial Commissioner for Nicaragua, whose wildest flights of embezzlement never exceeded a few hundred dollars. He respected a man who, like himself, could work in the grand style. To play upon the credulity of a continent – it was Napoleonic, it was like stealing a kingdom; it was not stealing at all. This, he shrewdly suspected, was what his good friend the Count was engaged upon. That delightful old man was working in the grand style.

Bronzes, ancient or modern, were Greek to Mr van Koppen. He could not tell the difference between the art of Clodion and of Myron – had, in fact, never heard the names of these good people and did not particularly care to hear them; he paid Sir Herbert Street for that part of the business. But he had picked up, in the course of his long humanitarian career, a good deal of general knowledge. Old Koppen was no fool. He was intelligent: intelligence, as the Count had said, being perfectly compatible with progress. The millionaire could put two and two together, as fast as most men; he was celebrated, even among his quick-witted compatriots, for an uncanny faculty of walking round people without getting off his chair. Common sense, he called it.

Many a time had he listened to Count Caloveglia's rounded periods anent the Locri Faun. Taking his own personal experience as a guide, he had come to the conclusion that a man does not explain things quite so satisfactorily, does not talk about things quite so enthusiastically, unless he has some business in hand. Everything fitted into a hypothesis which had been slowly maturing in his mind, namely, that he was confronted by a fraud, a

253

really noble fraud, a fraud after his own heart, a fraud deserving the fullest support of every sensible man and woman.

That vineyard, for instance, with those antiquities! A good many friends of his in the States had made their pile out of salted gold mines. Why not salt a vineyard? Oh yes; everything fitted in beautifully. The remoteness of that vineyard ... a town like Locri was obviously unsafe, too public a place for such important discoveries. The conscientious Sir Herbert would certainly want to make inquiries on the spot – inquiries which would prove that no Faun had ever been found there. And that would ruin everything. Therefore the statue had been 'carried' to the vineyard in ancient times by 'some young and ardent lover of art'. Carried, ha, ha! His knowledge of human nature made him doubt whether the Locri Faun had ever in its life made a further journey than to Caloveglia's shady courtyard from that mysterious, dusty shed at the back of his house. Or the Demeter either. That 'sadly mutilated head' was a feeler – a rehearsal. They both came 'from the same worskhop'. Excellent! That shed was the workshop – the birthplace of these two antiques; the Count himself their old Hellenic creator.

Andrea, no doubt, was in the secret.

These art experts! Here was Street, one of the best of them, a man of celebrity in his department, solemnly pronouncing for the authenticity of the fake – in the full and innocent conviction that it really was authentic. A sucking babe. This man, he could see by his simple society face, had not even made an arrangement with the Count as to a commission for himself in the event of a purchase being concluded. He was satisfied with his salary. These experts – what a crowd of fools they were! Especially the honest ones.

None the less, he was delighted with Sir Herbert's opinion. It was exactly what he wanted. For he meant to help the Count who, he was sure, would never accept a cent from him save under a pretext like that of the sale of the Faun. He loved old Caloveglia. There was something clean and purposeful about him. His friendship with such a man filled up what he knew to be a void in his own equipment as citizen of the world. And the Count was working – was lying – for a worthy purpose: a daughter's dowry. For that reason alone he was deserving of assistance.

Mr van Koppen was unmarried. Knowing life as he did, from its more seamy or mercenary side, he had never brought himself to accept a single one of several hundred offers of marriage which had been more or less overtly made to him – to his millions. He

254

loved the sex, as a whole; but distrusted them individually. He thought he knew exactly what they were after. Pearl necklaces and things. He was a good American; fond of bestowing pearl necklaces. But he liked to give them when, and to whom, he fancied; he meant to be his own master and to keep his painfully gotten millions under his own control. All of which, far from extinguishing, actually fostered that queer bachelor's feeling of reverential awe for the married state and its results. Every form of courage and success appealed to van Koppen – none more than the reckless impetuosity of a man who speculates in such a delirious lottery and sometimes actually draws a prize. Such had been Count Caloveglia's portion. His marriage had plainly been a love-match, a success; its result, this offspring – a daughter of whom any father might be proud. Mr van Koppen thoroughly understood the Count's position. These Italians need dowries for their girls. Well, he should have one! What did it signify? One pearl necklace the less, for some operatic charmer. Not worth talking about. Among all his various benefactions, none was ever projected with a lighter heart, with more sincere pleasure. It made him glad to be a millionaire.

All the details had been settled. The *Flutterby* was sailing in a day or two. The relic would be brought on board, at dead of night, by the faithful Andrea, who would return to the Count with a cheque in his pocket. It was a considerable sum; so considerable that Caloveglia had displayed great hesitation in accepting it. But the millionaire pointed out that the parties must be guided by Sir Herbert's opinion. What was the good, he asked, of employing a specialist? Sir Herbert Street had declared the bronze to be priceless, unique. His employer, therefore, insisted on paying what the other had called 'an adequate amount, if the value of such a work of art can be expressed in monetary figures at all'. There was nothing more to be said. The Count gave way, with graceful reluctance. A sham ancestry having been manufactured for the masterpiece (it was proved to come from Asia Minor) in order to elude the vigilance of the Italian Government, the Locri Faun could thereafter be freely displayed to the American public, and Sir Herbert Street was probably right in foretelling that it would be the showpiece of the millionaire's museum – artists and antiquarians flocking to see it from every part of the world.

And Mr van Koppen, as he drove along, was thinking of that cheque; he was converting the dollars into francs. They made rather an awkward sum. He decided to round it off, if only for the sake of appearances; a further reason for not sending the cheque till the last moment, together with a carefully worded letter to allay the Count's scruples. The old fellow might otherwise return the balance, in a fit of conscientiousness. Like himself, Count Caloveglia was infernally, and very properly, punctilious – in small matters.

Yes, there was some fun, at times, in being a millionaire. Or a sculptor either, for that matter! For it evidently took some doing – a little thing like that Locri Faun. It took some doing. And it was worth doing: that was the main point. A man who could bamboozle Sir Herbert Street – such a man deserved to be supported. And what if the truth ultimately leaked out? Had he not acted with the best intentions, under the written advice of an expert? Far from feeling uneasy, Mr van Koppen smiled at the thought of how his millions, backed by the opinion of a connoisseur of international reputation, had enabled him to play yet one more trick upon that great Republic whose fathomless gullibility no one had ever exploited to better purposes than himself. ...

Mr Eames was waiting for the bishop, according to appointment.

'How about Mrs Meadows?' he at once began.

'She was out, invisible. I waited nearly two hours and then lunched with Count Caloveglia. By the way, have you seen anything of Denis lately?'

'No. Why?'

'The old man seemed to be concerned about him. He asked me to make inquiries. Van Koppen thought that he might have got into trouble with some girl. But that strikes me as very unlikely. He may be a little homesick and lonely, so far from his mother.'

The bibliographer said:

'I understand Mr van Koppen is quite an authority on girls. As to Denis, I saw him last – when was it? Oh, not so very long ago. The day all those funny things happened; those portents. We walked up and down together on this very terrace. Perhaps he has left the island, like that wretched mineralogist who promised me – never mind! He seemed all right then. A little depressed, perhaps. Yes; a little depressed, now I come to think of it. But the Count need not be anxious. This island is a great place for scares and rumours.'

Mr. Heard was not satisfied.

'Do you believe the influence of Nepenthe can make Northern people irresponsible for their actions? Keith does. Or how about the sirocco? Can it upset their nerves to such an extent?'

'Not my nerves. I have heard of people making fools of themselves and then blaming the Creator. Often! And of course, if one

256

begins to brood over accidentals like the weather, one is sure to become a lunatic sooner or later. Weather was not made for that purpose. If you come to think of it, how few days there are when a man can honestly say that the weather is quite to his liking! It is nearly always too hot or too cold or too wet or too dry or too windy. I don't trouble myself about sirocco. Why should Denis? He is not nearly as much of a fool as many people look. And I would not listen to Keith. He moves among hyperboles.'

Mr Heard felt slightly relieved. What a sensible fellow this was; so matter-of-fact and sure of his ground. The ideal scholar. Sirocco did not exist for him. He stood aloof from human passions and infirmities.

It was plain that the bishop had never heard that story about the *ballon captif*.

'For my part,' he said, 'I am beginning to object to this South wind. I never felt it worse than today. Phew! Stifling! One can hardly breathe. My shirt is sticking to my back. Suppose we sit down somewhere?'

They found a bench, in view of the sea and the volcano. The population moved sedately up and down before their eyes.

'Is it always like this?' inquired Mr Heard.

'Spring is a little warmer than usual. Or perhaps one should say that summer has begun earlier. The sirocco is the same, year after year, although there is a kind of conspiracy among the foreign residents to say that it happens to be worse than usual that particular season. It never varies.'

'What does your Perrelli say on the subject?'

Mr Eames glanced at him distrustfully.

'You are trying to chaff me,' he said. 'Serves me right for talking so much this morning. I am afraid I bored you dreadfully.'

The bishop wanted to know.

'Then I may tell you that Monsignor Perrelli does not so much as mention the South wind. He names all the others and has some capital observations on the anchorages of the island as adapted to different winds and seasons. He has also extracted from old chronicles the records of the great storms of 1136, 1342, 1373, 1460, and so on; but never discloses the fact that they all blew from the south. He says the air is pleasant, tempered by gentle breezes from the sea. The word sirocco does not occur in his pages save once, when he laments its prevalence on the mainland.'

'The old humbug!'

A little shiver ran through Mr Eames. Then he observed, in a suave tone of voice:

'He was an historian of the period, an agreeable gentleman telling others of his kind what he knows will be of interest to them. That is what makes his work attractive to me; the personality of the writer. The facts that he records, taken in conjunction with those he slurs over or omits – they give one such an insight into changing human nature! You can construct the character of a man and his age not only from what he does and says, but from what he fails to say and do.'

'Modern historians are not like that,' said Mr Heard. 'They give you the truth to the best of their ability. It is rather dry reading sometimes. I would like to borrow your Perrelli for a day or two, if you don't mind.'

'I'll send it round, together with some old prints of this island and modern photographs. You will then see what I mean. The prints are not exactly true to nature; these people did not want to be true to nature. And yet they convey a better impression of the place than the modern pictures. Perhaps there are two truths: the truth of fact and that of suggestion. Perrelli is very suggestive; romance grafted upon erudition, and blossoming out of it! So imaginative! He has a dissertation on the fishes of Nepenthe – it reads like a poem and is yet full of practical gastronomic hints. Can you picture Virgil collaborating with Apicius?'

The bishop said:

'Horace might have got on better with that old *bon vivant*.'

'Horace could never have had a hand in this chapter. He lacks the idealistic tinge. He could never have written about red mullets as Perrelli writes when he compares their skin to the fiery waves of Phlegethon, to the mantle of rosy-fingered dawn, to the blush of a maiden surprised in her bath, and then goes on to tell you how to cook the beast in thirty different ways and how to spit out the bones in the most noiseless, genteel fashion. That is Perrelli – so original, so leisurely. Always himself! He smiled as he wrote; there is not a shadow of doubt about it. In another section, on the fountains of the island, he deliberately indulges in the humour of some old mediaeval schoolman. Then there is a chapter on the ecclesiastical conditions of the place under Florizel the Fat – it is full of veiled attacks on the religious orders of his own day; I suspect it got him into trouble, that chapter. I am sorry to say there is a good deal of loose talk scattered about his pages. I fear he was not altogether a pure-minded man. But I cannot bring myself to despise him. What do you think? Certain problems are always cropping up, aren't they?'

Mr Eames suddenly looked quite troubled.

'They are,' replied the bishop, who was not in a mood to discuss ethics just then. 'What are you going to do about it?' he added.

'About what?'

'This poetic omission on the part of Perrelli to mention the sirocco?'

'It has given me a deal of extra work, I can assure you. I have had to go into the whole question. I have tabulated no less than fifty-seven varieties of sirocco. Sailors' words, most of them; together with a handful of antiquated terms. Fifty-seven varieties. Twenty-three thousand words, up to the present, dealing with the South wind.'

'That is a fair-sized footnote,' laughed the bishop. 'A good slice of a book, I should call it.'

'My footnotes are to be printed in small type. In fact, I am thinking of casting the whole of this sirocco-material into an appendix. Too much, you think? Surely the number of words is not disproportionate to the subject? The South wind is a good slice of Nepenthe, is it not? ... Look! That cloud has made up its mind to come our way after all. There will be another shower of ashes. Sirocco, you observe. ....'

The terrace, meanwhile, had become crowded. Already the evening sun was slightly obscured behind a brown haze. Ashes were travelling fast. They began to fall, softly.

What was to be done? Everybody, mindful of the previous experience, was in favour of a second procession to take place immediately. The *parroco* held the same opinion. For form's sake, however, he despatched a confidential messenger to learn the views of Mr Parker, who was sitting dejectedly in his study with the incomplete Financial Report still staring him in the face. The Commissioner pulled himself together with praiseworthy alacrity and gave his whole mind to the question.

No. On due consideration, he was opposed to the idea of a procession. Having enjoyed, in various continents and various capacities, some experience of backing the same horse twice over, Mr Parker was not in favour of demanding a second largesse from the Saint. It might spoil everything, he said. Let them wait till next morning. If there was a deep fall like last time, the experiment might be worth trying. But not just yet! While admitting that something ought to be done, it struck him as a hazardous proceeding to play fast and loose, in this fashion, with the reputation of a Saint.

His Reverence, duly impressed, waited for half an hour. It was then seen that the Nicaraguan Representative had once more given the soundest advice. The downpour of ashes ceased abruptly at the moment when the sun sank into the sea. No mischief was done.

Late at night another phenomenon became visible. The volcano was observed to be in violent eruption. It blazed forth like a gigantic torch held into the heavens. Streams of lava poured down the mountain flanks, reddening sky and sea.

Nepenthe was consoled by the spectacle. The demon had at last found an outlet – a method of relief. There would be no more showers of ashes. The fact that villages were being overwhelmed under a deluge of flame, vineyards scorched and hundreds of innocent folk, their retreat cut off by fiery torrents, were even then being roasted to death, was no concern of the islanders. It only proved what every one knew: that the jurisdiction of their Patron Saint did not extend to the mainland.

Each of those villages had its own Saint, whose business it was to forestall accidents of this kind. If they failed in their duty through incapacity or mulishness, nothing was easier than to get rid of them; there were others to choose from – dozens of others, waiting for the job! Thinking thus, the islanders gave vent to an immense sigh of relief. They wished long life to their Patron Saint, with whose services they had reason to be satisfied. Their own crops and lives were safe from harm, thanks to the martyr Dodekanus. He loved his people, and they loved him. He was a protector worthy of the name – not like those low-bred bastards across the water.

CHAPTER 32

MR HEARD had just finished his early Italian luncheon. Sitting at his coffee and smoking a cigarette, in a mood of considerable contentment, he gazed over the mirror-like surface of the sea towards the volcano, whose pyrotechnical display on the previous evening had kept him awake to a late hour. Yet another glistering day! Each one warmer than the last, and never a change in the wind! Presently he would retire for an hour or two into his cool and darkened bedroom.

One little thing troubled his mind. There had been no reply to the note – a kind note of inquiry – which he had left at the Villa Mon Repos on the preceding day. Though he knew little of his cousin, he could not help feeling anxious. She was all by herself in that lonely little place, suffering – perhaps, and too proud or too shy to complain. Mr Eames' description of her had made him uneasy. Why should she look as if she had seen a ghost? What could that signify? The bibliographer was a level-headed person, by no means given to flights of imagination. Imperceptibly, he felt, there had been established an under-current of sympathy between himself and this solitary woman, whom everybody seemed to like. She was different from the ordinary type; the kind of woman whom a man could not help respecting. She contrasted favourably with some of his recent female acquaintances who, however charming or witty, dissatisfied him in this or that particular. His cousin's devotion to child and husband appealed to his heart. She seemed to be perfect of her kind.

Africa had boiled most of the starch out of Mr Heard. But his acquaintance with some of the saddest and wildest aspects of womanhood only deepened his conviction of the sanctity of the sex. Some called him old-fashioned or quixotic, because he was not altogether in sympathy with modern feministic movements; they called him an idealist, because he had preserved his belief in the sacred mission of women upon earth – his childlike faith in the purity of their souls. They were a humanizing influence, the guardian angels of mankind, the inspirers, the mothers, the protectors of innocence. It pleased him to think that woman had softened harsh dealings between man and man; that every mitigation of savagery, every incitement to worthy or heroic actions, was due to her gentle words, her encouraging example. From the very dawn of history woman had opposed herself to deeds of violence. What was it Count Caloveglia had said? 'Temperance. All the rest is embroidery.' How well the old man could put things! Temperance. ... His cousin, from what he could guess of her character, agreed with that description. Mr Heard would have maintained against the whole world that a woman, a true woman like this, could do no wrong.

And now he gathered that she was in trouble of some kind. Then why not allow him to help? He had asked for an early reply to his note. Well, perhaps it would arrive by the evening post.

Slightly vexed none the less, he laid down the stump of his cigarette, preparatory to retiring for the hot hours of the day. One owes something to oneself, *n'est-ce pas?* At that moment there was a knock at his door.

Denis entered. His face, shaded under a broad-brimmed hat, was ruddy with the heat. He wore light flannels, and was carrying his jacket on his arm. There was a large parcel in his hand. He looked the picture of health.

261

Mr Heard, on rising, gave him a critical glance. He remembered his trip in the boat, and the suicide's rock – that black, ominous cliff; he remembered the thoughts which had passed through his mind at the time. Was this the kind of boy to kill himself? Surely not. Keith must have been mistaken. And Count Caloveglia – was he mistaken too? Evidently. There was nothing tragic about Denis. He was brimming over with life. His troubles, whatever they were, must have been forgotten.

'I've been lunching with Keith,' he began. 'He made me tell him a fairy-tale.'

'Sit down and have some coffee! You came away very early.'

'He told me he wanted to go to sleep after luncheon. And one or two other nice things.'

Ah, thought Mr Heard, Keith was acting up to what he had said in the boat; he was being good to the boy; that was right of him.

'I'm sure,' he said, 'that Keith has been speaking kindly to you.'

'Kindly? It's like talking to an earthquake. He told me to dominate my reflexes. He called me a perambulating echo. He said I was a human amoeba –'

'Amoeba. What's that?'

'A sort of animal that floats about trying to attach itself to something which it can't find.'

'I think I see what he means. Anything else?'

'He said I was a chameleon.'

'A chameleon!'

'A chameleon that needed the influence of a good woman. Then he gave me this box of Cuban chocolates, to keep me from crying, I suppose. Have one! They're not nearly as nasty as they look.'

'Thanks. A chameleon. That is really interesting, as Keith would say. I have seen thousands of them. Outlandish beasts, that anchor themselves by their tails and squint horribly. Let's have a good look at you, Denis. No, I fail to detect any striking resemblance.'

'I believe he meant that I take on the colour of other people and have none of my own. Then he told me to go and murder somebody.'

'I wouldn't do that, Denis,' laughed the bishop. 'Murders are so dreadfully vulgar.'

'He said it might make a man of me. He forgets that I'm not quite his age.'

'You had better not tell him that! Any other advice?'

'Nothing new. He said I made a mistake in paying attention to what human beings said and did, and that I ought to forsake mankind for a while, and art and books and so on. You know the way he talks! He said it would give me a stronger individuality if I came into contact with nature and thought things out for myself instead of listening to other people. He advised me to sit among the rocks at midnight and in the hot afternoons, conversing with the genii of earth and air. It would correct my worldly perspective. I think he may be right, in a way. There is something in it. So I asked him to climb into the hills with me, then and there, in order to get into touch with elemental Powers. He said he thought highly of my character, but as to climbing about in this heat – he said he'd be damned if he would. Those were his very words. He wanted to sleep. He was too old for that sort of thing.'

'Very sensible, I'm sure.'

'You think so? Because then – then he told me that you were the proper person for an expedition of that kind. He suggested I should come and see you about it at once – it would allow him time to get his usual afternoon nap. That is why I'm here. So do! It isn't so very hot, once you get used to it. We are sure to see something funny.'

'Oh!'

This, thought the bishop, was a pretty example of that doctrine of benevolent egotism which Keith had expounded to him once or twice. A very pretty example!

'He said that?'

Denis nodded.

The notion was distasteful to Mr Heard. To go out into this torrid sunshine. ... He, too, was not exactly young; moreover, he was still rather delicate – he needed all the rest he could get. He was looking forward with positive delight to the coming hours in his cool bedroom.

'You really want me to climb to the top of a mountain at this hour of the day and sit there in the heat, waiting for some wretched demon to reveal himself? Aren't you a little too old for that sort of thing? Come now! Does it strike you as a reasonable proposition? With the thermometer at seventy-eight in this room?'

'Keith said you liked nothing better. He said you might take offence if I didn't ask you to come.'

He seemed to be disappointed.

There were not many people for whom Mr Heard would have put himself out just then in that particular way; and Denis, up to a few days ago, was certainly not one of them. The bishop had never been drawn towards this rather precious youth. He was not Mr Heard's type of boy. There was a lack of grit and stamina about him – something soft, both in manner and appearance; something dreamy, ambiguous, almost epicene. Mr Heard had not quite lost his old British instinct as to the fundamental useless-ness of all art. A young fellow who, instead of taking up some rational profession, talked about Cimabue and Jacopo Bellini ... there was something not quite right with him. Jacopo Bellini! But even while thinking what to reply, he was conscious of having undergone a slight change of feeling lately. He was growing more tolerant and benign, even in trifles like this. Jacopo Bellini: why not? Meanwhile, he bethought himself of a way of escape.

'Suppose you go alone? Or why not try the midnight expedi-tion first? I might manage midnight.'

'I've tried it.'

'Alone?' he laughed. 'No success?'

'None whatever,' said Denis. And it seemed as if a shadow flitted across his face at these words.

That cloud, that change of tone – what did they portend? Some-thing might be wrong, then, after all. Perhaps Keith had been cor-rect in his diagnosis when he observed that a susceptible mind like this could be shaken out of its equilibrium by the influence of Nepenthe – 'capable of anything in this clear pagan light'. It was not Mr Heard's habit to probe into the feelings of others – as to those of a person like Denis he did not pretend to understand them. Artistic people! Incalculable! Inconsequential! Irrespon-sible! Quite another point of view! Yet he could not help thinking of that doleful black rock, with the turquoise-tinted water at its foot. Remembering these things he felt a sudden access of sym-pathy towards this lonesome fellow-creature. Instead of pursuing the subject of the expedition he asked, quite abruptly:

'Tell me, Denis, are you happy here?'

'How odd that you should come with that question! I had a letter from my mother this morning. She wants to know the same thing. And hanged if I know what to say.'

Mr Heard made up his mind.

'Hanged if you know? Then I'll tell you. Write to say that you have met the Bishop of Bampopo, who seems a perfectly respect-able old fellow. Uncommonly respectable! Tell her you rather like him. Tell her she can find out all about him in Crockford or the Red Book. Tell her that he will be happy to correspond with her, if she will allow it. Tell her you feel sure he will look after you these last few days, before we all go away. Tell her – oh, everything nice you can think of. You'll do that, won't you? And now I will climb any mountain you like. Where are we going?'

'I have thought of a good place. Rather high up, but well worth it. I feel sure something funny is going to happen today. Don't you notice a kind of demonic influence in the air?'

'I notice a kind of infernal heat, if that is the same thing. Seventy-eight in this room! You will have to walk slowly. I am not in good condition just yet. Wait a moment. I must take my field-glasses. I never go without them.'

Mr Heard, resigned to his fate, was filled at the same time with anxiety. He could not drive Keith's words out of his head. Perhaps Denis was really up to some mischief. Who could tell? His eagerness – his curious language! The manifest absurdity of the whole enterprise! That note of exaltation in his voice. ... And what did he mean by saying that something funny would happen? Was he contemplating –? Above all, his dread of being unaccompanied! Mr Heard was aware that persons of unbalanced mind are apt to experience before some critical outbreak a pathetic terror of solitude, as though, dimly conscious of what was about to happen, they feared to trust themselves alone.

He meant to keep a sharp eye on Denis.

Often, in later times, he recalled that trivial conversation. Every word of it was graven on his memory. How more than strange that Denis should have dragged him away that afternoon, to that particular spot, at that very hour! By what a string of accidents had everything happened. ...

CHAPTER 33

IT was nearly two o'clock. To step out of doors was like passing into a furnace. Streets were deserted. The houses showed glaring white against the cobalt of the firmament; their inhabitants lay asleep within, behind closed shutters. Heat and silence brooded over the land.

Climbing slowly aloft by a lava-paved lane they reached the bibliographer's residence and paused awhile near its entrance. Mr Heard tried to picture the scholar's life in this two-roomed cottage; he regretted having had no chance of visiting that amiable person in his own abode. (Mr Eames was chary of issuing invitations.) A life of monastic severity. There was a small outhouse attached to one side of the wall; it was the kitchen, Denis explained; Eames' only servant being a boy whom he borrowed for an occasional morning's work from a neighbouring farm which supplied him with dairy produce.

'It isn't often used, that kitchen,' said Denis. 'He lives mostly on bread and milk. Does his own marketing in the early hours. I met him one day before breakfast, walking with a large brown basket on his arm. Said he was buying anchovies. There was a big haul of them overnight. He had heard about it. A penny a pound, he said. I noticed some lettuce as well. A couple of oranges. Fine chap! He knows what he wants.'

The bishop looked over the gate. An air of friendly seclusion reigned in this place. There was no pretence at a garden – not so much as a rose tree or a snapdragon; the vines, of daintiest green but sternly utilitarian, clambered up to the door-lintel, invading the very roof. He pictured to himself the interior. Bare walls and floorings, a print or two, a few trunks and packing cases utilized as seats, a bookshelf, a plain table littered with manuscripts; somewhere, in that further room, a camp bedstead whereon this man of single aim and purpose, this monk of literature, was even then at rest like all sensible folk, and dreaming – dreaming, presumably of footnotes. Happy mortal! Free from all superfluities and encumbrances of the flesh! Enviable mortal! He reduced earthly existence to its simplest and most effective terms; he owed no man anything; he kept alive, on a miserable income, the sacred flame of enthusiasm. To aspire, that was the secret of life. Thinking thus, Mr Heard began to understand the bibliographer's feelings for Mrs Meadows. She lived for her child – he for his work. They were alike; calm and self-contained, both of them; incapable of illusions, of excess in thought or conduct.

Without the doorway, in a small triangle of shade, sat his fox-terrier, alert, head poised on one side in knowing fashion, ready to bark if the visitors only touched the handle of the gate. Denis remarked:

'He told me that dog was sick the other morning, just like Keith.'

'It had probably been eating something. I suppose they generally do,' he added thoughtfully. 'Otherwise they couldn't be unwell, could they? What a heat, Denis! It's addling my old brains. More slowly, please.'

An hour went by. Fatigue was beginning to tell upon Mr Heard. They had left the cultivated ground behind and were now ascending, by a cindery track of pumice-stone, among grotesque blocks of lava and scoriae that glowed like molten metal. Tufts of flowery broom scented the air. The soil, so recently drenched by the mira-

culous shower of rain, was once more dry and dusty; its fragile
flowers wilted in the sirocco. And still the young man marched
ahead. Always upwards! The landscape grew more savage. They
bent round a corner and found themselves skirting a precipice. The
bishop glanced down in trepidation. There lay the sea, with not a
boat in sight. As he continued to look the horizon oscillated; the
ground sank under his feet and blue waters seemed to heave
and rise up towards him. He shut his eyes in a fit of dizziness and
grasped a rock. Its burning touch revived him.

Then on again. Always upwards.

'Do walk a little more slowly,' said the bishop, puffing and
wiping his face. 'We must be well above the level of the Old
Town by this time. A wild scramble. How much higher are we
going?'

'Here we are. This is the place I meant.'

'Charming, I must say! But aren't we a little too near the edge
of the cliff? It makes me feel funny, as if I were in a balloon.'

'Oh, we'll get used to it. Let's sit down, Mr Heard.'

Still distrustful of his companion, the bishop made himself comfortable and glanced around. They were high up; the view em-
braced half the island. The distant volcano confronting him was
wreathed in sullen grey smoke that rose up from its lava torrent,
and crowned with a menacing vapour-plume. Then an immensity
of sea. At his feet, separated from where he sat by wide stony
tracts tremulous with heat, lay the Old Town, its houses nestling
in a bower of orchards and vineyards. It looked like a shred of
rose-tinted lace thrown upon the landscape. He unravelled those
now familiar thoroughfares and traced out, as on a map, the more
prominent buildings – the Church, the Municipality, the old Benedictine Monastery, where Duke Alfred, they say, condescendingly
invited himself to dine with the monks every second month in such
state and splendour that, the rich convent revenues being exhausted, His Highness was pleased to transfer his favours to the
neighbouring Carthusians, who went bankrupt in their turn; he
recognized Count Caloveglia's place and, at the farther outskirts,
the little villa Mon Repos.

Where was she now, his cousin?

Reposing, no doubt, like all sensible folk.

And his eye wandered to the narrow pathway along the precipice where he had walked with her in the evening light – that pathway which he had suggested railing in, by reason of its dangers. A
section of the horrible face of the cliff was exposed, showing that
ominous coloration, as though splotched with blood, which he

had noticed from the boat. The devil's rock! An appropriate name. 'Where the young English lord jump over ...'

It was the stillest hour of the day. Not a soul in sight. Not a particle of shade. Not a breath of air. A cloudless sky, of inky blueness.

To Mr Heard's intense relief, Denis had settled down, apparently for ever. He lay on his stomach like a lizard, immovable. His head, sheltered by a big hat, rested upon his jacket which he had rolled up into a sort of cushion; one bare sunburnt arm was stretched to its full length on the seared ground. What a child he was, to drag one up to a place like this in the expectation of seeing something unearthly! Mr Heard was not quite satisfied about him. Perhaps he was only feigning.

Time passed. Do what he would to keep awake, the bishop felt his eyelids drooping – closing under the deluge of light. Once more there approached him that spirit of malevolence brooding in the tense sunny calm, that baleful emanation which seemed to drain away his powers of will. It laid a weight upon him. He fell into an unquiet slumber.

Presently he woke up and turned sharply to look at his companion. Denis had not stirred an inch from his voluptuous pose. A queer boy. Was he up to some mystification?

The landscape all around was scarred and deserted. How silent a place can be, he thought. An unhealthy hush. And what a heat! The lava blocks – they seemed to smoulder and reel in the fiery glare. It was a deathly world. It reminded him of those illustrations to Dante's *Inferno*. He thought to see the figures of the damned, writhing amid tongues of flame.

His glance fell once more upon the villa of his cousin. Strange! There were two persons, now, walking along the edge of the cliff. Mere specks. ... He took up his glasses. The specks resolved themselves into the figures of Mrs Meadows and Mr Muhlen.

The devil! he thought. What's the meaning of this?

They were moving up and down, at the same spot where he had moved up and down with her. They seemed to be on friendly terms with one another. Excellent terms. It looked as if they were laughing now and then, and stopping occasionally to glance at something, some book or other object, which the lady carried in her hand. The devil! At times his cousin seemed to be dangerously near the edge – he caught his breath, remembering that sensation of giddiness, of gulping terror, with which he had watched the falcon swaying crazily over the abyss. She was enjoying it, to all appearances. Then, as they retraced their steps, it was the man's turn to take the outside of the path. He suffered as little as she did, evidently, from vertigo. Laughing, and gesticulating. The devil! What were they talking about? What were they doing there, at this impossible hour of the day? Five or six times they went to and fro; and then, suddenly, something happened before Mr Heard's eyes – something unbelievable.

He dropped his glasses, but quickly raised them again. There was no doubt about it. Muhlen was no longer there. He had disappeared. Mrs Meadows was walking down towards her villa, in sprightly fashion, alone.

Mr Heard felt sick. Not knowing exactly what he was about, he began to shake Denis with needless violence. The young man turned round lazily, flushed in the face.

'Where – what –' he began. 'Rather funny! You saw it too? Oh, Lord! You've woke me up. What a bother. ... Why, Mr Heard, what's the matter with you? Aren't you feeling well?'

The bishop pulled himself together, savagely.

'Touch of the sun, I daresay. Africa, you know! Perhaps we ought to be going. Give me your arm, Denis, like a good boy. I want to get down.'

He was dazed in mind, and his steps faltered. But his brain was sufficiently clear to realize that he was face to face with an atrocious and carefully planned murder.

CHAPTER 34

ALL the traditions of his race, the uprightness of ages of decent law-abiding culture, the horror of the pure for what is impure rebelled against this thing which nothing but the testimony of his own eyes could have made him believe. He felt humiliated, as though he had received a blow; inclined to slink about and hide his face from other men. There was contamination in the mere fact of having been a witness. Oh, it was villainous. How carefully the hour and place had been chosen!

And he himself, during that evening walk, had given her the idea. He had said how easily a man could be thrown over at that spot. Very simple. ...

His mind would clear up, maybe, in course of time. Meanwhile he remembered about Retlow – *alias* Muhlen. It came to him in a flash. The man was his cousin's first husband; possibly her only legal husband, seeing that she may not have been able to secure sufficient evidence against him to justify a divorce – had, indeed, lost sight of the scoundrel altogether for several years prior to her elopement with young Meadows. It might well be that Muhlen had heard somehow or other of her presence on Nepenthe, and gone there for the purpose of renewing acquaintance with her. But this foul crime! For it cannot have been a sudden impulse on her part. She had been playing with him – leading him on. His visits to the Old Town, at that quiet hour of the day. ... No. She had carried out her infamous plan after ample premeditation.

Mr Heard stayed at home, burdened with a hideous secret. Practical questions began to assail him. What should he do? Wait! he concluded. Something would be sure to turn up. He was too dazed to think clearly, as yet. He also disliked that fellow. But one does not murder a man because one happens to dislike him. One does not murder a man ... foolish words, that kept on repeating themselves in his mind.

To pardon – yes. Mr Heard could pardon to any extent. The act of pardoning: what did it imply? Nothing more than that poor deluded mortals were ever in need of sympathy and guidance. Anybody could pardon. To pardon was not enough for a man of Mr Heard's ruthless integrity. He must understand. How understand, how interpret, a dastardly deed like this? What could her motives have been? Of what act or proposal could the man have been guilty to merit, even in her eyes, a fate such as this? For evidently, one does not murder a man because one happens to dislike him –

Denis came to inquire in the course of the morning. He was anxious to know how the bishop was feeling after yesterday's attack of sunstroke.

'I have been blaming myself bitterly for dragging you out,' he began. 'I – really –'

'Don't think about it! I shall be better soon. I'll remain indoors today.'

'You are not looking quite yourself just yet. What a fool I was! I can't tell you how sorry I am.'

'Not worth talking about. You'll stay to luncheon?'

The news of Muhlen's disappearance was spread about that same evening, and created no surprise whatever. Foreigners had a knack of coming to the island and mysteriously vanishing again; it was quite the regular thing to run up accounts all round and then clear out. Hotel-keepers, aware of this idiosyncrasy on the part of distinguished guests, arranged their scale of charges accordingly; they made the prices so high that the honest paid for the dishonest, as with English tailors. The other tradespeople of the place – the smiling confectioner, the simple-minded bootmaker, and good-natured stationer, the ever-polite hosier – they all worked on the same principle. They recouped themselves by fleecing the more ingenuous of their clients.

In the case of Muhlen's occultation there was even less surprise than usual. Everybody, judging by his lavish display of gold and showy manner, expected him to depart sooner or later in the orthodox manner – at night-time, by means of a sailing-boat secretly hired – conscientiously prepaid. His more intimate friends, the Magistrate and the Commissioner, were less surprised than anyone else. True, Signor Malipizzo was somewhat hurt, because Muhlen had practically invited him to stay at his own native town, where every kind of amusement was to be had, the female society being of the choicest. Exuberant women – and rich! It would have been a pleasant change after the trim but tedious gardens of Salsomaggiore. He had strong hopes, however, of receiving a letter from some safe place outside the dominions, making an appointment for the holidays. For form's sake, of course, he promptly initiated the ordinary judicial inquiries. It would look well in the records of the Court.

As for Mr Parker, who was brooding in the retirement of his villa whither the news had swiftly spread, he merely thought:

'Got off scot free. And without paying his Club account, I'll bet. Bolted. Lucky devil. That's where the casual visitor has the pull over a resident official like myself. Cleared out! I'm glad I never had any money to lend him. Touched a good few of them, I'll be bound.'

Within an hour or so the magistrate's formal inquiries led to a startling discovery. Muhlen's room in the hotel was broken open, and his property searched. No letters could be found conveying any clue as to his whereabouts. But – what was almost incredible – there was loose money lying about. A more minute investigation proved that the gentleman had dressed himself with considerable care prior to leaving the establishment for the last time. He had changed his socks and other underwear – yes, he had donned a clean shirt. The old one, blue-striped, which he had been seen to wear at breakfast, was lying negligently across the back of a chair with a pair of costly enamelled links, of azure colour to match, in the cuffs. Moreover, in a small box hidden beneath some collars in a drawer were found a few foreign bank-notes, a ring or two, and a handful of gold coins such as he was in the habit of carrying about his person. The judge, who superintended the researches, caused these valuables to be impounded, sealed, and deposited in the Court of Justice.

The discovery put a fresh and ominous complexion on the affair. When a man means to bolt, he does not leave portable jewellery – an enamelled pair of links – behind him. And even if, in the hurry and scurry of departure, he does overlook such elegant trifles, he never forgets to take his money; least of all a man like Muhlen.

A lengthy deposition was signed by the hotel proprietor. It set forth, in reference to Muhlen's general habits, that this gentleman had hitherto not attended to his account; he had not been urgently pressed for a settlement. One did not like to incommode foreign visitors with bills; it annoyed them so much that they sometimes migrated to other hotels and made debts there, debts which in certain unexpected cases were liquidated in full while the former and equally legitimate ones remained unpaid – which was disheartening. In regard to his recent mode of life, the document contained the suggestive fact that Muhlen had not taken his midday meal at the hotel for some time past. He was strangely fond of going out in the late mornings, the proprietor averred; it might be, to bathe; he returned at about five in the afternoon after lunching, presumably, in some small restaurant by the shore.

This declaration, signed by a respected citizen, soon leaked into publicity. Taken in conjunction with the discovery of his money it was an eye-opener to the whole community, and to nobody more than to the judge himself. Signor Malipizzo argued, with his usual penetration, that Muhlen had intended to return to his quarters as he had always done of late. The *animus revertendi* was abundantly proven by the sleeve-links and loose cash. He had not returned. Ergo, he had been prevented from returning. A man is prevented if something untoward happens to him. Ergo, something untoward had happened. Untoward things may be divided, for the sake of convenience, into two main classes, sections, or categories:

1. Accidents.
2. Foul play.

Which was it?

Signor Malipizzo dismissed as untenable the hypothesis of a clandestine withdrawal from local creditors. By way of clearing up the last vestige of doubt, however, and also for the sake of appearances (seeing that a wise magistrate is supposed to take nothing for granted) he called for depositions from the sailors and fishermen. It was a superfluous piece of work, a pure formality; he knew beforehand what they would say. They always said the same thing. They said it. Interrogated on oath they declared, one and all, that no person answering to the description of Muhlen had appeared on the beach for a long time; not for the last eight months and twelve days, to be quite accurate; much less had such a one engaged a vessel. The jovial but conservative sea-folk never varied their utterance on those many solemn occasions when a foreigner, for the purpose of evaporating, paid in advance for the hire of the boat, or was supposed to have done so. Albeit even ignorant people attached no significance to this statement, it went for what it was worth as cumulative evidence.

The sight of that loose cash would have been quite enough for a man of Signor Malipizzo's discernment. Muhlen had not bolted. Nor was he the kind of man to lose his life by an accident. Not he! Muhlen was careful of his skin. Ergo, his disappearance was due to something which came under the second class, section, or category. He had been done away with.

The magistrate, thinking of those summer holidays, began to be really vexed; so did Mr Parker, who soon learned the result of these inquiries and regretted that his mourning retirement prevented him from issuing forth and telling everybody what he thought of this new disgraceful scandal. His English blood revolted at the idea of a harmless tourist, a prominent member of the Alpha and Omega Club, being callously murdered. Would these people never get civilized? He was glad to hear, at all events, that the judge was doing something.

Signor Malipizzo was doing a good deal. He meant to sift the thing to the bottom. His energy, hitherto simulated, was now set genuinely at work to discover indications of the murderer – indications of his missing friend. But Nepenthe is not a good place for finding corpses. The island is full of fathomless rents and fissures. A good many foreigners, especially such as were known to carry loose gold in their pockets, had been suspected of falling into them without leaving a trace behind. Yet a thorough search was instituted, for he knew that criminals were not always as clever as they thought themselves; some insignificant relic might turn up – a shred of clothing or so forth. Such things were occasionally picked up on Nepenthe; nobody knew to whom they belonged. The Cave of Mercury, on being searched, yielded nothing but a trouser button, apparently of English manufacture. Inquiries were also made as to when the ill-starred gentleman had last been seen, and where. Finally, the judge drew up a list, a fairly long list, of all the suspicious characters on the place with a view to placing them under lock and key, in expectation of further developments. Such was the customary procedure; one must assume the worst. If innocent, they might of course regain their liberty in a year or two.

273

It stands to reason that a good many people had noticed Muhlen on the morning of his disappearance. One cannot walk about
Nepenthe at that hour of the day without being seen, and Muhlen
was sufficiently conspicuous. But everyone knew what was in store
for him if he admitted such a fact, to wit, an application of paragraph 43 of the 92nd section of the Code of Criminal Procedure,
according to which any and every witness of this kind is liable to
be segregated from his family and kept under arrest for an indefinite length of time, pending the instruction of a trial which might
take half a century. Nobody, therefore, was fool enough to admit
having encountered him – nobody save a half-witted youth who
fatuously confided to a policeman that he had met the gentleman
somewhere in the neighbourhood of the bibliographer's villa about
the hour of midday. Under ordinary circumstances Signor Malipizzo would have been delighted to lay sacrilegious hands on Mr
Eames, whose olympic aloofness had always annoyed him and
against whom a case could now be got up, on the strength of these
indications. Somewhere in the neighbourhood of his villa – that
was quite sufficient to warrant an arrest.

The boy in question happened to be a relation of his arch-
enemy, the parish priest. Better still. Chuckling at the happy co-
incidence, he forgot all about Mr Eames, and gave orders for the
other to be conveyed to the guardhouse, searched, and interrogated, arguing plausibly that a person of his mental instability
would be sure to give himself away by some stupid remark.

Things turned out better than he had dared to hope. Under the
prisoner's clothing was discovered a gold coin of foreign nationality attached, by a piece of string, round his neck. For all one knew,
it might have been Muhlen's. The interrogating carbineer who is
invested, during such preliminary inquiries, with quasi-judicial
functions – being permitted to assume the rôle of prosecuting or
defending counsel, or to remain sternly unbiased, as he feels inclined – desired to learn how he had come by this jewel.

He received it long ago from his mother, he said, as a talisman
against the moonsickness which had tormented him in childhood.
Replying, in stammering and dazed fashion, to further questions,
he gave it to be understood that nobody had ever set eyes on the
coin in question; he was afraid of showing it, lest someone should
take it from him by force. He loved the coin. He got it from his
mother.

'Ah!' said the friendly policeman. 'And your mother, now –
could she perhaps tell us when she gave it you?'

'My mother is in Paradise.'

'Dead, is she? H'm. That looks queer, my young friend. Very fishy. You should be more careful in little things like that. She ought to have been kept alive, you know. Anybody can say they had gold coins given them by dead mothers, don't you see? Rather a thin trick. Can't you suggest something better? Cheer up, boy! You needn't tremble all over. Look, I am writing it down, and you must put your name to it afterwards. Think a little. A living uncle, for instance – if he came into Court and testified that he had given you the coin, why, it might make all the difference and get you out of a nasty scrape. Surely you've got an uncle or something? How about His Reverence the *parroco*? Couldn't he swear –?'

'My mother is in Paradise.'

'In Paradise, is she? That's where you ought to be, my son. Just sign this declaration, please. Then perhaps you will meet your mother sooner than you expect. Can't read or write? Well, put your cross to it and may the Madonna help you! For I can't. I've done my best to be impartial, but God alone can steer a fool. He makes a speciality of it, they tell me. If so, you've got a sporting chance. ...'

Overjoyed with this incriminating deposition, His Worship gave orders for the prisoner's formal arrest. Aloud he remarked:

'What have I always said? Beware of simple folks. They are the deep ones. Their naïveté is nothing but a disguise. Here we have a case in point. This boy, from all accounts, is the pure type of the callous murderer. He stutters. He makes uncalled-for gurglings of a bestial nature. He has pendulous ears, and certain other stigmata of degeneration which are familiar to all conversant with criminal anthropology. Of course he denies everything. But mark my words! After six or seven months, when the prison diet begins to take effect, he will confess. I know the species; it is all too common. Meanwhile we must congratulate ourselves on having tracked down the culprit so soon.'

To condemn for homicide the cousin of a Catholic priest warmed the cockles of his free-thinking heart. In fact, on second thoughts, it was better than if he had caught the real murderer who might have turned out to be an atheist, which would have been bad enough – or possibly a freemason, which would have been really awkward. The news spread rapidly over the island, and caused wild rejoicings among the anti-clericals.

The rejoicings were of brief duration.

Torquemada, as usual, was in fighting trim. Like all God-fearing ascetics, he was a man-eater at heart. He made up his mind

275

long ago to eat the judge, whom he considered an offence to Heaven and earth – the official mouthpiece of the devil. Up to the present he had bided his time, waiting for a good opportunity. The time was now ripe.

Not that he greatly loved his cousin. The family to which the unhappy youth belonged was of no credit or use to himself, and this particular member was worse than useless, being afflicted with an unpardonable vice – lack of judgement. His stupidity had already got him into a number of minor scrapes. As a child he annoyed foreigners by ingenuous requests for money, stole flowers from neighbours' gardens because they were so irresistibly pretty, tied saucepans to their cats because they had such irresistibly long tails and made such irresistibly droll movements and noises in order to get rid of them, frightened old ladies by making faces at them; sometimes, by way of a change, he threw off a fit; later on, he had taken to smashing crockery, mooning about the vineyards, forgetting errands entrusted to him, throwing stones at passing carriages and making a general nuisance of himself. The *parroco* knew that he had been dismissed as incompetent by tradespeople to whom he was apprenticed, by farmers who had employed him as a labourer. He could not even repeat his Ave Maria without producing sinister crepitations from his gullet. And now he had crowned all by this surpassing act of imprudence. If he had only kept his mouth shut, like everybody else. But there! What could you expect from a fool?

A genuine murderer – it was most irreligious, of course. Still, some homicides were fairly justifiable, others almost meritorious: and a criminal of this kind showed, in every case, undeniable traces of manliness; one could not help respecting him in an oblique sort of fashion. But a fool! Torquemada, the zealous priest, the man of God, could never quite repress the promptings of his blood. He had all the fanatic's appreciation of violent methods; all the southerner's fondness for a miscreant, and contempt for a simpleton. A mere fool – what's the use of him on earth? Had the culprit been any ordinary Christian, His Reverence would not have dreamt of interfering; gladly would he have let him spend the remainder of his days in prison which everybody knew to be the best place for stupid people – it kept them out of mischief.

But this was not an ordinary Christian. He was a relation. A relation! That meant that one must show fight for him, if only for the sake of public appearances.

He held a hurried council with his family and, half an hour later, a second one with the more influential members of the priesthood.

It was decided, in both cases, that the occasion was favourable for a long-deferred contest between the Powers of Light and the powers of darkness, the Catholic Church and modernism, the Clergy of Nepenthe and the secular authority of law and order as personified by that judge in whom all evil, public and private, flowed together. A noble parting cheque which he had just received from Mr van Koppen for some urgent repairs to the parish organ came in handy. It would enable him to face the adversary with good hopes of success. To his friends, he said:

'An insult to my family! I shall not take it lying down. Let them see what a humble servant of God can do.'

So saying, he girded his loins for the fray, walked in person to the post-office and wrote out a lengthy telegram to the redoubtable Don Giustino Morena, the parliamentary representative of Nepenthe, who, as readers of the newspapers were aware, happened to be taking a brief holiday among his own people in the south. It was a judiciously flattering dispatch. It prayed the famous lawyer-politician to undertake the defence of a relation, an orphan, a mere child, unjustly accused of murder and arbitrarily imprisoned, and to deign to accept a pitiful honorarium of five thousand francs – the largest sum which a parish priest, poor but jealous of the honour of his family, could scrape together. If the great man accepted the offer, he might arrive by the next day's boat. There was a chance, thought the *parroco*, of his doing so. Don Giustino was an ardent Catholic; he might be favourably impressed by the modest petition of a clergyman in his constituency. He had promised over and over again to visit his Nepenthean constituents. He would now be killing two birds with one stone.

Five minutes, under ordinary circumstances, were wont to elapse ere an item of private news could percolate out of the post-office and become public property. Such was the portentous import of this message that it did not percolate at all. It flashed, and produced forthwith a feeling of joyous elation at the prospect of lively events in the near future – of a battle between the Vatican and the Quirinal. Coming on the top of Muhlen's murder – which was a decided improvement upon his alleged flight – it caused the citizens to talk in excited and almost random fashion about what was coming next. Alone, the members of the Alpha and Omega Club, thanks to the benign influence of Parker's poison, received the successive waves of information with composure, and preserved from beginning to end their sense of proportion.

'Heard the news? Muhlen's bolted.'

'I thought he would.'

277

'They say he owes a good deal.'

'Obviously. Else he wouldn't have bolted. Good riddance, anyhow.'

'That's what I say. But he owes me a lot of whiskies, the blighter.'

'You're lucky. Gone off with thirty francs of mine.'

'Damn his eyes. I expect we're not the only ones.'

'Not by a long chalk. Come and have a drink. ...'

'Heard the news? Muhlen's murdered.'

'Serve him bloody well right. The blackguard owes me two francs fifty. I'll bet it was some money business.'

'Not a bit of it. A little girl, you know. Got a knife in the stomach. About eleven at night, from all accounts. They heard him squealing a mile off.'

'I don't believe it. He was not that kind.'

'Not that kind? What do you mean?'

'Not that kind.'

'Not *that* kind? Really? Go on. You don't say so, by Jove! What makes you think it?'

'Think? I don't think. I happen to know. You pay for my peg and I'll tell you all about it. ...'

'Heard the news? Don Giustino's coming over.'

'The old assassin. What of it?'

'Good business! One in the eye for Mali – what's his name. There'll be the hell of a row. We ought to be grateful to Muhlen for this amusement.'

'Damned if we ought. Unless he got himself killed on purpose to amuse us. And even then it would have amused me more if he had paid me back those seventeen francs.'

'You're very hard to please today.'

'So would you be, if you'd been as raddled as I was last night. You ought to see the inside of my head, you ought. There's room for a coal barge, in there.'

'That's easily remedied. Toss up for drinks.'

'Don't mind if I do. ...'

Signor Malipizzo heard the news as he was sitting down to luncheon. At first he thought the priest had gone crazy. Don Giustino – good God! Five thousand francs. Where had he found the money? Then he remembered hearing about old Koppen's cheque for the organ. Those confounded foreigners, always mixing themselves up in local concerns! If the *parroco* were really poor, as these hypocrites of Christians professed to be, he could never have run to it. Don Giustino! What an awful turn of events.

And all because Muhlen got himself murdered. These confounded foreigners!

His heart sank within him. He had looked forward to keeping the priest's cousin for a year or two in gaol, previous to his trial. That would have to be altered. If Don Giustino came, the proceedings must be fixed for next morning – it was the merest act of courtesy towards a man of his standing, a man whom one must conciliate at any cost. He blamed himself for arresting that young idiot. It threatened to bring him into undesired prominence. Hitherto, by reason of his sheer insignificance, he had escaped the great Catholic deputy's eye. As Magistrate of Nepenthe who cared what political or religious views he professed or in what manner he administered the law? All this was now changed. He was in the limelight. It might end – who knows where? He had other enemies on the island besides the clericals; the arrival of Don Giustino might lead to a general revision of his judicial labours. To-morrow perhaps he would have to confront the monster. Don Giustino! He knew him by reputation. A camorrista of the blackest dye. He took no chances. He never threatened; he performed. Everybody knew that. Signor Malipizzo did not like the prospect of losing his lucrative job. Still less did he fancy the notion of receiving a charge of buck-shot in his liver, one evening from behind a wall. That was Don Giustino's cheerful way with people who annoyed him. Those infernal clericals; their sanguinary, out-of-date methods! Papacy and Camorra – interconvertible terms – who could plumb their depths? The Masons were different. They fought for the enlightenment of a people deluded by priestly snares and intimidated by the threats of assassins. Don Giustino. Holy Mother of God! What would tomorrow bring?

Thinking thus, the judge eyed his victuals resentfully. His appetite was gone – he was beginning to feel sick. Suddenly he pushed his plate away from him and hobbled out of the room, even forgetting to finish his wine. He limped across the broiling market-place to give the necessary orders to his faithful and experienced clerk who, having likewise got wind of that telegram, was not unprepared for some change of mind on the part of his chief.

'The young idiot must come up for trial tomorrow, if the assassin arrives.'

'A sound suggestion,' the grey-haired one replied. 'It will take the wind out of his sails. It will prove –'

'Of course it will. And now, Don Carlo, go and take your little nap. I will stay here, to put my papers in order. May your dreams be happy!'

The judge was dowered with extreme irascibility of temper, due to his chronic valetudinarian condition. He, too – within the limits of propriety – was not going to take things lying down. So much was certain. At first he was too agitated to be able to collect his thoughts. Gradually, as he moved about those rooms, calmness and confidence returned. He was alone. It was very warm and quiet here, amid these scenes of his many little triumphs. The look of the archives, the familiar smell of the place, were reassuring. He began to feel at ease once more. Ideas came to him.

'They will say I locked him up on account of his clerical connexions. That will never do. I must have non-clerical suspects under arrest, in order to prove that I am impartial and only desirous of eliciting the truth. Whom could we catch? The Russians! They have proved themselves law-breakers and criminals. The Russians! Suspicious characters. Their recent behaviour is quite sufficient for my purpose.'

He signed warrants for the arrest of the Messiah, Krasnojabkin and some fifteen others of those who had escaped his wrath on the previous occasion. They would be under lock and key within two hours. Don Giustino would never interfere on behalf of these aliens. Nor would anyone else. An inspiration! It would proclaim his zeal for the public order – his official independence of mind.

And – yes. There was one other little thing.

He hobbled to where the various *pièces justificatives* were lying in their sealed envelopes. He took up the receptacle containing the gold talisman which had been sequestrated from the priest's nephew, and broke it open. It could always be sealed up again. The coin, attached to its string, fell out; it was an old-fashioned medal – Spanish, apparently. He fingered it awhile. Then, opening the packet which held Muhlen's gold, he carefully examined the contents. Five or six of these coins were of the same kind; French Napoleons. That was lucky. Any stick was good enough to beat a dog with. This was a particularly good stick. He bored a hole through one of the Napoleons and placed it on the culprit's string, after removing the original talisman, which he bestowed in his own pocket. That done, he sealed up the two parcels again, conscientiously.

'There!' he said. 'He laughs best who laughs last. Don Giustino is a clever man. But the devil himself could not prove the prisoner innocent, in the face of evidence like this. Down with the Pope!'

Never had he felt so enlightened, so gloriously freemasonish.

CHAPTER 35

T H E Commendatore Giustino Morena – familiarly known as Don Giustino or, by his enemies, as 'the assassin' – was a southerner by birth, a city product. From low surroundings he had risen to be a prominent member of the Chamber of Deputies and one of the most impressive figures in the country.

As a child he was apprenticed to a cobbler. There, bending over his work on the pavement outside the shop door, his blue eyes and curly fair hair, his rosy cheeks, his winning smile, his precocious retorts, attracted the most favourable comment from the passers-by and secured him an unfailing supply of chocolates and cigarettes. People liked him so much that he quickly learned not only how to mend shoes but a good many other things which they were anxious to teach him. His grown-up friends vied with one another for a place in his affections, and a certain scandalous affair with knives, which somehow or other got into the daily press where it had no business to be, put the seal on his reputation in the quarter.

'That boy will go far!' the old men and women used to say. 'Only look at his blue eyes. Blessed the mother that bore him, whoever she was' – for nobody even pretended to know.

They were right; as old folks are apt to be. The victor in the disreputable affray happened to be a gentleman of middle age, a distinguished ornament of the Black Hand. No happier fate could have been devised for Giustino than to live under the patronage of such an individual. He took charge of the little fellow, and was not slow in discovering that his protégé possessed not only a muscular framework and ready wit, but the malice, the concentrated ruthlessness and rapacity of fifty devils rolled into one. Something could be made out of that boy, he concluded; the Society, always ready to adopt promising neophytes on the recommendation of a qualified practitioner like himself, would doubtless enrol him in due course. Meanwhile he instructed him, by precept and example, how to be religious in the manner most pleasing to the Madonna. He narrated the Lives of the Saints, forced him to attend Mass and confess himself to one of the Society's trusted priests and taught him, above all things, to hate the Government because it oppressed the Pope and the poor. One day he said:

'You must now attend evening classes. I think you will do well at our school of the Holy Cross. Your outfit is exceptional. Among other things you have the great advantage that the first and second fingers of both your hands are of equal length. That augurs well! God has favoured you, for many lads have to lengthen the first one artificially, which is apt to weaken the joints.'

The Master and Director drew good salaries from the numerous pupils at this institution. Everything useful to young boys was taught here save only religion. Seeing that all the scholars were drawn from families distinguished for their piety and adherence to the Pope, the Director considered a religious training to be superfluous – his pupils learnt these things on their mothers' knees. Giustino soon acquired the jargon; he passed his examination in the fifteen articles, in secrecy, swiftness of foot and nimbleness of hand. The latter was taught on a clothed wooden figure out of whose pockets the students were obliged to extract handkerchiefs, gold watches and jewellery with such dexterity that not one of the little bells, which dangled from its hat, gave forth the slightest sound; that stage passed, the art was practised on the person of the Director himself who, walking through the streets as an ordinary citizen, was supposed to have his pockets picked in the approved professional manner. Those who failed to come up to the standard were thrashed savagely three or four times; if they still failed, they were sent back to their parents with a polite recommendation that they should be taught some other trade. Giustino was seldom punished. On the contrary, the Director was so enamoured of his progress and blue eyes that he entered him as a fox long before the regular three years' course was up, and offered to tattoo the symbol of proficiency, a cross, on the back of his right hand.

The patron, while proud of his young friend, did not intend to spoil his chances in after life by an indelible bodily mark of this kind however honourably attained. He had other designs for him. To pass the next year or two, he made arrangements for Giustino, now grown lean and wolfish, to be officially received into the Black Hand. As probationer he was the delight of his superiors; he went through the various tests with phenomenal rapidity and gave abundant proofs of manliness. At the age of sixteen he had already killed three men – one of them being a policeman who was suspected of infidelity towards the Society. It was then that the protector, who was no fool, spake to him a second time, saying:

'As you know, my son, I can neither read nor write. Those were not considered respectable accomplishments, in my day, for a lad of spirit or a man of honour. Devil's work! But we live in an effeminate age. Virtue is at a discount. The wise man, while observing these things with regret, adapts himself to them. He marches with the times. They call us reactionaries. It depends upon boys like you to show the world what reactionaries are good for. The whole town has already learnt to respect your manly instincts. You must now go further and learn to read and write. You will then enter the University. There you will study law and politics. You will then enter Parliament. There you will represent our cause. The means – the money? Trust the Society! Only be a credit to your friends, defend the poor, and never forget to say your prayers. Then the good God will reward your efforts.'

This is precisely what the good God did. Within a short space of time the young deputy had made a name for himself; he was recognized as one of the few representatives of the Black Hand whose word could be implicitly relied upon. He had a share in everything; commissions and percentages poured in upon him. After making an example of half a dozen tiresome persons by having them quietly stabbed or shot – nothing was ever proved against him though everybody knew it was his work – he experienced no further opposition in his political career. Morena never threatens, they said; he performs. A safe man! From a timorous Liberal Government, his avowed enemies, he extorted the title of Commendatore; not because he attached any value to such outward distinctions but because, like a true Camorrista, he never lost an opportunity of showing that he could do what he pleased with everybody, Government included. It was an open secret that the next vacant portfolio of Justice would be at his disposal. All this of course was years and years ago.

To these arts of statecraft he added a quite unusual legal acumen and forensic ability. For the last fifteen years he had been in receipt of large annual retaining fees from the principal commercial firms of the country; that of one shipping company alone amounted to fifty thousand francs. They found it worth their while since, without doing a stroke of work for them, he gave his tacit support to their most nefarious undertakings. A useful man! As a lawyer in private cases his reputation was tremendous. Judges and juries had been known to faint with emotion at his dramatic gestures, his fiery eloquence. He could pull anybody out of a scrape. Wherever he spoke the Court was crowded to listen to his impassioned arguments, to look upon the cold fire in his blue eyes, his carefully adjusted dress, his fair hair turning to grey, his smooth face which he kept shaven for no other reason – so he used to declare – than because he reverenced the fashions of the old papal régime. 'Just like an Englishman,' people said.

He had lately put on flesh; it inspired confidence. Moreover, he never married; that was also something out of the common – it pointed to independence, to lack of ordinary human frailties. In short, he was so perfect a compound of vice and intelligence that even his dearest friends could not put their finger on the exact spot where the one began and the other ended. And the whole of this unique mixture was placed at the disposal of the Vatican. Don Giustino was the implacable enemy of modernism, a living disproof of the vulgar assertion that freemasonry is the sole key to success in modern Italy. A formidable man! And growing more formidable every day, as his wealth increased. His income was already such that he could afford to be honest; nothing but the force of old habits kept him from developing into a positive saint.

It stands to reason that a person of this calibre would have sniffed at a paltry remuneration of five thousand francs offered by an obscure country priest. But Don Giustino was a good son of the Church. He had never forgotten the recommendation of his old patron to succour the humble and distressed; he specialized, as a lawyer, in defending murderers and rescuing them from the secular arm. They were enthusiasts suffering under a sense of wrong; they belonged to the class of the honest poor; they were victims of governmental greed and social injustice. 'Motives, not deeds!' he would say. And the motives of the poor must be judged by other standards than those of the rich. They have other lives, other temptations. Trust the people. The people, under proper guidance of the priests. ...

Although it was hardly likely that the great man would deign to accept Torquemada's invitation, yet half the town was assembled at the harbour to await the arrival of the evening boat and catch a glimpse, if possible, of the famous Camorrista. And there he was! He leaned over the taffrail, easily recognizable from his pictures in the illustrated papers. He was dressed in a felt hat, brown boots, and light grey clothes – just like anybody else Presently he descended to the quay, followed by a tall and solid-looking young valet. He was wreathed in smiles. A whiff of political life, of busy deeds in the capital, exhaled from his person. The Mayor of Nepenthe, a devout Catholic, deferentially shook hands and introduced the *parroco* and other notabilities. They drove up together. It was all delightfully breezy and informal. But men were aware that in this little episode there lurked more than met the eye; that the arrival of Commendatore Morena was an occasion worthy to be chronicled in the annals of the island. Not only was it his first appearance as deputy among his constituents. That alone would have been an event. The avowed purpose of his visit, to rescue a criminal from the properly constituted authorities, gave it the character of a pro-Vatican demonstration – a slap in the face for King and Constitution.

An intimate little dinner had been arranged by the parish priest in order to give the principal clergy and a few favoured laymen of their party an opportunity of paying their respects. No one knew what took place at this repast save that the distinguished guest was in wonderful humour; he joked and laughed and told funny stories; he was enchanted with the wine and the excellent local crayfish and announced his intention of buying a little villa wherein to spend the evening of his days, after his public labours were over. An ideal spot! Lucky people, he called them. It was most unfortunate that he would be obliged to leave by to-morrow's midday boat, and so miss the greater part of the festival of Saint Eulalia.

Another little item of news was allowed to filter out and sedu-lously propagated, to the effect that the Commendatore had re-fused, politely but firmly, to accept any remuneration for his ser-vices. Such a thing could not be thought of! Pleasure and duty rarely coincided as in this case, where it was both a pleasure to come to this charming island and a duty to say a few words in Court about this unfortunate young man – to defend the oppressed to the utmost of his miserable ability, and thereby approve himself a good son of the Church.

'Your servant in everything!' he added. 'And if you would now accept from me a humble donation of one thousand francs to be distributed, as His Reverence thinks best, among the needy poor of Nepenthe, you would indeed make me your debtor for life!'

Such was the great man's speech, as reported. It was a pure in-vention on the part of Torquemada, who, being a high-principled ecclesiastic, had clear-cut orthodox views anent the utility of pious legends. He knew it would sound well among the populace. He hoped it would vex the envious magistrate into a fit of the colic. He argued that the great man himself, in the event of its coming to his ears, would not be otherwise than gratified by a godly fable so strictly in keeping with his character.

Don Francesco alone, the smiling terrestrial beast, the lover of wine and women, held aloof from the entertainment, alleging a gastric indisposition and doctor's orders. He did not see eye to eye with Torquemada on matters such as these. Don Francesco dis-liked all measures of violence, camorra or freemasonry, Vatican or Quirinal – disliked them so much that he would have hated them had he been built, like the *parroco*, on hating lines. He was too

285

unwieldy, too fond of life, too indulgent towards himself and others to experience at mention of Don Giustino's name anything but a certain feeling of discomfort – a feeling which his acute intelligence, embedded under those rolls of fat, enabled him to formulate with warmth and precision.

'I know quite well,' he said to Torquemada, 'that he calls himself a good son of the Church. So much the worse for the Church. I understand he is a prominent member of the Government. So much the worse for the Government. And I realize that, but for his intervention, this harmless individual might spend the remainder of his life in prison. So much the worse for all of us, who derive justice from so tainted a source. As to dining at the same table with him – no. Does not the whole world know his history? The animal! He would make me vomit. And you will believe me when I say, my dear *parroco*, that I do not look my best on such occasions.'

Torquemada shook his head, mournfully. It was by no means the first time that he had suspected his popular colleague of being a lukewarm Christian.

CHAPTER 36

THE market-place was filled to over-brimming. Everybody discussed the near events in the Court of Justice. It promised to be a bad day for Signor Malipizzo. And yet people could not help admitting how clever he had been to lock up those Russians. It was the best thing he could have done under the circumstances. It proved his freedom from anti-Catholic prejudices. It made him look icily objective.

Torquemada, on hearing that the prisoner's gold coin corresponded with those others which had been in the possession of the murdered man, thought it deplorable. Here was plain evidence of his cousin's guilt! Most deplorable. Still, the victim being not only a foreigner but a Protestant was a considerable mitigation of the offence from the moral and religious point of view, and possibly from the legal one as well. Anyhow, what did legal aspects matter? Had he not engaged Don Giustino? Innocent or guilty, the prisoner would be released. And, on second thoughts, he discovered him to be worthy of the great man's golden eloquence. He was not altogether a fool. There was a touch of manliness about him; he was decidedly a brighter lad than he looked. He deserved to be released.

Ten o'clock sounded.

The Court had never been so crowded. There was barely standing room. Sunlight poured in through the windows which had not been cleaned for many long months; the atmosphere was already rather oppressive. It was a stuffy place at all times, reeking of old tobacco smoke and humanity.

Everybody was still save the old grey-headed clerk who fussed about with papers. Signor Malipizzo, after a deferential but dignified bow to the famous lawyer, had taken his seat on the raised platform facing the public whence he was wont to dispense justice. Nailed against the wall, directly over his head, was a large white paper bearing the printed words 'LA LEGGE'; the law. It dominated the chamber. On one side of this could be seen a coloured portrait of the Sovereign in the bersagliere uniform; a fierce military glance shot out of his eyes from under that helmet whose plume of nodding feathers made it look three sizes too large for the head. On the other side hung a representation of the Madonna, simpering benignly in a blue tea-gown besprinkled with pearls and golden lace. The spittoon, which His Worship required continually during the audiences, was wont to be placed immediately below this latter picture; it was the magistrate's polite freemasonish method of expressing his reverence for the Mother of God. Everybody noticed that on the present occasion this piece of furniture was located elsewhere. It stood below the Sovereign's portrait. A delicate compliment to the formidable lawyer-champion of Catholicism, sworn enemy to the House of Savoy. People commented favourably on this little detail. How artful of him! they said.

All eyes were fixed upon Don Giustino. He sat there quietly. If he was bored he certainly did not show it. Now that he was here he would give these good people a taste of his quality. He knew all about the gold coin; he was profoundly convinced of the prisoner's guilt. This was lucky for the young man. Had he thought otherwise he would probably have refused to take up the case. Don Giustino made a point of never defending innocent people. They were idiots who entangled themselves in the meshes of the law; they fully deserved their fate. Really to have murdered Muhlen was the one and only point in the prisoner's favour. It made him worthy of his rhetorical efforts. All his clients were guilty, and all of them got off scot free. 'I never defend people I can't respect,' he used to say.

He began his speech in a rambling, desultory sort of fashion and quite a low tone of voice, as if he were addressing a circle of friends.

A charming place, Nepenthe! He would carry away the

pleasantest memories of its beauty and the kindliness of its inhabitants. It was like a terrestrial paradise, so verdant, so remote from all danger. And yet nothing on earth was secure. That volcanic eruption the other day – what a scare it must have given them! What a lucky escape they had, thanks to the Divine intervention of the Patron Saint! Hardly any damage done; no victims worth mentioning. The fertile fields were intact; mothers and fathers and children could once more go out to their daily tasks and return in the evening, tired but happy, to gather round the family board. Family life, the sacred hearth! It was the pride, the strength, the mainstay of the country; it was the source whence the rising generation drew their earliest notions of piety and right conduct. Nothing in the world could replace home influence, the parent's teaching and example – nothing! And this poor boy, now threatened with imprisonment, had a mother. He had a mother. Did the Court appreciate the import of those words? Did they realize what it meant to shatter that hallowed bond, to deprive the parent of her offspring's help and consolation – the child of its mother's fostering care? Let them consider the lives of all those great men of the past who were known to have had mothers – Themistocles, Dante, Virgil, Peter the Hermit, and Madame de Maintenon – why had they achieved distinction in the world? What was the secret of their greatness? A mother's affectionate guidance in youth. They had not been torn, as children, from her loving arms.

A good many people were already sobbing. But the orator had noticed that something was wrong. He consulted a small scrap of paper and then continued in the same conversational tones as before.

He had no mother. He was an orphan. An orphan! Did the Court realize what it meant? No, he dared not ask them to picture to themselves all that was implied in that bitter word. An orphan. Nobody to instil those early lessons of piety ... to grow up wild, neglected, despised. ... It was impossible for a man to avoid going astray in such terribly unnatural conditions. Everybody else had parents to counsel and direct them; he alone was bereft of this blessing. It was cruel, it was illogical, to apply the same standard to him as to those fortunate other ones. Let the Court call to mind the names of those who had deviated from the narrow path of duty; did they not all belong to this unhappy class? It might safely be inferred that they had no mothers! Such persons were to be pitied and helped, rather than condemned for what was the fault not of their natures but of their anomalous situation in life. To rescue a motherless young soul from the brink of perdition was the noblest task of a Christian. And this was still, thank Heaven, a Christian country, despite the ever-swelling invasion of that irreligious foreign element which threatened to break up the old faith in God. The Madonna was still worshipped; together with the Saints. Their precious relics and other holy amulets still proved their efficacy in the hour of danger.

Amulets – ah, that reminded him.

To kill a man with a view to possessing yourself of his substance was an unpardonable crime. Now what had this boy done? Let them take the so-called robbery first. Well, no robbery had been committed, in spite of the notorious fact that this Protestant, this foreigner was known to be loaded with money. His client had fought down the temptation, the almost irresistible temptation, of appropriating the gold. Let them remember that! The minutest investigation failed to reveal anything save a single coin which he had attached to a string and hung about his neck. Motives, not deeds! What were his motives for this strange act? An unconscious application of the homoeopathic principle. He had taken it as a safeguard, an amulet, in the childish belief that it might protect him on future occasions against insults such as those he had undergone.

Then, while the audience were still puzzling what the last words meant, he suddenly indulged in one of those abrupt transitions for which he was famous, and burst out:

'Down with foreigners! We Catholics know what foreigners are, how they work for evil in places high and low. One cannot take up a daily paper without seeing some exposure of their many-sided viciousness. They contaminate the land with their godless depravity. Nobody can count on immunity. The highest officials in the land, the very Ministers of the Crown, are subjected to their vile disguised attempts at bribery and corruption; no humble peasant girl, no child, is safe from the befoulment of their filthy minds. We know them – our police records, the archives of our Courts of Justice, testify to their demoralizing agency. A pest, a contagion! Who can tell what proposals were made in this particular case – what degrading proposals, backed by the insidious offer of foreign gold? A weak character might have succumbed. But the victim was made of different stuff. He belonged to another type – the heroic type. Suffering anguish of soul, he yet preferred honour to baseness. In self-defence –'

At this point the great Deputy ceased to speak. Signor Malipizzo had swooned away. He had to be carried out of Court.

It mattered little, for the proceedings were at an end, save for a few formalities. The case was won.

289

People were rather annoyed at being deprived of one of Don Giustino's far-famed perorations. It could not be helped. Better luck next time. Then they asked themselves why the Judge had fainted. Some thought it might be the heat, or a touch of his old complaint. The majority were agreed that the attack was due to the Deputy's eloquence. And it was true that he was greatly impressed by the speech, but not quite as much as all that. He had decided to faint at a critical moment, for the sake of appearances. It was clever of him. He did it beautifully too; he had been rehearsing half the night. Don Giustino, on his part, shared the common opinion and was charmed with this tribute to his genius. Altogether, the local judge had made a favourable impression on him; his attitude had been irreproachably correct. He was not a bad fellow, for a freemason. One might do worse than leave him in possession of his present appointment on Nepenthe.

The Deputy freed his prisoner; it was unavoidable. But the Russians remained in gaol, and this was always something to the credit of Signor Malipizzo. ...

Madame Steynlin, on hearing of Peter the Great's arrest, was stricken dumb. She wept the bitterest tears of all her life. Then, with returning calmness, she remembered Mr Keith, whose friendship with the magistrate was the common talk of the place. Would he be able to do anything? Impulsive by nature, she called on that gentleman and poured out her griefs to him. Mr Keith was sympathetic. He declared he understood perfectly. He promised to do his utmost, that very day.

The Master, meanwhile, languished in prison. He had nobody to take his part, not even among the Little White Cows; the new section, that clique of young extremists, were only too delighted to have him out of the way. The communal doctor alone interceded on his behalf, imploring the judge in the name of the sacred brotherhood of freemasons that he, the Messiah, should be excarcerated in order that he, the physician, might be enabled to continue the daily treatment to which the old man had grown accustomed and for which he was being regularly remunerated. 'Think of my wife and children!' he said to the magistrate.

Signor Malipizzo on this occasion did not mean to be baulked of his prey. He was in bad humour; Don Giustino had got on his nerves. By means of a lightning-like discharge of symbols intelligible only to the Elect he retorted that a physician, who depended for his livelihood upon a legitimate practice among *bona fide* patients, was not fit to be a freemason.

Then the doctor urged the humanitarian aspects of the case.

The old man needed the treatment which could be given in prison just as well; the fees would doubtless be paid sooner or later.

The magistrate proved inexorable, adamantine. What was good enough for a native, he argued, was good enough for a vicious old alien. A stomach-pump in prison! What more? They would be wanting fried fish and asparagus next.

As a special concession to the Master's age and rank a separate upper chamber, described as very airy, had been allotted to him in the local gaol. The poor old man did not know how he got there; they had thrust him into this strange place and locked the door on him. Long hours had passed. He sat on an uncomfortable cane-bottomed chair, his hands folded across his stomach. There was already a slight sense of oppression in that region of his body. His head, too, felt heavy. Without knowing how or why, he had fallen into a trap, after the manner of some dumb beast of earth. When would they take him out again? And when would that kind gentleman with the machine arrive?

Daylight entered through a small but thickly grated window. Looking out from where he sat, he could detect neither men nor houses nor trees – nothing but four rectangular patches of deep blue. The sea! Often had he wondered about the sea, and why it was there. It had ever been an enigma to him, this purposeless mass of water. Not even good to drink. He knew nothing of those fables of the pagans – of old Poseidon and white-armed Leucothea and the blithe crew of Triton and silver-footed Thetis moving upon the placid sunlit waters; nothing of that fair sea-born goddess whose beauty swayed the hearts of men. His Venus ideals had been of a more terrestrial nature – the wives or daughters of army generals and state functionaries who desired advancement, and sometimes got it.

Not even good to drink! There was nothing like this in Holy Russia. God would never have allowed it. The uselessness of this sea had always been to him a source of perplexity and even vague apprehension. The spectacle of this shining immensity troubled his world-scheme. Why did God create water, when land would have been so much more useful? Often had he puzzled on the subject. ... Why?

But now, in the evening of his life and the extremity of his anguish, the truth was made manifest. A revelation drew nigh. It just came to him.

The fishes.

It was a dying gleam of intelligence, his last inspired thought, his swan-song. How else could the fishes live save in the water?

291

All these long years he had remained ignorant of the truth. Ah, if only his disciples were at hand, to jot it down into that *Golden Book*!

But why – why must the fishes live in water? And why so much water for so few fishes? Why cannot fishes live on land? Then everybody would be satisfied. Inscrutable are the ways of God. ...

And his glazed eye moved wearily from that disquieting expanse of blue along the wall of his chamber which had once been white and was now scrawled over with obscene jests and drawings, product of the leisure hours of generations of prisoners. The writing, like all writing, was unintelligible to him. But some of the artistic efforts left little to the imagination. He was saddened, less by homely pictures than by the unfamiliar script. He had always distrusted the written word. Why all these strange letterings – so unnecessary, so dangerous to the life of an orthodox Christian? What one brother has to tell another – why write it down?

He saw the straw pallet destined for his nocturnal repose. It reminded him dimly of a similar resting-place during his monastic life. Then, too, he had slept on a couch near the floor. Flickering visions came to him of those days, so long ago, ere yet the First Revelation was given to the world. A breath of old Russia was wafted into his nostrils. He remembered the lusty, jovial country folk, the songs and dances at hay-making, the fragrance of the land, the sluggish rivers rolling their brown mud about the plains, the mild long-drawn evenings. He felt again that all-pervading charm of sadness, of tender yearning, that hangs in the pale Russian sky and penetrates to the very soul of that endless country.

Gloomy autumn days – wet leaves and lowering horizons. The long winter within doors. Faces appeared to him, faces of old, an endless procession of faces clear-cut as ever ... his brother monks, bearded and unkempt ... debauched acolytes ... pilgrims from the Holy Land ... glittering festal robes ... vodka orgies, endless chants and litanies, holy lamps burning, sombre eikons with staring eyes ... the smell of greasy luke-warm cabbage soup, of unwashed bodies and boot leather and incense. Holy Russia – it all moved before his eyes in a kind of melodious twilight. Then the First Revelation. The Man-God.

Man-God. The word filtered through his intelligence. How strange it sounded. The Man-God – what could it mean?

A sudden change. A life of glory and intrigue. Food on platters of gold, sparkling wines and laughter. A diamond cross, an imperial gift, the reward of faithful services. Everybody cringing.

Showers of bribes. Women – always women. A divine life! Nothing but women. ...

Darkness. Something had happened; they had carried him into a place full of endless penances, floggings, starvings. Then they accused him of doing wrong. What was it? The flesh of warm-blooded beasts. ... He had preferred the service of God to that of his earthly master. For this they banished him and made him suffer. He was dying now – dying to save mankind. He was giving up his life for sinners. Someone else had once done the same thing. Who was it? He could not remember. People who read and write – they know these things. Some saint, possibly; or at least a man from another province – someone he had never met or spoken to. A good Russian, whoever it was. But the name – the name had slipped out of his mind. He always had a good memory for faces, but a bad one for names.

He was so ill and oppressed too. Worse than before. He felt himself rotting earthwards, like a fungus of his own native forests under autumn rains. His body remained inert but his eye, roaming away from the straw pallet, fixed itself upon the door. When, when would that kindly gentleman with the instrument arrive?

CHAPTER 37

CONCERNING the life and death of Saint Eulalia, patroness of Nepenthean sailors, we possess ample and accurate information.

She was born in 1712 at a remote village in the Spanish province of Estremadura. Various divine portents accompanied her birth. Her mother dreamed a strange dream about a sea-serpent; her father was cured of a painful gouty affection; the image of Saint James of Compostella in the local church was observed to smile benignly at the very hour of her entry into the world. At the age of two years and eleven months she took the vow of chastity. Much difficulty was experienced in keeping the infant alive; she tormented her body in so merciless a fashion. She refused to partake of food save once in every five weeks; she remained immovable 'like a statue' for months on end; she wore under her rough clothing iron spikes which were found, after death, to have entered deeply into her flesh. She was never known to use a drop of water for purposes of ablution or to change her underwear more than once a year, and then only at the order of her confessor who was obliged to be in daily contact with her. The heat of her body was such that it could not be touched by human hands. During her frequent trances she spoke accurately in sixty-nine different languages; there was no hair whatever on her head, which was 'spotless as an egg'. She put baskets of sea urchins into her bed and, as a penance for what she called 'her many sins', forced herself to catch the legions of vermin that infested her brown blanket, count them, separate the males from the females, set them free once more, and begin over again. She died at the age of fourteen years and two months. Her corpse forthwith became roseate in colour, exhaled a delicious odour of violets for twenty weeks, and performed countless miracles. On dissection, a portrait of Saint James of Compostella was discovered embedded in her liver.

Saint Eulalia appeared too late to find her proper niche in Monsignor Perrelli's *Antiquities* or to be commemorated in some worthy architectural monument by the Good Duke Alfred; too late – and this is doubtless a lucky circumstance – to become the victim of one of Father Capocchio's offensive sneers. Whoever is interested in her saintly career may purchase at Nepenthe, for the small sum of sixpence, an admirable biography by a young Canon of the Church, Don Giacinto Mellino. It gives a full account of her life and of those nine hundred and seventy-two miracles of hers which have been authenticated by eye-witnesses. No need, therefore, to expatiate further.

It stands to reason that Mr Eames possessed a copy of this treatise. An ideal annotator, he rarely indulged in speculation; his business was to discover and co-ordinate references. Nevertheless, in regard to the earthly life of this particular saint, he used to say: 'There are some things a man cannot help puzzling about.' It irked him – her success on Nepenthe. He knew the sailormen to be a horny-handed, sceptical, worldly brood. Why had they imported the cult of Eulalia from Spain; why had they chosen for their patroness a mawkish, suffering nonentity, so different from those sunny goddesses of classical days? He concluded, lamely, that there was an element of the child in every Southerner; that men, refusing to believe what is improbable, reserve their credulity for what is utterly impossible; in brief, that the prosaic seafolk of Nepenthe were like everybody else in possessing a grain of stupidity in their composition – 'which does not bring us much further,' he would add. ...

At the time of this year's festival Mr Eames was supremely happy. Another pamphlet had come into his hands, an anonymous pamphlet making fun of the Duchess, whose reception into the Roman Church had been fixed for the day of Saint Eulalia's festival. It bore the objectionable title 'The Dipping of the

Duchess' and had presumably been indited by some wag at the Alpha and Omega Club who disapproved of water in every shape, even for baptismal purposes. The stuff was printed on the sly and hastily circulated about the island – some people maintained that Mr Richards, the respectable Vice-President of that institution, was its author. It was a scurrilous anti-Catholic leaflet, grossly personal and savouring of atheism. The Duchess, on hearing of it – everything got about on Nepenthe – was so distressed that she decided to cancel, or at least postpone, the ceremony of her public conversion. At a meeting of urgency convened by the priests, who were bitterly disappointed at her attitude, it was agreed that this was no time for half-measures. A round sum of money was voted wherewith to buy back the pernicious pamphlet from its respective owners with a view to its destruction.

In the space of a single day every copy vanished from the island – every copy save one, which had found its way into Mr Eames' collection. He meant to keep that copy. He would have died sooner than yield it up. When the clerical deputation arrived at his villa with soft words and promises of more solid lucre, he professed the uttermost amazement at their quest. Mr Eames, the soul of honesty, the scorner of all subterfuge and crooked dealing, put on a new character. He lied like a trooper. He lied better than a trooper; that is to say, not only forcefully but convincingly. He lied as only a lover of bibliographical curios can lie, in defence of his treasure. He thanked them for their courteous visit and bade them keep their gold. He professed himself a poor recluse innocent of the world's ways and undesirous of riches, adding, as a mere after-thought, that he had not so much as heard of the noxious broad-sheet in question. There must be some mistake. Society people might know something about it; that gentleman who called him-self a bishop for example, that sallow gentleman from Africa, who spent so much of his time in social gaieties – he might very likely have received a copy. If they wished, he would gladly make inquiries, discreet inquiries, about the matter.

It was Mr Eames' second lapse from grace. Gentlemen do not tell falsehoods. He did not want to be a gentleman just then. He wanted that pamphlet.

The reverend visitors withdrew convinced, amid showers of compliments and apologies. After seeing them safely off the pre-mises and even, for greater security, halfway down the hill, Mr Eames returned, drew out the jewel from where it lay in a secret hiding-place among others of its kind, and hugged it to his heart. He proposed to reproduce the pamphlet *in extenso*, in that particular appendix to his edition of Perrelli's *Antiquities* which dealt with 'Contemporary Social History'. ...

Mr Heard knew nothing of all this as, jostled among the crowd, he watched the procession on that bright morning. It reminded him of the feast of Saint Dodekanus which he had witnessed twelve days earlier; it was even more extravagant. But he now felt himself seasoned to this kind of display. Besides, he had seen funnier things in Africa; though not much funnier. Once more his thoughts went back to those laughing black people, he remembered all of them – the Wabitembes, the M'tezo, the Kizibubi – what a set of jovial ruffians! How they would have enjoyed this sunshiny nonsense. And the Bulangas. Really those Bulangas –

There was a light touch on his shoulder. He turned, and found himself face to face with Mrs Meadows. She was smiling and looking ever so happy.

'Well, Tommy!' she said. 'You don't seem to be very pleased to see me. Why haven't you come to tea lately? And why are you looking so glum? He's got his leave, after all. I had a cable two days ago. He'll pick me up here in a fortnight or three weeks. Aren't you glad you needn't escort me to England?'

'Awfully glad!' he replied, trying to be jocular. The words stuck in his throat. He had expected to meet – if he met her at all – a skulking, contrite criminal. This woman was jubilant. An amazing, terrifying state of affairs.

'There is something the matter with you, Tommy. Perhaps you have caught my headache. You remember how inquisitive you were? And how you complained of the roses? If you come up now you will find fresh ones waiting for you.'

Her glance was unclouded. No human being ever looked less conscience-stricken. It was as though she had convinced herself of the righteousness of her deed, and thereafter dismissed it from her mind as something not worth bothering about. Blithe as a bird! If he had not seen with his own eyes –

'Has it gone, your headache?' he inquired, not knowing what to say.

'Gone away altogether. I have heard so much about this procession that I thought I would drive down and have a look at it. I missed the last one, you know. Besides, I wanted to see some friends here whom I've been neglecting lately. I feel quite guilty about it,' she added.

He could not help saying:

'You don't look guilty.'

'Ah, but you mustn't judge by appearances!'

296

'You blamed the sirocco, I remember.'

'I don't blame it any longer. Surely a woman can change her mind? But what is the matter with you?'

'Perhaps the South wind,' he ventured.

She remarked laughingly:

'I don't believe the wind is in the South at all. But you always were a funny boy, Tommy. If you are very good you will see some pretty fireworks presently. As for myself, I shall have to drive home for Baby's early dinner.'

'Fireworks in broad daylight?' he asked. 'That is something new.'

'In broad daylight! Aren't they queer people? They can't wait till it gets dark, I suppose.'

At that moment they were joined by Keith and three or four others. He had no more chance of speaking to her alone; she drove away, not long afterwards, waving her parasol at him and leaving him in a state of dazed perplexity.

He had been thinking night and day about his cousin, certain of her criminality and profoundly convinced of her moral rectitude. What had Muhlen done? He had probably threatened her with some exposure. He was her legal husband – he could make himself abominable to her and to Meadows. The future of the child, too, was imperilled. He might be able to claim it; or if not that – the bishop's notions of bastardy laws were not very clear – he could certainly rely upon his friend the magistrate to take the child out of the mother's custody or do something horrible of that kind. The happiness of that whole family was at his mercy. She had been goaded to desperation. Mr Heard began to understand. To understand – that was not enough. Anybody could understand.

Keith took his arm and remarked:

'Come and see my cannas! They are perfect just now. I must tell you a story about them – it's the wildest romance. I am the only person in Europe who understands the proper cultivation of cannas. I shall have scented ones soon.'

'Don't they smell?' inquired the bishop absent-mindedly.

'Not yet. You are looking a little tired, Heard, as if you had not slept well lately. Perhaps you would like to sit down? We can watch the fireworks from the terrace. You ought to read Pepys' Diary. That is what I have been doing. I am also rather low-spirited just now. The end of another spring, you know – it always makes me feel sad. Pepys is the antidote. He is a tonic. Every Englishman ought to be compelled, for the good of his soul, to go through Pepys once in three years.'

297

'I must read him again,' said the bishop, who was not particularly interested in the diarist just then.

'His universal zest! It seems to be extinct nowadays; it is a charm that I have not discovered in any living Englishman. What a healthy outlook! Not a trace of straining anywhere. He took life with both hands. How he threw himself into his work, his amusements, his clothes and women and politics and food and theatres and pictures. Warm heart, cool head. So childlike, and yet so wise. There's only one thing that troubles me about him – his love of music. It was so obviously sincere. He not only liked it; he actually understood it. Music, to me, is a succession of sounds more or less painful. I can't even whistle. It's too bad.'

The bishop said:

'If the lives of all of us were written down with the same remorseless candour, how few would stand the test.'

He was thinking of the Devil's Rock.

'I don't trouble about tests,' replied Keith. 'The whole herd of humanity adapts its pace to that of the weakest lamb. The capacity of the weakest lamb – that is the test. I don't consider myself bound to such a vulgar standard. And how spectacular we are, in matters of so-called right and wrong. That is because we have painfully cultivated the social conscience. Posing, and playing to the gallery! Mankind is curiously melodramatic, my dear fellow; full of affected reverence for its droll little institutions. As if anybody really cared what another person does! As if everybody were not chuckling inwardly all the time!'

'Surely there are heights and depths in the matter of conduct?'

'I don't trouble about heights and depths. Does it not all depend upon where we take up our stand? Must we always remain stationary like vegetables? A bird knows nothing of heights and depths. You sit here at night-time and look at the stars. They are firm-fixed, you say. Well, they are not firm-fixed. Therefore it is the wrong way to look at them. I have also written a diary, Heard. It is my legacy to posterity and will be published after my death. It relates of actions not all of which Count Caloveglia would call pretty. Perhaps it will give some people the courage of their unspoken convictions.'

The bishop suddenly asked:

'If somebody you knew had committed a crime, what would you say? Somebody you really respect – a person like Mrs Meadows?'

'Your cousin? I should say that whatever Mrs Meadows does is well done.'

298

'You would approve?'

'Of course I would. People like that are bound to be in the right.'

'Really ...?'

The fireworks were splendid; altogether, Saint Eulalia's day proved a tremendous success. The festal joy was only marred by the unseemly behaviour of Miss Wilberforce, who profited by the occasion to let off some fireworks, or at least steam, of her own.

In broad daylight too.

This was something new, and rather ominous.

The dear lady was becoming quite a problem.

CHAPTER 38

MEN looked down from the market-place that afternoon and beheld a gaily-coloured throng moving about Madame Steynlin's awkwardly situated promontory. Her house and its wide terrace overhanging the sea were filled with guests. The entertainment differed from the receptions of the Duchess. It was more rustic and unrestrained – more in the nature of a picnic. Everything possible had been done to convert that tongue of land, that refractory stretch of trachyte, into a garden. Paths were blasted through the rock; those few scarred olives, the aboriginals, had been supplemented by whatever flowers and shade-giving trees could be induced, with assiduous waterings, to strike roots into the arid soil. It was still rather a transparent place.

A number of new people had lately arrived on Nepenthe in favour of whom the hostess, with the frank cordiality of her nature, had issued invitations broadcast. There was the celebrated R.A. and his dowdy wife; a group of American politicians who were supposed to be reporting on economic questions and spent their Government's money in carousing about Europe; Madame Albert, the lady doctor from Lyons whose unique combination of magic and massage (a family secret) had brought the expiring Prince of Philippopolis to life again; an Italian senator with his two pretty daughters; a bluff hilarious Scotchman, Mr Jameson, who, as a matter of fact, had done seven years for forgery but did not like to have it brought up against him; some sisters of charity; a grizzled sea-captain, who was making discreet inquiries about a safe place for a shipwreck, having been promised by the owners twenty per cent of his vessel's insurance money; a dilapidated Viscount and his soi-distant niece; two fluffy Danish ladies who always travelled together and smiled at everything, though the younger one smiled in such a horribly knowing fashion that you could not help disliking her; Mrs Roger Rumbold, who addressed meetings to advocate Infanticide for the Masses; Mr Bernard of the Entomological Society – author of *The Courtship of Cockroaches*; another young man of pleasant exterior who was held to be an architect because his brother used to be employed in a well-known engineering firm, and several more.

The exclusive Mr Eames was absent. He sat at home, thinking how narrowly he had escaped imprisonment at the hands of Signor Malipizzo, in connexion with Muhlen's disappearance. The closest shave of all his life! It showed how right Keith had been in bidding him keep on the right side of the law – on the right side of the judge – rather than trust to the promptings of a 'good conscience'. The Duchess likewise sent her excuses. She was so troubled about the pamphlet that Don Francesco hardly dared to leave her side. He, therefore, was also absent; so was the bereaved Commissioner. Mrs Meadows had driven home again long ago. Van Koppen intended to sail in the early hours of next morning. The bishop and Denis were likewise on the verge of departure. A break-up was at hand.

Mr Keith alone refused to budge. He was waiting for the first cicada whose strident call was due, he declared, in a week's time. Till then he proposed to remain on Nepenthe.

'Fancy waiting for an insect,' said his friend van Koppen. 'I believe, Keith, you've got a sentimental streak somewhere.'

'I have been fighting against it all my life. A man ought to dominate his reflexes. But if the insect keeps good time – why not?'

He was in an elegaic mood, though he meant to drive away his cares later in the evening by the 'Falernian system'. He felt the exodus in the air. Another spring drawing to its close – everybody scattering! He was filled, too, with that peculiar pensiveness which troubles complex people when they have done a kindly act. Virtue had gone out of him.

He had wrought a miracle.

The moist look in the eye of his hostess testified to the miracle; so did her frock which, being of pink muslin, harmonized with the state of her mind but not with her complexion. Peter the Great had escaped from prison. Not only he, but all the others were at liberty once more, including the Messiah, who, after some attentions on the part of the communal doctor, had been put to bed like a little child. The rest of them filled her trim walks with their gleeful laughter and bright raiment; they devoured abundant wines and food at those refreshment tables which groaned under the weight of good things. One could trust Madame Steynlin to attend to the commissariat department. She knew how to gladden the human heart. That of Peter the Great was gladdened to such an extent that he soon began to perform a Russian peasant dance, a *pas seul*, to the delight of the assembled guests. It was a cheery interlude with a disastrous ending, for the rough terrace being different from what he expected, he stumbled and fell full length upon the ground. There he lay, laughing like a young giant refreshed with wine.

'I don't know how you have done it, Mr Keith,' she said, 'and I am not going to ask. But I shall never forget this kindness of yours.'

'Would you not do the same for me? I imagine, between ourselves, that the judge has been a good deal flustered with his trial and the intervention of Don Giustino. Perhaps he lost his head. We are all liable to that, are we not? He is a nervous man; but quite a good fellow if one keeps on the right side of him. It is so easy to keep on the right side of people. I often wonder, Madame Steynlin, why men are so full of bitterness towards each other. It is one of the things I shall never live to understand. And another is this problem of music! Will you help me to grasp the pleasure which you seem to derive from it? Helmholtz does not bring me much further. He explains why certain sounds are necessarily disagreeable –'

'Oh, Mr Keith! You would go to a professor. I fear you are not very musical. Have you never felt inclined to cry?'

'I have. But not in a concert-room.'

'Nor yet in a theatre?'

'Never,' he replied, 'though it saddens me a little to see grown-up men and women stalking about in funny dressing-gowns and pretending to be kings and queens. When I watch *Hamlet* or *Othello*, I say to myself: "This stuff is nicely riveted together. But, in the first place, the story is not true. And secondly, it is no affair of mine. Why cry about it?"'

'That looks as if you were heartless and unimaginative. And you so compassionate! I do not understand you. I do not understand myself either. We are always groping about in the dark, are we not? We are always puzzling about our own problems instead of helping other people with theirs. Perhaps one should not think so much of oneself, though it is an interesting subject. Tell me, if music says nothing to you, why not leave it alone?'

'Because I want to be able to extract pleasure from it, as you do.

301

That is what makes me curious. I like to understand things, because then I can begin to enjoy them. I think knowledge should intensify our pleasures. That is its aim and object, so far as I am concerned. What are other joys – those of the illiterate and incurious? A dog scratching his fleas in the sunshine. They too are not wholly to be despised –'

'What a dreadful simile!'

'A precise one.'

'You like to be precise?'

'It is my mother's fault. She brought me up so carefully.'

'I think that is a pity, Mr Keith. If I had children I would let them run wild. People are too tame nowadays. That is why so few of them have any charm. These poor Russians – no one tries to understand them. Why is everybody so much alike? Because we never follow our feelings. And yet, what is a surer guide than the heart? We seem to live in a world of echoes.'

'A world of masks, Madame Steynlin. It is the only theatre worth looking at. ...'

The lady was too happy to consider how the miracle had been wrought, though she suspected dirty work at the bottom of it. She never discovered how simple had been the method of Mr Keith, who had merely given His Worship to understand that he had done enough bribing for one season and that, unless Krasnojabkin were promptly released, there would be no bribing whatever next year. The judge, with his usual legal acumen, perceived the cogency of his friend's argument. He met Mr Keith's wishes more than half-way. On an impulse of downright good-nature – there was no other interpretation to be put on it – he released all the Russians, including the Messiah. They were excarcerated then and there on a decree of 'provisional liberty', which looked well in the records of the Court and, being interpreted, signified immunity from further judicial molestation. The incident was closed.

People talked about it none the less. They discussed Don Giustino, his past career and present prosperity. As for Mr Muhlen – he was already almost forgotten. So was the Commissioner's lady. Madame Steynlin alone brought herself to say a few kind words about both of them. She was ready to say kind things about anyone. The magic of love! Her heart, under the influence of Peter, had opened so wide as to embrace not only the Russian colony, but even the nine thousand families of Chinese cultivators who, according to a paragraph in the morning's newspaper, had perished in a sudden inundation of the Hoang-Ho.

The poor people! she said. She did not see why one should not

302

sympathize with the griefs of a Chinaman. Humble, honest folks, without a doubt – swept off the face of the earth, through no fault of their own, by a cataclysm! There was quite a discussion about it on her terrace that afternoon.

Mr Heard, feeling also very charitable, found himself taking her part against someone who said it was impossible to sympathize with the troubles of a yellow man – they were too different, too remote from ourselves. He thought that much individual hardship had been suffered, undeserved, unchronicled; homes destroyed, children drowned before the eyes of their parents. And nobody seemed to care.

CHAPTER 39

LATER on, he turned his back upon the crowded walks and found himself on a remote terrace overlooking the sea. It was quiet here, in view of the sunset – his last sunset on Nepenthe.

Leaning over the parapet he enjoyed, once more, the strangely intimate companionship of the sea. He glanced down into the water whose uneven floor was diapered with long weedy patches, fragments of fallen rock, and brighter patches of sand; he inhaled the pungent odour of sea-wrack and listened to the breathings of the waves. They lapped softly against the rounded boulders which strewed the shore like a flock of nodding Behemoths. He remembered his visits at daybreak to the beach – those unspoken confidences with the sunlit element to whose friendly caresses he had abandoned his body. How calm it was, too, in this evening light. Near at hand, somewhere, lay a sounding cave; it sang a melody of moist content. Shadows lengthened; fishing-boats, moving outward for their night-work, steered darkly across the luminous river at his feet. Those jewel-like morning tints of blue and green had faded from the water; the southern cliff-scenery, projections of it, caught a fiery glare. Bastions of flame. ...

The air seemed to have become unusually cool and bracing.

Here, on a bench all by himself, sat Count Caloveglia. As the bishop took a seat beside him they exchanged a few words. The Italian, so affable as a rule, was rather preoccupied and disinclined for talk.

Mr Heard remembered his first encounter with that old man – the Salt of the South, as Keith had called him. It was at those theatricals in the Municipality. Then too the Count had been remarkably silent, his chin reposing in his hand, absorbed in the spectacle – in the passionate grace of the young players. He was absorbed in another spectacle now – the old sun, moving in passionless splendour down the sky.

Only a fortnight ago, that first meeting. Less than a fortnight. Twelve days. How much had been crammed into them!

A kind of merry nightmare. Things happened. There was something bright and diabolical in the tone of the place, something kaleidoscopic – a frolicsome perversity. Purifying, at the same time. It swept away the cobwebs. It gave you a measure, a standard, whereby to compute earthly affairs. Another landmark passed; another milestone on the road to enlightenment. That period of doubt was over. His values had righted themselves. He had carved out new and sound ones; a workable, up-to-date theory of life. He was in fine trim. His liver – he forgot that he ever had one. Nepenthe had done him good all round. And he knew exactly what he wanted. A return to the Church, for example, was out of the question. His sympathies had outgrown the ideals of that establishment; a wave of pantheistic benevolence had drowned its smug little teachings. The Church of England! What was it still good for? A stepping-stone, possibly towards something more respectable and humane; a warning to all concerned of the folly of idolizing dead men and their delusions. The Church? Ghosts!

His thoughts wandered to England. Often had he sighed, in Africa, for its drowsy verdant opulence – those willow-fringed streamlets and grazing cattle, the smell of hay, the flowery lanes, the rooks cawing among slumberous elms; often had he thought of that village on the hill-top with its grey steeple. Well, he would see them all in a few days. And how would England compare with the tingling realism of Nepenthe? Rather parochial, rather dun; grey-in-grey; subdued light above – crepuscular emotions on earth. Everything fireproof, seaworthy. Kindly thoughts expressed in safe unvarying formulas. A guileless people! Ships tossing at sea; minds firmly anchored to the commonplace. Abundance for the body; diet for the spirit. The monotony of a nation intent upon respecting laws and customs. Horror of the tangent, the extreme, the unconventional. God save the King.

So much the better. This soulful cult of tradition, this clinging to the obvious and genteel as it were an anchor of safety – it nipped in the bud the monster-making faculty of low horizons and bleak, wintry stretches of earth. Bazhakuloff! Those Russians, it struck him, had been providentially sent to Nepenthe for his delectation and instruction. He was glad to have beheld a type of this nature, inconceivable in England. That grotesque, with three million followers! It had been a liberal education to look into his vacuous face, into those filmy eyes dripping with saintliness and alcohol. The Little White Cows! Chimaeras, engendered in hyperborean mists.

And still Count Caloveglia said nothing. He gazed at the sun, whose orb now rolled upon the rim of the horizon. Slowly it sank, fusing the water into a golden pool. A hush fell upon nature. Colours fled from earth into the sky. They scattered among the clouds. The enchantment began, overhead.

At last the old man remarked:

'I suppose that is why I am no colourist. That is why I worship the inexorable rigour of form. We of the South, Mr Heard, are drenched in volatile beauty. .... And yet one never wearies of these things! It is what you call a glamour, an interlude of witchcraft. Nature is a-tremble with the miraculous. She beckons us to explore her strange places. She says: Tread here, my friend – and here; tread where you have never trodden before! The sage surrenders his intelligence, and grows young again. He recaptures the spirit of his boyish dreams. He peers into worlds unknown. See! Adventure and discovery are lurking on every side. These painted clouds with their floating banners and citadels, yonder mysterious headlands that creep into the landscape at this hour, those islets emerging, like flakes of bronze, out of the sunset-glow – all the wonder of the Odyssey is there!'

He spoke out of politeness and soon fell silent again. His thoughts roamed far away.

They were thoughts commensurate with the grandeur of the scene.

Count Caloveglia was no colourist. He was a sculptor, about to reap the reward of his labours. The cheque would be in his pocket that night. Three hundred and fifty thousand francs – or nearly. That is what made him not exactly grave, but reserved. Excess of joy, like all other excess, is not meet to be displayed before men. All excess is unseemly. Nothing overmuch. Measure in everything.

Measure even in the fabrication of Hellenic masterpieces. He had created one of them (the Demeter did not count); it sufficed his modest ambitions. The Faun was his first forgery, and his last. To retrieve the fortunes of his family he had employed those peculiar talents which God had given him. He would remain henceforward an artist. He shrank from the idea of becoming a wholesale manufacturer of antiques.

Three hundred and fifty thousand francs. It sufficed. Thinking of those figures, he began to smile with contentment. He smiled – but no more. And as he continued to muse upon the transaction

305

his look melted, imperceptibly, into one of reverential awe; there was a solemnity about that sum, an amplitude, a perfection of outline that reminded him, in a way, of the proportions of some wonderful old Doric temple. The labour of a lifetime would not have enabled him to collect so much, had he tried to sell bronzes of his own workmanship. A bust or statue by Count Caloveglia – it would command a certain small price, no doubt; but what was the reputation, the market value, of the most eminent modern artist as compared with that nameless but consummate craftsman of Locri?

The Count saw things in their true perspective. His mental attitude towards Sir Herbert Street and his American employer was not tinged with the faintest cloud of disrespect; for van Koppen, indeed, he cherished a liking which bordered on affection. He detected in the astute American what nobody else could detect – an element of childlike freshness and simplicity. As far apart, in externals, as two distant trees whose leaves are fluttering on either side of some tangled forest, he yet felt that their roots were interwoven below ground, drawing common life and nourishment and sympathies from that old teeming soil of human aspirations. Nor was he vainglorious of his achievement. His superiority over the art-expert he took as a gift of the gods. Vanity was abhorrent to his nature. He was not proud but glad – glad to have been able to reconquer his legitimate social position; glad, above all things, to have forged a link with the past – a key to admit him into the fellowship of Lysippus and those others whose august shades, he opined, were even then smiling upon him. The Locri Faun was his handiwork. He was 'entitled to dine well', as he had told Denis. That was what he now purposed to do. One master-stroke had repaired his fortunes. It sufficed. Nothing overmuch. Count Caloveglia knew the story of Polycrates, the too-fortunate man. He knew what lies in wait for the presumptuous mortal, who oversteps the boundary of what is fair and good. Nemesis!

Three hundred and fifty thousand francs. There would be an ample dowry for Matilda. And, as regards himself, he could return to his passion of youth; he could afford to become a sculptor again and even, if so disposed, a collector – though not exactly after the style of his excellent friend Cornelius van Koppen.

'That was a suggestive encounter, was it not, between the Deputy and our local judge?'

He spoke, as before, out of civility.

'Very suggestive,' assented Mr Heard. 'Two blackguards, I call them.'

306

The bishop was particularly glad to learn, as everybody on the island had learnt, the minutest details of this sordid legal affair. It seemed likewise to have been providentially arranged, in order to afford him an insight into the administration of local law, and some notion of what would have been in store for his cousin had she applied for relief from Muhlen's persecutions to Signor Malipizzo, his intimate friend. There would have been no justice for her – not from that quarter. He would probably have forbidden the child to be moved out of his jurisdiction, pending the progress of a trial which might never end. Nor could the English Court, with its obsolete provisions on this head, have regarded Muhlen otherwise than as her legal husband – the child of her later union as illegitimate. Bastardy: a taint for life! How well she had done to put herself beyond a rancorous letter of the law; to protect her child and family according to the immutable instincts of mankind!

The Nepenthe magistrate had shown what he was capable of, in his bestial dealings with a half-witted lad and those harmless Russian lunatics – the first one saved through the intervention of a cutthroat politician, and the second ... well, he did not exactly know how the Muscovites had been able to regain their freedom but, remembering what Keith had told him about Miss Wilberforce, her periodical imprisonments and his periodical bribes, he shrewdly suspected some underhand practices on the part of that gentleman at the instigation, very possibly, of the charming Madame Steynlin. Signor Malipizzo's cruel travesty of justice – how unfavourably it compared with his cousin's altogether satisfactory, straightforward and businesslike handling of Muhlen's little affair.

Doubtless she suffered intensely. He called to mind her looks, her voice, during that first interview at the villa Mon Repos; he thought it likely that, but for her child and husband, she would have taken her own life in order to escape from this villain. And doubtless she had weighed the matter in her own mind. Sensible people do not take steps of this gravity without reflecting on the possible consequences. She must have tried her hardest to talk Muhlen over, before coming to the conclusion that there was nothing to be done with the fellow. She knew him; she knew her own mind. She knew better than anyone else what was in store for her if Muhlen got the upper hand. Her home broken up; her child a bastard; herself and Meadows – social outcasts; all their three lives ruined. Mrs Meadows, plainly, did not relish such a prospect. She did not see why her existence should be wrecked because a scoundrel happened to be supported by a disreputable paragraph of the Code. Muhlen was a troublesome insect. He must be brushed aside. Ridiculous to call such a thing a tragedy!

He thought of the insignificance of a human life. Thousands of decent upright folks swept away at a blow. ... Who cared? One dirty blackmailer more or less: what on earth did it matter to anybody?

An enigma? His cousin was not an enigma at all. Keith had called her a tiger mother. That was correct. Not every parent could do what she had done. Not every parent was placed under the necessity. Not every parent had the grit. If all of them fought for their offspring after this fashion, the race would be stronger and better. Thinking thus, he not only understood. He approved. Mrs Meadows had saved her family. She was perfect of her kind.

Suddenly he remembered that other parent on the passenger boat when he came to Nepenthe – that ugly peasant-woman dressed in black, with the scar across her cheek – how she had tried to console her suffering child. What had Muhlen said? 'Throw it into the water! It's often the only way of ridding oneself of a nuisance.' Into the water. His own words. That was where he, the nuisance, had gone. It was unpleasant, maybe, to hurtle through eight hundred feet of air. But men who specialize in making themselves objectionable after Muhlen's peculiar fashion deserve all they get. Sensible women do not put up with such nonsense, if they can help it.

One owes something to one's self, *n'est-ce pas*?

Decidedly so.

Everything was clear as daylight. And he found he had bothered himself long enough about Muhlen; there were so many other interesting things on earth. A contemptible little episode! He decided to relegate it into the category of unimportant events. He was glad that the whole affair had remained in the background, so to speak, of his Nepenthe experiences. It seemed appropriate. Odd, all the same, that the most respectable woman on the island should be a murderess.

'Dear me!' he mused. 'How very queer! It never struck me in that light before. Shows how careful one must be. ... And a relation of mine into the bargain. H'm. Some people, if they knew, would call it a compromising situation. Well, I begin to think it rather creditable than otherwise to our family. We want more women of this kind on earth. All mothers ought to be tiger mothers. ...'

'Don't you notice, Count, that there is an unwonted sparkle in the air this evening? Something cleansing, clarifying?'

'To be sure I do,' replied the other. 'And I can tell you the cause of it. Sirocco is over for the present. The wind has shifted to the North. It brightens all nature. It makes one see things in their true perspective, doesn't it?'

'That is exactly what I feel,' said Mr Heard.

CHAPTER 40

THE symposium, that evening, might have degenerated into something like an orgy but for the masterful intervention of Denis, who was not going to let Keith make a fool of himself. It took place in the most famous of all the caves of Nepenthe – Luisella's grotto-cavern dedicated, by common usage, to the worship of Venus and Bacchus.

There were two or three living rooms on the surface of the ground. Walking through the first of these you clambered down some slippery stairs into what was once a breathless subterranean vault hewn out of the soft and dry pumiceous rock and used, as was customary, for storing barrels and other paraphernalia. In the course of time, as more barrels accumulated, the grotto was excavated further and further into the entrails of the island. There seemed no reason why it should ever cease growing when suddenly, one day, the perspiring workmen were struck in the face by a cool blast of wind laden with marine moisture. They knew what this meant. They had encountered one of those mysterious and dangerous fissures that lead down to unknown depths, opening upon the world of sunshine often at the water's edge, four hundred feet below. It was deemed prudent to suspend excavations. These rents in the interior of the earth had a knack of enlarging themselves, without a word of warning, from cracks of a few inches to black gulfs several hundred feet across. The cavern ceased to grow. As a matter of fact, it turned out to be just large enough.

That current of air ventilating the grotto made the fortune of these orphan girls – Luisella and her three sisters. The barrels and other lumber once removed, the recess became a breezy night-tavern, its natural vaulting being first whitewashed and then adorned, by a master-hand, with thrilling pictures of crimson fish afloat upon caerulean waves, and piles of bossy pumpkins, and birds of Paradise with streaming golden feathers, and goats at pasture among blue lilies, and horses prancing over emerald mountains, and trees laden with flowers and fruits such as no mortal had ever seen or tasted. It was an ideal place for a carousal.

They could cook, those girls. Their savoury stews and vegetable soups and *fritturas* of every description were known far and wide. It was universally agreed that nobody could make a more appetizing mayonnaise sauce for cold fish and lobsters. No mayonnaise was quite like theirs; no, not quite. Its flavour lingered on the palate; it haunted your memory in distant lands, like the afterglow of some happy love-affair. Nice girls, too; well-mannered; not very difficult to caress, and never jealous of each other. 'It's all in the family,' they used to declare.

'Am I right, then, or am I wrong?' asked Mr Keith, whose pomposity was melting away under successive bottles of his own wine, specially imported to grace the table.

The honest Vice-President of the Club, Mr Richards, was pretty far gone, but could always be relied upon to say something apposite. That was due to his legal training. Once a thriving solicitor, he had been struck off the rolls in consequence of some stupid trustee business which turned out all wrong and thereafter driven along devious paths known only to himself: hence his residence on Nepenthe. He replied:

'That depends entirely, my dear sir, upon what you postulated.'

'The older I get,' observed Mr van Koppen, 'the more I realize that everything depends upon what a man postulates. The rest is plain sailing.'

'I never heard a truer remark,' said Keith, 'not even from you! One has only to posit a thing, and it's done. Don't you agree, Bishop? Here is what we would call a worn-out earthenware plate. It is not a plate unless I tell it to be a plate. You may call it anything you like – it can't answer back. But we need not pursue the argument. Speaking for myself, I am feeling as comfortable as a beetle in a rose.'

The Vice-President remarked:

'We all know what it means when Mr Keith becomes horticultural in his similes. It means the same thing as when I become legal. Gentlemen! I propose to grow legal within the next half-hour or so.'

'You promised to tell the history of your cannas,' said Mr Heard.

'You were going to tell it me, too,' added Denis.

'I did. I was. And I will. But let me ask you this: have you ever heard of a teetotaller conspicuous for kindliness of heart, or intellectually distinguished in any walk of life? I should be glad to know his name. A sorry crew! Not because they drink water, but because the state of mind which makes them dread alcohol is unpropitious to the hatching of any generous idea. *When men have well drunk*. I like that phrase. *When men have well drunk*. I am inclined to think that the Aramaic text has not been tampered with at this point. What do you say, Heard?'

'Nothing is more improbable,' replied the bishop. 'And the water, you perceive, was changed into wine; not into cocoa or lemonade. That conveys, if I am not mistaken, rather a suggestive implication.'

'I have been perusing Seneca's letters. He was a cocoa-drinker, masquerading as an ancient. An objectionable hypocrite! I wish people would read Seneca instead of talking about him.'

Van Koppen observed:

'What a man postulates is truer than what exists. I have grown grey in trying to make my fellow-creatures understand that realities are less convincing than make-believe.'

'Given the proper atmosphere,' said the bishop, laughing, 'everything becomes inevitable. If you were wrong, Mr van Koppen, where would our poets and novelists be?'

'Where are they?' queried the American.

'How shall that come out of a man,' continued Mr Heard, 'which was never in him? How shall he generate a harmonious atmosphere if he be disharmonious himself? It is all a question of plausibility, of verisimi – simili –'

'I never heard a more profound remark, Koppen; no, nor a more subtle one; not even from you. Nor yet from you, Heard. And I can tell you something to the point. I was talking this afternoon with a gentlemen about the stage. I said it made me sad to see flesh-and-blood people pretending to be kings and queens. Because it cannot be done. No sensible person can bring himself to believe it. But when you watch some of these local marionette theatres the illusion is complete. Why is a poppy show more convincing than the Comédie Française? Because it is still further removed from reality. There is so much make-belief that you cease to struggle. You succumb without an effort. You are quite disposed, you are positively anxious, to make concessions to the improbable. Once they are made – why, as you say, it is plain sailing.'

'All life is a concession to the improbable,' observed the bishop rather vaguely.

Mr Richards remarked:

'These questions must be approached with an open mind. An open mind, gentlemen, is not necessarily an empty one.'

'A fine distinction!'

'Very well. Mr Keith proposes to abolish theatres. I second the motion. Nothing is easier. Let me draw up a memorial to the House of Lords. We will appeal to them on moral grounds. I know the proper language. *Whereas by the grace of God your petitioners humbly protest that there is too much kissing on the stage* – ah! Talking of kissing, here comes our friend Don Francesco. He shall put his name to the memorial and seal it with an oath. No Englishman can resist a Monsignor. And nothing like a solemn oath. People always think you mean it.'

That amiable personage strode down the stairs in dignified fashion, greeting the guests with a sonorous:

'*Pax vobiscum!*'

He could not be induced to stay long, however. He had been perturbed all day on account of the Duchess, who now threatened to join the Moravian Brotherhood; she was so annoyed about a little thing which had happened. He did not quite believe it, of course; but, like a well-trained priest, took nothing for granted and was prepared for every emergency where ladies are concerned.

'Just one glass!' said Keith.

'Let me drink to your health ere we part,' added the bishop. 'I am sorry to leave you. Our friendship will endure. We meet in September, during the vintage season. Keith has been talking to me. I am as wax in his hands. Your smile, Don Francesco, will follow me across the ocean. Just one glass!'

'Ah, well!' said the priest. 'The next best thing to leading others astray is to be led astray oneself.'

He gulped down a couple of tumblers and dutifully took his leave, turning round, as he reached the staircase, to make a playful gesture of benediction towards the assembled company.

'Don't leave your bottle half empty,' Keith called after him imploringly. 'It looks untidy.'

'And so unhappy,' added the bishop. 'Dear me! This is most singular. I seem to see two lamps instead of one. It must have been those apricots.'

Keith interposed:

'Or perhaps you strained one of your eyes bathing. It has happened to me, occasionally. Darkness is the best remedy. It rests the optic nerve.'

'Shall we take a turn or two outside?' asked Denis.

It was past midnight as the two climbed out of the cave into the night air. A cool north wind blew across the market-place. The bishop was filled with a sense – a clear-cut, all-convincing sense – of the screamingly funny insignificance of everything. Then he noticed the moon.

It dangled over the water, waning, sickly, moth-eaten, top-heavy, and altogether out of condition – as if it had been on duty for weeks on end. In other respects, too, its appearance was not quite normal. In fact, it soon took to behaving in the most extraordinary fashion. Sometimes there were two moons, and sometimes one. They seemed to merge together – to glide into each other, and then to separate again. Mr Heard was vastly pleased and puzzled by the phenomenon – so pleased that he gave utterance to one of the longest speeches he had made since his arrival on Nepenthe. He said:

'I have seen many funny things here, Denis. But this is the funniest of all. The spectacle seems to have been providentially arranged, as a sort of *bonne bouche*, for my last evening on the island. Dear me. Now there are two again. And now they are behind each other once more. A kind of celestial hide and seek. Most interesting. I wish Keith could see it. Or that dear Count Caloveglia. He would be sure to say something polite. ... The inconstant moon! I know, at last, what the poet meant by that expression, though the word inconstant strikes me as hardly forcible enough. The skittish moon, I should be inclined to call it. The skittish moon. The frivolous moon. The giddy moon. The quite-too-absurd moon. ... There it goes again! Very curious. What can it be? ... Why, this is the reverse of an eclipse, my boy. The disk is darkened during an eclipse. It disappears *in vacuo*. In the present case it is brightened and rendered, so to speak, doubly apparent. What would you call the reverse of an eclipse, Denis? Anti-eclipse. That sounds rather barbaric to my ears. One should never mix Greek and Latin, if it can possibly be avoided. Well?'

'We must have a good look at this thing from your window, and then find out all about it.'

'Oh, but I could not possibly take you from your friends! I know my way home perfectly well. You will not dream of accompanying me.'

'Indeed I will. I walked with you to that house when you first arrived here, and helped you to unpack. Don't you remember? And now you must let me take you there on our last evening. ...'

By the time Denis returned to the grotto a more exuberant and incoherent tone had been generated among the guests. He was not pleased. He felt inclined to be stern. A number of reprobates from the Club had dropped in, and Keith, whom he meant to keep straight for one night at least, was saying silly things and giving himself away. So was the excellent Mr Richards.

313

'This is a good island,' observed that gentleman. 'We discourse like sages and drink like swine. Peace with Honour! ... How that old Jew took our English measure, eh? How he laughed in his sleeve at our infatuation for a phrase like that. Peace with Honour! The sort of clap-trap that makes a man feel so jolly comfortable inside, so damned satisfied with everything, as after a good feed. And that sentimental primrose-business. Dizzy as flower-expert! What cared he for primroses? Votes and money-bags was what he was after. But he knew the British Public. And that accounts for the pious domestic button-hole. Who ever heard of a Jew telling the difference between a primrose and any other kind of rose? They're not such blasted fools.'

'Excuse me,' said Keith, rising from his seat in an afflatus of in-spiration. 'Excuse me. I know the difference. It is primarily a ques-tion of nutrition. Glucose! I am a great believer in glucose. Be-cause, even if it could be proved that the monks of Palaiokastron stripped the vine of its leaves and thereby hastened the maturity of the grape without reducing its natural supply of sugar –'

'You don't shine,' interrupted Denis, 'when you talk like that.'

'Because even if this could be proved, which I greatly doubt, yet nothing on earth will make me believe that glucose is otherwise than beneficial to vegetation. Because –'

'Do sit down, Keith. You are monopolizing the conversa-tion.'

'Because the glucose resides within that verdant foliage like truth in her well, like the oyster within its pearl. The monks of Palaiokastron – they got it straight from Noah. I am a great believer in glucose. Which is absurd. Because –'

'Oh, shut up! You are making a perfect exhibition of yourself. Can't you oblige me, for once in the way?'

Denis was growing seriously alarmed for the reputation of his friend. He had changed of late; he was beginning to know his own mind. He meant to put a stop to this humiliating scene. As the other, regardless of his pleadings, continued to babble dithy-rambic nonsense concerning glucose and self-fertilization and artificial manures and inflorescence and Assyrian bas-reliefs and Stilton cheese, he suddenly gripped his arm and pulled him, with a crash, into his chair.

'Sit down, you double-distilled owl!'

This was the first virile achievement of his young life and directed to a worthy end. For it was obvious to the meanest intelligence that Mr Keith was considerably drunk. Too surprised to utter a word of protest, the orator paused in his declamation, beaming blandly at nobody in particular. Then he remarked, in quite a subdued tone of voice:

'We are all at the mercy of youth. Mr Richards! Could you oblige me with a fairy-tale?'